THE RISE OF IMMORTALS

THE RISE OF IMMORTALS

AZALON

BOOK ONE

K. VANG

NU VOICE
PRESS

NU VOICE
PRESS

First published by NU VOICE PRESS 2025
An imprint of Hubhawks Pvt. Ltd
www.nuvoicepress.com

This is a work of fiction. Space and time have been rearranged to suit the convenience of the book. Except for public figures, hotels, and institution names, any resemblance to persons living or dead or the real events are purely coincidental. The opinions expressed in the book are those of the characters, and should not be confused with that of the Author.

ISBN: 978-81-982661-6-3

Typeset by Saanvi Graphics, Noida

Printed at Nutech Print Services - India

Published by Nu Voice Press

To my family and friends who dared me to dream.

Author's Note

WELCOME TO *AZALON*, a realm locked in a fierce struggle between humans and Immortals, where the war drums of kingdoms beat relentlessly against undead forces, heroes are forged from ordinary men, and humans are no longer the hunter but the hunted. *The Rise of Immortals* is the first book in an epic series that has been years in the making, exploring timeless human struggles—love, loyalty, betrayal—while combating an evil threatening to engulf its world.

I was once oblivious to the depths of love and sensed I was not alone, inspiring me to write a romance about a pure, innocent love that gradually evolves into something deeper and more mature, an enduring, passionate love. I wanted to craft a world ravaged by wars, one that would resonate with epic fantasy lovers, while delving deep into complex human emotions involving relationships, power struggles, and sacrifice.

My characters are not simple heroes or villains—they are complex beings, shaped by their destinies and the harsh realities of their world. Through the eyes of Deon, a loyal commander torn between duty and forbidden love, and Zelana, a princess who is the last demi-goddess, destined to threaten the balance of power, we witness humanity's desperate fight for survival against the Immortals. Marcus, the ruthless Immortal King, commands a world where power must be absolute and strength unyielding while mercy is seen as weakness, a sliver of doubt could embolden others to usurp his throne. In Krimzon, we are plunged into a cold, dark realm where bloodthirsty Immortals roam freely, and morals have no bounds. Marcus must dominate both the living and the dead where survival often means sacrificing one's humanity.

I poured my heart onto every page, hoping to create a universe rich with emotion, intrigue, and drama. I invite you to immerse yourself in the world of *Azalon* where ancient powers clash with modern finesse. May the vivid imagery, stirring romance, and fierce battles keep you turning the pages and leave you eagerly awaiting the next installment of this dark yet hopeful saga.

Love,

K. Vang

Azalon
N
S
W
E
Wailing Sea
Enchanted Ocean
Misty Ocean
Infernal Sea
Glimmer Sea
Winter Strait
Moonstruck Channel
Merci Harbor
Ivory Depths
Red Bay
Dark Waters
Faery Basin
Snowy Meadows
Frostwald
Zelonia
Starhaven
Lashia
Ferria
Sanshe
Glimmerock
Mesa Valley
Ember Falls
Krimzon
Iron Glades
Stormhold
Esperia
Windpass
Bridgethorn
Snowford
Aspenridge
Azurecrest
Spectra Springs
Zelonia City
Tumble Heights
Velvetville
Starcrest
Crystalshade
Cherry Blossom
Silver Peak
Sanshe Mines
Eastern Village
Dravenville
Fire Mines
Zelana's Cabin
Glimmer Desert
Northern Village
Mesa Mines
Jasperpines
Goldstone City
Overport
Western Village
Bronze City
Nightshade City
Ironville
Skyheights
Evergate
Dark Fires Cave
Southern Village
Storm City
Marshsong
Sabrehaven

Prologue

A NIGHT OF UNPRECEDENTED terror unfurled its dark wings in the Kingdom of Esperia as rapid footsteps pounded on the ground, echoing beneath the starless night. Plunging through the dense forest, Crown Prince Winston Thorneblade led the desperate escape, feeling the weight of his future crown growing heavier with each stride. Behind him, his sister, Princess Lenora Thorneblade, and the last of the Royal Guards followed him closely.

Tension and fear thickened while the Immortals closed in on them like dark shadows, ominous and foreboding. These formidable foes pursued them with an unwavering resolve to shroud Esperia and its royals forever into the depths of oblivion.

As the distance between them closed, the entourage pushed forward with increased desperation, but the Immortals' menacing presence encircled them from all sides in a final confrontation.

"Take the princess and escape into the forest, Your Highness," offered Graham Evans, the lead Royal Guard, with urgency. "We'll distract them."

A chorus of mocking laughter erupted from the Immortals; their predatory gazes fixed on the frightened men as Lenora's eyes brimmed with tears.

"I'm done running," Winston declared courageously as he drew his sword, its steel gleaming under the dim moonlight.

Recognizing the Crown Prince's determination, the Royal Guards knelt in unison in front of the royal siblings, moved by his courage.

"It was an honor..."

Winston nodded as he witnessed the unwavering loyalty of his Royal Guards, his heart clenching in his chest. "For Esperia!" he cried out, charging fearlessly toward the Immortals.

Loyal to the end, the Royal Guards stood and unsheathed their weapons, joining him in this final stand. Their swords moved in a lethal dance, slashing and slicing through the Krimzonites with a ferocity born of desperation and valor.

Lenora watched them as she stood back helplessly, tears flowing down her cheeks.

The battle raged, fierce and unforgiving. Blood splattered across the faces of the Royal Guards and one by one they fell, their bravery unyielding even in the face of the Immortals' ruthless onslaught.

Minutes felt like hours and soon Winston found himself gasping for air, standing alone, the last defender of Esperia. With a protective fierceness, he slowly backed deeper into the forest with his sister behind him, ready to lay down his life to shield her.

"Lenora..." the Crown Prince murmured as he tightened his grip on his sword, his heart pounding relentlessly in his chest. "I will hold them back, but when I fall, do not allow yourself to be captured."

"I will quickly follow you, Winston," Lenora responded, clutching the small dagger hidden in her cloak, ready to accept her fate.

Suddenly, the ground shook with an army of horses approaching them from behind. The thunderous gallop resounded through the dense forest like a drumbeat, growing louder and more ominous with each passing second.

A flurry of arrows cleaved the night air, descending like a vengeful storm upon the Krimzonites. This unexpected assault threw the Immortals into disarray as they were met with an unexpected force—an army of riders, their bodies and faces fully encased in gleaming metal armor, forming an impenetrable line behind the Esperian royals.

The Commander swiftly leaped off his horse with an agile grace, wielding two pistols, releasing a rapid volley of bullets. Each shot found its mark with perfect accuracy, effectively neutralizing the Immortals, as they fell, one by one, to his deadly aim.

The immediate threat quickly subsided, and a tense quiet settled over the battlefield.

"Are you Sanshe?" Winston asked as a surge of relief washed over him.

"Greetings from King MuaYeng," the Commander spoke, his tone carrying the authority of a seasoned warrior.

"I will repay Sanshe's generosity with my loyalty," Winston assured him with deep appreciation.

In the midst of their darkest hour, Lenora's eyes met the Commander's, who emerged as her unexpected savior.

I can't believe I might live to see another sunrise, she thought in silence.

Despite the chaos around them, the Commander couldn't help noticing how her disheveled blonde hair framed her vivid green eyes, now shadowed by loss, yet still clinging courageously to hope.

Spears suddenly descended like rain from the heavens.

The Commander and his unit skillfully deflected the deadly projectiles with swift, precise kicks, sending the spears hurtling back into the ranks of the advancing Immortals, where they found their marks with deadly accuracy.

Amid this newfound chaos, the Krimzon army parted, creating a path for their king, the ruthless Marcus Chamberlain, to advance to the front lines.

He was an Ancient—one of the first Immortals transformed in the Dark Fires Cave during the pact made with Maldev, the spawn of evil from Hell—and the eldest son of King Theo Chamberlain and Queen Katherina Hawthorne.

Marcus's strength and combat skills far surpassed that of most Immortals, making him the most feared figure in all of Azalon. He had ruled Krimzon for the last two centuries, ever since the death of his father and brother during the legendary Clash of Azalon. Under his iron-fisted rule, he commanded the three most powerful and respected factions within his realm—Kumar, Ravenshadow, and Silverbane—solidifying his dominance over the realm and bringing death across all of Azalon.

"King Marcus..." Winston murmured as the Commander and his unit brandished their swords.

"Defenses up!" the Commander shouted.

The Sanshe army dismounted and stepped forward, immediately shielding the Esperian royals while swords banged against shields in a rhythmic battle cry that grew in intensity. Louder and louder, the war sound spread through the Sanshe army, sowing seeds of fear and disarray in the Krimzon ranks.

"Ops move!" ordered the Commander.

The air thrummed with the tension of the imminent clash as the Ops squadron surged forward, their movements synchronized and fatal. They leaped into the air, unleashing a storm of bullets upon the enemy, their actions a dance of death and defiance against the Krimzonites.

In the thick of battle, they made landfall amidst the enemy. Their mechanical arms sprung to life with lethal efficiency, engaging in brutal, close combat with the Immortals. Their enhanced limbs delivered deathly blows and sword strikes, countering the superior strength of their foes. Limbs of the Krimzonites covered the battlefield while their blood soaked the earth.

"Sanshe!" Marcus growled, his eyes widening in anguish.

"Unit One, advance!" the Commander ordered, propelling his men into a synchronized advance.

The battlefield was a blur of motion as the Sanshe army marched forward as one, striking and shielding in a relentless rhythm, their formation an impenetrable barrier of steel and resolve.

Marcus dismounted from his horse, his figure looming large and menacing. He lunged at the Sanshe Commander; his blade aimed with deadly intent.

The Commander quickly dodged, his defenses unbreakable as he countered with a powerful shove, sending Marcus staggering backwards.

The clash between the Commander and the King of Krimzon intensified with a maelstrom of kicks, punches, and counter strikes. The Commander swiftly delivered a flurry of blows to Marcus's head, causing him to lose composure and descend into disarray. He culminated his attack in a barrage of gunfire that tore into the King's torso mercilessly.

Marcus cried out in pain, enraged. "Who are you?!"

"The man that will end your reign," the Commander responded without fear.

"I will come for you!" Marcus vowed vengeance, blood dripping from his wounds.

The Krimzonite Army swiftly formed a protective ring around their King, their shields raised to intercept the incoming gunfire. A primal roar tore through the chaos, signaling their retreat. The Krimzonites slowly disappeared into the shadowy embrace of the forest, leaving behind the echoes of a battle that would long be remembered by Esperia.

"We must return to Sanshe with haste," the Commander's voice cut through the aftermath.

The army regrouped with trained efficiency. A soldier brought two horses to the Esperian royals.

"I don't know how to ride," Lenora confessed, embarrassed under the weight of so many eyes.

The Commander approached her, drawn to her aura of natural beauty and innocence. He gently lifted her onto the horse and effortlessly swung up behind her. As he took the reins and turned the horse around, the army silently parted, forming a path for them.

"Follow me," the Commander instructed as he set off with Winston behind.

The Commander's arms encircled the Princess, securing her against the swift movements of the galloping horse. Lenora's heart raced as she leaned back slightly, feeling the solid warmth of his chest against her and the rhythm of his breathing aligning with the pounding of hooves on the earth.

"Thank you for coming," she managed to murmur, gazing up at him in wonderment.

"It's what we do," he replied simply, his focus never wavering from the path ahead.

She tried to catch a glimpse of the face behind the helmet, the name of this enigmatic Commander still unknown to her. All she could see were his eyes—striking hazel slits filled with determination.

Why do you stir such curiosity within me? she pondered, her gaze lingering on him, lost in thought.

The landscape blurred around them as they raced through the woods, the horse carrying them deeper into the unknown to face the promise of both daunting challenges and new beginnings.

CHAPTER ONE

The Ambassador

A ROYAL CARRIAGE TRAVERSED leisurely across the vibrant, lush meadows of Zelonia as dawn's golden light broke over the horizon. The landscape shimmered with a blur of green, dotted with wildflowers that swayed gently in the warm breeze. As the carriage glided into the city, life stirred within its streets, the populace beginning their day in a harmonious symphony of activity, blending seamlessly with the natural beauty surrounding them.

Inside the luxurious confines of the carriage, Deon Vang, a distinguished man from Sanshe, gazed out the window, admiring the wonders around him.

It has been almost two decades since my visit to Zelonia. She is still as beautiful as I remember.

A month had swiftly flown by since Deon's return from Esperia, a journey marked by both peril and triumph. In recognition of his exemplary service, the King of Sanshe elevated him to the esteemed role of Ambassador, the third most powerful position in the Sanshe Kingdom.

For decades, diplomatic engagements between Sanshe and Zelonia had been complex, often marked by distrust and cautious diplomacy. Many discussions had yielded little in the way of concrete results. Since the geopolitical landscape had shifted dramatically in the last few years, Deon saw a glimmer of opportunity as this shared struggle against the Krimzon Kingdom provided a new context for negotiations, one that could pave the way for genuine cooperation.

Seated across him was Chue Lor, the Sanshe Advisor-in-Chief, with whom Deon had been assigned to a joint commission to address the mounting challenges facing Sanshe. Together, they faced the daunting task of navigating this delicate alliance in the hope of shaping a new future.

As the carriage departed from the bustling city, the men's eyes were drawn irresistibly to the commanding structure rising with stately grace and regal poise, sitting majestically atop a verdant hill—the Zelonian Castle. Its fluttering banners proudly displayed the kingdom's emblem—a golden eagle in flight. Its grand spires and formidable walls bore witness to centuries of prosperity, dutifully safeguarding the realm nestled below.

The carriage wheels hummed a steady rhythm against the cobblestone as they ascended the winding road toward the castle gates. The Zelonian guards' maroon and gold tunics gleamed in the sunlight, adding a touch of splendor to the scene as a nostalgic smile touched Deon's lips, softening his features.

The carriage slowly rolled to a graceful stop. It was in this moment of stillness that the full weight of his role as the Ambassador of Sanshe sank in, making him realize that he was tasked with bridging a chasm of centuries filled with tangled histories and old wounds. The prospect felt a bit daunting, especially knowing he would be in the presence of the Zelonian royals. They were not mere mortals but elite humans, demigods, the direct descendants of the revered Goddess Alexi.

Deon stepped out from the royal carriage and paused for a moment to adjust his jacket, a gesture exuding a calm composure that belied the swirl of emotions within him. Immediately, his eyes were drawn upwards, captivated by the intricate carvings on the archways that spoke of centuries-old craftsmanship.

His attention was swiftly captured by a beautiful young woman standing on the balcony—her eyes were surprisingly already fixed on him. He felt her allure reach out across the distance as a subtle smile graced her lips, deepening his nervousness and intriguing him all the more.

"Could she be the Zelonian Princess?" Deon wondered aloud, squinting his eyes, feeling momentarily lost in her enchantment.

Her beauty was breathtaking, characterized by her alluring blue eyes, luscious lips, and golden hair cascading down her back like a shimmering waterfall catching the sunlight in a mesmerizing display.

Stepping out of the carriage, Chue looked up to where Deon was entranced. He saw an attractive young woman, in a delicate light blue and gold gown, her poise radiating a serene confidence that showed her royal bearing.

"How could she not be?" he murmured, his tone filled with a quiet admiration.

The Princess was a vision of regal grace, the embodiment of youthful elegance and beauty, holding Deon's gaze effortlessly, captivating him breathless.

"Welcome to Zelonia!" greeted King Lucas Celeste, approaching the Sanshe entourage with Commander Dominic Dupont following closely behind.

The King of Zelonia's words brought Deon back to the present, prompting him to face him. "Your Majesty, it's a pleasure to be in your presence," he responded, swiftly regaining his composure.

From the balcony above, the Princess maintained her observant gaze, watching the formal greetings between her father and the Sanshe delegation. Her uncharacteristic silence drew the attention of Crown Prince Samuel, her brother, as he joined her to observe the men.

"You can still retreat to your chambers before their arrival," he remarked playfully.

"I will do no such thing," the Princess assured him, her smile broadening.

Samuel was the future king of Zelonia and a second-generation demigod. With striking blue eyes and dark blonde hair, his handsome features bore a resemblance to the gods themselves.

The Princess's gaze remained fixed on the distinguished men, taking in their appearance with a discerning eye. "The Sanshe representatives are younger than I expected."

"Do not underestimate them," Samuel voiced out, unease etched across his forehead, while their father led the Sanshe men into the castle. "Make sure you meet the Ambassador's gaze, or he won't take you seriously."

"My eyes will never leave his," teased the Princess, deepening the Crown Prince's worries.

Before Samuel could respond, the doors to the Meeting Hall swung open and the royal siblings fell silent as they turned to greet their guests.

As the Sanshe delegation followed the King deeper into the chamber, their eyes swept across the opulent room, impressed by the splendor of the luxurious décor—gold silk curtains draped gracefully around the massive windows allowing natural light to enhance the room's grandeur. The delicate fragrance of roses permeated the air, adding a subtle yet unmistakable touch of natural beauty to the stately surroundings.

Deon exuded effortless charisma as his eyes moved across the room, offering a confident smile, warm greetings, and exchanging firm handshakes with the dignitaries introduced by the King.

The Princess came to know that the man she had been observing was indeed the Ambassador as he made his way from one Councilman to the next. His youth, coupled with his captivating presence, suggested a man forged in significant achievements and complex international relations.

Deon's eyes inadvertently met the Princess's gaze. *What are you doing here?* he pondered to himself, maintaining a poised façade, while a subtle smile flickered across her lips once more, awakening an interest within him that had lain dormant for years.

He has green eyes, she noted as she slowly took in the full measure of his appearance, from his notable height to his well-proportioned frame, giving him a presence that was both commanding and entrancing. From what little she could discern, he had a muscular build beneath his tailored attire—a black and gold suit, made for royalty. His dark brown hair was meticulously styled, completing the air of refinement that surrounded him.

The Ambassador appears to value luxury, discipline, and order, she concluded silently.

"Along with the Royal Council, the Crown Prince and Princess will be joining us," Lucas announced with pride as he turned to Deon. "I believe you remember my son, Crown Prince Samuel."

"How could I not?" Deon responded, smiling warmly as he stepped toward the Crown Prince. "It is an honor to meet you again," he greeted, extending his hand. "I am Deon Vang, the Sanshe Ambassador."

"Your name is quite familiar," observed Samuel, his brow furrowed slightly, shaking his hand.

"We sparred during my last visit, eighteen years ago," Deon replied, his smile widening as he released the Crown Prince's hand.

The revelation seemed to catch Samuel off guard. "Were you that boy in the gardens?" he exclaimed, recognizing the young playmate who had now returned as the Ambassador.

"Time flies, doesn't it?" Deon's laughter rang out, light and unburdened.

"Indeed. Strangely, I still recall that day," the Crown Prince responded, his own laughter joining Deon's as a warm, reflective look crossed his face.

"We had some good times," Deon nodded in agreement.

Their memories vividly transported them back to the royal gardens of Zelonia, where a spirited seven-year-old Deon and five-year-old Samuel engaged in a playful chase. Their laughter and the sound of wooden swords clashing in mock battle resonated amidst the fragrant blossoms.

"I bet you can't catch me!" The Prince teased him with a challenge, the chase taking on a new level of excitement as he darted past a dense bush, temporarily vanishing from sight.

"I'll get you!" Deon called out, following Samuel along the narrow path, rushing toward the foliage.

He was taken by surprise as the Prince reappeared and tapped him on the chest. Stumbling backwards and falling to the ground, Deon rubbed his buttocks with laughter.

"On guard!" Samuel declared with a mischievous grin.

Their playful duel was abruptly interrupted by the arrival of King Lucas and Queen Sophia, instantly softening the atmosphere in the garden.

"Now, Samuel, play nice," reminded Sophia gently, while holding a baby in her arms.

"I was just playing hide-and-seek with my friend," replied Samuel, heading toward his mother. "Come meet my little sister, Deon."

Deon hesitantly rose and joined the royal family. His eyes lit up as he saw the adorable infant, cooing and swaying in her mother's arms. He extended his finger, which she grasped firmly, enchanting him with her curious eyes.

"She seems to have taken a liking to you," observed Lucas.

Deon exchanged playful babbles with the infant as the royal family watched them in amusement.

"Let's go play, Deon!" interjected Samuel, eager to resume their game.

Deon tried to gently withdraw his finger, but she began to cry, her tiny face wrinkling in distress. Instantly concerned, he halted his attempt.

"There, there…I'm still here," he reassured her with his soothing voice, calming the little Princess as she resumed her joyful babbling.

"Looks like you'll have to go play with your other friends," Lucas teased his son as the royal couple shared a knowing laugh. "Deon's already caught your sister's eye."

Their voices echoed from a distant time as Deon remembered that fateful evening vividly.

"This is my daughter, Princess Zelana," Lucas introduced with a warm smile.

The King's words returned Deon to the present as he finally

faced the enchanting Princess, staring into her alluring blue eyes, feeling himself getting lost in their depths.

Zelana was beautiful and a second-generation demigod, carrying the legacy of divine strength and power, revered throughout Azalon as the most enchanting princess in all the realms.

"Princess Zelana..." Deon greeted. Her name felt new, but her essence was unmistakably familiar. "It is a profound honor to meet again," he confessed, respectfully taking her hand and lowering his head to gently press a kiss upon it, a gesture of chivalrous admiration.

"The pleasure is mine, Ambassador Deon, but I don't think we've met," Zelana replied politely, unaware of the charming connection they had shared many moons ago.

Deon slowly lifted his head as their eyes met again, his lips curving into a tender smile. "I wouldn't expect you to remember. You were still in diapers..." he playfully replied with a wink, bringing a light-hearted tone to their interaction.

Zelana's cheeks tinged with a blush, her smile growing more luminous. "Rest assured, I've moved beyond those days," she quipped, displaying her quick wit.

Laughter cascaded through the room, infectious and warm, effectively melting away the stiff formality that had initially shrouded their meeting.

Deon's smile spread slowly, allowing himself a moment to truly appreciate her visage. His eyes gently traced the contours of her face, admiring the soft, harmonious lines that composed her elegant features. His attention moved down to the gentle curve of her lips; their fullness held an undeniable charm. As his eyes met hers once more, he noticed how the light danced playfully in her gaze. Every movement she made was imbued with an effortless elegance, her poise softening the air around her, drawing him inexorably deeper into her graceful aura.

I'm in trouble, he thought silently to himself.

As the moments unfolded, Zelana found herself increasingly captivated by Deon, her heart quickening each time their eyes met. The intensity of his unwavering gaze stirred a flurry of emotions within her.

How did you rise to such prominence at such an early age? She wondered silently. *What are you thinking behind those deep, expressive eyes?*

The longer Zelana observed him, the deeper her curiosity grew about the man whose smile radiated sincerity and warmth, softening his authoritative demeanor and revealing a personable charm. His strikingly handsome features continued to tug at her heart, entrancing her deeper.

It must be your charismatic presence that escalated your ascent. Her thoughts continued to dance inside her mind, her intrigue growing as her hand remained in his—their touch lingering longer than necessary, an unintended intimacy that seemed to pause time itself.

Samuel noticed their prolonged contact and stepped in with a hint of awkwardness in his voice. "Perhaps you might want to let go of his hand now, Zelana."

"I'm so sorry," she stammered, flustered, as she quickly withdrew her hand, a flush of embarrassment coloring her cheeks.

"Some things remain the same, I see. You clung to Deon's thumb with your little baby fingers just as tenaciously years ago," Lucas reminisced with a chuckle.

Zelana gasped at the unexpected revelation of their childhood interactions as her blush deepened. "I assure you, I've outgrown that habit as well," she added humorously with flair, enriching the light-hearted banter and bringing another wave of laughter through the room.

Deon grinned, his eyes twinkling with amusement as he watched the princess use humor to manage the uncomfortable situation and recover from the playful embarrassment, leaving him deeply impressed.

"I'm Chue Lor, the Advisor-in-Chief," Chue introduced himself as he stepped toward the princess and gracefully took her hand, kissing it lightly. "I thought I'd step in to spare you further blushes, Princess Zelana," he quipped gallantly.

Laughter filled the chamber once again, echoing the warmth that had come to define the evening.

"Your chivalry is most welcome," the Princess replied with a warm smile.

Chue extended his hand in greeting to the Crown Prince. "It's an honor to meet you."

"A pleasure..." Samuel shook his hand firmly.

CHAPTER TWO

THE NEGOTIATOR

THE ATMOSPHERE IN the meeting hall buzzed with the subdued murmur of conversation.

"Please have a seat and let's enjoy some brunch," Lucas offered generously before sitting down at the head of the long mahogany table, signaling the beginning of the social hour.

Lucas was a first-generation demigod, the son of King Merci Celeste and Goddess Alexi. His parents were the founders of Zelonia, established after their triumphant victory over Krimzon in the legendary Clash of Azalon. Known for his progressive leadership, he was celebrated for his willingness to evolve with the times, empowering women to take on leadership roles and participate in combat.

Servers glided in, offering snacks and pouring wine for the guests as the gentle clink of glasses filled the room. An array of fresh fruits and delicate pastries were served, inviting the guests to enjoy them while they mingled.

Deon took a sip of wine, allowing the flavors to settle on his palate before speaking. "This wine is exceptionally smooth, with a robust flavor that lingers pleasantly."

Zelana observed Deon closely, noting his raised eyebrow of appreciation.

"I'm glad it meets your taste, Ambassador Deon. It hails from the Lashia Kingdom, one of our oldest allies. They have the most esteemed vineyards in Azalon," Lucas nodded with a warm smile.

"Lashia, you say? I've heard of their storied vines. They truly live up to their reputation," he praised.

"Indeed, they've been cultivating grapes on those hills for generations," Samuel interjected, reaching for a strawberry and tasting it.

"Their unique climate and soil contribute to the distinct taste you're enjoying," Zelana commented, intriguing those present, especially Deon.

How is it that you know such minuscule details, Princess? he pondered in silence, swirling the wine gently in his glass, admiring its intense color. "It's not just the taste but the aroma as well. There's a hint of oak and maybe… blackberry?"

"Very perceptive," the King replied, pleased with Deon's discernment. "They were aged in oak barrels, and the blackberries grow wild in the area, adding a subtle note to the bouquet."

"It really is a remarkable integration of flavors," Chue added to the conversation.

As Deon indulged in another sip, his eyes couldn't help but wander back to Zelana, observing her poised demeanor as she delicately nibbled on a grape.

How do you manage to look so charming even while simply eating a grape? He thought to himself, his admiration for her elegance barely concealed as a subtle smile escaped his lips.

"I must say, Your Majesty, Lashia's vineyards have outdone themselves this year," remarked Lord Makeo Kamaka, a seasoned politician whose life was deeply rooted in family and a sense of duty. He had dedicated forty years of his life in service to the kingdom, where his sharp intellect and strategic mind were invaluable assets.

"Have you tried the white wine from Northern Village? It brings out the subtle flavors in spicy cuisine," added Commander Rowan Campbell, a middle-aged gentleman who had served for two decades as the esteemed leader of the Royal Guards. He was known for his ruthlessness, striking fear into the hearts of those who dared to threaten the royal family.

"Indeed, Commander Rowan, it pairs remarkably well with potatoes. It seems we may need to start growing some grapes ourselves," General Gaius Cornelius commented as he sipped from his glass. A man with thirty years of battle-hardened experience, the General had led the Zelonian army with a blend of discipline and respect. His tall, muscular frame was honed by decades of rigorous combat training, his very presence commanding respect and instilling confidence on the battlefield among his troops.

A round of laughter filled the room as Dominic chuckled. "It seems someone is already drunk."

Dominic was a notable Commander in the Zelonian Army and the King's bodyguard. Born into a world that offered him nothing as an orphan, he carved his path with sheer determination and exceptional combat abilities, earning his place beside the King.

Servers returned to the meeting hall with trays of the afternoon meal, starting with a fresh salad, followed by a main course of baked chicken, accompanied by noodles and a medley of vegetables.

The room filled with jovial banter as the Royal Council continued their chatter with the Sanshe representatives. The air was rich with the bond of new friendships. Each bite of food and sip of wine seemed to fuel their discussions, blending laughter with pleasurable conversations.

"To new opportunities and promising discussions," Lucas raised his glass with enthusiasm and optimism as he surveyed the assembly of distinguished guests. "May it be as rich and rewarding as this vintage wine we share today."

Cheers resounded harmoniously through the hall as glasses clinked, and together they took a collective sip of wine, savoring the complex flavors. As the last drops lingered on their palates, they set down their glasses and the clatter of silverware settled while the servers whisked the final dishes away. The conversations subtly transitioned to more serious matters, leaving everyone eager for the deliberations that awaited.

With a composed and regal demeanor, Lucas cleared his throat lightly, drawing the eyes of all those present toward him. "Now that we have shared a splendid meal and our appetites are satisfied, it is time we turn our attention to the pressing issues at hand," he began, his voice authoritative yet inviting, filling the suddenly hushed space as he turned to Deon, who sat poised and attentive.

"As our esteemed guest, I would like to invite Ambassador Deon to initiate our conversation. Please, feel free to present the topics and concerns you wish to address." Lucas's formal invitation shifted the room's focus to Deon.

"First and foremost, His Majesty, King MuaYeng of Sanshe, extends his warmest greetings. He has great confidence and trust that together we can overcome the challenges that lie before us," he began as his words were met with nods of affirmation from the Councilmen.

"Furthermore, I must express my profound gratitude to Your Majesty for the exceptional and delightful meal prepared in our honor, adding to the splendor of this gathering," Deon continued after a brief pause. "I am equally grateful to the esteemed Royal

Council for this invaluable opportunity to convene and engage in meaningful dialogue. Please grant me your understanding, as I intend to speak frankly."

"I prefer honest and open conversations myself," Lucas replied in a conducive tone.

"Sanshe has evolved into a haven for refugees fleeing from neighboring lands, each seeking safety from the relentless grip of Immortals engulfing their kingdoms. This sudden surge of asylum seekers has placed considerable strain on Sanshe's resources. We're finding it difficult to feed our expanding populace, creating a situation that demands immediate and innovative solutions. It appears Zelonia has encountered similar challenges and yet managed to sustain and even thrive, ensuring sufficient food supply for your citizens. We are keen to understand and possibly emulate your strategies to better address our current situation," Deon shared, laying out the situation with clarity and seeking a collaborative approach to solving the issue, inspired by Zelonia's effective solutions.

Lucas leaned forward, his demeanor reflecting a proactive stance. "We've taken significant strides in agricultural advancement in Zelonia. We have developed a range of advanced farming tools that have the potential to increase food production rates by up to fourfold. Adopting our tools and agricultural methodologies could significantly address the challenges Sanshe faces in feeding its growing population. These innovations are available for purchase."

"I've personally witnessed the efficiency of these tools, Your Majesty. Our King is aware of their potential. Not only do we want to acquire these remarkable machines, but we aspire to understand the underlying technology and craftsmanship that goes into creating them," proposed Deon.

Lucas's eyes moved slowly across the faces of the Councilmen, pausing to consider the implications of such an exchange while murmurs between the members filled the room.

Deon cleared his throat and continued, "We are interested in a partnership that would allow for a transfer of knowledge and skills. By learning to produce these machines domestically, we can lay a sustainable foundation for our agricultural sector and ensure long-term food security for our people."

"Farming has always been a specialty in Zelonia, a sacred jewel bestowed upon us since the descent of the revered Goddess Alexi," Samuel spoke with a reverent tone. "We prefer to safeguard this knowledge and offer our tools for export."

The Councilmen nodded in agreement as Zelana observed Deon closely, knowing the majority would be against his proposition.

"The tales passed down by my mother, Lady Sonia Alderidge of Zelonia, depict Goddess Alexi not just as a savior of Zelonia, but a guardian of all Azalonian people, generously sharing her agricultural wisdom with those who sought it. Her intent was clear—to fulfill the fundamental needs of humanity, allowing all societies to prosper and thrive," Deon responded thoughtfully.

The room fell silent, and a subtle smile of intrigue formed on Zelana's lips. She was impressed at how he used the enduring values Zelonia was built upon to his advantage.

"I urge Your Majesty and the Royal Council to embrace the essence of Goddess Alexi's legacy and reconsider the sharing of not just the tools but also the knowledge that powers them. Such an act would be in true alignment with the divine Queen's intent, ensuring the collective growth and well-being of all nations," Deon suggested. "Not to mention, the sheer size of these farming machines is colossal. Transporting them on standard wagons is nearly impossible."

Deon's comment drew laughter from the Royal Council, easing the tension in the room.

"Furthermore, if our blacksmiths are not versed in the construction of these machines, we will face a dire predicament should they malfunction. It could lead to a catastrophic delay in food production, a risk Sanshe cannot afford," argued Deon.

"And the availability of replacements isn't guaranteed," Zelana finally spoke, her voice soft yet imbued with a quiet strength.

"Indeed, a valid point, Princess Zelana," Deon acknowledged, visibly impressed by her insightful participation in the discussion.

Samuel remained unwavering in his stance. "Our unique farming techniques are a cornerstone of trade with other nations. Sharing the knowledge to create these marvels would compromise our trade immensely."

"I understand your concern, Crown Prince Samuel. Sanshe has ample resources—silver, gold, gems—to procure these tools, but our situation transcends mere trade," Deon sighed, pausing before delving further into the crux of the matter. "Sanshe and Zelonia are the last bastions of hope humanity has left, teetering on the brink of annihilation. A single misstep and one of us could cease to exist. Should Sanshe face famine, it would not only be a catastrophe for us but also leave Zelonia without a crucial ally in these perilous times," he reasoned, his words resonating with earnestness. "I strongly implore you to reconsider."

The men absorbed the gravity of Deon's stark depiction of their shared reality as the room fell silent once more; yet none of them dared to speak.

"Perhaps we're being a bit hasty in our decision," Zelana interjected, breaking the silence, speaking from a position of power. "What will Sanshe offer in return for this exchange of knowledge?"

"Sanshe recognizes the immense value of Zelonia's expertise," Deon said, facing the Princess and addressing her directly. "We are committed to compensating the time and effort of your blacksmiths fairly for the crafting of each tool and the training involved in educating our own."

"This approach seems equitable. I am confident we can forge a partnership that honors the skill of Zelonia's craftsmen while also fostering the building of Sanshe's self-reliance," summarized Zelana, aligning the implications of his proposal to her expectations. "However, you must also compensate for the intellectual rights involved with each tool."

Deon was pleasantly taken aback that the Princess had not only grown into a beautiful young woman but was quite intelligent for her age, as his brows furrowed in respect for her shrewd negotiation skills.

"Could you elaborate on these intellectual rights you speak of?" he asked, digging for further details.

"The rights to craft, to use, and to sell any tool or machinery. These rights must be clearly defined, compensated, and formalized in our agreements," clarified the Princess with precision.

"That sounds rather intricate," Deon countered firmly. "I fear the process may delay the execution."

"The contracts can be simple and straightforward. We can refine the details later," Zelana assured him with a subtle smile. "We will also require a reciprocal exchange of knowledge that mirrors this agreement." She paused and clarified, "Sanshe weapons..."

Deon recognized her shift toward a more sensitive topic. *That is quite bold of you, Princess.*

"You must be referring to cannons and pistols," he surmised with a slight smirk. "Princess Zelana, today's discussions were meant to focus on agricultural tools and machinery. Perhaps we could reschedule another visit to discuss and explore matters of weaponry."

"Ambassador Deon," Zelana referred to him by name as he did her. "Sanshe needs to secure food for its growing population while Zelonia needs to strengthen its defenses. If we are to survive the looming threat of Krimzon, there must be cooperation on both sides, wouldn't you agree?"

"You indeed negotiate with vigor, Princess," Deon admitted with a serious expression, his mind racing to navigate the complex negotiation she had skillfully steered. "However, I must confess that this discussion will necessitate additional deliberations with the Sanshe King."

"Ambassador..." Zelana leaned forward, staring daringly into his eyes. "Your very presence here assures me of King MuaYeng's confidence in your capabilities. We both know that you have the authority to negotiate these terms."

Deon was captivated by her discerning insights, feeling a deeper spark of intrigue ignite within him as he rubbed his chin in quiet admiration. Despite recognizing her valid points, he simply squinted his eyes and maintained a composed silence, a veneer of resistance, curious to observe how she might further articulate her proposal to sway his decision.

"Consider the endless possibilities," Zelana continued, her voice steady, exuding both wisdom and vision. "We propose to dispatch our finest farmers, blacksmiths, and artisans to Sanshe as part of a comprehensive knowledge exchange initiative. Similarly, Sanshe could reciprocate. This initiative would offer apprenticeship programs for our citizens and give them the freedom to choose and excel in their preferred trades. This would enable both nations to benefit and flourish from their collective expertise and success."

"Your vision is quite progressive and thought-provoking," Deon observed, almost unable to hide his growing respect and admiration for her innovative and strategic mindset.

"Then how can you not be moved?" asked Zelana, gazing deeply into his hazel eyes.

"Your conviction is indeed compelling, but..." he paused to think, her intense gaze slowly dismantling his diplomatic guard.

"What reservations still linger, Ambassador?" the Princess inquired, a gentle smile playing on her lips.

Deon cast a brief glance toward Chue, searching for a hint of guidance, yet found only an inscrutable expression on his friend's face. After a moment of contemplative silence, he turned back to the Princess, who awaited his decision with unwavering attention.

"Your arguments are persuasive, Princess. You've convinced me that pursuing this path will undoubtedly enrich both our realms," he declared with a new resolve.

In that moment, the room erupted in applause as the Princess's hand immediately drifted to her lips, a subtle attempt at masking her surprise and excitement. Yet, her eyes, alight with the exhilaration of her vision being acknowledged and embraced, betrayed her.

Samuel was unable to believe that Zelana had succeeded, his laughter resonating warmly through the chamber with pride, watching his sister revel in her well-earned victory.

Deon couldn't steer his gaze away from Zelana as he noticed a soft blush color her cheeks, eliciting an unexpected smile from him. He was witnessing not only a Princess before him, but a determined woman brimming with ambition.

Quickly composing herself, the Princess gently lowered her hand. "We are poised to forge history together, Ambassador Deon," Zelana declared as applause continued to wash over them.

"I look forward to our collaboration," agreed Deon, his smile widening in response as he watched her turn gracefully toward her father.

"What are your thoughts on this partnership, Your Majesty?" she questioned with reverence, seeking the King's endorsement to bind the future of the two realms.

Lucas chuckled with a father's pride. "Princess Zelana will proceed to champion the rest of this discussion on behalf of Zelonia," he commanded, giving his final nod of approval.

Deon was momentarily surprised by the King's decree.

"I anticipate hearing positive developments soon, Ambassador Deon," the King remarked, an endorsement of his trust in the competence of both Deon and Zelana in finalizing the negotiations.

"I assure you that you will not be disappointed, Your Majesty," replied Deon with respect.

"We'll leave the finer details to your capable hands," the King said with a light chuckle before standing up, concluding the day's meeting.

Deon's gaze returned to the Princess as their eyes locked. He recognized the depth of her negotiation skills and understood the need to elevate his approach.

CHAPTER THREE

AGREEMENTS

AS THE ECHOES of the final footsteps faded and the door softly clicked shut, the room shifted from its formal ambience to an intimate setting with Deon and Zelana finally alone.

He observed her sitting with regal poise before him. It was only moments ago when her spontaneous reaction offered a rare glimpse into her unguarded persona, not constrained by the weight of her crown. He felt an increasing desire to understand the person behind those expressive blue eyes.

"I think it would be more comfortable if we weren't so far apart," he suggested with a stoic expression.

"Please join me," she responded, gesturing with a caress of her hand to the seat next to her, her eyes alight with a gentle inquisitiveness.

"Don't mind if I do," Deon responded, rising to his feet and moving toward her, his every step marked by a fluid, confident grace that spoke of his strength not just in stature but also in character.

As he took a seat beside her, the closeness allowed him a clearer view of the delicate features of her face, more striking at this distance. "Where did you learn to be so persuasive?" he asked.

"Observing you," she responded with a subtle smile.

Deon's expression softened. "But the more I hear you speak, the more you leave me speechless," he admitted, a hint of a burgeoning affection growing within him.

"I've never had that effect on anyone but you…" she flirted, her eyes locked onto his with intrigue.

"Why do I find that hard to believe?" Deon teased with a wink.

There was something about his wink that sent an exhilarating shiver through her as her eyes sparkled and a curious smile played on her lips.

"If I didn't know better, I'd think you were flirting with me…" she murmured, her heart fluttering uncontrollably as her cheeks flushed with a soft rose hue.

Deon's face broke into a smile, caught off guard by her words, and he replied half-seriously, half in jest, "I wouldn't dare… you're the Princess of Zelonia."

"I doubt that has stopped you before," the Princess countered with a teasing glint in her eyes, her gaze alluring, softly challenging him to step over the line he had drawn.

Deon let out a light chuckle, finding her boldness and wit genuinely captivating, delighted by the unexpected depth of their interaction.

I must not lose my composure, he reminded himself, recognizing the need to maintain some decorum while on duty. He cleared his throat, shifting his gaze slightly as he anchored back to the negotiations they were tasked to complete.

"So… Princess, it seems this was a strategic move of yours from the start, aiming for Sanshe's military assets," he said, gently steering them back to the matters of state.

You are quite disciplined, her thoughts raced, deepening her intrigue as she noticed him swiftly shifting the conversation back to politics.

"We both need each other, Ambassador Deon," she replied with a soft, enticing whisper. "I can't foresee how we can win this war against Krimzon without standing united."

Deon felt the sincerity in her words, and with a solemn nod, he reached for a quill and parchment paper, ready to translate their spoken agreement into action. "How do you want to proceed?"

"I can prepare Zelonia's proposals and payment outlines," Zelana suggested, her hands moving with purpose as she mirrored his actions.

"Alright," he responded. "I'll draft Sanshe's, and we can refine them together, ensuring every detail aligns with our mutual goals."

"Perfect," she agreed as she dove into writing her agreement.

The room instantly filled with the rustle of papers and the scratching of quill on parchment. Deon's admiration for Zelana grew, observing her unwavering focus and commitment. He began to work on Sanshe's proposals, his actions deliberate and thoughtful, mirroring the seriousness of the task. Time passed unnoticed with the occasional crossing out and meticulous rewriting of the proposals.

Zelana finished writing the last point of Zelonia's agreement and glanced at Deon's work. She was awestruck by the neatness of his handwriting and the thoroughness of his approach, each line reflecting his careful attention to detail and deep understanding of the stakes involved. She voiced some concerns and their subsequent discussions transformed into strategic ideas, resulting in them sharing, debating, and refining their points.

After hours of negotiating, characterized by a steady exchange of concessions and agreements, they finally came to a mutual consensus. The contracts were finalized, embodying a balanced representation of both kingdoms' interests and establishing a foundation for future cooperation and prosperity.

"I didn't anticipate we'd wrap this up so soon," Deon remarked, a hint of surprise mingling with a deep sigh of relief, leaning back in his chair, the tension easing from his shoulders as he allowed himself a moment to savor their accomplishment.

"We came into this knowing our goals and stood firm, ensuring equity and fairness," Zelana reflected, her voice imbued with pride.

"Our collaborative effort and the efficiency of today's discussions were remarkable, Princess," he admitted. "Most negotiations that I've chaired usually stretch over days, if not weeks."

"I'm relieved the contracts are complete, but I can't help feeling anxious. I hope it satisfies the King of Sanshe's expectations," she shared, feeling a bit nervous.

"Don't worry, leave His Majesty to me," Deon replied, his voice carrying a calm assurance.

"I trust that you will make our visions a reality," murmured the Princess with a subtle smile.

Her words warmed Deon's heart, who found himself lowering his guard as he admired her quiet beauty.

The lilting strains of music wafted into the room, tugging at Zelana's spirits. She stood up and walked over to the window, drawn by the lively melodies and the buzz of activities from the streets below.

"I nearly forgot it was Summer Fest…" the Princess murmured, peering out at the colorful scene.

Deon's gaze lingered appreciatively on Zelana's physique, noting her slender yet voluptuous figure as he stood and joined her at the window, taking in the vibrant festivities. "It looks inviting."

Zelana turned to him, her eyes alight with a playful spark of spontaneity. "Would you like to get lost with me in Zelonia?"

"I'd get lost with you anywhere, Princess Zelana," Deon replied as his face lit up with a playful grin.

"You're officially flirting with me," she teased, a hint of mischief twinkling in her eyes.

"I wouldn't dare," he flirted openly with intent. "We can't have the Zelonian Princess falling for me."

His audacity left her momentarily breathless as her pulse unexpectedly quickened.

"Mister Ambassador, you've become quite bold," she murmured softly, her smile enchanting him.

"Your presence emboldens me, Princess," he admitted while his heart pounded excitedly in his chest.

"Let's strip away all the pretense tonight and be exposed and raw," she proposed playfully, her eyes dancing with amusement, intensifying the emotions Deon was struggling to keep under control.

"Careful what you wish for," he warned, half-teasing, yet half-serious.

Zelana giggled softly as she moved gracefully toward the door, each step brimming with exhilaration.

Swept up in the moment's infectious energy, Deon gathered the freshly inked contracts from the table, hurrying to catch up to her.

"Deon?" Chue was shocked to see his friend step out and quickly hand over the contracts.

"Don't lose those," he said, his eyes twinkling with the magic of the moment, quickly falling into step beside Zelana.

As they walked side by side, the corridor felt more intimate as they laughed and talked effortlessly. It was the beginning of a fate that would bind their hearts in ways neither of them could fully understand—testing, challenging, and ultimately defining their destinities.

CHAPTER FOUR

First Date

UNDER THE STARLIT sky, Zelana and Deon found themselves lost in the vibrant heart of the Zelonian city, their presence melting seamlessly into the lively crowd. The streets around them were bustling with activity, a tapestry of colors and sounds painting the evening air. They walked side by side, their expressions lit with the excitement of shared discovery, as the radiant colors of the market stalls and the diverse array of goods on display mesmerized them.

"The energy here is incredible," Deon remarked, his voice carrying a mixture of wonder and admiration, echoing the lively sights and sounds around them.

"The city never ceases to amaze me," replied Zelana with a hint of longing and fascination.

"How often do you get the chance to enjoy it?" he asked curiously.

"Rarely," she confessed. "My parents always worry about potential dangers lurking in the shadows."

"I'm somewhat astonished that the King would entrust you to my care then," Deon admitted, his words tinged with gratitude and a hint of playfulness. "Although, he is having us discreetly followed."

"Oh, Commander Dominic?" Her laughter, melodic and unguarded, filled the air. "He's harmless," she assured him, her eyes sparkling with amusement.

Deon's chuckle mingled with hers. "I've seen the man. 'Harmless' isn't quite how I'd describe him."

"I promise I won't let him hurt you," teased the Princess.

Deon laughed wholeheartedly, his voice echoing through the streets.

"But something tells me you won't be needing my protection," she added casually.

"And why do you say that?" he inquired curiously.

"You look like someone who has bled in many wars," she observed, eyeing his physique.

"Do I?" Deon asked teasingly, feeling flattered as a sudden warmth rushed to his face. The unfamiliar sensation of her admiring gaze pierced through his well-maintained composure.

"More than most," she replied, realizing he caught her staring. She glanced away, blushing slightly.

The air was alive with the scents of exotic spices and the cheerful chatter of the crowd as they succumbed to the temptations and paused by small food stalls lining the streets, sampling the local cuisine from skewered meats to other delectable bites, reveling in their flavors.

"Mmmm... this is exquisite," Zelana declared, savoring the meat's rich, succulent flavor.

Deon boldly reached over and cheekily swiped the last piece of her chicken, popping it into his mouth. "The flavors are amazing," he agreed with a grin.

"Ambassador Deon!" she exclaimed, feigning shock. "Who said you can take my food?"

"You told me to be myself, exposed and raw," he reminded her, his eyes sparkling with mischief.

"Well then..." The Princess playfully leaned over and took a bite of his remaining steak, an expression of pure enjoyment on her face.

Deon's laughter rang out under the twinkling lights of the Zelonian streets, his eyes crinkling with genuine amusement as she brought her hand to her lips, attempting to stifle her soft giggles.

"You're so different from other Princesses..." he murmured, admiring her charming presence.

His words stirred something deep within Zelana that moment, igniting foreign emotions she had not experienced before as she lowered her hand, her gaze lingering on his handsome, exotic features.

"You must know many princesses," she surmised, searching his face for clues to his relations.

"There are quite a few Royals taking refuge in Sanshe," he admitted with a warm smile, choosing his words carefully. "My role as a diplomat brings me into their circles often."

"Is there one you admire?" she asked, her heart skipping slightly.

Deon found himself pausing as his gaze drifted away, lost in contemplation. "Perhaps..." he confessed softly with hesitation. "But she's unaware of my feelings."

The air seemed to thicken with tension as Zelana felt an unexpected sting in her chest at his admission, a selfish pinch of jealousy halting her. "Why haven't you confessed to her?"

Deon stopped and faced her as he confronted a sad truth. "She's... out of my reach."

Zelana paused; her previous insecurities slowly morphed into empathy.

"It's hard to imagine a man so bold and assured as you quietly harboring unspoken affection," she murmured as her expression softened, sensing the depth of his pain.

"I'm discovering that unrequited love is the most painful," he admitted softly.

The lights cast a soft glow around them, creating an intimate atmosphere that enhanced her allure, making her look more breathtaking as he found himself becoming more captivated by her with each passing moment. Deon's heart, usually steady and composed, now throbbed with raw intensity as Zelana slowly backed away toward the crowd.

"You promised to get lost with me," she whispered, her eyes twinkling with a playful challenge, never leaving his as she invited him to shed the weight of his emotions and follow her into the night.

How are you doing this to me? He thought, slowly losing himself to the moment and hastening his steps toward her.

The Princess turned and weaved through the lively crowd, her gentle laughter beckoning him onward, guiding him through the maze of people.

Deon's heart beat with excitement, utterly hypnotized by her charm as he continued to chase her while she playfully attempted to lose him. Surprisingly, she led them to the heart of the city square where they seamlessly blended into the crowd.

As Deon caught up with her, he became captivated by the enchanting smile that lit up her face and the sparkle of excitement in the Princess's eyes. The lively music and the sight of people dancing under the soft glow of the streetlights added to the magic of the moment, leaving him completely mesmerized.

"Dance with me," he whispered and extended his hand to her.

She slipped her hand into his as he led her onto the cobblestone floor, quickly immersing themselves amidst a sea of dancers. Their laughter mingled with their attempts to imitate and mirror the dance steps of those around them, drawing them closer together.

"In case you haven't noticed, I'm completely lost," he playfully confessed with a chuckle, proceeding to perform his own improvised moves, endearingly coordinated with the music.

"I would have never guessed," she teased, captivated by his genuine and irresistible charm.

Deon laughed heartily as he watched the Princess embrace the traditional dance, linking arms with the women, her feet moving in tune with theirs, creating a dynamic line of dancers. He joined in the men's cheers and clapping, adding to the festive atmosphere.

The line broke off and he swiftly pulled her back to him, wanting her close. Zelana's feet moved with precision and flair while Deon's steps were expertly timed to the lively beat. He spun her around and they lost themselves in the enchantment of the moment, moving to the rhythm of the infectious music. The song then waned while joyous applause rang out, leaving them exhilarated.

"I haven't had this much fun in a long time," Zelana confessed, slightly out of breath, her eyes shimmering with joy and something deeper as she looked up at him.

"I feel the same way," Deon replied, echoing her sentiment.

The music shifted, slowing to a soft, romantic melody that draped the city square in an intimate shroud. Around them, couples drew closer, some exchanging tender kisses, enveloped in the magical ambience.

Deon made a decisive, bold move, twirling Zelana into his embrace, with her back to his chest.

"Is this how you dance in Sanshe?" she asked nervously, her body tense with the closeness of his.

"Perhaps..." Deon replied, holding her closer as he nestled his nose to her hair, inhaling the sweet rose scent that encapsulated her essence.

"What is this fragrance?" he murmured close to her ear.

"Myztica..." she replied in a breathy whisper.

"Myz...tica..." he echoed, his voice a soft caress in her ear.

Deon gently twirled her to face him, his hands settling securely around her waist, drawing her even closer as their foreheads touched.

What is this feeling? Zelana's heart fluttered, her body surrendering to the closeness, as they swayed gracefully to the mesmerizing tune, lost in each other's eyes.

Time slowed as the world around them blurred and the crowd faded, leaving only the two of them dancing intimately under the starlit sky.

As Deon's breath lingered just above her lips, his heart raced, temptation washing over him as he saw the same look of unspoken desire in her eyes.

I want to kiss you.

He thought, breathless, slowly leaning down, inching closer, his restraint slipping.

Applause suddenly erupted around them as Deon froze—his lips a whisper away from hers.

A bittersweet ache swelled in his chest as he gazed into her eyes, realizing that the melody had ceased, and the magic had ended. He was once again the Ambassador and she, the Zelonian Princess.

"I wish this night didn't have to end," he whispered, pained at the thought of letting her go.

Zelana stared into his eyes, breathless, her heart mirroring the same unspoken emotions.

As they stood, breaths apart, their hearts pounded with anticipation, unable to escape the forbidden feelings that lingered between them—the evening of brief respite unexpectedly transformed into an unforgettable encounter, one that would linger in their memories long after the night ended.

CHAPTER FIVE

FINALLY FREE

DEON RETURNED TO his room, letting the door slam shut behind him. His heart pounded from the night's encounter; a feeling that intensified with every passing moment. It had been years since he felt a desire this consuming, a hunger that could plague him all night as he stared at himself in the mirror, trying to steady his breath, trying to regain control.

But it was useless. Zelana consumed his thoughts. His mind was filled with vivid, seductive images of her—the softness of her lips, the way her body had leaned into him, so trusting, so wanting, and yet so unattainable. He clenched his jaw, battling the urge that continued to simmer relentlessly.

Leaning back on the dresser, Deon reminded himself of his duties—he was the Ambassador of Sanshe, not some reckless man who could afford to fall for the Princess. And yet, as he thought of Zelana, every rational thought crumbled—her eyes, filled with the same unspoken desire, pierced through his defenses; her luscious lips, gently parting so close to his... had tempted him beyond reason.

I wanted to kiss you.

The thought slammed into him, raw and undeniable, but he had stopped—just before crossing the line, the pull of duty too strong, too ingrained to ignore, but the temptation was intense… very intense.

With a frustrated sigh, Deon ripped off his jacket and shirt, letting them fall carelessly to the floor. He stripped off the rest of his clothes, as if shedding the burden of restraint he had fought so hard to maintain all night. He needed to cool off—to clear his head.

He moved purposefully toward the corner of the room and opened the partition. Stepping into the large tub, he yanked on the lever, releasing a torrent of cool water from the huge barrel overhead. The cold cascade shocked his body, pouring relentlessly over his skin. But, even as the water rushed down his body, it did little to extinguish the craving for her touch gnawing at him, relentless and unforgiving. It was a yearning refusing to let go, clinging to him despite the numbing chill.

I should have kissed you.

The thought clung to Deon, filling him with a haunting sense of regret. His heart was still racing, his skin tingling as he stood drenched under the cascading cold stream. All he could think about was Zelana—the rose scent that clung to her, intoxicating him, and the way her body had fit so perfectly against his as he slipped his hand around her slender waist. He could still feel the warmth of her skin beneath his fingers as he gently caressed her back while they danced, her soft curves pressed against him, making him desire her helplessly as he pulled her close… too close.

He raked a hand through his wet hair, frustration coursing through him. Forbidden emotions overwhelmed him helplessly. The need… the raw need to feel the softness of Zelana's body and devour her slowly consumed him. He hadn't thought of a woman this way for years. Until Zelana.

Deon's breath hitched as he tried to steady himself, his hands pressed firmly against the wall. He had denied himself intimacy for years, ever since Victoria. Victoria Schulz... the woman who had once been his everything—until she wasn't. The day she left, Deon suppressed his deepest desires, learning to dim the flame and live without it, choosing duty over passion.

I want to be vulnerable again. A small smile tugged at his lips. *My heart wants to beat for someone other than her.*

Deon finally felt the remnants of his love for Victoria wash away, leaving behind only a quiet acceptance.

I'm finally free of Victoria.

Deon leaned his back to the cold, stone wall as his thoughts drifted irresistibly back to Zelana. Mere thoughts of her left him breathless as his heart began to pound with an undeniable longing.

"Zelana..."

Deon groaned her name under his breath, his voice heavy with desire as the cold water ceased to drip, fully drained from the barrel. He found himself savoring the burning ache that consumed his body, refusing to fade, his resistance slipping.

As his craving slowly consumed him, he slumped down into the cool water, letting himself sink deeper into the tub, submerging himself under the water, lost in the depths of his emotions.

Minutes passed as Deon emerged, catching his breath, yet his yearning for her still clung to him. He leaned back and sighed as a quiet truth settled upon him that moment...

No amount of cold water could wash away the desire I feel for you.

CHAPTER SIX

INSIGNIA

THE FOLLOWING MORNING dawned bright and sunny, mirroring the optimism that filled the meeting hall. The heavy velvet curtains were drawn back, allowing the morning light to spill across the polished marble floor as the members of the Royal Council of Zelonia sat at the mahogany table, meticulously reviewing the documents.

Makeo read the Zelonian contract aloud while Gaius matched up the Sanshe contract in detail. The air was thick with anticipation as Deon, Zelana, and Chue waited anxiously, watching closely for the Council members' reactions.

Deon sat silently beside Lucas, his posture relaxed. Yet, his presence exuded a quiet, commanding confidence. His gaze swept across the table, settling on Zelana. Her expression remained poised, attentively engaged in the ongoing discussions.

I can't stop thinking about you, he mused silently as his eyes lingered on her, admiring the radiant glow she brought to the golden gown she wore.

As though sensing his thoughts, Zelana glanced at Deon, a subtle smile playing on her lips as she took in his appearance, dressed in a maroon and gold suit that enhanced the robust hue of his complexion.

You become more handsome each time I see you, she reflected silently, holding his gaze.

"I am thoroughly impressed," Lucas voiced his approval, interrupting the tense atmosphere. "Let us proceed to a vote. Those in favor, please raise your hand."

In unanimous agreement, all the Councilmen raised their hands, a gesture that brought a satisfied smile to the King's face, marking a decisive moment of consensus.

"Excellent," the King declared as he exchanged approving glances with Deon and Zelana. "Both of you have reasons to be immensely proud," he commended, affirming the success of their joint effort.

"I want to express my deepest gratitude to Princess Zelana," Deon began, his acknowledgment causing a slight lift of eyebrows among some of the Councilmen. "Collaborating with the Princess has been an enlightening experience," he continued, his gaze shifting to meet hers. "Her astute insight, steadfast dedication, and unwavering commitment to the welfare of Zelonia and its people have significantly advanced our negotiations. She fostered a spirit of mutual respect and understanding that promises a flourishing future for both our realms."

The chamber filled with soft murmurs as the Councilmen nodded in agreement, their attention shifting between Deon and the Princess. A blush touched Zelana's cheeks under the weight of Deon's public praise, but she quickly regained her composure.

"Thank you, Ambassador Deon, for your gracious words," Zelana responded elegantly, her melodious voice resonating softly in the hushed room. "It is a rare privilege to work with someone who is not only a skilled diplomat but who also holds a deep reverence for the values and traditions of the people he engages with. Your openness, expertise, and profound respect for our heritage have made these negotiations not only productive but also enjoyable. The seamless nature of our collaboration signals a boundless potential for what we can achieve together across Azalon."

Deon acknowledged her words with a respectful nod, his admiration for her vision deepening.

Lucas observed their exchange with a thoughtful expression, nodding appreciatively. "When leaders can unite with such mutual respect and vision, the path forward is surely one of success." He chuckled softly, affixing his insignia to the contracts, sealing Zelonia's commitment.

Applause erupted throughout the room as Deon and Zelana exchanged proud glances, reflecting a shared sense of accomplishment.

"I eagerly await King MuaYeng's insignia alongside mine on these documents," Lucas stated enthusiastically.

"I don't foresee any issues," Deon replied with a confident assurance. "I will coordinate a delegation of specialists for each sector and arrange for their arrival in Zelonia."

Samuel leaned in with interest and pressed, "And how soon do you expect to mobilize this team?"

Deon paused momentarily, sharing a brief but meaningful glance with Zelana. "Would commencing next week be agreeable?" he proposed, setting an ambitious yet achievable timeline that surpassed even Zelonia's expectations.

"That would be excellent," replied the Crown Prince, clearly impressed.

"Your promptness is truly praiseworthy, Ambassador Deon," Lucas expressed, solidifying the positive impression Deon had cultivated within the Zelonian court.

"I came with intentions to deliver," Deon responded with a warm smile, assuring his commitment to meeting the expectations set upon him and taking pride in executing his duties with efficiency.

"And how fares my old friend, the General of Sanshe?" Lucas inquired, his smile warming with fond memories, signaling his interest in Deon's familial ties.

Deon's expression brightened at the mention of his father. "Thank you for your gracious concern, Your Majesty. My father remains robust and active. He is currently overseeing the training of new refugees from the Kingdom of Esperia, ensuring their seamless integration into our military forces."

"You're the Sanshe General's son?" Zelana inquired, surprised, seeking clarification.

"Yes, I am," Deon affirmed, his voice carrying a blend of humility and pride. Sensing the Princess's keen interest, he added, "Alongside my ambassadorial duties, I also hold a commission as a Commander in the Sanshe military."

Zelana's eyes sparkled with deepened admiration and respect, absorbing this new dimension of Deon's life. His disclosure also heightened Lucas and Samuel's interest, intrigued by Deon's dual roles and his intricate connection in both military and political spheres.

"I heard about the prolonged battle in Esperia. It's tragic that they faced such a brutal defeat. Did King MuaYeng extend any support? Given that Esperia is just a half day's ride south of Sanshe," Lucas asked curiously, his tone serious with concern.

Deon's face took on a somber expression as the King mentioned the arduous battle at Esperia. "We received word of the dire situation in Esperia during the fourth week into the conflict. King

MuaYeng acted swiftly, commissioning me to lead our Special Ops unit to aid the Esperian royals. Regrettably, by the time we arrived, the castle had fallen, and many of their people were either slain or taken prisoner, destined for Krimzon."

"More human lives used as pawns in the coming Krimzon wars," Samuel muttered angrily, expressing his frustration about the ongoing conflict. "The only kingdom nearby that's still standing is Lashia."

"It is indeed a harsh reality," Deon admitted gravely. "We were able to rescue Crown Prince Winston and Princess Lenora, but tragically, the King and Queen were lost in the onslaught at the castle."

Lucas exhaled deeply, his heart heavy over the loss of an old friend. "At least the bloodline of Esperia will survive through Winston and Lenora," he reflected, offering a somber tribute to the royal family.

The Councilmen nodded in agreement with the King, sharing in the sentiment, yet remained silent.

"I proposed to King MuaYeng that we should seize the moment and end Krimzon's tyranny while we still draw breath," Deon confessed under the weighty scrutiny of Lucas's focused gaze. "For centuries, humanity has been on the defensive, allowing Krimzon to systematically dismantle our kingdoms one by one. If we continue to cower in fear behind our walls, there will come a day when there is no one left to stand against them."

It became increasingly apparent to Lucas that Deon was far from a simple envoy. His words hinted at a man with not only strategic foresight but also the readiness for direct confrontation when necessary. He had appeared before the Zelonian Royal Council as the Sanshe Ambassador, expertly negotiating the fate of his nation. But today, Deon revealed a different facet of himself—a man who wielded power over the lives of thousands, an esteemed Commander who strategized high-stakes military operations that hovered between life and death, determining the fate of many lives.

"Our next discussions should pivot to military strategy," declared Samuel confidently, "Zelonia will stand shoulder to shoulder with Sanshe against Krimzon."

A spark of dauntless determination lit Deon's eyes. "I look forward to it, Crown Prince Samuel."

Lucas continued to study Deon in silence, his gaze thoughtful and assessing.

"What exactly is a Special Ops unit?" asked Rowan.

"It's one of the many elite tactical divisions within the Sanshe military. My unit is the most lethal, operating strictly under the direct command of the King," Deon elaborated, subtly emphasizing the trust and responsibility bestowed upon him. "Each division is specialized and categorized based on combat capabilities and the skill set of its members."

"And what responsibilities do you hold as the Commander?" Gaius interjected.

"Our roles likely mirror each other, General," Deon acknowledged with a nod of respect. "I strategize and oversee the execution of every operation, navigating through perilous conditions with meticulous precision, achieving our objectives efficiently and minimizing risks," he explained with the experience and expertise of a seasoned warrior.

Intrigued, Lucas posed a challenging question. "Suppose during a mission you sense impending failure, what is your course of action?"

"Retreat," Deon replied without hesitation, "The safety of my unit is paramount. It's crucial we survive to fight another day, to ensure that we can continue to defend our realm and overtake our enemies."

Lucas's nod was thoughtful, acknowledging the strategic depth of Deon's answers. His gaze lingered on the Ambassador, recognizing a man guided not only by strict military discipline but also by a strong moral compass, driven by ambition, wisdom, and unwavering courage.

"Very impressive," Lucas finally voiced, his tone rich with respect. "It's evident that King MuaYeng has remarkable talents in his service, like yourself, Ambassador Deon."

His words, weighted with rare praise, caught Zelana and Samuel by surprise. It was uncommon for their father to express such high regard for individuals, especially those from beyond the borders of Zelonia. His endorsement signaled a deep appreciation for Deon's capabilities, subtly strengthening the diplomatic bonds between their kingdoms.

"I'm truly grateful for your generous words, Your Majesty," Deon responded with respectful modesty.

Seizing the opportunity to further gauge the young Commander's capabilities, Lucas asked with evident respect, "I have one more request of you."

"I am at your service," Deon replied charismatically with a confident readiness.

Lucas rose to his feet, his stature signaling the significance of his forthcoming request. "Would you be willing to demonstrate some of Sanshe's combat techniques?" he inquired, his voice a blend of challenge and invitation, keen to witness the military prowess of Deon's homeland firsthand.

Deon felt a sudden surge of adrenaline mixed with a hint of apprehension, understanding the King's intent to assess his skills directly. The request placed him squarely under the scrutiny of not just the King but the entire Royal Council. His mind raced with the potential implications of his performance, possibly enhancing or tarnishing the diplomatic ties.

"It would be my honor," he finally affirmed, accepting the challenge with a dignified nod, despite the whirlwind of thoughts.

No matter the outcome, I will support you, Deon, Zelana assured him silently as the fear of the repercussions—physically and politically—loomed over her. Yet, a spark of curiosity flickered within her, eager to witness the skills he possessed.

"Excellent," Lucas replied with a pleased smile, admiring him for his courage. "To the arena."

Without waiting for a response, Lucas led the way with the Royal Council in tow to witness a demonstration of Sanshe's renowned combat techniques.

CHAPTER SEVEN

TESTED

THE ARENA WAS hallowed ground, where countless legendary warriors had tread for centuries, fighting for the honor of their nations—a place that had borne witness to the fierce and riveting displays of merciless combat. As Deon stepped onto the arena, he could almost sense the echoes of the past—the metallic scent of blood spilled in fierce combat, the visceral clang of steel against steel, and the roaring cheers of the crowd as they rallied behind their chosen gladiators.

The air was crisp, carrying the murmurs of leaves that seemed to echo the hushed anticipations of the Royal Council. Each whisper was the subtle stirrings of fate, poised to record the challenges of the day into history. Deon now stood on the very soil where military diplomacy had been forged for centuries, his heart set on proving his worth and solidifying the alliance through his combat demonstration.

From their elevated seats, Lucas and the distinguished members of the Royal Council observed with rapt attention. The atmosphere was thick with expectancy as Deon and Dominic, both stripped to the waist, prepared for the impending challenge.

Zelana's attention was captured by Deon's impressive physique, her breath catching at the sight of his sculpted form. His chiseled pecs and firm, defined abdominal muscles were a clear indication of his rigorous training and discipline, eliciting a subtle blush to her cheeks.

Connor Williams, a dedicated Zelonian officer, approached the men, presented them each with a wooden sword, and then backed away.

"With all due respect, do not hold back, sir," intoned Deon with a respectful bow.

"Nor you," Dominic reciprocated in kind, his return bow laced with equal respect, before initiating the duel with a rapid, targeted slash.

As the battle progressed, Deon expertly deflected Dominic's aggressive strike, swiftly countering with a series of rapid slashes, each executed with precision and speed. Dominic was compelled to adopt a defensive strategy, retreating step by step under the force of Deon's unyielding offensive. The exchange was a dance of blades, captivating the audience with the artistry and intensity of their combat.

In a strategic move to reclaim control, Dominic lowered his stance and aimed a kick at Deon. But with agility and poise, Deon executed a nimble flip over Dominic, landing deftly behind him. Without missing a beat, he delivered a sharp slash across Dominic's back, followed immediately by a swift kick that knocked Dominic to the ground.

Taking a moment to catch his breath, Dominic looked up to find Deon extending a hand to help him to his feet. Graciously accepting the gesture, Dominic allowed himself to be pulled to stand.

"I concede…" he spoke words he didn't expect to hear from himself.

The audience was deeply impressed by the display, breaking into applause as Deon turned to face the Royal Council, wearing a look of pride and accomplishment.

"Well done," Lucas complimented with a genuine admiration for Deon's masterful display.

"Thank you," Deon acknowledged with a respectful nod.

Deon's attention then shifted to Zelana, whose expression radiated pride, her eyes sparkling with unmistakable admiration—and perhaps of a deeper affection.

"You're exceptionally quick, Ambassador Deon," Dominic commented, his tone laced with respect. "It was challenging to mount an offense with your blade constantly threatening to strike me."

"I've found that adopting a defensive stance too early can often lead to a disadvantage," Deon said, sharing his tactical insight. "It allows the adversary to dominate psychologically, and once that upper hand is established, a physical defeat often ensues."

Clearly engaged by Deon's strategic depth, Lucas nodded in agreement. "I've observed similar outcomes on the battlefield," he remarked, his interest in Deon's experiences deepening. "Tell me, have you ever faced the King of Krimzon in direct combat?"

Deon's expression was serious, recalling their confrontations. "I have clashed with King Marcus on several occasions," he began, sharing his assessment of the adversary. "His formidable strength enhances his strikes, yet his considerable bulk makes him slower. In terms of skill, we are comparable."

Deon then activated what appeared to be mechanical enhancements as they immediately covered his arms, eliciting gasps from the Councilmen. "But with these mechanical arms, I can match his strength. My true advantage hinges on my skill, speed, and precision, particularly when facing him."

The assembly watched with close attention and growing amazement as Deon articulated his strategy and highlighted his capabilities. His blend of physical skill, technological integration, and tactical acumen elevated his status as a distinguished warrior and a strategic asset in the ongoing struggles.

"To enhance our effectiveness against these formidable foes, I usually recommend that my forces focus on developing both, skill and speed," Deon shared, extending his battlefield experiences to the leaders.

Samuel's interest visibly sharpened. "That's an intriguing approach," the Crown Prince mused, his tone infused with curiosity. "I've traditionally relied heavily on my strength in battle."

"I wonder how mechanical enhancements compare to the strength of elite humans," Lucas chimed in thoughtfully, glancing between his son and Deon.

Acknowledging his father's implicit challenge, Samuel addressed Deon with a mix of playfulness and competitive spirit. "Shall we dance, Ambassador Deon?"

Deon smirked and replied with a light-hearted jest, "As long as you don't mind me stepping on your toes." His quip drew a round of laughter, lightening the atmosphere.

With a smile, Samuel stripped off his jacket and shirt, embracing the spirit of the challenge as he confidently stepped onto the training grounds. The air was electric with anticipation as all those present prepared to witness this unique matchup of skill and technology.

"This is so nerve-racking," Zelana murmured under her breath as she inhaled deeply, nervously watching her brother and Deon about to engage in combat.

The arena was primed for a captivating exhibition of prowess and power, promising both, insight and entertainment. As the impromptu match began, Deon discarded the wooden sword, opting instead for a demonstration of hand-to-hand combat.

Samuel wasted no time, swiftly launching into action, unleashing a flurry of punches aimed at Deon's torso. Deon, with nimble grace, evaded and parried each blow, displaying his exceptional agility and mastery in close combat. With a fluid movement, he dodged and slammed his mechanical hand to the Crown Prince's back, delivering a firm push, causing him to stagger forward.

Seizing the moment, Deon advanced with calculated speed and precision. Samuel, regaining his footing, turned just in time to intercept a well-aimed punch from Deon. The two locked in a struggle of force, Samuel's hand covering Deon's fist, pushing against each other. Perspiration began to form on the Crown Prince's brow, reflecting the intensity of their engagement. As Samuel's strength waned, Deon's punch broke through, landing squarely on his jaw, the impact sending him spinning and ultimately collapsing on the ground.

"You possess commendable strength," Deon offered generously, extending a hand to assist the Crown Prince rise to stand.

Samuel rubbed his jaw with a wry smile and accepted Deon's hand. "Yet, you've outmatched it," he conceded, his competitive spirit undimmed. "Sanshe has evolved significantly."

"We like to believe our efforts are showing results," Deon acknowledged, his eyes briefly meeting Zelana's gaze, her expression conveying a deep admiration that stirred a thrill within him.

"Your father must be proud, Ambassador Deon. You exhibit both, exceptional intelligence and formidable combat skills," Lucas interjected, deeply impressed.

"I am humbled, Your Majesty," Deon responded with heartfelt gratitude.

With a discreet motion, he deactivated his mechanical enhancement as it receded up his arm, the quiet hum of the machinery swiftly subsiding as Deon gathered his clothes.

The demonstration had not only solidified Deon's reputation as a formidable warrior but also deepened the respect of the Zelonian dignitaries.

"I trust you enjoyed your evening in the city yesterday, Ambassador," remarked the King, venturing into more personal territory.

"Zelonia's beauty is unparalleled, accentuated by the company of Princess Zelana," Deon responded, unabashed and forthright with a candid and bold enthusiasm, despite his surprise with the question.

The King was impressed by Deon's frankness as his eyes moved to his daughter, whose cheeks had blossomed with a delicate flush, visibly moved by Deon's flattering remarks.

"We are in search of a mentor for Princess Zelana, someone to refine her skills in strategy and combat. Would you consider such a role, Ambassador Deon?" Lucas proposed unexpectedly, hoping to secure a formidable future for his daughter and by extension, his kingdom.

Did the King just ask me to mentor his daughter? Deon's mind raced, momentarily caught off guard as he turned to Zelana, her radiant smile seeming to hint at the eagerness for his acceptance.

How could anyone decline this offer? He thought to himself, finding a warmth settle over him. But doubts crept in—*Can I truly step away from my responsibilities in Sanshe? Can I bear to let King MuaYeng and my father down?*

Questions weighed heavily on his heart as he silently contemplated King Lucas's flattering offer.

"I am deeply honored by your trust," Deon responded after a thoughtful pause. "However, I must consult with King MuaYeng before I make such a commitment."

Lucas nodded, his expression one of understanding patience. "Naturally, we wouldn't proceed without his approval," he agreed, projecting a diplomatic tone. "Let us revisit this matter when you return next week. Perhaps by then, you can provide us with an answer."

Deon acknowledged with a respectful bow, "Thank you for your understanding, Your Majesty."

"Please join me for lunch in the Zelonian Gardens in an hour," the King suggested warmly.

"It would be my pleasure," Deon expressed.

Lucas and his Royal Council departed from the arena while Zelana rose from her seat and moved toward Deon, gazing at him with deeper respect and a hint of something more.

"Will you be joining us?" Deon inquired, hoping to spend more time with her. "I will most likely be departing to Sanshe after lunch."

"My father didn't extend an invitation," Zelana responded with a subtle disappointment.

Sharing her sentiment, Deon awkwardly turned to his companion. "I'll meet you at the guest house shortly, Chue."

Chue nodded, understanding the unspoken request for privacy, and discreetly made his way out.

CHAPTER EIGHT

THE FAREWELL

SILENCE STRETCHED BETWEEN them, dripping of tension, as Deon and Zelana stood mere steps apart, facing each other. They struggled to maintain their usual poise, their nervousness visibly seeping through for the first time in each other's presence. Deon's eyes searched Zelana's, trying to read the emotions swirling within them, while her gaze flickered with uncertainty. Unspoken questions and decisions yet to be made marked a rare moment where both seemed momentarily unsure, their usual eloquence replaced by a charming disarray.

"Ambassador..." Zelana's voice broke the stillness, soft and tentative.

"Princess..." Deon addressed her, perfectly coordinated, as if their thoughts were intertwined.

A gentle laughter escaped them, softening the moment's intensity. Deon, caught up in the spontaneity, ran his fingers through his hair—a gesture of endearing nervousness—while a lovely blush painted Zelana's cheeks, enhancing her natural beauty.

"You first," he said, his voice low and warm, extending the moment with a chivalrous grace that invited her to open her heart.

"I am deeply impressed by your combat skills," the Princess murmured in appreciation.

"Hearing that from you means a lot," he replied with a heartfelt smile.

"I'm eager to see more," she added, her enthusiasm undisguised.

Deon shifted his weight, a slight awkwardness in his stance. "I'd love to stand beside you one day on the battlefield, but I'd prefer sharing more memories with you in the city."

His mention of the city made her smile widen, reminding her of his words lingering within her. "It seems you meant those words last night..."

"Last night was truly... unforgettable," he admitted earnestly, his words hanging between them, charged with unspoken emotions.

A playful spark ignited in Zelana's eyes as she pondered aloud curiously, "Did my company momentarily make you forget about the other princess?"

"What other princess?" Deon squinted his eyes with a coy smile, feigning ignorance perfectly.

Zelana giggled at his playful denial. "Perhaps we should venture even further out next time."

"I'm counting the days," he replied with heartfelt anticipation.

"It's rather silly of me..." she confessed, her fingers nervously twirling a strand of her hair, "...to have once thought you were merely a simple envoy from Sanshe."

"Who says I'm not?" he teased, his eyes twinkling with amusement.

Zelana averted her gaze, as a soft, bashful smile graced her lips.

"You're quite mysterious. I never would have guessed you were also a Commander—a man with the authority to lead thousands on the battlefield, and the Ambassador, the third most powerful man in Sanshe," she observed, her eyes meeting his once more. "You wield so much power...."

"If I had known you had such a fascination with men in power, I would have mentioned being a Commander sooner," Deon replied, feeling his pulse quicken.

"There's something undeniably irresistible about you," she flirted openly, her eyes sparkling with a playful intrigue. "It seems you have mastery over the command of someone's thoughts as well."

The smile on Deon's face slowly dimmed, feeling touched. "Now who's the one flirting, Princess?"

"I wouldn't dare..." Zelana teased, echoing their light banter from the night before. "We can't have the Ambassador of Sanshe falling for me."

"Because I am a man of Sanshe?" He added with a grin, matching her tone in jest.

"And you will remain in Sanshe..." she guessed, pressing him subtly for a response.

How did you know? Deon wondered, a flicker of hesitation crossing his face.

"Being given an opportunity to mentor you is a great honor, but..." his voice trailed off, and her heart sank as he struggled to find the right words to convey the conflicting emotions swirling within him.

"It seems highly unlikely..." she softly cut in, finishing his thought.

Deon dropped his gaze, lost in contemplation, regret etched across his features. Seeing his composure waver, Zelana smiled, barely masking the depth of her disappointment.

"I understand my father's request was a bit ambitious, considering your commitments in Sanshe," she said with gentle grace. "It was perhaps naive of me to hope you might agree."

"I'm sorry, Princess..." he murmured, mustering enough courage to meet her eyes once more.

"It would be unfair to expect you to abandon your responsibilities to mentor me," she assured him thoughtfully.

Her words, though kind, carried an unspoken pang of sadness that weaved Deon's heart with a bittersweet ache.

"I trust the King will find a suitable mentor for you, someone worthy of nurturing your talents," he tried to offer comfort, though his voice revealed a sense of helplessness.

"I'll devote myself to training so that one day I might stand proudly beside you," Zelana murmured, her voice barely above a whisper.

Deon observed her, pained to see her usual confidence falter. "I don't often say this, Princess..." he began, hesitating for a brief moment before continuing. "But from the moment we met, your grace and intellect have ceaselessly impressed me," he confessed, his admiration flowing freely without restraint.

"You're too kind," she replied, a delicate smile striving to veil the turmoil beneath.

As the moment of their parting drew near, they were both struck by an overwhelming sense of unspoken longing, a sentiment neither had expected, surfacing profoundly. The memories of their time together resonated with them like the lingering notes of a sad song, echoing the bittersweet farewell that neither was prepared to face.

"May your journey be gentle, Ambassador Deon," she whispered, her eyes clinging to his just a heartbeat longer.

"I will carry your words with me, Princess Zelana," he reluctantly responded, feeling a sudden tightness in his chest, struggling to let her go.

Zelana offered him a small smile and nodded, then slowly turned to walk away. With each step she took, the distance between them grew and the ache in her heart deepened. The smile that had once brightened her features gradually dimmed, leaving her expression wistful, as she gently placed her hand over her heart.

Stop longing for him, she silently urged herself, trying to soothe the sharp pain of unrequited feelings he had mentioned the night before. Yet, as she walked away, Deon consumed her thoughts—his smile, voice, and the emotions that had steadily taken hold of her whenever he was near.

CHAPTER NINE

PRINCESS HUASHI

AFTER A JOURNEY of two days and a night, Deon and Chue finally arrived at Sanshe in the velvet cloak of evening. The Kingdom of Sanshe, nestled in a lush valley surrounded by towering mountains, was a land where nature and civilization danced in harmonious existence. The landscape was adorned with ancient forests that whispered tales of old, with crystal clear streams meandering through these woods, cascading into waterfalls that shimmered like veils of silk under the sunlight.

The Sanshe Kingdom welcomed the delegates home with its signature allure—rows of cherry blossom trees, their petals fluttering delicately in the soft breeze, creating a fragrant pathway leading to the kingdom. The grand doors opened, revealing the bustling Sanshe city with the majestic castle displayed in the background, the architecture a perfect blend of strength and elegance, reflecting the resilience and cultural depth of its people. It stood proudly on the shores of the vast Aisha Ocean, its tranquil waters mirroring the sky's twilight hues, stretching out to meet the horizon.

As the royal carriage glided down the familiar streets of Sanshe, the beauty of Deon's homeland unfolded around him, yet his mind was elsewhere, drifting helplessly back to Zelana. Each breath he took carried the echo of her smile, the melody of her laughter, and the lingering warmth of her entrancing gaze. The way she looked at him during their last meeting was of admiration and perhaps something deeper, leaving a profound impact on his heart—aching with a deep longing; an emotion he hadn't felt so intensely in a long time.

As they approached the Sanshe castle, the starlit sky cast a serene glow over the cobblestone ground, transforming the ordinary into the ethereal. Underneath this celestial canopy, the spirited daughter of King MuaYeng, Princess Huashi Yang, paced restlessly beside the entrance of the castle. Her porcelain skin was illuminated by the soft moonlight as her long, sleek hair, dark as night, glided down her back. Her light brown eyes reflected a natural enchantment, captivating those who dared to meet her gaze.

Huashi's heart fluttered as she heard the sound of a royal carriage winding its way toward her. Through the window, she caught glimpses of familiar faces, prompting her to quicken her pace toward them, with her loyal lady-in-waiting, Kalia, keeping stride beside her. The carriage door swung open and the men stepped out, their faces lit with warm smiles.

"It's been almost three months," she exclaimed excitedly.

Chue descended with a wry smile and teased her, "Have you been keeping count?"

A flicker of annoyance crossed her face before turning to Deon. "You missed my eighteenth birthday."

"Apologies," Deon replied, his smile widening. "I'm sure your father threw you a grand celebration."

"He did, but it wasn't the same without you," Huashi confessed, her tone softening as her eyes locked with his. "I look forward to seeing how you plan to make it up to me."

"I'm sure you have it all planned out," Deon retorted with a grin.

"You're on your own this time," the Princess teased with a challenge. She quickly slipped her arm into his and gazed up at him. "I hope you haven't eaten. I've prepared a special meal for us in the gardens."

"We haven't, in fact. That was very thoughtful of you," Deon responded, touched by her gesture.

"I'm quite famished," Chue chimed in, his stomach audibly agreeing.

"The dining hall is still open," she retorted dismissively. "I only prepared enough for Deon and me."

"I prefer the dining hall anyway," Chue quipped, shrugging off the Princess's slight, and strolled away, hurt and disappointed, leaving the two to their uncomfortable reunion.

Deon shook his head, frustration weaving through his tone as he pushed her hand off him. "You're eighteen now, yet you still act impulsively without considering the consequences of your behavior," he swiftly lectured and turned away, his departure marked by decisive strides.

"I waited all day for you. I just wanted some time alone," Huashi pouted as she followed him persistently. "Is that too much to ask after months apart?"

Deon's steps faltered at her unexpected words as he turned to face her, his words retaining their firm edge. "A Princess should use discretion when expressing her feelings. What if someone heard you? They might misunderstand the nature of our conversation," he continued, his voice lower, tinged with concern rather than rebuke.

"Deon..." she murmured, her voice breaking with vulnerability as she spoke his name. "Must I always be formal with you? I'm tired of being discreet, always wary of my words and actions..."

"You're no longer a child, Princess Huashi," he replied sternly. "Your words and behavior reflect not just on you, but on Sanshe as well."

"I miss how things used to be between us," she confessed desperately. "I miss you."

"I'm exhausted and would prefer to discuss this later when we're not so..." he paused, trying to find the right word. "Distracted."

"I'm not distracted at all. I have so much I want to share with you," Huashi insisted, stepping closer.

Deon sighed, a look of resignation crossing his face. "You're not considering my feelings—just your own... like always," he said, hoping to make her see his perspective.

"I'm going to be selfish just this once," Huashi declared with defiance, her eyes pleading. "I command you to have dinner with me."

"How many times have I told you that I only serve your father?" he clarified, his tone a blend of exasperation and firmness, fully aware of her playful yet persistent maneuvers.

"Therefore, you serve me," she countered swiftly, a mischievous certainty brightening her expression.

Deon's brow furrowed slightly. "There is a line..."

"...that must never be crossed between us. I know," she interjected smoothly, finishing his sentence with practiced ease, having heard his warnings countless times before. "But I assure you, my father will think nothing of our dinner together."

Frustrated with her insistence, Deon capitulated and turned around, walking toward the gardens as his steps reflected a reluctant acceptance. Huashi's smile broadened triumphantly, quickly matching his pace, excited at the prospect of finally having Deon alone to herself.

CHAPTER TEN

Grown Up

DEON AND HUASHI strolled toward the secluded gardens of the palace, the stars twinkling above the manicured hedges and blooming flowers, setting a romantic backdrop for their dinner. The gardens, a favored retreat of the Princess, were illuminated with candles, and the subtle sounds of a nearby fountain added a soothing melody to the air.

Upon arriving at a small, elegantly set table under a flowering gazebo, Deon pulled a chair for Huashi to sit as he noted the care she had taken in the table arrangement. Fine china and crystal glasses gleamed under the soft glow of lanterns that hung from the gazebo, and a bouquet of fresh wildflowers sat in the center, their scent enhancing the atmosphere as he seated himself next to her.

Huashi observed Deon, pleased with his silent appreciation, as servants quietly presented the first course, an aromatic soup infused with herbs from the royal gardens. The Princess watched Deon's reactions closely, eager to see his enjoyment as he dipped his spoon into the soup and tasted it.

"Splendid," Deon commented with a genuine smile. "Pork dumpling soup, my favorite."

"I wanted to welcome you back with familiarity and a touch of novelty," replied the Princess.

They progressed to the main course, a dish of roasted quail with a rich, fruity glaze accompanied by seasoned vegetables. The aroma was inviting, and the presentation impeccable.

"Chicken?" Deon inquired, looking at the dish curiously.

"Better," Huashi responded with a playful smile. "Quail…"

"I have to admit, I've never had quail before," he remarked curiously.

"You will love it, Deon," she assured him confidently. "I was acquainted a month ago and had to share it with you."

Deon cut a piece, forked it into his mouth, and chewed thoughtfully. His nod and the smile that followed were all the confirmation she needed. She felt ecstatic seeing him pleased as she cut into the meat and ate.

The conversation between them began to flow more freely. Deon, initially reserved, started to relax, charmed by Huashi's efforts and the intelligent conversation she was able to hold. They reminisced about shared memories from their younger days, laughing over past escapades and the lessons learned from them while also discussing her aspirations and hopes for Sanshe's future. He listened intently, offering his insights and support as she opened up to him.

"I really wish I knew what grandfather VangKong looked like," she mused with a bright smile. "If we recorded history with paintings, future generations wouldn't have to wonder as I do."

"I'm impressed, Princess," Deon remarked with a tease. "Perhaps you have grown up after all."

Her eyes sparkled at his compliment. "I probably shouldn't be telling you this, but Duchess Maychee has been enlightening me and the other princesses with some eye-opening lessons about marriage."

"Marriage?" He raised an eyebrow, acknowledging that she was indeed of age.

"The intricate details of how babies are made," she added, a blush creeping onto her cheeks.

Deon squinted slightly, taken aback by her frankness. "Interesting..."

"Did you know that—"

"Princess..." Deon cut her off gently but firmly. "I think those lessons are best kept private."

Huashi nodded, her demeanor becoming reflective. "I'm glad you're back, Deon. I miss nights like these, where we can talk about anything and just be together."

"You always remind me what normal life can be," he responded, grateful. "I appreciate that."

Her eyes glistened, touched by his words. At that moment, a server arrived to clear their table, and another brought dessert—honeyed fruits with cream.

"Another of my favorites," he murmured with a smile, tasting the fruits.

"Pleasing you has always made me happy," she responded, catching his gaze once more, the intensity of his look momentarily causing her heart to flutter.

Deon studied the beautiful Sanshe Princess, sensing a subtle hint of deeper emotions from her that momentarily unsettled him. He lowered his gaze, continuing with his dessert, yet a growing emptiness began to creep into his heart. Despite his best efforts to remain present, his thoughts inevitably drifted to Zelana—her face, her voice, the lingering scent of her perfume that seemed to gently invade his senses, stirring his heart.

Huashi watched him, noticing his eyes downcast, seemingly lost in thought. "You mentioned being distracted earlier. Did something happen during your visit to Zelonia?"

Her voice brought Deon back as his eyes met hers once again. "Nothing I couldn't handle."

The intimate atmosphere she had arranged for them couldn't dispel the unease that settled over Huashi as she stared at him with growing suspicion.

What are you hiding? She wanted to ask him, sensing that perhaps for the first time, he was keeping something from her.

Deon's gaze lifted to the night sky, his eyes settling on the soft glow of the full moon. Strangely, he felt a distant connection, as if the vast sky between them wasn't quite so wide after all.

What have you done to me, Princess Zelana? He asked silently, a quiet sigh escaping his lips.

CHAPTER ELEVEN

The Moon

THREE DAYS HAD passed since the Ambassador's departure, yet his absence felt like an eternity. Zelana sighed softly, the night's tranquility only deepening the emotions swirling within her.

What have you done to me, Ambassador Deon? she pondered to herself, her voice a mere whisper as she stared at the full moon. Its soft glow illuminated her beautiful face with a silvery light as she sat alone on the stone bench, surrounded by the quiet stillness of the Zelonian courtyard.

Lowering her eyes, Zelana's gaze became lost in the dance of falling leaves while she listened to the distant murmur of the palace fountains, her heart aching endlessly. Beside her stood Natalie, her loyal lady-in-waiting, maintaining a respectful silence, sensing the deep reverie of her Princess.

The crisp air of autumn whispered through the trees, the gentle rustle of leaves carrying with it the scent of distant memories—memories of a man whose presence continued to linger in her thoughts.

Samuel's footsteps approached lightly, breaking the silence of the night as he strolled through the courtyard to his room. He noticed his sister sitting in thoughtful silence as he whistled softly, catching her attention, walking up to her, and settling beside her.

"Someone seems to be in a good mood," Zelana teased, noticing the wide smile on her brother's face.

"And someone seems a bit lost," Samuel replied playfully, a knowing glint in his eyes.

"I have no idea what you're talking about," she replied playfully with a subtle smile.

"His name starts with a D and ends with an N," he added with a smirk.

Zelana let out a soft giggle. "Stop reading my mind," she teased as he chuckled lightly.

"Tell me. How does it feel to dominate him?" he inquired as her smile faded slightly.

"I feel terrible. I manipulated him… using Sanshe's desperation to get the weapons we needed," she admitted, thinking back to their intense negotiations. "Deon pressed relentlessly, but in the end, he had no choice but to give in—for the survival of his kingdom. If it weren't for the ongoing threats of the Immortals, that agreement would never have been forged."

Samuel nodded knowingly. "It had to be done. He's a tough man to crack."

"You'd be surprised. When we were alone, drafting the contract, Deon was more… human. Not just the fierce Ambassador you met," she said, her voice softening.

"You don't say…" he said, raising an eyebrow.

"At the Summer Fest that evening, Deon was simply himself—open, unguarded, charming, and… manly," she remarked, her eyes glazing over with memories.

"He is not royal," he reminded her, surprised by his sister's dreamy tone. "Don't get any ideas."

"It was just an observation," she replied, her gaze dropping.

Samuel noticed a subtle change in his sister's expression. "Zelana," he began softly, his tone firm but gentle. "I'm not like Mother and Father. I don't mind if you spend time with him, even flirt a little. Just remember," he added, his gaze steady, "he can be nothing more than a passing breeze."

"I'm tired of these expectations imposed on me," she sighed, frustrated.

"Might I suggest you consider a courtship with Crown Prince Nikolai? He's skilled in combat, clearly interested in you, and most importantly, one of our own," Samuel offered, his voice coaxing.

"I can't get there with him," Zelana confessed, her voice soft with emotion.

"And yet, after spending no more than a day with the Ambassador, you can't stop thinking or talking about him," he remarked, raising an eyebrow.

"There's something about him," she whispered wistfully. "Those stolen moments in the city... they changed everything."

"I think I know how you feel," he admitted quietly, his thoughts drifting to the Princess who had captured his attention.

"Are you courting someone in secret?" she asked, her curiosity flaring.

"We aren't there yet..." he replied with a playful smirk.

"Now I'm curious to know who has dared to catch my brother's attention?" she pressed, her eyes gleaming with intrigue.

"You'll know when the time is right," he said, skillfully dodging the question.

"Samuel..." Zelana teased, a mischievous lilt in her voice.

He laughed, shaking his head. "Don't you dare say anything to anyone."

"I promise, my lips are sealed," she assured him, though her curiosity still burned brightly.

A small smile tugged at his lips. "She brought me another homemade soup, and after tasting it, I started to think, 'This woman can really cook.' Then all these crazy thoughts filled my head—of her being a wife, a mother..." Samuel murmured with a sigh. "I've been thinking about her for months..."

Samuel's words stirred something in Zelana, her thoughts drifting back to that night in the city.

"You must know many princesses," she had surmised, searching Deon's face for clues to his relations.

"There are quite a few Royals taking refuge in Sanshe," Deon had admitted with a warm smile, choosing his words carefully. "My role as a diplomat brings me into their circles often."

"Is there one you admire?" she had asked, her heart skipping slightly.

Deon had paused, lost in contemplation. "Perhaps..." he finally confessed softly with hesitation. "But she's unaware of my feelings."

Zelana blinked, her mind snapping back to the present. Samuel was still talking, but before he could continue, she interrupted him, suddenly blurting out her thoughts. "Why are you guys so mysterious?"

Samuel stared at her, bemused. "Have you heard anything I've said?" he asked as Natalie burst out laughing beside them.

"Sorry, my mind wandered," Zelana admitted, giggling along.

"Natalie, if I hear a peep—" Samuel began, half-joking.

"You won't," Natalie quickly promised, stifling her laughter under his playful warning.

"Confess your love to her so you don't have to threaten us to keep quiet," Zelana teased with a subtle smile. "I don't understand the secrecy."

Samuel's expression softened into something more serious. "I can't risk Father sending her away to Sanshe. He told me explicitly not to court any of the princesses taking refuge in Zelonia, and now... I'm conflicted."

"How many kingdoms are left standing in Azalon? How many will fall in the next few months?" She leaned in closer, her voice low with concern. "The only princess Father adores is Princess Lulu, but isn't she engaged to a Crown Prince from one of the kingdoms in the east? I forgot the name..."

Samuel sighed deeply, standing. "I'd feel relieved if it were her. But I'd rather not think about a marriage of convenience right now."

"I have to consider it on a monthly basis," she whispered sadly.

"When I become King, I will change these traditions," the Crown Prince promised confidently.

"Long after I'm sent away to marry," she retorted, a subtle sadness in her voice.

Samuel exhaled heavily. "You don't know that, Zelana."

"I don't know a lot of things," she admitted softly.

"Good night, ladies." He swiftly walked off into the shadows.

Zelana glanced at the moon, its steady, silvery glow illuminating her face. The uncertainty of her future lingered in the cool night air.

Will I have the strength to forge my own destiny?

CHAPTER TWELVE

Quiet Yearning

In the ambassador's office at Sanshe, Deon sat surrounded by the trappings of his duties. The room was strewn with papers and diagrams, evidencing the intensity of his work. The clock had long passed into the early hours, but he remained diligently focused on his task, while Chue was succumbing to the late hour, yawning and showing signs of exhaustion.

"It's two in the morning, we need sleep," he uttered, his voice heavy with fatigue as he slumped into the chair at his desk.

"Get some rest, I'll finish up," Deon responded without looking up, his attention fixed on the documents in front of him.

Chue was too tired to protest and soon surrendered to sleep, his head resting on the desk, his snores filling the quiet room.

Deon smiled at the sight of Chue's slumber before turning his focus back to the Zelonia agreement. As he reviewed the document, his smile deepened when his eyes glossed over Zelana's beautiful handwriting and the charming way she had expressed her points in the contract.

A wave of emotion washed over him, and his smile faded as memories of the first moment he laid eyes on her, on the balcony, flooded back to him. He suddenly felt his chest tighten once more, strangely no longer foreign. It was an ache born of emotions he hadn't anticipated or fully understood that haunted him since he'd returned.

"Princess Zelana..." he murmured her name softly, barely a whisper in the quiet room, as he continued to bear the pain that tortured his heart.

As the clock ticked away, Deon continued to immerse himself in work, the only way to distract his mind from wandering back to her. The more he focused on the tasks at hand, the less he dwelled on the emotions stirring within him, emotions he wasn't prepared to confront. Yet, it only offered temporary respite. For in those quiet moments in the solitude of the night, when his guard was down, her image would resurface, reigniting the tumultuous blend of quiet yearning and confusion.

CHAPTER THIRTEEN

The Jeweler

In the bustling heart of the Sanshe court, the late afternoon sun cast playful glints of light off the shop's windows as Deon, clad in a simple yet elegant tunic, stood inside the finely adorned Royal Jeweler's shop, his figure framed by the ornate window. His brow was furrowed in concentration as he spoke quietly with the Royal Jeweler, gesturing subtly toward a display of exquisite gems.

Huashi and her lady-in-waiting happened to stroll past the shop outside as Kalia caught the unmistakable figure of Deon through the window. With a nudge, she drew the Princess's attention.

"Why do you think Deon's with the Royal Jeweler?" she whispered excitedly.

"Oh my gosh," Huashi murmured as her heart skipped a beat, pausing to observe Deon as her eyes widened with surprise and delight. "He did say he was going to make it up to me for my birthday," she replied. The idea of him customizing a jewelry piece for her sent a thrill through her.

"I wonder what he's getting…" Kalia mused, peering over the Princess's shoulder to get a better look at the scene unfolding in the shop.

Huashi's gaze fixed on Deon's earnest expression as he continued to consult with the jeweler. "I have a feeling it's a necklace."

"It could be a ring," Kalia said, indulging in a wistful thought, as the women giggled excitedly.

Huashi continued to watch, a flush of nervousness coloring her cheeks, as her heart was a flutter with the possibilities, each one more enchanting than the last.

Inside the shop, Deon nodded in satisfaction at something the jeweler showed him, a small, satisfied smile tugging at his lips. Unaware of the watchful eyes upon him, his decision was made with care and precision, considering the preferences he knew so well—preferences that matched the elegance and grace of the Princess.

Outside, Kalia linked her arm with Huashi's as they slowly resumed their walk. "It's about time he proposed."

"Do you really think that's what he's going to do?" asked Huashi in a dreamy daze.

"Yeah, you're eighteen and your father would definitely approve," remarked Kalia with a smile.

Huashi's mind was adrift with anticipation and wonder as she smiled excitedly, barely noticing the path before her. The possibility of a ring, symbolic and intimate, filled her with a hopeful joy.

CHAPTER FOURTEEN

The Invasion

UNDER A MOONLESS sky, the Snowy Meadows Kingdom found itself in the throes of an unimaginable horror. The battlefield was a nightmarish scene, shrouded in the darkest of nights. The relentless Immortals, with their supernatural strength, swept across the battlefield like a dark tide, overpowering the valiant Snowy Meadows soldiers. Their courage was unwavering, but one by one they fell, their mortal strength no match for their adversaries.

On the nightmarish battlefield, Marcus's presence made all who saw him shudder. With his astounding strength and otherworldly powers, he cleaved through the Snowy Meadows soldiers who had the misfortune to face him, leaving a trail of destruction and despair in his wake.

His voice, deep and commanding, cut through the chaos as he bellowed to the wavering Snowy Meadows soldiers, offering them a twisted ultimatum. "Turn your swords the other way and fight for Krimzon, or I will bring death upon you. Choose your fate!"

Frightened and feeling hopelessly outnumbered, some Snowy Meadows soldiers hesitated, their loyalty wavering in the face of such dark power. In an act of betrayal, they turned their swords against their comrades, choosing self-preservation over honor, one treacherous decision at a time.

"Look at those feeble humans," said Marcus, exchanging a glance with his right-hand man, Commander Lorenzo Vargas, another Ancient, as they shared a chilling chuckle, sneering at the weakness of those who would willingly betray their own kind.

On the bridge that overlooked the chaotic battlefield, Princess Kalina Ashbourne was on her horse as her hair blew softly in the wind. She was the only daughter of King Leigh Ashbourne and Queen Isabel Wallace of the Snowy Meadows Kingdom. With striking green eyes, flowing blonde hair, and a slender frame, Kalina possessed a natural beauty that complemented her alluring aura.

Below in the snowy, blood-soaked field, Kalina watched the advance of the Krimzonites, while her father fought alongside his soldiers, leading his people in their darkest hour.

Kalina turned to her mother, who was riding alongside her, with determination in her eyes. "We must seek aid from Zelonia. Father can't hold them back alone."

Isabel nodded sadly, knowing that their beloved kingdom stood on the brink of disaster, her face etched with horror as she watched the soldiers turn against each other.

"Go, Kalina. Hurry," Isabel implored, knowing their only hope lay in their neighboring kingdom.

Kalina spurred her horse and raced toward Zelonia—a race against time, a journey that might turn the tide of battle and save their homeland from destruction.

Leigh was surrounded by the last of his Royal Guards, their faces etched with determination and grim acceptance of their fate, as the Krimzonites set fire to the castle. The flames quickly grew in intensity and size, greedily consuming the castle's structure from corner to corner. They watched in shock and despair as the grandeur and legacy of Snowy Meadows were devoured by the inferno.

Marcus approached Leigh with a wicked smirk on his face, his gaze filled with malicious intent. "How does it feel watching your kingdom burn to ashes and your men turn against you?"

"A Kingdom may fall, but another will rise," Leigh replied, remaining resolute. "You will never be able to annihilate the human race, you blood-sucking devils!"

Marcus chuckled loudly. "Pathetic human! Why would I wish for your extinction? I need humans alive to serve me." His words carried a sinister undertone, hinting at a fate far worse than death.

The King and his men charged at Marcus and Lorenzo fearlessly. In a single, ruthless motion, Marcus raised his sword and severed Leigh's head from his body. The lifeless form of the Snowy Meadows King crumbled to the ground, blood spraying from his body and staining the pristine snow.

The loss of their King sent shock waves through the remaining soldiers, gripping them with fear. They joined the villagers and scattered into the snowy mountains, desperate to escape the impending carnage. The Krimzonites, their faces twisted with anticipation, rushed after them, eager to feast.

Marcus called out to his troops, issuing a chilling command. "Don't slay them all. We need more sustenance at home."

The Immortals chased after the terrified townsfolk. The land echoed with cries of fear and terror through the night, a haunting chorus of agony and hopelessness.

CHAPTER FIFTEEN

Heart of Zelonia

IN THE TRANQUIL Zelonian courtyard, under a blanket of stars, Zelana sat engrossed in a book written by her late grandmother, Goddess Alexi. The gentle murmur of the night breeze and soft rustle of leaves created a serene atmosphere, perfect for her to lose herself in the wisdom of the ancient pages.

The delicate sound of silk brushing against the stone announced Queen Sophia Visconti's approach. Noting her daughter's wistful expression, she moved gracefully to sit beside her, tucking a loose strand of hair behind Zelana's ear with a tender smile.

Sophia was a first-generation demigod, renowned for her beauty, grace, and deep compassion for the people, as she also came from humble beginnings as the only daughter of Bellarose Visconti, a Lady from the kingdom of Stormhold, and the mighty God Azar.

"*The Heart of Zelonia...*" Sophia's voice gently interrupted her daughter's reading.

Zelana looked up, her eyes shimmering with emotion. "I can't imagine a time when people were so desperate for food in Azalon that they lost the will to live," she began softly. "Grandmother Alexi was tasked by the gods to teach humans how to survive by farming. She disguised herself as an old man and even descended from the Heavens to share this knowledge. Yet, it's heartbreaking that the people no longer had the strength to listen—except for one ten-year-old boy—Grandfather Merci."

"At that time, survival was a luxury known to few," Sophia nodded solemnly.

"It's so sad, but also empowering that she didn't give up, even when it was just an orphan boy who embraced her teachings," the Princess continued, her voice thick with emotion. "He tilled his small farm, planting different crops each season, feeding his entire village. As others saw the success of his methods, people traveled from near and far to learn his secret."

"I see that same determination in you and Samuel every day," the Queen remarked proudly.

"I don't know if I could ever do what Grandfather did," Zelana admitted as tears welled in her eyes.

"It runs in your blood, my sweet," Sophia assured her lovingly.

Zelana's voice softened as she recalled the passage she had just read. "Grandmother Alexi protected him until he turned twenty. She wrote that Grandfather loved her so much, even as the old man she pretended to be, that it broke her heart to leave him and return to the Heavens. That's why she revealed her true Goddess form to him. I can only imagine what went through his mind, seeing a beautiful, divine being in his humble home."

A soft, tender laugh escaped Sophia. "And to hear her confess her love to him..."

Zelana giggled, covering her mouth with her hand, her imagination painting the scene vividly.

"A Goddess falling in love with a poor orphan during the village wars, resulting in her exile from the Heavens and having to fight countless battles alongside the villagers against the evil threatening Azalon at the time..." Sophia mused with a soft sigh.

"It's a love story beyond words," Zelana whispered, her voice brimming with emotion, the awe of their story clear in her eyes. "And despite everything, the orphan rose to become the most powerful King in all the realms, founding Zelonia with his love by his side."

"You resemble her so much, Zelana," the Queen murmured softly with affection. "You have her golden hair and light blue eyes... and perhaps her stubbornness too, always challenging traditions."

Zelana's eyes sparkled with pride. "I am the first princess to negotiate for the kingdom—successfully, I might add—and I will be the first to wield a sword in battle to defend Zelonia."

Before Sophia could respond, a sharp, insistent knock echoed through the air, reverberating off the heavy wooden gates framed by vines and ancient stone. The tranquility of the night shattered as the knocking grew louder, its urgency impossible to ignore. Zelana and Sophia exchanged a quick glance, the warmth of their intimate conversation abruptly replaced by a sense of unease.

"It seems the Crown Prince of Ferria may have arrived sooner than expected," Sophia remarked, her voice now more serious.

"I'm not meeting him tonight," Zelana objected, cutting off her mother.

But before either could say more, the sound of hurried footsteps broke through the stillness, and Dominic entered the courtyard as two ladies accompanied him, both drenched and visibly shaken from their journey. Their clothes clung to them, dampened by the snow. Sophia and Zelana were both caught off guard by the sudden, grim arrival as they rose from their seats.

"Queen Isabel? What happened?" inquired Sophia, her voice filled with alarm, a mix of shock and concern etched on her face.

"All is lost," Isabel managed to say, her voice barely above a whisper. Isabel, her regal composure undone by the night's harrowing events, had tears brimming in her eyes. She was a picture of despair, her usual poise replaced by a vulnerability seldom seen in a Queen.

Dominic, in a rush to return to the King and rally the troops to Snowy Meadows, discreetly stepped away and left the royal ladies to converse amongst themselves.

"Come, sit with me," Sophia gently suggested, extending a hand of comfort toward Isabel, her tone soothing in the face of distress.

Kalina guided her mother toward the garden bench. As Isabel sat down, the enormity of her loss and the horrors she had escaped seemed to crash upon her all at once. She broke down, her heart-wrenching sobs resonating through the quiet courtyard.

"Do tell me what happened," Sophia urged, her heart aching for her friend.

Gathering the remnants of her strength, Isabel recounted the tragic tale. "Snowy Meadows is up in flames right now," informed the Queen, her voice breaking under the weight of her grief as her words painted a picture of devastation and despair.

"The Immortals unexpectedly marched on our castle as the sun set, ruthlessly pillaging and burning everything in sight. The scene was a nightmarish vision—bloodshed and chaos everywhere. Our own soldiers turned on each other like cowards," she described, her voice breaking with emotion.

"Princess Kalina and I barely escaped with our lives while my dear husband fought off a horde of Immortals with the last of his guards, drawing attention to himself, fighting valiantly to give us a chance to flee," she added softly.

"King Leigh will be remembered for generations. His selfless act of valor in the face of such overwhelming odds is the mark of true royalty—putting the safety of his family and Kingdom above his own," Sophia expressed, acknowledging her profound respect for him.

Sophia's words offered some comfort as Isabel continued to weep. Kalina knelt before her mother, unable to hold back her own tears. Zelana, moved by their pain, knelt and gently comforted her.

A sudden mournful horn pierced the night, its haunting cry reverberating through the courtyard. It was a sad reminder of the fragility of peace and security in their world.

"The battle horn..." Zelana whispered nervously, knowing her father and brother were leaving for Snowy Meadows to wage war against the Krimzonites.

"King Lucas is on his way to bring King Leigh back to you," Sophia assured.

"May the heavens protect him and the Zelonian army," Isabel prayed, amidst her tears.

"May the Heavens bless us tonight," they intoned together, their voices harmonizing in a chorus of hope and faith as the war horn sounded once again in the distance.

In a powerful moment of solidarity, the royal ladies clasped their hands together, united in their prayer for the safety of their loved ones and the success of the Zelonians.

CHAPTER SIXTEEN

PRINCESS SIERRA

UNDER THE SCORCHING sun of Sanshe's training grounds, the esteemed heir to the kingdom, Crown Prince Zhong Yang, engaged in vigorous swordplay with Deon. Their movements collided in a dance of steel—fluid and forceful—each strike and parry were an eloquent display of their skill and years of training.

The metallic song of their clashing swords reverberated through the air, capturing the attention of the Princesses, including Princess Sierra Alanis of Mesa Valley Kingdom and her lady-in-waiting, Elena, who had come to entertain themselves, watching the men charge fiercely at each other.

Zhong's tall, muscular frame, complemented by his striking brown eyes and raven black hair, amplified his natural charisma. He possessed an undeniable charm that effortlessly captivated those within his presence, particularly women. With Deon at his side, the two were irresistible, commanding attention with their presence wherever they went.

"Princess Sierra is here... again," Zhong muttered under his breath, catching sight of her arrival.

"She is your fiancée," Deon pointed out, expertly blocking a swift jab from Zhong as the crowd cheered along with Huashi, applauding from the stands.

Zhong paused to wipe away the sweat beading on his brow, his movements slowed as his focus shifted from the duel to the woman staring at him from the stands. "I'm done."

"You say that every time, yet nothing changes," Deon retorted, launching a strategic slash toward the Crown Prince, which was skillfully blocked, and the crowd roared with Sierra cheering with pride.

"I'm deadly serious this time," Zhong grunted in annoyance, initiating a counterattack as his sword whistled through the air. Beads of sweat shimmered and scattered with each movement.

"You end things, then you let her back in," Deon remarked, deflecting the Crown Prince's strike.

"It's complicated, but I can't take it anymore. I literally feel like I can't breathe..." Zhong muttered bitterly under his breath, visibly troubled as he sheathed his sword, the clink of the metal against his scabbard echoing in the tense air. "I wonder if I'd feel this way if I actually had feelings for her."

Before Deon could respond, Sierra had already crossed the distance, overhearing the tail end of their conversation.

"What did you just say?" she asked, her voice laced with suspicion as the other Princesses slowly filed out of the training grounds, wanting to avoid the drama.

Zhong met her gaze with cold determination. "I'm calling off our engagement," he declared boldly.

Sierra's lips barely twitched, but the flash of hurt in her eyes betrayed her. "This again?"

"I'm sick of seeing you everywhere," he confessed, his frustration boiling over.

The slap came hard and fast, stinging his cheek.

"I wouldn't be clinging to you if it wasn't for your constant flirting with other women, Zhong!" she said, her voice unrestrained, fire in her words.

Zhong's eyes narrowed, glaring at her with raw disdain. "Did it ever occur to you that maybe I did all that on purpose? To be free of you?"

Sierra's lips trembled as she held back the tears threatening to spill. "I'll... I'll start flirting too. Let's see how you feel."

"Go ahead," Zhong said with a grin, unfazed by her threat. "Latch onto someone else. It'll just give me more reason to leave."

"Do you really think you can just leave that easily?" Sierra spat, her voice shaking with bitter mockery. "If it wasn't for Mesa Valley, Sanshe would be nothing. The fate of our kingdoms was sealed by our grandfathers long before we had a choice. After ten years of enduring you, I deserve to be Queen."

Zhong's grip tightened on his sword hilt, his knuckles turning white. For a moment, he wavered, but the words came, cutting her like a blade. "You deserve nothing!"

He stood, trembling with the force of his words, shocked at the cruelty that escaped his lips. His chest heaved seeing tears finally flow down her cheeks as he fought to regain control of his emotions.

"I won't be trapped into marrying you," the Crown Prince added, his voice colder, his words more final as he turned to leave.

"Zhong..." Sierra's voice wavered, thick with desperation as she reached out, her fingers cold against his skin as she tugged at his arm, halting him and forcing him to face her.

"Let go..." Zhong hissed, his voice cracking with fury.

She bit her lower lip, gathering her strength. "If that's how you really feel, return all the aluminum my kingdom has supplied

Sanshe the last two decades, and I'll end the engagement myself. Otherwise, we're bound—until death."

Her words revealed the complex entanglement of political and personal interests binding them together. There was no romance, no warmth, only a relationship arranged years ago, now reduced to a transaction devoid of love or respect.

"To hell with that," Zhong growled, shrugging off Sierra's grasp before turning his back on her and walking away, without looking back.

"All I've ever desired was your affection and to be by your side as Queen..." Sierra's voice broke, but she kept her head high, even as her hands trembled at her sides, frozen in place.

I know that feeling well, Deon thought, observing her silently, *but I no longer allow it to have power over me.*

"I don't understand why you have so much disdain for me," she murmured softly, more to herself than anyone else, while her face exuded a storm of emotions—hurt, sorrow, disappointment. "I never thought my love for you would drive you away from me."

Deon slid his sword into its sheath with a gentle sigh, his gaze softening. "Perhaps giving Crown Prince Zhong some space will help. After some thought, he might change his mind... or not."

Sierra's body trembled as she sobbed helplessly. "We're supposed to be wed on my twenty-first birthday. It's only months away. I can't lose him... not now."

"Love cannot be forced, Princess Sierra," Deon managed to say, choosing his words with care. "Sometimes, when you've done all you can, the only choice left is to let go."

Before she could say more, Deon withdrew from the emotionally charged scene.

CHAPTER SEVENTEEN

ROYAL LETTER

ZHONG BARGED INTO the King's lounge, where his father, King MuaYeng Yang, the revered reigning monarch of Sanshe, was absorbed in a serious conversation with Chue about a forthcoming journey to Zelonia. With determined strides, he approached the grand table, placing both of his hands firmly upon it. His father awkwardly glanced up from the documents he was scrutinizing with Chue.

"I refuse to go through with the wedding!" Zhong burst out, his eyes blazing with fury as he confronted his father. "You can disinherit me for all I care. I will not marry that wicked woman!"

MuaYeng rose from his chair, his expression one of sheer disbelief.

"Enough with the theatrics!" exclaimed the King, losing his patience.

Chue sensed the King's rising agitation, quickly stepping in. "We've discussed this repeatedly, Crown Prince Zhong. Remember, your grandfather was compelled to agree to this for the sake of peace."

"It's his vow, not mine!" Zhong retorted steadfastly. "We don't owe Mesa Valley anything! They traded us aluminum for years, thinking it to be worthless. Only when we began using it for weapons did they fear our growing power. Mesa Valley felt threatened, and my grandfather's promise of me marrying Sierra was merely a ploy to calm their anxieties. They have never been true allies."

MuaYeng exhaled a weary sigh, his gaze drifting away as he became immersed in his thoughts.

"Our commitment must stand. Abandoning them in their misfortune is not an option," added Chue.

"Their downfall wasn't about luck. They were simply too weak, overrun by the Krimzon Kingdom within a week," Zhong reminded them with a tone of conviction. "Our battles with the Immortals have spanned centuries! Mesa Valley isn't as powerful as it once was. They pose no threat to us now. And let's not forget, we've more than compensated for their aluminum over the last three years, providing their people with food, shelter, and clothing. Crown Prince Esteban and his sister should not bind us to this promise any longer."

MuaYeng turned to face his son, intrigued. "Why do you loathe Princess Sierra?"

"She is the most self-centered and conniving woman I've ever met. She speaks down on Sanshe and disrespects me constantly, reminding me of the aluminum as if it were a personal favor bestowed by her." Zhong continued without mincing his words, "I'm finding myself becoming cruel just like her. Sierra is not fit to be my Queen, let alone be the mother of my children, who are the future of Sanshe."

Chue weighed the situation with caution. "Ending the engagement might incite unrest within Sanshe. Mesa Valley has formed bonds with many nations while their people lived in the refugee camps."

Zhong turned to Chue in frustration. "Do you want me to live under constant threat from Mesa Valley? To be a puppet King, forever answering to Sierra and her brother?" He paused, then faced his father. "If that's the case, you might as well make Crown Prince Esteban the future King of Sanshe, and I'll go venture out elsewhere. I refuse to be ruled by Mesa Valley in my own realm."

MuaYeng let out a deep breath after a moment of reflection, then seated himself and began to pen a letter. The room was tense as Zhong and Chue observed each word being written. The contents of the letter visibly shocked them. Once finished, MuaYeng sealed the letter with his royal insignia and handed it to his son.

"Go to Zelonia with Deon and Chue tomorrow. Your destiny is now in your own hands, my son," MuaYeng finally spoke, gazing up at Zhong with a blend of solemnity and respect.

"Thank you, Father," Zhong murmured, still taken aback, understanding the gravity of the King's gesture, and accepted the letter with a humble, appreciative bow.

CHAPTER EIGHTEEN

Anticipation

THE ZELONIAN INSTRUCTIONAL Academy was bathed in the soft light of the afternoon sun, casting long shadows across the ornate floors of the classroom. Zelana stood alone by the balcony, the gentle rustle of the wind and the occasional chirping of birds her only companions. Her gaze wandered across the lush greenery of the courtyard, yet her thoughts were tangled in a quiet yearning for someone distant.

Suddenly, she caught sight of a young man in regal attire, his posture tall and composed as he spoke with her father. The rich fabric of his clothing told her all she needed to know—this was the Ferrian Crown Prince. A sigh escaped her lips, barely audible but heavy with the weight of her thoughts. *Another day to play the Princess of Zelonia...* she mused silently, already bracing for the familiar motions of polite conversation, flattery, and feigned interest.

Please, don't be another one of those Crown Princes, she silently pleaded, *boasting of conquests and titles, while my mind drifts elsewhere.*

Crown Prince Nikolai Kuzmin, the sole heir to the Frostwald Kingdom, entered the room, a flash of nervousness crossing his face seeing Zelana already there, alone.

Will this be the moment she sees my heart? He wondered, glancing at the small box he clutched in his hands. He quickly hid it behind his back as he quietly approached her, stopping just a few steps away. As he stood there quietly, he couldn't help but waver momentarily, his throat tightening as the words hovered on his lips.

"I didn't expect to find you here so early, Princess Zelana," he finally found his voice and greeted her warmly while his fingers rubbed the small box behind his back.

Zelana turned, blinking away her distant thoughts. "I couldn't sleep," she replied, her faint smile barely reaching her eyes. "The morning was too beautiful to waste, so I came to watch the sunrise."

"Next time, come find me. I love watching the sun too," Nikolai offered with a small smile, feeling idiotic for what he just said.

"Absolutely," she responded with feigned excitement, returning a warm smile.

"I have something for you," the Crown Prince said, bringing the small box forward, his hands trembling slightly as his grip tightened, fearful of her rejection.

"Crown Prince Nikolai..." she murmured softly, taken aback by his gesture. "You're always bearing gifts. I feel bad I never have anything for you."

This is the third time in six months. What should I do? Zelana thought to herself, staring at the box.

"I can't help thinking about you when I want to share little things with someone," he admitted, opening the box and revealing a large iced cookie. "I baked this in class yesterday."

"A heart?" Zelana's fingers brushed lightly against the cookie.

"My heart, figuratively speaking," Nikolai clarified in a playful tone, his eyes flickering nervously.

"You're always so thoughtful..." Zelana began, yet her voice trailed off, not knowing what else to say.

"Shall we share it?" he proposed, breaking the cookie in two and offering her a piece while their friends slowly filed into the classroom. "It's supposed to be strawberry."

She hesitated for a moment, then accepted the piece. "How did you know I like strawberries?"

"Lucky guess," he replied as they took a bite.

Her eyes lit up. "It's quite good," she remarked with a soft giggle.

"I'm glad you enjoyed it." Nikolai leaned against the balcony railing, his voice dropping slightly as his gaze lingered on her longer than usual. "We've known each other for over a year now. It feels like no time has passed."

Zelana lowered her eyes, sensing the shift in his tone. "It has gone quickly," she agreed, her fingers nervously tracing the edge of the railing, already sensing where the conversation might lead.

"There's a reason for that," Nikolai continued, his voice soft but insistent. "Time flies when we're around people who matter."

Zelana's fingers traced the folds of her gown, a silent rhythm to calm the nervous flutter in her chest. Every second in Nikolai's gaze felt heavier than the last. She forced her gaze back to his, but her chest tightened as she saw the hope in his eyes—hope she wasn't sure she could meet.

"You've always been that someone special for me," he affirmed, his voice filled with emotion as his eyes searched hers again, more serious this time.

"The loss you've endured would break anyone, but you've come out stronger," she replied softly. "I'll always be here when you need to talk."

"I know, that's why I was wondering..." he paused, the vulnerability in his eyes softening, "if you had considered my offer?"

Zelana's pulse quickened as Nikolai's words hung in the air. Her throat tightened. She had known this conversation was inevitable, yet now that it was here, the weight of it felt suffocating, pressing against her like a sudden chill in the afternoon warmth.

"I..." she paused, searching for the right words. "Can you remind me?"

Nikolai let out a small, nervous laugh. "My feelings haven't changed, Princess Zelana," he confessed, the words tumbling out. "I'm still hopeful that we could become something more and progress together on a personal level."

Zelana felt her heart quicken as her eyes flicked down to the ground, avoiding his hopeful gaze, glancing down at the half-eaten cookie, her fingers trembling slightly.

"Crown Prince Nikolai..." she managed to utter, her voice softer than before. "There's so much happening right now..."

Seeing her hesitate, he felt his heart sinking. *You're going to reject me, again.*

"Everything seems so uncertain in Azalon... the Krimzonites... and the negotiations with Sanshe..." her voice trailed off, unsure how to let him down slowly.

"I wasn't aware," Nikolai replied as he nodded, his smile faltering, doubt crossing his mind.

A part of me wants to comfort you and give you the answer you've been waiting for, but how could I when someone else lingers on my mind constantly?

She gripped the railing just enough to ground herself as her eyes met his gaze once again. "I wish I could give you a better answer," she admitted, her voice barely a whisper.

"I understand," he responded, the disappointment in his eyes unmistakable.

Zelana's heart ached at the expression on his face.

"I'm not one with much patience, but I'm learning to be more… for you," he said, his voice quieter. "If there's anything I can help you with, please let me know, Princess. I may not be the best warrior or the most intelligent, but I'm sure you can find me useful."

"I wouldn't hesitate for a moment," she assured him, the tension around them finally clearing.

"I… uh… I noticed another suitor arriving this morning," he said, changing the subject slightly with a careful tone, trying to keep his expression composed. "Will you be sending him away, like the others?"

"Most definitely," she promised. "I wouldn't entertain a courtship with someone so far away when I have you and others that have shown me your hearts and proven to me your sincere intentions."

Nikolai's smile returned. "I hope I'm the first on that list."

Zelana's eyes flickered with a sadness she couldn't quite hide. "There is no list, Crown Prince Nikolai," she clarified in a soft tone. "There can only be one man I give my heart to."

"Let it be me," he said in a low voice as his expression grew serious.

Before Zelana could respond, Makeo, their instructor, entered the classroom.

"We should probably find our seats," she suggested, taking the opportunity to step away.

Nikolai sighed as he followed her, his heart still heavy with hope, even as hers remained undecided.

As they sat down next to each other, Zelana glanced over at Nikolai, noticing his shoulders slumped in quiet defeat. Her chest tightened.

How much longer can I leave him waiting?

CHAPTER NINETEEN

PRINCESS LENORA

LENORA APPROACHED THE Sanshe Armory with delicate steps, her heart beating a little faster as she neared the entrance. The moment she walked inside, a subtle murmur spread through the room and she felt the eyes of the men glance her way. Despite her usual confidence, she felt a quiet sense of uncertainty that clung to her as she scanned the room, trying not to attract too much attention.

The lead blacksmith, a man marked by years spent in the trade with weathered hands, stepped forward, his eyes kind yet curious. Wiping his hands on an old, worn cloth that had seen better days, he kindly asked, "How may I assist you, milady?"

"Is Commander Deon here?" Lenora inquired softly, hoping to pass unnoticed.

The blacksmith's eyebrow arched with interest. "He is. May I know who's asking?"

"Princess Lenora…" she revealed with a reluctant whisper.

Contrary to her desire for discretion, the blacksmith's voice boomed, "Commander Deon! You have a visitor—Princess Lenora!"

A rosy blush crept onto Lenora's cheeks as the other men in the armory exchanged glances, their murmurs turning into low chuckles. She lowered her gaze, feeling vulnerable and exposed.

In mere moments, Deon appeared from around the corner. His approach commanded her attention effortlessly as Lenora's breath caught when their eyes met.

There he was—the man who had once been a faceless hero to her, now standing mere paces away. She had imagined this moment so many times since that fateful night in Esperia, but seeing him now, it was different. He was even more handsome than she'd imagined. His dark hair and rugged features exuded a quiet strength, and the way he moved carried an air of confidence that was impossible to ignore.

Finally, the man behind the mask, she thought to herself, as her heart fluttered against her chest.

Her gaze traced the sharp angles of his face, the way his eyes seemed to hold so much more than what he allowed others to see. The aura around him drew her in, and for a fleeting moment, she was lost in the magnetic pull of his presence.

Deon paused before her, his memory of her returning as his expression transformed to one of serious curiosity. "Princess Lenora, what a pleasant surprise," he greeted. His tone was of someone who remembered her far more vividly than he let on.

"Good afternoon, Commander Deon," she managed, her pulse quickening. "I was wondering if you have a moment to spare?"

Deon hesitated briefly, a flicker of something unreadable passing across his features before he replied, "I was just about to have lunch." He was polite, yet there was a restraint in his voice, as if he were holding back more than he was saying.

The Princess's eyes lingered on him a second longer than appropriate. "May I join you?"

Deon's eyes searched hers, his calm demeanor barely concealing the surprise her bold request stirred in him. He shifted slightly, then offered a graceful sidestep. "How can I be of service, Your Highness?"

Lenora bit her lip, realizing her request might have come off as too forward. "I… I wanted to thank you for saving me and my brother, Crown Prince Winston. I had hoped to express my gratitude sooner, but I was told you were away on a mission."

"It's what I do, Princess. There's no need to thank me," he replied gently as his expression softened to her words. His demeanor was no longer guarded. He even seemed a little touched by her vulnerability.

Catching the warmth in his voice, her gaze drifted from his eyes down to his lips, and for a moment, she lost herself. His presence was intimidating, igniting something deep within her, drawing her to him in a way she couldn't fully comprehend, yet it intrigued her.

Deon cleared his throat, breaking the moment. "It's rare to see women here in the armory. Allow me to escort you back to camp." His words held an air of formality, as if to keep the situation professional, even though something in his gaze told her otherwise.

He opened the door for her as Lenora's heart fluttered once more, touched by his courteous gesture.

"Are you always this chivalrous?" she asked, a soft smile playing on her lips as they stepped out into the sun, which seemed to shine brighter with him beside her.

Deon chuckled softly, glancing at her, admiring the subtle physical semblance she had with Zelana.

"With you, it seems to come naturally," he replied, his voice low and teasing as the sun cast a soft glow over them while they walked side by side.

Lenora's cheeks flushed at his words as she looked up at him, tucking a loose strand of hair behind her ear. "Well, I suppose I should feel honored then, although I imagine you have that effect on many."

She cast him a sideways glance, wondering how he would respond.

"Perhaps," Deon replied, his gaze briefly meeting hers before looking ahead. "But not everyone makes me want to be so... chivalrous."

"And what exactly do you think it is about me, Commander, that brings out this side of you?" she asked playfully, yet her eyes searched his intently, eager to understand her effect on him.

Deon paused for a moment, his smile fading as his expression turned more serious, choosing his next words carefully. "You're a guest in my kingdom, what other reason did you think it could be?"

A small flicker of disappointment crossed Lenora's face, noticing him becoming more guarded as the warmth between them slowly dimmed. "If I knew, I wouldn't have asked," she retorted awkwardly.

He found her reaction to his change in demeanor a bit irritating. "How are you acclimating to Sanshe?" he inquired, retreating to formality and steering their conversation to serious matters.

Lenora let out a soft sigh, feeling the distance between them grow. "If I'm to be honest, it's a significant change from what I'm accustomed to. Being immersed in such a varied populace and hearing so many different tongues being spoken, I often catch myself wondering if I'm the subject of their discussions."

Deon maintained a composed exterior but felt a subtle unease at her admission.

"Sanshe is a vibrant tapestry of cultures. It's natural to feel a bit overwhelmed and somewhat disoriented initially, but rest assured, Princess Lenora, the people here are generally too preoccupied with their own lives to indulge in gossip, especially about someone of your stature," he consoled, trying to assuage her concerns. "I understand the challenges of adjusting to a new environment, but please recognize the importance of embracing the opportunities to experience and learn from the rich diversity Sanshe offers."

"I appreciate your attempt to offer reassurance, Commander," Lenora replied with a soft smile, yet her thoughts were still wrapped in her discomfort. "It's just a bit daunting at times, living so closely among the common folk. Their habits… the noise… even their smells. They stay up late into the night, rise at dawn, and for what? It's so baffling to me."

"For some refugees, work starts early. For others, they work late into the night," Deon clarified patiently. "It's what keeps the camp running, allowing us to maintain some semblance of normalcy."

He hoped his words might broaden her perspective, but Lenora pressed on, seemingly unaffected by his explanation as they approached the camp's entrance, and their steps slowed to a stop.

"Being surrounded in this sea of unfamiliar faces, languages, and customs… I feel like an outsider," she expressed, revealing a subtle frustration.

Deon's brow furrowed, trying to be empathetic. "Feeling out of place is understandable, but Sanshe is a sanctuary for everyone, encompassing people from all walks of life. We pride ourselves on providing protection and hospitality to all who seek refuge here."

Lenora let out a soft sigh, dismissing his reassurances. "All the more reason the food should cater to different tastes," she remarked with a slight grimace. "I often choose to go without rather than endure what is served here. I miss the comforts of the castle—the privacy, the luxury—standards befitting someone of my status."

Deon's patience finally wore thin as her persistent grievances continued to pile on.

"May I remind you, Princess, that we're all trying our best to survive," he said, his voice now stripped of its earlier warmth. "If the Sanshe King hadn't intervened, you wouldn't be reminiscing about life in the castle; you'd likely be dead, rotting in the forest or worse, enslaved in Krimzon, serving the Immortals."

Lenora's expression shifted to one of surprise at his candidness as his words sank in, stinging her pride and leaving a bitter taste of humiliation.

"I am the Princess of Esperia," she replied, her tone rising defensively as the camp's inhabitants' attention turned to them, drawn by the intensity of their exchange. "Your words are quite bold for a mere soldier."

"It would serve you well to relinquish some of your pride and entitlement. The crown of a fallen kingdom like *Esperia* carries little influence here in Sanshe," clarified Deon calmly, yet his words were harsh as he tried to maintain his composure. "The Sanshe King has generously welcomed all those in need, irrespective of their former glory, *Princess Lenora*. A bit of gratitude might make this transition smoother for you. And if you work to integrate and contribute, as others have, it might make life here a little more bearable."

Deon's words hung in the tense air, heavier than Lenora expected. She opened her mouth to retort, but found herself momentarily speechless, her mind scrambling to make sense of his bluntness. Before she could gather herself to respond, Deon turned on his heel, leaving her stunned and flustered; her shock mirrored in the faces of the onlookers. Watching him go, her anger resurged back to the surface.

"Commander Deon!" Lenora called after him, outraged. Her fingers curled into the fabric of her dress, trying to hold on to her composure. Her eyes, however, betrayed the frustration and hurt she tried to conceal. "How dare you talk to me so disrespectfully?!"

Gwen, her lady-in-waiting, hurried to her side, attempting to soothe her amidst the scrutiny of the crowd. His departure felt abrupt, leaving a strange hollowness between them, needing attention.

Deon exhaled deeply, his strides steady and resolute as he continued walking. His thoughts somehow drifted irresistibly to Zelana, her warmth instantly replacing the abrasive exchange he had just endured with Lenora. He knew deep in his heart that Zelana would linger—unforgettable, for years to come.

A smile tugged at his lips as he recalled a few tender moments—how endearing she had looked while eating her grape. Her playful teasing that ceaselessly caught him off guard, and those shared glances between them—so intense, carrying a depth that words could never capture. In those moments, everything seemed effortless, from the subtle smiles to their fingers accidentally touching, they found joy in each other's company.

Behind him, Lenora's lips tightened in disbelief, and her fists clenched at her sides, struggling with the hurt and fury that was overwhelming her. She couldn't reconcile the man who had walked away from her with the kind gentleman she had met earlier. The distance between them was both physical and emotional, and it continued to grow.

"Commander Deon, we need to talk," Lenora called to him again, her voice softening, breaking through his thoughts, bringing him back from his reverie.

A flicker of annoyance surged through him as he realized Lenora had followed him, only a few steps behind. Without turning back, Deon waved his hand dismissively, signaling his disinterest.

Just then, Zhong approached Deon, a knowing chuckle escaping his lips, having witnessed the entire exchange from a discreet distance.

"Looks like I'm not the only one with women troubles," Zhong teased lightly.

Deon halted, a smile tugging at his lips as he faced his friend. "At least I can walk away. You, on the other hand, don't have that luxury."

"Women…" Zhong shook his head and exhaled a sigh of resignation as his expression turned somber, thinking of Sierra. "I need a drink."

"That makes two of us," Deon replied with a smirk as they headed toward the dining hall.

CHAPTER TWENTY

THE UNEXPECTED

AS THE SUN dipped below the horizon, the flickering candles cast a warm glow over the Sanshe dining hall, where the hum of conversation mingled with a soft tune playing on the piano. At the heart of this bustling ambiance, Zhong and Deon were seated together for dinner, immersed in their meals, savoring the delicate flavors while sharing playful chatter. Zhong's gaze drifted to the window, catching sight of Lenora gracefully proceeding toward the throne room.

"It appears Princess Lenora is off to see my father," Zhong remarked casually, a flicker of amusement crossing his face.

Deon merely nodded. "My name will come up in their conversation," he predicted with certainty.

"And it will amount to nothing," Zhong agreed with a chuckle.

Deon swirled his wine contemplatively. "The sense of entitlement of fallen Royals around here is maddening," he expressed his vexation under his breath.

"If I ever find myself in a foreign kingdom, mimicking the haughty air of these Royals..." Zhong started to say before Deon swiftly interjected.

"I'll be quick to humble your ego."

His tease elicited a hearty laugh from the Crown Prince.

"That's the Deon Princess Lenora had a taste of today," the Crown Prince retorted with a twinkle in his eyes. "By the way, I'll be joining you to Zelonia."

Deon paused, his fork suspended in mid-air, as he processed the unexpected announcement. Surprise and intrigue danced across his features. "Is the King aware of this?" he inquired, eyebrows raised.

"I've been discussing with my father the importance of forging alliances with other nations," Zhong explained, a spoonful of rice poised in his hand. "He finally agreed, so I'm set to visit Zelonia."

Deon's expression softened into a grin. "Well, this journey just got more interesting."

Zhong leaned in inquisitively. "Did the Zelonian Princess really spearhead the trade negotiations?"

Deon paused momentarily, swallowing his bite before answering. "Indeed, Zelana drafted all the terms to the agreements with me."

Zhong's face shifted, his curiosity deepening. "What's your impression of her?"

"She possesses wisdom beyond her years," Deon articulated thoughtfully.

The Crown Prince's curiosity sharpened. "Is she attractive?" he asked, probing further.

"Her presence exudes a natural elegance and effortless charm," Deon responded promptly, capturing her essence in a way that resonated beyond her physical beauty.

Zhong's intrigue deepened. "Interesting way of answering my question." As a striking woman in a flowery dress glided by, catching his eye, he pressed further. "Is she a beauty like her?"

Deon glanced at the woman, a small smile forming on his lips.

"There's no one in Sanshe quite like the Princess of Zelonia," he said with quiet conviction.

Zhong's smirk broadened, savoring the confirmation. "She's that amazing, huh?"

Deon took a leisurely sip of his wine. "Meet her and decide for yourself."

The Crown Prince nodded, his gaze returning to the woman in the flowery dress, who now seemed to be looking his way. "She's staring at me as if she knows me."

"You're not exactly a stranger in Sanshe," Deon reminded him with a chuckle.

Grinning, Zhong rose from his seat. "Perhaps it's time I get to know her."

With a determined stride, Zhong approached the young woman, quickly engaging her in conversation.

As Deon reclined in his chair, sipping his wine, his gaze lingered idly on Zhong, who was effortlessly charming the young lady. But as he watched, a familiar ache washed over him—a deep longing to be in Zelana's presence once more. His mind wandered aimlessly to that enchanting night in Zelonia City. The memory slowly came alive—he could almost feel her softness as he held her close, swaying under the twinkling stars.

The yearning to relive that magical moment tugged at Deon's heart, as her fragrance, a delicate hint of roses, vividly lingered. He could faintly feel her in his embrace, nestled against him under the starlit sky, moving together to a melody that seemed to be made for them as the world faded away.

As Deon's breath had lingered just above her lips, his heart raced, temptation washing over him as he saw the same look of unspoken desire in her eyes.

I want to kiss you.

He had thought, breathless, slowly leaning down, inching closer, his restraint slipping.

Applause had suddenly erupted around them as Deon froze—his lips a whisper away from hers.

A bittersweet ache had swelled in his chest as he gazed into her eyes, realizing the melody had ceased and the magic had ended. He was once again the Ambassador, and she, the Zelonian Princess.

"I wish this night didn't have to end," he had whispered, pained at the thought of letting her go.

Zelana had stared into his eyes, breathless, her heart mirroring the same unspoken emotions.

Deon's words reverberated within him, a silent whisper of his unspoken desire, as he blinked, returning to the moment. Every time he thought back to that night, remembering the tender look she had in her eyes, his heart clenched. He so desperately craved to envelop her lips with his, he wanted to surrender to the temptation, to indulge in the moment, but he hesitated, choosing restraint over his desire for her.

Since Victoria, he had avoided the thought of being intimate with anyone, but after meeting Zelana, he felt a shift within himself. Zelana intrigued him effortlessly as he tried to impress her while knowing she was a Princess, someone he couldn't reach. Her beauty and poise had captured his heart, and for the first time, he felt insecure, wishing he were of royal blood, equal to her in status.

Yet, her eyes met his with warmth and understanding, accepting him without judgment—even when he disappointed her, deciding to decline the flattering offer of her father to be her mentor.

Will I ever meet another woman as beautiful, intelligent, and charming as Princess Zelana? he pondered, the thought gripping his heart as the truth echoed with painful clarity—no.

The longing for Zelana was almost unbearable, suffocating. He had tried to bury his feelings, but they refused to leave him until it was all he could think about as his thoughts drifted back to her last words.

"There's something undeniably irresistible about you," she had flirted openly, her eyes sparkling with a playful intrigue. "It seems you have mastery over the command of someone's thoughts as well."

The smile on Deon's face slowly dimmed, feeling touched. "Now who's the one flirting, Princess?"

"I wouldn't dare..." Zelana had teased, echoing their light banter from the night before. "We can't have the Ambassador of Sanshe falling for me."

"Because I am a man of Sanshe?" he had added with a grin, matching her tone in jest.

"And you will remain in Sanshe..." she had guessed, pressing him subtly for a response.

His mind grasped her last words slowly at first... then it hit him—he could be a man of Sanshe *and* Zelonia. The thoughts that were once clouded by the constraints of his loyalty became clear, driven by a newfound certainty.

It doesn't have to end.

Deon rose from his seat, his pulse quickening, knowing he couldn't lose her. He had to find a way to be with her. With decisive and swift steps, he left the dining hall and made his way toward the training camp grounds, intent on seeking out his father.

CHAPTER TWENTY-ONE

A Father's Blessing

FOR THE FIRST time, Deon hastened toward the training camp, desiring something more than power or prestige, and he was ready to sacrifice everything for it. With each stride his steps grew lighter, eventually quickening, driven by his emotions for Zelana.

Upon entering the training grounds, Deon found his father, General Yengxue Vang, engaged in rigorous strength training exercises with his men—each steadfastly holding pails of water in each hand, demonstrating their discipline and endurance, a routine he knew all too well.

Observing his father, Deon's thoughts drifted to his upbringing—being raised with a strong foundation of morals. He was also instilled to value every life, love deeply, and indulge in the honor that comes with fulfilling one's duty.

Yengxue spotted his son and ceased his training. "What brings me the honor of your visit, son?" He approached Deon, clapping him on the back.

"I wanted to see my old man before I depart to Zelonia," Deon replied with equal warmth.

"When do you leave?" he asked casually, noting his son's serious demeanor.

"Tomorrow at dusk," Deon answered as his father nodded. "We plan to rest at Eastern Village."

Yengxue led Deon away from the training area toward his tent, which served as his office and resting quarters due to the relentless demands of his duties.

"Remain vigilant throughout your journey," Yengxue advised, leaning back against his desk.

"Aye, aye, sir," Deon grinned, drawing a smile from his father. "Don't forget to drink your herbal tea, eat well, and get enough sleep while I'm away," he reminded him with a smirk.

Yengxue chuckled lightly. "You sound just like your mother," his eyes twinkling with affection.

"She always took good care of you," he shot back playfully. "I never worried when she was around."

"I miss your mother every day," Yengxue sighed as his expression softened to one of concern, regarding his son intently. "Is everything all right? You seem rather fatigued."

"I was up late working on the preparations and will probably stay late again finalizing my duties here," he explained, momentarily averting his gaze, contemplating how to broach the subject on his mind.

"Finalizing your duties?" Yengxue pressed, sensing his son's unease.

"When I was in Zelonia last week, King Lucas made me an offer," he explained, meeting his father's gaze. "I've decided to accept it, and hope to have your blessing, Father."

"What kind of offer?" Yengxue asked, his brows arched in surprise.

"He's asked me to work closely with the royal family," Deon replied, choosing his words with care.

"That's incredible!" Yengxue's eyes lit up, proudly. "You must have made quite the impression on the King. But I'm not surprised; after all, you are my son," he added with a grin.

Deon chuckled lightly at his father's unabashed pride.

"What role did King Lucas envision for you?" He leaned in with interest, eager to learn more.

"I am to mentor his daughter, Princess Zelana," Deon revealed, observing his father's reaction closely.

Yengxue exhaled sharply, feeling apprehensive. "You do realize that being a mentor is a demotion from your roles as Ambassador and Commander here in Sanshe."

"That was precisely my initial reservation, and why I declined the offer at first. But upon further reflection, I've come to see it differently," he replied, hinting at the serious contemplation put behind his decision.

"This is uncharacteristic of you, Deon," Yengxue remarked, a bit confused.

"Father, have you ever been in a situation where you felt like you'd lose something far more valuable than title or power?" Deon questioned with a serious expression.

He paused, sensing the depth of his son's conflict. "The only time I felt that desperate was when your mother fell gravely ill, and I learned she was dying. I would have forsaken it all if it could save her."

"I'm standing at that crossroad right now," Deon murmured, his voice thick with emotion.

"Is this about Princess Zelana?" he asked, suspiciously.

With a heavy sigh, Deon acknowledged his intuition as Yengxue recognized his son's true motive.

"She's a Princess. Not just any, but one of divine lineage, a descendant of Goddess Alexi," Yengxue remarked in astonishment.

"I thought you might appreciate that I aspire to be with someone so revered," Deon responded, a playful smile tugging at his lips despite the seriousness of the conversation.

"Deon..." Yengxue began, his voice softening as he gazed at him with a newfound clarity. "There are countless princesses within Sanshe whose unions could secure our future. The fallen kingdoms are at our mercy. You could choose any princess here to be your bride, and arrangements could be made by tomorrow if you wished."

"But Father, no one here captures my interest," he replied with a somber expression.

"Not even Princess Huashi?" Yengxue inquired curiously.

"She always felt like a little sister to me," Deon admitted, his gaze dropping.

Yengxue sighed deeply, words failing him as he absorbed his son's declaration.

"Princess Zelana has become the first thought I wake up to and the last before I sleep," Deon confessed from the depths of his heart. "If anyone is to mentor her, it must be me. It's the only way I can be certain she's equipped to face the evil that lurks in Azalon."

"I have never witnessed such devotion from you toward any woman," Yengxue acknowledged as he observed Deon thoughtfully, countering with reason. "You are my only son and my support for your decisions has been unwavering. However, how can I willingly send you into the midst of gods? King Lucas would not take kindly to a Lord of common birth harboring feelings for his daughter."

"Father, I understand your worries and respect them," Deon replied with affection, "But remember, as warriors, death smiles upon us each day we step on the battlefield. Should that knowledge ever deter us from standing up and protecting those we love?"

Their intense conversation was abruptly interrupted as a herald's voice rang out, sharp and commanding, from outside the tent. "Prepare for His Majesty!"

Both Yengxue and Deon quickly regained their composure, turning toward the tent's entrance as the curtain parted to reveal MuaYeng, his presence filling the space with an air of authority.

"What was that you were saying, Commander?" the King asked, catching parts of their discussion.

Deon held the King's intense scrutiny without flinching. "I was reminding my father that as warriors, we are acquainted with death's presence on the battlefield, yet this familiarity doesn't stop us from charging forward."

MuaYeng sensed tension in the tent as he sought clarification. "What exactly is this about?" he probed, his eyes shifting between Deon and the visibly frustrated Yengxue.

"It concerns Deon's future plans, Your Majesty," Yengxue revealed with a hint of reluctance.

Deon hesitated, yet he laid bare his intentions. "Upon completing the negotiations in Zelonia, I intend to resign from my roles as both Ambassador and Commander."

"Why would you resign?" The King's expression turned to one of surprise. "If there are issues, let's address them now."

"I am deeply grateful for everything, my King. There is no particular incident prompting this decision. My allegiance to Sanshe is unwavering," Deon paused, then added, conveying a sense of finality. "I just wish to explore new horizons."

MuaYeng connected the dots in his mind and ventured, "Is this about Princess Lenora? I heard the two of you had a few words this afternoon."

"My conversation with the Princess is inconsequential to this decision," Deon swiftly clarified.

"I know you well, Deon," the King said, unswayed and probing further. "You wouldn't resign without a compelling reason. What exactly is driving this change?"

Deon paused to collect his thoughts, aware of the King's persistence in uncovering the full story.

"Your Majesty, I appreciate the opportunities and trust you have bestowed upon me. However, I believe my capabilities are no longer being fully utilized here, and there's a greater need for my skills elsewhere. An offer has been extended from Zelonia which aligns closely with my aspirations to further challenge my skills and contribute in new ways. It will also foster stronger bilateral relations between our kingdoms," Deon revealed, sharing his vision. "This change would also allow others in Sanshe to step up and leave their mark. My hope is that Your Majesty sees my heart and can appreciate the intent behind my decision."

MuaYeng exhaled deeply as he listened intently. "It appears King Lucas has recognized your value and wished to steal you for himself," he remarked as he acknowledged the strategic move by the Zelonian monarch.

"Your Majesty..." Deon sensed the King's emotional turmoil. "I am but one of many capable warriors under your command. The true strength of Sanshe's military lies with the General—my father. Under his leadership, I am confident that Sanshe will not only endure but grow, thrive, and achieve greatness."

MuaYeng turned his attention to Yengxue, unmoved. "Have you given him your consent?"

Yengxue exhaled deeply. "Commander Deon has always been one to forge his own path. As his father, all I can do is offer my blessing. May the Heavens shine upon you this day, my son."

"Blessings abound," Deon accepted, comforted to hear his father's support in the presence of the King.

After a contemplative pause, MuaYeng made a firm declaration. "I forbid you from resigning."

"My King... I must implore you to reconsider..." Deon pleaded, feeling constricted once again.

"My decision is final. Crown Prince Zhong will proceed to Zelonia with Chue to conclude the negotiations. You will stay and reflect on your commitments here. I refuse to lose you to King Lucas," the King stated firmly as he turned and exited the tent.

"Your Majesty, please—" Deon began as he stepped out after the King in a bid to be heard, but MuaYeng continued on his path, unyielding, forcing Deon to accept his decisive command.

CHAPTER TWENTY-TWO

Heroic Tales

THE AIR WAS warm, carrying the faint scent of autumn, and the sounds of distant conversations in different parts of the garden echoed softly in the night. Natalie stood behind Zelana as she sat across from the proud Crown Prince of Ferria, Emeric Vitus, tall with striking green eyes and light brown hair. They shared dessert while he recounted his tales of bravery and shared his grand visions with her.

"Ah, Princess Zelana, you should have seen it," Emeric said, his voice dripping with pride as he leaned back on the garden bench, holding a half-eaten pastry in his hand. "The Krimzonites were relentless, but you see, Ferria still stands because of my courage and tactical brilliance."

Zelana nodded politely, offering him a soft smile. "Quite impressive, Your Highness," she replied, though she dreaded the conversation, trying to focus on his words. She then noticed a figure moving among the shrubs behind Emeric.

Crown Prince Andreas Fadel, the mischievous and charming Crown Prince from the western kingdom of Glimmerock, suddenly peeked his head out from behind a bush. His dark brown eyes sparkled with mischief, and his black hair, tousled from his hiding place, only added to his roguish charm.

He put his finger to his lips, silently signaling her, *Shhh*...

She pressed her hand to her lips, fighting back the smile that threatened to break through as Andreas made exaggerated faces behind Emeric's back, mimicking his grandiose gestures.

Emeric, completely oblivious, continued, "I was outnumbered, but I never gave up or faltered. With a sword in one hand and the banner of Ferria in the other, I led my men to victory."

Zelana stifled a laugh, her eyes flicking between Emeric's serious expression and Andreas puffing out his chest dramatically, mocking Emeric's bravery and clearly enjoying her struggle.

"You're quite skilled on the battlefield," she managed to say, her voice barely steady.

Emeric leaned forward, taking her reaction as admiration. "You see now why it's only logical for Ferria and Zelonia to join forces—together, we could rule over Azalon. A marriage between us would secure many triumphs for our future generations."

Andreas clutched his chest as if overcome by Emeric's words.

Zelana couldn't hold it in any longer and let out a soft giggle, quickly covering it up with a cough.

Emeric paused, confused by her sudden laughter. "Did I say something amusing?" he asked, puzzled.

"Oh, no, no," Zelana quickly replied, waving her hand dismissively. "I just... remembered something funny, that's all." Her eyes darted briefly to Andreas, who now had one hand over his heart and was pretending to be in deep reverence for Emeric's speech.

Emeric raised an eyebrow but shrugged it off. "As I was saying," he leaned in slightly, his eyes alight with determination, "our marriage would be the strongest alliance the world has seen. Together, we would build a legacy—our names forever remembered as the ones who brought down Krimzon."

Zelana nodded, doing her best to appear interested, but her attention kept slipping back to Andreas, who was now crawling behind Emeric on all fours, completely unseen by the Ferrian Crown Prince. He paused, glancing up at Zelana with a wicked grin before striking another ridiculous pose—this time, pretending to draw a sword from his side in an overly dramatic fashion.

Her lips twitched as she stifled a giggle, but Andreas wasn't done. He stood up, towering behind Emeric, and mimicked a royal stance, puffing out his chest and straightening his invisible crown.

Zelana put her hands together and squeezed, trying to stay composed as Emeric, oblivious to the antics behind him, leaned closer.

"I can see you as my Queen, Princess," he said, his voice full of passion. "And I can already see our children—they have your blonde hair and my green eyes..."

But before he could continue, Andreas loudly cleared his throat behind him.

Emeric froze mid-sentence, his eyes narrowing in confusion. "What...?" He slowly turned around, his expression morphing from regal composure to pure bewilderment, coming face-to-face with Andreas.

"Who are you?" Emeric asked, his voice strained. "And what in the world are you doing here?"

"Crown Prince Andreas, Your Highness. I was on my way to meet a friend, but I couldn't help overhearing your... captivating tale. Truly inspiring," he replied, his voice dripping with insincerity.

Emeric straightened himself. "This is a private conversation, Crown Prince Andreas," he said, irritated. "Didn't you say you have somewhere else to be?"

"Oh, indeed I do," Andreas replied, his expression growing mock-serious. "But when I saw a fellow Prince delivering such a heartfelt declaration to Princess Zelana, I simply couldn't tear myself away."

Emeric's patience had clearly worn thin, his jaw tightening as he turned back to Zelana. "Shall we continue this conversation tomorrow, in private?"

"Of course, Crown Prince Emeric. I appreciate the time we've spent together," she replied politely.

"Until tomorrow then. Noon?" he asked in clarification.

"I'll be here," she confirmed with a small smile.

Emeric gave Andreas one last look of barely concealed annoyance before bowing to Zelana and turned, walking away from the garden, his posture stiff with irritation.

As soon as he disappeared, Andreas dropped his royal pretense, grinning. "Well, that was entertaining," he said, walking over to the bench where Zelana was seated.

She shook her head at him, still smiling. "You couldn't resist, could you?"

"Not in the slightest," he replied, sitting beside her. "But I must say, I saved you from at least another hour of listening to his heroic exploits. You owe me."

Zelana laughed, her heart lighter. "I suppose I do, though I'm not sure what you'll demand in return."

"Hmmm..." he mused, tapping his chin thoughtfully. "I'll think of something. But for now, I'm happy to bask in the glory of my successful interruption."

Zelana giggled, the garden suddenly feeling much more vibrant with Andreas by her side. "You're impossible, you know that?" she teased, leaning back against the bench.

"I've heard that once or twice," he replied, his tone light and carefree. "But I like to think of it as a charming impossibility."

Zelana couldn't deny the ease she felt around him. "I'm sure all of Glimmerock adored their Crown Prince with his impossible charm."

"They tolerated me, I suppose," he said with a mock sigh. "Though not as much as I hope you do, Princess." His expression softened, the teasing edge to his voice fading as his eyes found hers.

She had always appreciated Andreas's ability to bring lightness to any situation, but as he held her gaze, there was a sincerity she hadn't quite expected.

"And what about you, Princess Zelana?" Andreas asked softly. "Do you find me tolerable?"

Zelana paused, unsure of how to answer. Andreas was unlike any of the other suitors who constantly asked to court or marry her. He was playful, easygoing, and, above all, unpredictable. But beneath the teasing, she felt there was something deeper—a sincerity she sensed in recent months.

"I've always found you... more than tolerable, Andreas," she finally admitted in a playful tone.

The smile that spread across his face was slow and genuine. "Well, that's a relief. I was starting to think my charm was failing me."

Zelana couldn't stop the grin that pulled at her lips. "Your charm is fully functioning."

Andreas let out a light chuckle as they sat quietly, enjoying each other's presence.

"So..." she broke the silence, her eyes gleaming with curiosity, "care to explain why you were spying on me from the bushes?"

He chuckled, amused at her question. "Spying is such a harsh word. I prefer 'strategic observation'."

"Oh, is that what it was?" she teased with a smirk. "And what were you strategically observing?"

Turning to face her, Andreas's grin widened mischievously. "I was merely ensuring you weren't falling asleep listening to Crown Prince Emeric's heroic tales. You looked like you could use some... alternate entertainment."

Zelana couldn't suppress her laugh. "So, you decided to make faces at him behind his back?"

"It worked, didn't it?" he replied with playful satisfaction. "You smiled. Mission accomplished."

Zelana shook her head, still giggling. "Well, since you've completed your mission, how about another one—walk me to my room?"

Andreas leaned in closer, his voice lowering with a playful glint in his eyes. "Only if you invite me in."

Zelana brushed off his suggestion with a smile and rose to her feet as she teased, "On second thought, never mind."

Andreas stood up, mock-pouting. "I'm wounded. But I'll settle for walking you to the door."

CHAPTER TWENTY-THREE

I See You

ZELANA AND ANDREAS' light banter continued as they strolled through the palace gardens toward the royal courtyard, the soft glow of lanterns lighting their path.

"If you don't mind me asking, how many princes have come through here to win your hand?" Andreas asked with genuine curiosity.

Zelana smiled softly, her gaze turning thoughtful as they walked. "Too many to count. Each one with their tales of valor, their promises of glory, and their grand visions for our kingdoms." She glanced at him with a hint of amusement. "It's always the same song and dance."

"Ah, yes. The heroic tales of slaying beasts, conquering lands, and the occasional 'I'll unite our kingdoms in marriage to defeat the Krimzonites'," Andreas said, mimicking the grand gestures he imagined the others would use. "Quite the romantic pitch."

Zelana giggled at his impression, shaking her head. "Sometimes it feels like they see the alliance with Zelonia more than they see me."

Andreas looked at her, his expression softening. "I don't doubt that. But I see you, Princess Zelana, the real you—the one who's more than just a political union."

She paused, his words catching her off guard. The playful banter between them stilled for a moment, replaced by something deeper, as they reached the courtyard.

"And what exactly do you see?" Zelana asked as her gaze met his.

"A beautiful, intelligent, and strong woman who cares so much for people. You listen to their stories even when they're... well, as dull as Crown Prince Emeric's." He grinned again, though he was serious.

"Thank you," she said softly, her usual sharp wit momentarily lost.

As they continued walking, an unspoken question tugged at Andreas, a persistent thought he couldn't quite shake. When they finally reached her room, Zelana paused at the door, turning to face him with a playful glint in her eyes.

"Mission accomplished, Crown Prince Andreas," she teased.

He grinned, matching her tone. "Another notch to add to my ever-growing list of victories."

Natalie opened the door, waiting patiently for Zelana to enter.

"Good night," Zelana said, turning to step inside.

"Princess Zelana," he began, drawing her attention back to him. "Can I ask you something... personal?"

Zelana tilted her head, intrigued. "When do you not ask personal questions?"

He laughed softly. "Fair enough." He hesitated, weighing his words carefully before continuing. "What are your feelings toward Crown Prince Nikolai?"

Zelana's smile faltered, caught off guard by the question. "Crown Prince Nikolai?"

"Yeah." Andreas nodded, studying her closely. "You two have been spending a lot of time together, and well... he's not exactly subtle about how he feels."

Zelana lowered her eyes, her fingers playing with a loose strand of her hair. "Nikolai is... sweet. Loyal. He's been nothing but kind to me."

Andreas waited for more, but when she didn't continue, he leaned forward a bit. "But?"

She sighed softly, brushing her hair behind her ear. "I don't know if I feel the same way he does."

Andreas observed her thoughtfully, noticing a slight tension in her posture. "It's not easy, is it? Trying to balance not hurting someone and figuring out what you want."

She nodded hesitantly, feeling a bit vulnerable, before glancing at Andreas. "Why do you ask?"

"Just curious," Andreas replied with a shrug, trying to play it off casually. "I mean, you've got Crown Princes vying for your attention. It must be quite the experience."

Zelana smiled subtly, sensing deeper meaning behind his words. "Thanks for walking with me."

"Good night, Princess," he murmured softly into the quiet night.

As Zelana disappeared behind the door, the playful spark in his eyes faded slightly, replaced with something more contemplative. He stood for a moment longer, his thoughts lingering on her words, unable to shake the feeling that her heart was still searching for something—someone—that hadn't yet been found. And perhaps, just perhaps, he could be the one.

CHAPTER TWENTY-FOUR

Conviction

FOR THE FIRST time in his life, Deon let his personal feelings take precedence over his responsibilities as he reached the doors of the Sanshe throne room, where the fates of nations were often decided. His heart pounded in his chest as he paused momentarily, mustering the courage to confront the finality of the King's decree.

"Ambassador Deon seeks an audience with Your Majesty!" the royal guard formally announced, his voice echoing through the grand corridor.

A tense silence followed, until Chue's voice, firm and unyielding, answered from behind the closed doors. "The King has no desire to meet with him."

The royal guard looked bewildered, but it was Deon who felt the weight of the words crash down upon him. Deon fell to his knees before the massive doors of the throne room, accepting his fate.

"What are you doing, Ambassador?" questioned the Royal Guard, puzzled by Deon's actions.

"I will wait here until the King is ready to see me," Deon replied, grounded in his conviction.

The corridor filled with hushed whispers, high-ranking

members of Sanshe's court exchanging murmurs of intrigue and speculation as the Ambassador remained kneeling, his posture unwavering. Each time the grand doors of the throne room creaked open to admit a Councilman, Deon's gaze would lock briefly with MuaYeng's, their eyes meeting in a silent exchange, each standing firm in their conviction before the doors closed once more, leaving Deon to wait in the tense stillness.

Zhong, on his way to meet his father, came to an abrupt halt when he saw his friend kneeling in the corridor. His heart sank with disbelief.

"Deon!" he called, hurrying over to him. "What in the name of the gods are you doing?"

Deon remained silent, his posture rigid, eyes fixed on the doors ahead.

"Is this about Princess Lenora?" Zhong asked, his frown deepening.

"No, this has nothing to do with her," Deon responded, his voice flat, void of any emotion.

"Then why are you doing this?" Zhong's confusion grew.

Deon paused, knowing that the truth would only complicate things. "It's nothing you need to be concerned about, Zhong."

Zhong stared at him in shock, hurt flickering in his eyes. "Why are you shutting me out?"

"Don't worry about me," Deon answered calmly while continuing his silent demonstration.

"Since when have we had secrets, Deon?" he inquired, his voice cracking slightly with emotion.

Deon sighed inwardly, aware of how much his silence was hurting his friend, but he kept his focus on the doors, knowing that if he spoke, it would only drive them further apart.

"I can't believe you right now!" Zhong shouted, his frustration finally breaking as his anger surged, searching his friend's face, desperate for an answer.

Deon's gaze remained on the doors, his eyes refusing to meet Zhong's fully.

"Whatever this is about, I'll speak to Father," Zhong said, his voice softening, feeling desperate, the mystery killing him. "It'll all work out. You don't need to be so… dramatic."

Deon's gaze flicked briefly to him. "We're brothers in all but blood. I don't want to fight with you."

"You've changed since you returned from Zelonia," Zhong blurted out, feeling a sense of loss as he noticed people gathering around them to observe. "Get up, Deon. You're drawing attention."

"Leave me to fight my own battle, Zhong," he stated, his composure unwavering.

Zhong recoiled, a knot tightening in his chest. He stared at Deon, the brother he had always known, and yet now, he felt as though he didn't recognize him. Without another word, Zhong turned and stormed toward the throne room, shoving open the doors.

Deon's eyes met MuaYeng's once again, his silent message unmistakable—he wasn't only protesting, but declaring that he *would* carve his own path forward.

All my life, I've devoted myself to the King, to my duties, and to my country. But now… it's time for the King to return that loyalty, he thought in silence with unwavering conviction.

Time seemed to stretch, each minute dragging on like an eternity, as the Royal Council's meetings finally ended. One by one, the members filtered out of the throne room, casting curious glances at Deon, who was still kneeling resolutely by the entrance.

The door was held open as the King's eyes fell on Deon, a silent standoff between them. His figure was still as determined as when he first arrived. He didn't speak, but his plea for an audience was clear.

Inside the throne room, Chue turned to the King, feeling sympathetic toward his friend. "Will you grant Deon an audience now, Your Majesty?"

"Absolutely not," MuaYeng grunted, remaining resolute in his stance, deepening the mystery.

"Why are you refusing to meet him?" Zhong asked, perplexed.

"I have no words for him," the King replied, his voice cold with a stubborn defiance as his grip on the throne's armrest tightened with each passing moment.

The Crown Prince lost his patience. "Is this because of Princess Lenora?" he pressed, attempting to understand the issue.

MuaYeng's patience snapped. "Why would you assume I'd discipline Deon over that?" His voice boomed through the chamber like thunder, causing those present to flinch at his sudden outburst.

An oppressive silence settled over the chamber, the tension thick and suffocating, as Zhong took a step back, startled by the ferocity of his father's reaction. Agitated, the King stood and stormed to the King's Lounge, leaving an uncomfortable silence in his wake.

CHAPTER TWENTY-FIVE

Heartache

ZELANA SAT ON her bed across from Natalie as the soft glow of the half-moon cast dim shadows across the room. She absentmindedly folded the last of her skirts, her thoughts distant, as her heart seemed to ache more deeply than usual.

"I sense another rejection incoming tomorrow at noon," Natalie teased, her voice light and playful, breaking the quiet stillness that had settled in.

A subtle smile tugged at Zelana's lips. "If it were you, you would've walked away immediately and avoided him completely," she replied with a gentle laugh.

Natalie laughed along, folding a shirt. "You know me too well."

Zelana finished tidying up, then rose from her bed and stepped over to the window. She stared out into the darkness, her reflection faintly visible against the glass. The night felt heavy, burdened by an inexplicable weight that pressed down on her heart.

"Why am I feeling so gloomy tonight?" she wondered aloud, a hint of sadness in her voice.

"It must've been the rain this afternoon. Cloudy days always ruin my mood," Natalie responded, closing the wardrobe after putting the clothes away.

Zelana sighed, her thoughts drifting far beyond the palace walls once again. Deon's absence had left an emptiness inside her that felt all the more unbearable tonight.

"Days like this make me long for him more," she whispered softly, the words barely escaping her lips.

Natalie's expression softened. "He's made quite an impression."

Zelana nodded, the ache in her heart intensifying. "If he lived close, I'd ride to see him right now," she confessed with a mischievous smile, her eyes momentarily brightening at the thought.

Natalie smiled warmly. "I'd make sure no one knew," she said with a twinkle in her eyes, always loyal.

Zelana began counting the days in her head, attempting to suppress the sorrow that clung to her. "He should be here in two days," she murmured with anticipation.

Natalie stepped closer, observing her thoughtfully. "I can finally meet him," she said softly.

Zelana smiled, a longing swirling in her chest, as her gaze lifted to the moon hanging low in the sky.

"You will find the ambassador most admirable," she said dreamily as her eyes brightened with the vivid imagery of him. "Deon's charisma and strength are met equally with his intellect and diplomacy, a rare blend that makes him profoundly skilled in both the diplomatic court and the military field. He stands out among the most eligible bachelors of Azalon."

Natalie's eyes warmed as she listened, intrigued by the passion in the Princess's words. "From what I hear, he's also quite attractive."

Zelana blushed. "None of the princes who have come calling over the years can hold a candle to him," she responded, her voice a soft confession.

"It seems the young ambassador has not only captured your attention but perhaps a bit of your heart as well," she gently teased, becoming more surprised by the Princess's deep fondness for him.

"Is that why my heart's been aching?" Zelana murmured, gazing at Natalie with questioning eyes.

She paused thoughtfully. "I believe it's the uncertainty—wondering how he feels about you—that brings the pain, but I could be wrong."

A flicker of sorrow crossed Zelana's face. "He does have feelings for another princess," she admitted quietly as Natalie's expression softened with sympathy.

"Who is she?" she inquired curiously.

"He didn't say, but I believe she's from Sanshe," Zelana murmured softly, lowering her gaze.

"Don't worry your little heart over it," Natalie said gently, offering a reassuring smile. "You'll have more time with him soon—maybe you'll learn where his heart truly lies."

Zelana's mind drifted back to that magical night in Zelonia City, a subtle smile gracing her lips.

Deon had gently twirled her to face him, his hands settling securely around her waist, drawing her even closer as their foreheads touched.

What is this feeling? Zelana's heart fluttered, her body surrendering to the closeness as they swayed gracefully to the mesmerizing tune.

Time slowed as the world around them blurred and the crowd faded, leaving only the two of them dancing intimately under the starlit sky.

As Deon's breath lingered just above her lips, she stared into his eyes, heart racing, breathless.

Was he going to kiss me?

She had wondered nervously, noticing him leaning down, inching closer, her restraint slipping.

The music had suddenly faded and he froze—his lips a whisper away from hers…

Zelana exhaled softly, her thoughts drifting back to the present. The memory of that night still lingered, bittersweet, tugging at her heart with a quiet ache.

"I fear each stolen moment only deepens the emptiness his absence leaves behind," her voice barely a whisper, the truth unsettling.

Natalie fell silent, wishing there was more she could do to ease her Princess's pain.

Despite the lingering sadness, the thought of seeing Deon again offered a sliver of hope—a glimmer of light, enough to pierce through the clouds hovering over her heart.

CHAPTER TWENTY-SIX

Envy

THE GOLDEN GLOW of the palace lanterns illuminated their path as Huashi and Lenora, along with their ladies-in-waiting, strolled through the opulent corridor leading to the lush Sanshe Gardens. The distant sound of their footsteps echoed through the hall as Lenora's eyes caught a figure kneeling silently in front of the throne room.

"Is that Commander Deon?" Lenora asked, cutting off Huashi's explanation about the royal spa.

Huashi's gaze shifted immediately. "Deon..." she called to him, quickening her pace toward him.

There was a softness to his expression that surprised Lenora. His gaze flickered to her briefly, distant and indifferent, as if she wasn't even worth his acknowledgement.

"What's going on?" Huashi asked, concerned.

"The King must have reprimanded him because of me," Lenora stated before he could respond.

"That seems a bit harsh," Huashi murmured as her brow furrowed at the assumption. She swiftly grabbed a pillow from a nearby plush couch and approached him, kneeling beside him. "Here, put this under your knees, Deon. I'll speak to father and take full responsibility."

"I'm grateful, but I have to decline. I'm not being punished, Princess Huashi," Deon responded, offering a warm, reassuring smile that took her by surprise.

"Then why are you kneeling?" she asked, perplexed.

"He's protesting," Lenora accused, her concern deepening. "He wants to drive me out of Sanshe." Deon sighed as his gaze faltered for a moment, a flicker of irritation passing over his face.

"Princess Lenora," he began, remaining composed, "not everything revolves around you."

Lenora's face paled, visibly hurt by his words. "Why are you so rude to me?" she asked, her voice trembling slightly as she struggled to understand his harsh tone.

"I've been honest, but not rude," Deon retorted with no apology.

Frustration and anger flared across Lenora's face as she tugged at Huashi's arm. "Let's go."

Huashi shook off her hand, her voice rising in frustration. "What exactly is going on here?"

Deon simply smiled. "Don't worry about me, Princess."

"This is a waste of time," Lenora muttered in exasperation, grabbing Huashi's arm once again, pulling her away decisively toward the lush expanse of the Sanshe gardens.

As they walked, Huashi's worry deepened. "I've never seen Commander Deon so humbled before the King," she remarked, glancing back with concern.

"I didn't think he had that side to him," Lenora shot back sharply. "I've only been here a month, and from the moment I encountered him, Commander Deon has been nothing but a total ass."

Huashi halted abruptly beside the gazebo, turning to face Lenora with a stern expression. "Don't you dare try to smear him," she warned. "Commander Deon has always been nothing but kind to me and the other princesses. Just because you've had your difficulties doesn't mean you get to paint him unfairly."

"You must not have had many encounters with him then," Lenora speculated, her brows knitting in skepticism. "I've been having a difficult time adjusting to Sanshe, and when I confided in him about it this afternoon, he didn't offer any sympathy. Instead, he dared to lecture me."

"I've known him all my life," Huashi began, her words catching Lenora off guard. "And yes, he lectures me all the time, Princess Lenora. In fact, if it weren't for Commander Deon, I wouldn't even be talking to you right now as the Sanshe Princess. You wouldn't be worth my time."

Lenora blinked in surprise, her confidence faltering under Huashi's firm rebuke.

"He detests selfishness and arrogance," she continued calmly, but her voice was firm. "He's taught me humility and it's made me a better person. Perhaps you could learn from him as well."

The sting of Huashi's words pierced her heart mercilessly. "I didn't realize the two of you were so close," she managed to say, her voice softening.

A nostalgic smile briefly crossed Huashi's features as she stared at the flowering paths around them.

"Commander Deon and I used to stroll through these very gardens every day, watching the sunset and talking until the stars came out," she confided softly.

"It sounds like you don't meet anymore," Lenora remarked, hearing the wistfulness in her tone.

Huashi paused, her smile fading. "Not like we used to," she admitted quietly, her eyes lingering on the flowers trailing the path as if searching for something that had long since passed.

"What changed?" Lenora asked gently.

"The conflicts with Krimzon and the other kingdoms escalated. When he was promoted to Commander, his duties became more demanding," she explained, her expression darkening. "And now, with his role as Ambassador, I see him even less."

The contrast between Lenora's experience with Deon and Huashi's deep, lifelong respect for him stirred something unfamiliar within her—a pang of envy.

"Are you... romantically involved?" Lenora inquired, feeling that strange emotion tighten in her chest.

Are you interested in Deon? Huashi wondered silently, her eyes sweeping over Lenora's figure.

Huashi narrowed her eyes, as if trying to decipher Lenora's intent. "But what is it to you if we were?" she replied, her tone suddenly guarded.

Lenora hesitated, feeling self-conscious under Huashi's probing gaze. "I just... wondered," she mumbled, unsure how to express the sudden flood of emotions that surged within her.

"If I'd court him since he's not of royal blood?" Huashi quickly completed her thought.

"Well, you wouldn't have to court him, per say. You could command him to do whatever you pleased as the Princess," she replied casually, daring her to share more.

What is she insinuating? Huashi pondered, her eyes widening, unsure whether to be amused or offended.

Lenora paused, sensing the tension. "I'm sure your father would agree that because he's not royal—"

"My father adores Commander Deon," Huashi cut her off without hesitation. "He would approve of our union if we chose to be together."

Lenora was startled by her confidence. "Are you certain? You are the daughter of one of Azalon's most powerful kingdoms," she said slowly, trying to make sense of their relationship. "I would assume your father would arrange a marriage for you to strengthen alliances."

How rude! You're trying to impose your own values on us! Huashi eyed her suspiciously, her demeanor shifting more formal and distant.

"Sanshe wouldn't be the kingdom it is today without Commander Deon's contributions. He puts his life on the line every day for you and me, Princess Lenora. My father would choose the Commander over any Crown Prince vying for my hand," Huashi replied, her gaze intense and unwavering, as if daring Lenora to challenge her.

"I didn't realize he was such an important figure in Sanshe," Lenora murmured, her tone subdued, embarrassed over her earlier misunderstandings.

"He deserves your respect and appreciation," Huashi added sharply. "If it wasn't for Commander Deon, you wouldn't be leeching off us and benefiting from Sanshe's protection—wouldn't you agree?"

Lenora was surprised by Huashi's condescending and dismissive words, each one cutting deeper than the last. "I do appreciate him. I'll work on mending my relationship with him," she managed to reply, her voice cracking slightly, lacking confidence.

How dare you try to get closer to Deon, Huashi thought as a wave of jealousy flickered through her.

"Commander Deon has far more important matters to handle than your trivial issues. I'll speak to my father to arrange for you and Crown Prince Winston to move into the castle with the other royals," she assured her, her tone ice cold. "If you have other concerns, come to me—don't go bothering the Commander. Do you hear me?"

Lenora felt a lump rise in her throat as she forced a smile. "Thank you. I look forward to moving into the castle," she murmured, maintaining a veneer of gratitude, although deep down, all she wanted was to flee and cry.

"Now, if you'll excuse me," Huashi said, giving her a curt nod, and then turned sharply and walked away, her disdain unmistakable.

Lenora managed a slight bow, her hands trembling. The moment the Princess disappeared down the path, her composure crumbled. The tension that gripped her chest was too much to bear as she collapsed onto the bench, tears spilling freely down her face.

"Princess, are you alright?" Gwen quickly rushed to her Princess's side and sat down beside her.

Lenora's heart was heavy with the weight of Huashi's harsh words. "She humiliated me..." she admitted as tears continued to flow.

"Princess Huashi isn't known to mince words," Gwen admitted softly, trying to comfort her Princess.

"I'm in a foreign land, surrounded by strangers... utterly alone," Lenora's voice broke, the vulnerability she had tried to hide now laid bare. "I have no allies, no friends."

"You have me," Gwen reminded her gently, her smile warm and reassuring.

Lenora's throat tightened as more tears welled. The humiliation, the harsh truth—for the first time, she felt truly powerless.

"I have no influence here. Neither do you," Lenora admitted, her words heavy with despair.

"If a man of common birth can hold so much power in Sanshe, imagine what a princess can do with her beauty and charm," Gwen suggested subtly.

Lenora felt her heart calm, her tears slowing as Gwen's words sank in.

She's right. I can't allow myself to be helpless. Not here, not now.

With a steadying breath, Lenora wiped the tears from her face, a spark of determination glimmering in her eyes.

You will regret ever underestimating me, Huashi, she vowed silently, her heart now pulsing with a new sense of purpose.

CHAPTER TWENTY-SEVEN

Resilience

IN THE DIMLY lit corridor leading to the throne room, Chue stood beside Deon, whose knees had endured hours of torment. Concern etched across his face as Chue called out to the monarch once more.

"Commander Deon is still waiting for your audience, Your Majesty."

Inside the throne room, Huashi and Zhong stared at their father as he sat upon his throne, his head propped up with his hand, a picture of regal discomfort—his expression exuded pain and frustration, yet he remained resolutely silent.

They heard Chue's desperate plea once again as Zhong turned to his father, flustered. "Are you going to stay stubborn all night?"

"Please see Commander Deon, Father," urged Huashi, concerned for both of their well-being.

MuaYeng remained silent, visibly exhausted, his resolve unwavering despite his fatigue.

"Go to bed," the Crown Prince implored, his voice softening. "You're about to fall over."

MuaYeng slowly lifted his head, his gaze piercing toward the door of the throne room. "I'm not sleeping until Deon leaves," he declared stubbornly.

"What has Commander Deon done that's upset you so?" the Crown Prince pressed, his temper flaring once again, his voice echoing through the high-ceiling room.

"I don't want to talk about it," the King replied, the sadness in his voice reflecting the depth of the emotional toll on him.

"Surely whatever issue lies between you two isn't worth this ordeal," muttered Huashi, her frustration reaching a breaking point as she observed the tense standoff. "Commander Deon has been kneeling since early afternoon. Whatever the reason, it can't possibly justify such self-torture."

"See him, Father, and talk this out," the Crown Prince pleaded, "I don't want you to fall sick over this."

"You don't understand," MuaYeng sighed deeply, feeling the weight of his crown grow heavier as the minutes passed. "If I see him and he begs me one more time, my heart will break."

"Beg you for what?!" the Princess exclaimed in desperation as she knelt before her father and glared up at him, her words sharp and filled with worry.

After a moment of painful hesitation, the King's voice cracked, conceding. "Let him in…"

Relieved, Zhong quickly descended the stairs toward the door and pushed it open, stepping out, while his friends stared at him with forlorn gazes.

"The King will see you now, Commander Deon," Zhong declared with a sigh of relief.

"Hurry before the King changes his mind," Chue urged as he quickly grabbed Deon's arm.

Deon took a deep, steadying breath, gathering the strength to rise. "Thanks, but I'll manage."

Chue nodded in understanding and released him.

Deon stood slowly, each movement a struggle as his legs and knees screamed in protest after hours of kneeling. But with fierce determination, he pushed against the heavy doors. As they swung open, he stepped into the throne room, managing a smile that was as much a mask as it was an expression of his resolve.

The opulent grandeur of the room—its towering ceilings and majestic decorations—swallowed him whole. He had traversed the throne room countless times, shouldering the weight of governance, making decisions that affected millions. This was the world he had known, the realm he had served his entire life. But as familiar as these halls were, they now felt distant, as if belonging to another life.

His heart now drifted to a land far away—Zelonia, a place he barely knew. His thoughts were consumed by a Princess he had only met briefly, yet their encounter had left a deep mark on his soul. He longed to meet her again, to dance with her once more—this time a dance of destiny, one that could potentially demand every sacrifice he could make.

As Deon moved through the throne room toward the King, each step was heavy with what he was leaving behind and what lay ahead. The physical discomfort of hours spent kneeling paled in comparison to the deep emotional turmoil swirling within—a heart torn between duty and desire. An encompassing pain throbbed in his chest. He contemplated the path that lay ahead, as terrifying as it was exhilarating.

Reaching the base of the steps that led to the throne, Deon could feel the penetrating, scrutinizing gaze of the King upon him. His eyes were filled with expectations and unspoken questions. As Deon gathered himself to kneel once more in respect, MuaYeng unexpectedly intervened.

"You've knelt long enough," the King stated firmly, his hand raised in a gentle but commanding halt.

Deon felt relief washing over him, loosening the tension that had knotted his muscles and clouded his thoughts. He straightened slowly, meeting MuaYeng's gaze with gratitude.

"Thank you for seeing me, my King," Deon spoke with a bow, his voice filled with deep affection.

The tension in the throne room was palpable as Zhong and Huashi, who stood on each side of their father, observed the unfolding scene, their expressions a mix of curiosity and concern.

"I hope you've reflected on your words and actions this afternoon," MuaYeng addressed Deon with a stern tone that brokered no argument, devoid of emotion.

Deon nodded as he met the King's gaze with unwavering respect and calm resolve. "I have," he began, his voice filled with a gentle yet firm conviction. "It dawned on me that you are my King, yet you've always treated me more like a son."

Deon's heartfelt words began to erode the icy resolve in MuaYeng's heart.

"Since I was five years old, you took me in and gave me the same combat training that you gave Crown Prince Zhong. You allowed me to read the same history books he read. You even mentored me yourself," Deon reflected thoughtfully with a touch of nostalgia. "I was born a Lord, yet you bred me to think and behave like a royal. I know that I am the man I am today because of you. I'm grateful to the Heavens that I was born into Sanshe and lived under such a strong and benevolent King."

The raw honesty and acknowledgment of his deep gratitude visibly affected the King, softening the edges of his stern façade. "Why would you want to go serve another King then?" MuaYeng asked, his voice rising, the words slipping out more as a pained plea than a question.

"Your Majesty, my service to Zelonia does not lessen my loyalty or my love for Sanshe," he said, his voice filled with emotion.

"Deon..." Huashi called to him in shock, now realizing his intentions.

"I aim to bring honor to our kingdom through diplomacy and forge an alliance that will strengthen us. I see this not as leaving but as fulfilling the destiny you have prepared me for—extending the influence and values of Sanshe far beyond our borders," Deon continued assuring the King, recognizing his insecurities and the underlying fear of losing him.

Huashi stared at him in disbelief, realizing his request.

"My presence in Zelonia would be Sanshe's presence. My success will be Sanshe's success. I would be serving you in a different capacity," Deon persuaded, hoping to convince the King of the merits of his mission. "My leaving will be a blessing and not a curse. I will make you proud, my King."

"I don't see a problem, Father. Sanshe will always be Commander Deon's home," Zhong interjected, supporting Deon's plea, visibly moved by the depth of his commitment.

"And home is where my heart will forever lie," added Deon, his smile warm and reassuring.

MuaYeng's expression was a complex mix of anger and pain as his resolve crumbled under the weight of his affection for Deon. "Go, if you must!" he exclaimed, the words torn from him in a burst of emotion, breaking his heart.

Moved by the King's anguished concession, Deon lowered himself to the ground with a profound sense of reverence, his heart brimming with affection as he gracefully knelt and bowed before him.

"Thank you for your blessing… Father," his voice trembled slightly as he voiced *that* word.

Tears welled up in MuaYeng's eyes, his heart warming at the sound of Deon calling him 'Father.' Memories rushed in like a flood—quiet moments when they confided in each other to tender moments when Deon would tease the King privately so no one could hear. Deon was always reserved with his affection but his actions spoke volumes about his unspoken respect and love for him.

MuaYeng's heart softened in that moment, and he said, fighting back tears, "You will always be a son of Sanshe no matter where your duties take you, Commander Deon."

The silence that followed the emotional exchange was profound as the King lowered his eyes and quickly stood up, leaving the chamber, not wanting anyone to see his vulnerability.

Chue and Zhong exchanged stunned looks that conveyed their inability to articulate the intense scene they had just witnessed.

As Deon rose to his feet, steadying himself, his mind continued to linger on his King, when a slap—sharp and sudden—returned him back to the moment. The sting on his cheek mirrored the sting in his heart as he slowly turned to face Huashi, standing before him, tears streaming down her face. Each tear was a shimmering reflection of the pain his decision had inflicted on her, slicing through his defenses. The imprint of her palm burned onto his cheek, but it was nothing compared to the emotional weight behind the gesture, truly leaving its mark.

"How dare you leave Sanshe?" Huashi's voice trembled in anger, her words echoing in the silent hall, each syllable heavy with betrayal and pain.

Deon couldn't respond; no words could heal the wound he had inadvertently caused. His stoic façade barely concealed the tumult of emotions roiling within him. Despite his own pain, his stance was one of understanding and compassion, recognizing the depth of what Huashi must be feeling.

"How dare you leave me?" she cried out again in an emotional outburst, her heart breaking as Deon stood still and let her unleash hell on him, her hands thumping against his chest with a desperation that spoke volumes about her feelings for him.

Deon's heart broke for the second time that night as he reached out and pulled Huashi into a tight embrace, offering her the only comfort he could as she sobbed uncontrollably against him.

"I hate you..." Her body shook with each cry. "I hate you..." Her harsh words muffled into the fabric of his shirt as she poured out her anguish and fear of abandonment. "I hate you, Deon!"

Chue and Zhong observed them helplessly, reminded once again of the complex relations formed throughout the years within the Sanshe court. The men glanced at each other and quietly slipped out of the throne room, leaving them alone.

The hall around them fell silent and suddenly felt impossibly large and empty as Deon held her tighter, battling between his personal feelings and the pain he caused. "Hate me. Despise me. Forget me, Princess Huashi," he murmured, his voice breaking with emotion.

His words were like salt on Huashi's wounds as her cries began to subside, feeling more pain. She freed herself from his embrace and gazed up at him sadly. "I can't forget you even if I want to, but you already know that, don't you?" she whispered, her heart shattering before him.

Deon stared into her eyes helplessly. "You are strong and beautiful, Princess. One day, you will meet a man of your stature, worthy of your heart," he attempted to console her.

More tears escaped Huashi's eyes as her heart crumbled inside, realizing it was Deon's way of letting her down slowly. Yet, it only hurt her more, knowing his intentions.

Deon reached up to wipe her tears, but she took a step back from him.

"All my life, I've loved you," Huashi confessed from the depths of her bleeding heart. "Yet, I mean nothing to you," she whispered as more tears slid down her face while she slowly backed away and turned around, rushing out of the throne room.

Deon watched her retreating figure as the doors slammed behind her, the pain engulfing him. He had never intended for his departure to Zelonia to cause such heartache. The reality that his decision had deeply wounded someone he cared about became a heavy burden, so heavy that he had to do something he'd never done before—chase after her.

CHAPTER TWENTY-EIGHT

Amends

IN THE QUIET sanctuary of the royal gardens, Lenora sat inside the gazebo with Gwen, her gaze occasionally drifting out to the flowers where the last light of the day cast long shadows. The atmosphere was laden with reflection and a subtle unease as Lenora thought back to her conversation with Huashi that had left her questioning her interactions with Deon, wondering how her words had unwittingly crossed the line.

She felt a wave of guilt wash over her, her previous misjudgments of Deon now seeming harsh and unfounded. Suddenly, her eyes caught sight of a young woman rushing through the gardens, her movements swift and purposeful. Then a man, not far behind.

"That's the Sanshe Princess and Commander Deon," Gwen noted in surprise.

"Quiet…" Lenora whispered as they both stood up and hid behind a vined column, watching discreetly.

In the dimly lit garden, Deon caught up to Huashi and gently grasped her arm, halting her. She turned, her heart racing, as their eyes met in the quiet stillness.

"Princess Huashi, you've misunderstood me," he said softly, catching his breath.

"Then help me understand," she replied, her voice trembling, tears tracing paths down her cheeks.

Deon's heart ached at her sorrow. "You're someone I've treasured deeply all my life," he murmured, stepping closer and gently wiping her tears. "I can't leave like this, knowing you're hurting."

His words and gentle touch warmed her heart as Deon reached into his pocket, pulling out a small black velvet box, extending it toward her.

With trembling hands, Huashi accepted the box and opened it with care. Inside lay a beautiful floral hairpin with a red ruby as its centerpiece. The gem sparkled like a myriad of tiny, brilliant fires.

"It's beautiful," she breathed, her emotions raw as she sadly realized that his meeting with the Royal Jeweler was for someone else.

Deon smiled, a hint of pride in his voice. "I knew you'd like it."

With gentle fingers, he took the hairpin from the box and carefully placed it in her hair, arranging it so that it caught the light with every movement. "Happy eighteenth birthday, Princess Huashi."

Her heart fluttered at his gesture. "Thank you," she whispered, managing a small, heartfelt smile. She tilted her head playfully and asked, "How does it look on me?"

Deon stepped back, his gaze softening, taking her in fully. "Like everything else you wear—perfect."

Huashi smiled, taking a moment to savor his sincerity. "Why do you always spoil me?" she murmured, as she gently caressed the glinting hairpin nestled in her hair. "It must have cost you a small fortune."

"What are coins for if you can't spend it on people you care about?" he responded, his voice light but his eyes serious.

His statement made her smile widen, a touch of warmth spreading through her despite the turmoil of the evening. "I remember how you used to spend on Victoria, as if you never ran out of gold."

"Now I have you to spend my countless gold coins on," Deon murmured, gazing sweetly into her eyes.

Huashi's heart started fluttering again, amidst the comfort of his presence. Unable to suppress her emotions any longer, she laid her head against his chest, just like she had done countless times as a child. Deon instinctively wrapped his arms around her, pulling her close.

"Please don't go," Huashi whispered in desperation.

"I'm sorry, Princess..." he said softly, holding her tighter, his heart about to burst. "I'm going to miss you. You've always been the little sister I never had."

His words made tears well up in her eyes again as he confessed his feelings for her.

"I truly hope that with time, you can come to understand and perhaps forgive me," Deon's voice was soft, filled with a sincere desire to mend the rift between them, created by the emotional storm.

"I'm going to miss you so much," she choked out, surrendering to the inevitability of his departure.

Deon fought back his own tears as he slowly let her go and gazed into her eyes. "Promise me you'll listen to your brother and father. Don't go out alone late at night, you hear?"

"I promise..." she replied softly. "You will come back to visit, won't you?"

"Of course," Deon assured her with a playful smile. "When you're old and gray."

Huashi stepped back and mockingly glared up at him.

"You…" she began, her voice trailing off teasingly as she bit her lip, caught between annoyance and affection. "You better hope they don't throw you out the moment you get there."

Deon laughed, his voice echoing through the garden in amusement. "Don't curse me, or you'll need more than a bucket of quails to cheer me up."

Huashi giggled softly, the tension of the evening easing slightly.

"I'm tired," she confessed as she grabbed his sleeve, her voice suddenly soft and pleading. "Will you give me a piggyback ride to my room… one last time?"

"Princess Huashi…" he admonished, giving her a look of exasperation and fondness.

"Please?" she implored with a tinge of sadness in her voice.

With a resigned smile, Deon crouched down, and Huashi eagerly climbed onto his back.

"Oh, no. I can't seem to get up," he teased, pretending to struggle.

"You're just getting old," she joked playfully with a giggle as she rested her head against his shoulders.

"No…" he protested as he stood up, securing her with his strong arms. "You need to stop eating sweets."

They continued moving together down the familiar garden path, teasing each other playfully.

As the figures in the garden grew distant, Lenora and Gwen quietly emerged from their hiding spot, their footsteps light on the soft earth. Lenora's mind whirled with thoughts of Deon's gentle care for Huashi, his tender touch, and the way he held her close. Every gesture left an indelible mark on her heart, stirring emotions she hadn't expected.

"It seems like Commander Deon is leaving again," Gwen observed softly, noting the unexpected farewell between him and Huashi.

Lenora's heart clenched, envy bubbling beneath the surface. "And they're closer than I realized," she murmured, her voice betraying the surge of emotions coursing through her. Watching them together had stung more than she wanted to admit—Huashi had a piece of Deon she could only dream of.

CHAPTER TWENTY-NINE

PRINCESS KALINA

BENEATH THE CLEAR, luminous sky in the bustling market square, Princess Kalina assessed a beautiful painting of a lush garden, held up by her lady-in-waiting, Miranda.

"What do you both think?" Kalina inquired, turning to her companions.

Uncharacteristic silence followed, prompting Kalina to glance over her shoulder. Princess Jenessa Guardcrest and Crown Princess Anika Sharma were no longer paying attention to the painting, their gazes fixed intently down the street. An elegant royal carriage was weaving its way through the throng of marketgoers, stirring curiosity among the onlookers.

"It seems more contenders have come for Princess Zelana's hand," Jenessa commented, lightly fanning herself against the day's warmth.

Jenessa was the sole survivor of the Ember Falls Kingdom, striking with her dark skin, brown eyes, and medium-length black hair.

As the royal carriage drew nearer and glided elegantly past them, Anika caught glimpses of the gentlemen through its windows. "Quite dashing, I must admit," she said with a trace of amusement.

With her long, black hair and deep brown eyes, Anika was a stunning figure of regal beauty, entrusted with royal responsibilities from an early age as the heir to the Star Haven Kingdom.

Kalina noticed the royal carriage slowing to a halt. "They're stopping," she remarked.

Jenessa sensed an opportunity and suggested eagerly, "Should we approach and introduce ourselves?"

"I would advise against that," Connor warned, his arms crossed, as he and his two Zelonian Guards stepped forward.

Jenessa responded with an eye roll. "Oh, Officer Connor, you can be such a drag," she murmured.

"Your shopping excursion appears complete. Perhaps we should return now," Connor said.

Anika quickly diverted his attention to a stall displaying an array of vibrant handkerchiefs. "But look at this scarf, Officer Connor, isn't it lovely?" Her fingers gently grazed the material with fondness.

Jenessa quickly joined in the ruse, commenting on the beauty of the items, ensnaring Connor's focus.

Seizing the distraction, Kalina leaned toward Miranda and whispered, "Stay with them."

Miranda nodded with a knowing smile, while Kalina slipped quietly away from the group. Her movements were graceful and unobserved, as Jenessa and Anika continued their animated diversion, expertly keeping Connor occupied with their enthusiastic chatter.

Kalina drew closer to the royal carriage, her hand resting lightly upon a market post, as she watched the men descend. She now had a clear view of their distinguished looks and regal bearing.

Her discreet observation didn't go unnoticed, as one of the men caught sight of her, their eyes meeting, sparking an immediate, silent connection. His smile, warm and inviting, acknowledged her allure, and she reciprocated with a subtle smile of her own.

As his companions ventured into The Lagoon, the man hesitated briefly before following, lingering just enough to glance back at Kalina, a silent invitation, beckoning her to follow.

After taking a moment to ponder the encounter, Kalina decided to enter the restaurant. Its vibrant ambience of conversation, laughter, and clinking of glasses created the perfect setting for her discreet observation.

She walked over to the bar and ordered a drink, "A Sultry Sunset, please."

The server acknowledged her order and began preparing her drink. Kalina kept her watchful gaze on the table where the men had settled. She maintained a composed exterior, blending seamlessly with the restaurant's lively atmosphere.

At the table, Deon leaned in and broke the casual conversation. "Men, we're being observed."

Zhong was quickly intrigued. "By whom?"

"The blonde lady at the bar, on your right," Deon responded as his friends subtly scanned the room under the guise of casual glances.

Recognition dawned on Zhong as his gaze shifted to the woman, who, feeling his eyes on her, accepted her drink with a graceful, yet slightly self-conscious gesture.

"Friend or foe?" questioned Chue, half-amused and half-cautious.

"I bet she fancies one of us," Deon chimed in with a light-hearted grin.

"Let's find out," declared Zhong.

"Don't..." cautioned Deon, but it was too late.

Zhong was already on his feet, making his way toward the captivating stranger sitting at the bar.

Kalina, her drink in hand, felt the man's presence as he came and sat at the seat next to hers, sending ripples of excitement through her.

"A Taste of Midnight, please," he ordered casually as the server nodded and crafted the cocktail known for its robust blend of dark liquors and exotic spices.

"A strong choice for a strong man," Kalina commented, taking a sip from her drink.

"I do enjoy a little spice in my life," Zhong responded with a light-hearted yet suggestive tone.

Kalina glanced at him, his aura of self-assured charm drawing her into its gravitational pull. "You're not from around here, are you?"

A smirk played across Zhong's lips, amused by her attempt to deceive him. "Why ask something you already know?" he retorted candidly. "You witnessed my arrival by carriage."

Kalina's smile broadened. "It seems you've noticed me as well."

"How could I not?" he responded, genuinely taken by her allure. "Your eyes are captivating; a serene green like the fields I passed by at dawn."

Her confidence swelled with his compliment as she leaned into him flirtatiously. "There's more of me you'll find intriguing."

"Is that so?" Zhong's eyes swept over her in an appreciative manner while the server delivered his drink. He took a sip, savoring its complex flavors. "Nothing beats the Taste of Midnight in Zelonia," he declared, his eyes lingering on her curiously.

"I can't help but wonder how you'd taste at midnight," her voice lowered suggestively, emboldened by the flirtatious exchange they'd been sharing.

The intensity of the moment caught Zhong off guard. He quickly finished his drink in one gulp. "Why don't you find out?" he countered with a challenge.

In the charged atmosphere, Kalina's heart raced with anticipation, her gaze locked intensely with Zhong's, but the moment was abruptly interrupted as her attention snapped to the window, catching sight of Connor and the other Princesses standing outside, their faces etched with concern and haste.

"Meet me at the stroke of midnight at Swan Lake," she quickly voiced in sudden urgency.

Before Zhong could respond, Kalina placed a coin on the bar counter and hurried to the back exit, vanishing into the market square. Her abrupt departure left him momentarily stunned.

Zhong stood up and rejoined his friends, who welcomed him with laughter and light-hearted teasing, ribbing him about his failed romantic encounter they had just witnessed.

CHAPTER THIRTY

Crown Prince Zhong

In the heart of Zelonia, the majestic throne room represented the Kingdom's grandeur and rich history. Beautiful red curtains, adorned with gold trimmings, cascaded down the walls, framing the room in a display of opulence. Below, the floor was a sea of pristine marble, a canvas of luxury extending across the vast chamber. At the center, a plush red carpet, vibrant and rich, representing a symbol of power and authority, stretched toward the three steps that led to the thrones where King Lucas and Queen Sophia sat with an air of dignified elegance.

Lucas, with a demeanor that commanded respect, balanced his authoritative presence with a touch of kindness in his eyes. Beside him, Sophia exuded a quiet strength and wisdom, her poise reflecting the years of benevolent rule and compassionate leadership.

Surrounding them, the Royal Guards were a silent but formidable presence, their stoic expressions and upright stance a physical representation of their oath to protect the royal family and the kingdom.

As the grand doors of the Zelonian throne room swung open, the Sanshe delegation made their entrance, each step more prominent than the last. At the forefront was Zhong, followed closely by Deon and Chue, each stepping into the opulent chamber with poise and grace befitting their roles.

Standing before the royals, the delegation offered slight bows; the gesture spoke volumes of the respect Sanshe held for Zelonia, a reverence for the ancient lineage and the esteemed rulers before them.

"Your Majesty, I am Crown Prince Zhong Yang of Sanshe," greeted Zhong, lifting his head to face the Zelonian monarch.

"The Kingdom of Zelonia extends a warm welcome to you and your esteemed companions," Lucas replied with a subtle smile, his voice both kind and commanding.

"Thank you. My presence is a testament to Sanshe's commitment to our collaborative future," Zhong declared with charisma, his words earning a nod from the King. "My father, King MuaYeng, has fully endorsed the agreements between our nations. However, he wishes to add a specific clause, a matter best discussed privately."

The request from Zhong had clearly taken Lucas by surprise, but the seasoned monarch responded with the composure befitting his position. "Let's continue this discussion in my private lounge."

Rising from his seat with a regal grace, Lucas led them toward the side chamber, a space where the walls had witnessed many pivotal decisions and negotiations.

Dominic stepped forward to guide the others. "Please follow me," he instructed.

The delegation followed Dominic's lead, only to be met with a hand half raised in the air, signaling them to halt their footsteps.

"I will speak to the King alone," Zhong said in a commanding voice.

Chue's expression was of surprise as his eyes shifted to the letter held in the Crown Prince's hand.

"As you wish, Your Highness," Deon conceded, masking his own curiosity with professionalism. "We will be here should you require our assistance."

Zhong acknowledged him with a brief nod and followed Dominic. His footsteps were soft, echoing in the grand hallway.

Once out of earshot, Deon turned to Chue, his brows furrowing in contemplation. "Why the secrecy?"

Chue hesitated before responding, a note of unease in his voice. "It must have something to do with King MuaYeng's letter."

Deon looked squarely at Chue and pressed further, "What's in it?"

Chue felt conflicted. Telling Deon would break the trust of the King and the Crown Prince.

"I'm not sure myself," he fibbed nervously, fully aware of the contents in the letter.

Deon stared at his friend suspiciously, the air between them thick with betrayal and distrust.

CHAPTER THIRTY-ONE

The Clause

THE KING'S LOUNGE was a room rich with the history of Zelonia and adorned with timeless art, bathed in the golden light of the afternoon sun.

Lucas seated himself at a polished table, exuding a calm authority, as Zhong took a seat next to him.

"Here are the signed contracts for your review," Zhong stated, handing the documents to the King.

Lucas's eyes were attentive and sharp, reviewing each contract. After a few moments, he responded with a warm, appreciative smile. "Ambassador Deon has indeed done excellent work," he remarked, a note of respect in his voice for the diligent efforts of the Sanshe ambassador.

There was a brief pause as Zhong processed the King's words, a slight awkwardness momentarily passing over his features. "He is a great asset to Sanshe," he concurred, as his mind suddenly drifted to Deon's plea to his father prior to the trip.

The corridor filled with hushed whispers, high-ranking members of Sanshe's court exchanging murmurs of intrigue and speculation as the Ambassador remained kneeling, his posture unwavering. Each time the grand doors of the throne room creaked open to admit a Councilman, Deon's gaze would lock briefly with MuaYeng's, their eyes meeting in a silent exchange, each standing firm in their conviction before the doors closed once more, leaving Deon to wait in the tense stillness.

The Crown Prince immediately dismissed the thought and handed an envelope to the King.

"This letter comes directly from my father, intended solely for you, Your Majesty. It details the clause that is essential for the agreement. If you choose to decline, the contracts will be deemed invalid," explained Zhong, leaving no room for misunderstandings.

Lucas's curiosity heightened as his fingers carefully broke the seal that encompassed the private thoughts and royal confidences of the Sanshe King. Unfolding the parchment, his eyes moved across the words that seemed to take on a life of their own while a profound silence enveloped the room.

Zhong watched intently, his anxiety barely concealed beneath his composed exterior, consumed with anticipation, as he waited for the King's reaction.

The King finally looked up, rising to his feet, his expression of utter surprise.

Zhong slowly stood from his seat and gracefully descended to one knee. "Your Majesty..."

During this crucial moment, Lucas found his gaze unintentionally locking with Deon's through the glass doors. In that brief exchange, he sought some hint of persuasion in the young Ambassador's eyes, but Deon offered nothing more than a respectful nod, his expression carefully neutral. It dawned on him that Deon was unaware of the letter's contents.

"Please get up," Lucas said after some reflection.

Zhong complied and stood, facing the King with a quiet confidence.

Lucas fixed his gaze on him, taking a moment to truly see the Crown Prince—his poise, the earnestness in his eyes, and the subtle strength he exuded.

"I will need to discuss this matter with my Queen," stated Lucas after more contemplation.

"Of course, Your Majesty," Zhong responded with a respectful nod, understanding the delicacy of the situation. "I will await your decision with all due respect and patience."

Lucas's eyes continued to observe the Crown Prince. "I shall have accommodations prepared for you and your delegation. In the meantime, please make yourselves comfortable in the royal lounge."

"Thank you kindly, Your Majesty," replied Zhong as he nervously stepped out of the King's lounge.

CHAPTER THIRTY-TWO

GREETINGS

THE ROYAL LOUNGE of the Zelonian palace was a sanctuary of sophistication and tranquility where the Sanshe delegation found a moment of respite. The room harmonized the grace of royalty with the warmth of a family home.

"By the way, what was in the letter you handed to the King?" inquired Deon, glancing at Zhong as Chue clasped his trembling hands together.

"It's nothing you need to be concerned about," Zhong replied, his voice cold and detached.

"Are you really doing this right now?" Deon asked in disbelief, as he realized Zhong had thrown his own words back at him.

"You're the one who shut me out first," Zhong retorted, his anger obviously still lingering.

"I didn't know how to relay my intentions without making things worse," he admitted with a sigh.

"It was just a personal letter between two old friends," replied the Crown Prince, his words intentionally vague, shrouding the contents of the letter in a veil of secrecy.

"How can I effectively execute my responsibilities if I'm being kept in the dark about potential shifts in Sanshe's strategies?" Deon argued, not easily dissuaded.

Zhong remained silent, staring ahead, just as Deon had done in Sanshe in front of the throne room.

Even after I've conceded, he's still clinging to his absurd power play, Deon thought as he lowered his eyes in frustration, silently fuming.

The tension between them lingered, heavy and unspoken. Zhong's eyes remained forward, not ready to bend and heal the fragile distrust that had settled between them... not yet... not now.

"I'll oversee the task assignments and make sure everyone is clear on their duties," Chue said with a sigh, changing the focus, sensing the tension intensify between his friends.

"Keep your secret," Deon said, eyeing Zhong. "But don't be surprised when it blows up in your face."

Zhong finally turned and glared at Deon, feeling a hint of regret, but he had to put Deon back in his place. *No one defies me and gets away with it,* he thought as a smirk slowly crept onto his face.

"I'll meet with Princess Zelana to gather the necessary experts and resources to fulfill Sanshe's requirements," Deon outlined, turning to Chue.

Suddenly, the doors to the lounge swung open, silencing every voice, as Crown Prince Samuel made his entrance, displaying a natural authority fitting of his royal status, while the Sanshe delegation rose to their feet in a unified gesture of respect.

"I'll be leading the next phases of our meetings, so you'll coordinate with me moving forward, Ambassador Deon," Samuel announced, greeting warmly. "Nice to see you again."

Deon responded with equal warmth, "Always a pleasure, Crown Prince Samuel." They exchanged handshakes, followed by a friendly pat on the back, hinting at their closeness and mutual respect as Zhong observed their interaction with suspicion.

Chue extended his hand. "It feels like we just met yesterday," he teased.

"My thoughts exactly, Chue," replied Samuel, accepting his handshake in acknowledgment.

Samuel then turned his attention to the Crown Prince, offering his hand. "I'm Crown Prince Samuel. I look forward to our collaborations, Crown Prince Zhong."

Zhong stepped forward to meet his gesture, shaking his hand firmly. "It's an honor. I hope for deeper ties between our nations in the days to come."

"The feeling is mutual," Samuel affirmed, reciprocating the sentiment with a warm smile. "There will be time for our discussions, but they can wait until after you've rested. I can imagine your journey here was exhausting. Your accommodation is ready. Let me guide you there," he offered graciously, prioritizing their well-being as he led the delegation through the corridors.

"How far is Swan Lake from here?" Zhong inquired casually as they traversed the opulent passageways, his mind swirling with thoughts of a certain someone.

The question caught Deon and Chue off guard as they exchanged annoyed glances, reflecting their astonishment at the Crown Prince's unexpected boldness.

"It's quite close, just a ten-minute carriage ride down the road," Samuel responded promptly, his eyes narrowing slightly as he studied Zhong. "What draws you to Swan Lake?"

"At one of our stops on the way here, we overheard someone speaking highly of it," Zhong managed to answer, maintaining his façade.

"Swan Lake is a tranquil spot, favored by many for its serenity, especially at sunset," Samuel added.

"Then I must pay a visit before I return to Sanshe," Zhong replied, glancing at his friends with a smirk.

CHAPTER THIRTY-THREE

BATTLE OF WILLS

THE MEMORY OF the alluring woman from the bar lingered on Zhong's mind as he prepared for his clandestine rendezvous. Adjusting his collar with deliberate care, a pleased smile played on his lips. He dabbed cologne onto his neck, his eyes never leaving the mirror as he admired his reflection. After a final, self-assured glance, he turned and walked to the door, opening it only to find Deon standing in the corridor, unexpectedly waiting for him.

"You're not meeting her," Deon declared, stepping forward and blocking the corridor with his presence.

Unperturbed, Zhong responded with a smirk, "Oh yes I am."

The Crown Prince casually brushed past Deon, their shoulders colliding in a silent battle of wills.

"We should avoid behaviors that might tarnish our reputation at the Zelonian court," Deon advised, keeping his tone steady while turning around to face his retreating friend.

"I highly doubt she's connected to royalty," Zhong countered, dismissing his concerns and continuing his purposeful stride.

"We need to talk," Deon called after him.

"I have nothing to say to you," Zhong shot back coolly.

With a resigned sigh, Deon quickened his steps, following him, his steps falling in sync with Zhong's.

"And where do you think you're going?" the Crown Prince asked, raising an eyebrow as he approached the royal carriage.

"You're not going alone..." Deon replied, climbing in without waiting for permission.

A soft chuckle escaped Zhong's lips, amused by Deon's unexpected company. "She's mine."

He stepped inside and the royal carriage set off into the nocturnal embrace of the lake shore.

Deon scoffed, leaning back. "Not interested."

Zhong's grin widened. "You only have eyes for a redhead with wandering affections," he teased, throwing Deon's past love life against him.

"At least Victoria meant something to me," Deon replied, his voice edged with restraint. "You, on the other hand, chase after anything that..." His voice trailed off, not wanting to widen the rift.

"Go on. Say it..." Zhong dared him, but Deon kept silent, a smirk tugging at his lips.

I know when to hold back, Deon replied silently, turning his gaze toward the window.

"If you were a Crown Prince, you'd be doing the same exact thing," Zhong said in his defense.

No, I wouldn't... Deon uttered to himself as the carriage continued toward the lake, the night enveloping them in its silence.

CHAPTER THIRTY-FOUR

Rendezvous

As THE ROYAL carriage halted near the serene lake, Zhong alighted swiftly with Deon closely behind.

"I'm going alone," he instructed firmly, making his way toward the lakeside.

Deon persisted, walking beside him. "I'll keep my distance," he promised.

Zhong shook his head in mild annoyance.

Reaching the lake's edge, they immediately spotted a figure in the gazebo. Zhong gave Deon a cautionary glance. Deon tactfully concealed himself behind a tree, maintaining a watchful eye yet respecting Zhong's privacy.

The Crown Prince continued toward the lake, shrouded in a mysterious fog that drifted over the water, lending an air of enigma to the night and the woman who had lingered in his thoughts all day.

Kalina sensed someone's approach and rose gracefully to meet the gaze of the man from the restaurant.

"You came..." she murmured with reluctance as her heart pounded nervously in her chest.

"Didn't you want a taste of me at midnight?" Zhong teased, advancing closer with an intense gaze.

She made a daring move, clasping her hands to his neck, pressing her lips to his in a light kiss before retreating slightly to gauge his reaction.

"That's not how you taste a man," he said, his voice low and intimate, realizing her inexperience.

Zhong gazed into Kalina's eyes, their intensity mirroring the desire simmering between them as he leaned in closer, his hand gently grasping the back of her neck, pulling her toward him. His lips brushed against hers, sending a shiver down her spine as his fingers threaded through her soft hair.

Kalina's lips parted slightly as his tongue explored her, deepening the desire that pulsed through them. The kiss lingered, a perfect blend of passion and tenderness, leaving both Zhong and Kalina breathless and yearning for more as they finally pulled away, their foreheads resting together, savoring the electrifying moment they had just shared.

"So, that's how you taste," Kalina breathed out, her gaze locked onto his, captivated with the intensity of the kiss.

"Did it live up to your expectations?" he asked playfully.

"I think I'm addicted," she confessed as her feelings for him deepened.

Zhong immediately drew closer, his lips meeting hers again, more passionate and demanding. He backed her up against the gazebo's column as their kiss deepened. His lips moved to her neck as she gasped, breathless in the wake of their escalating passion.

"Who's there?" an unfamiliar voice called out from the distance as Zhong immediately pulled away.

"Are you with someone?" he asked urgently, his senses heightened.

"It must be night patrol," she replied as two beams of lights bobbed, approaching from a distance.

"I have to go," Zhong stated, moving swiftly toward the nearby trees.

"Wait…" Kalina's plea trailed off as she reached for him, but he had already vanished into the shadows as the patrols' lanterns illuminated her startled face.

Meanwhile, hidden nearby behind a tree, Deon saw a figure darting toward him. He soon realized it was Zhong, moving with surprising speed.

"I didn't think you'd be back so soon," Deon remarked, stepping out, half-amused and half-concerned.

"We need to leave… now," Zhong urged as he ran past him.

Deon quickly rushed after him. Together, they raced back to the carriage, ready to flee the scene and avoid any further encounters with night patrol.

CHAPTER THIRTY-FIVE

PRINCESS ZELANA

IN THE HEART of the Zelonian garden, a tapestry of vibrant flowers bloomed elegantly, their scents, rich and sweet, wafted through the air, enchanting the senses of all who wandered through. The gentle babble of a nearby brook harmonized with the melodic chorus of birds, crafting a calming symphony.

Secluded in the corner of the garden, the King and Queen were seated at an ornate table, immersed in a serious conversation. Sophia appeared visibly distressed, her expressions conveying frustration and concern. Lucas attempted to provide comfort but seemed at a loss.

"Your Majesties," Zhong greeted, approaching the royal couple with confidence.

"Please sit down," invited Lucas, his expression grave. "We have important matters to discuss."

Zhong took his place across from them, the air heavy with unspoken tension.

Nearby, Samuel was passing through the garden with Deon and Chue, heading toward the armory. The scene at the table caught Samuel's eye—particularly the sight of his mother's troubled expression. Concern immediately etched his features, prompting him to halt.

"What could be troubling the Queen?" Samuel mused aloud, drawing the attention of Deon and Chue to the royal family's private moment.

They observed as Zhong suddenly stood up, his posture shifting into one of deep respect—or perhaps apology—before he knelt solemnly in front of the Queen. His unexpected actions evoked curiosity and concern in the onlookers.

"It appears to be a private affair," Chue commented thoughtfully, suspecting it involved *the letter*.

It unsettled Deon to think Zhong might be withholding something crucial as he continued to observe the royal couple's reactions for clues, his mind stirring with suspicion.

Samuel was torn between concern for his mother and their need to respect the moment. "We should continue to the armory," he decided, directing their steps away from the unfolding scene, recognizing the need to maintain their scheduled responsibilities.

"Sanshe's blacksmiths should already be there," Deon confirmed, his thoughts shifting to the task ahead, though Zhong's actions continued to linger in the back of his mind.

As Deon turned to proceed down the garden path, he was caught off guard, pleasantly halting to find Zelana standing before him. Her appearance was like a vision from a dream, making his heart race. In that moment, he forgot the world around him, utterly captivated by her presence.

I've missed you, he murmured silently as the gentle sway of her gown trailed behind her in the breeze, accentuating her natural beauty, effortless elegance, and undeniable allure.

"Welcome back, Ambassador Deon," Zelana greeted him, her voice soft and melodic, her smile subtle yet enchanting, while her eyes sparkled like diamonds, rivaling the brilliance of the morning light.

Deon slowly blinked as her voice pulled him back to the moment. He took a step closer, gently taking her hand and pressing it to his lips, his gaze never leaving hers.

"Princess Zelana Celeste, I trust you've been well," he murmured, his voice soft with emotion.

Her eyes tenderly traversed his features. "I've been eagerly awaiting your return, Ambassador Deon Vang," she confessed, her words making his heart skip a beat.

Deon gently released her hand, a smile tugging at his lips, while his mind raced.

She's openly flirting with me now.

"Had I known of your anticipation, I would have hastened my journey back," he replied with a wink, effortlessly matching her playfulness with his own charm.

Zelana's cheeks flushed with a rosy tint, and Chue, standing nearby, observed them with growing concern, noticing their bond deepening with each shared glance.

"I heard you arrived last night," she murmured, her smile warming.

"And got lost looking for you," Deon admitted with a tease, his heart throbbing nervously in his chest.

He's become bold, thought the Princess, a soft giggle escaping as she covered her lips with her hand.

"Good day, Princess," Chue awkwardly interrupted, offering Zelana a bow, which was a blend of respect and slightly clumsy unease.

Zelana acknowledged him with her usual grace. "It's wonderful to see you again, Chue."

At that moment, Dominic arrived with a message. "Princess, your father is waiting."

"Thank you, Commander Dominic. I'll be on my way," she replied, her gaze returning to Deon.

"We should continue with our duties as well," Samuel interjected, leading the way.

Chue followed him while Deon lingered a moment longer.

"Princess Zelana…" Deon spoke her name, savoring the way it felt on his lips. "If you can spare a moment, I'd like to take a stroll with you later this afternoon."

Her eyes lit up with a flicker of mutual longing. "You can probably find me in the gardens. Hopefully you won't get lost this time."

Deon chuckled softly. "Come find me if you don't seen me before sundown."

"I'll alert all the guards," she replied playfully, her smile broadening.

Deon laughed as he pivoted to rejoin his companions. "I should get going."

Zelana nodded thoughtfully as he turned to walk away, but her observant gaze caught a subtle inconsistency in his movement. "You're limping, Ambassador."

Deon froze in his steps, unprepared for her keen observation. Slowly, he turned back to face her, grappling with a memory he thought he had long buried.

Deon could still see Victoria's eyes, always watching him, but never truly seeing *him. She talked about everything—except the two of them. He had always worn his helmet in battle, not out of fear, but to protect the face he knew she adored.*

"Commander Deon! You're back and just as handsome as ever," Victoria would often say, her smile bright as they carried on with their day.

He had once been flattered by her words, thinking little of them—until one fateful day when he returned from a brutal battle, limping, his body and face marked with fresh wounds. Despite his suffering, he rushed to see her, anticipating her reaction with a hint of unease.

"Commander Deon! You've finally returned," Victoria had greeted him that day, sweeping over his wounds with a detached, scrutinizing gaze. "You're scarred… I hope it heals."

Excitedly, Victoria went to grab a flyer. She busied herself with it, seeming to not notice him in pain, her focus elsewhere—on her plans, her desires.

"There's a show I've been dying to see. Want to go tonight?" she asked, her eyes filled with anticipation, insensitive to his injuries.

Deon's heart sank as he mustered the energy to respond, his body screaming in agony. "I don't feel like going out," he had admitted softly, hoping she might notice the pain etched across his weary form.

"I've waited a whole month for you," she had said with a hint of exasperation, not pausing to ask him why or truly see him. "You have no idea how bored I was while you were away."

Staring at her in disbelief, Deon collapsed onto a nearby sofa, his mind torn between trying to understand her and managing his own suffering.

"Come on, Deon. Don't be a downer," she had pleaded, sitting beside him with a playful pout, completely oblivious to the deep fatigue weighing on him.

Giving in once more to her desires, he had forced himself to stand, his muscles aching with every movement. "Alright, let's go."

Victoria rose to her feet, still blind to the man who had returned from the brink—broken and bruised.

Deon felt a gentle touch on his arm, pulling him back to the present.

"Where does it hurt?" Zelana murmured softly, her fingers brushing his arm with tenderness.

"Just a minor mishap the other night," he replied casually, though his voice betrayed a hint of emotion.

"There must be more to it," she murmured, her perceptiveness piercing through his façade.

"It will have to be a tale I share another day," he said with another wink.

"Alright," she nodded, though the worry in her eyes didn't wane. She reached into her blouse, retrieving a small pouch, and offered it to him. "Take these. One every hour until you feel better. They're surprisingly pleasant for medicinal herbs."

Deon paused, struggling to keep his composure, deeply touched by how much Zelana cared for him. The tenderness in her gaze made it harder to mask the feelings that stirred within him. He accepted the pouch, opening it to find small, green, candy-like remedies. He placed one in his mouth, surprised by the soothing taste reminiscent of green tea.

"Thank you, Princess," he murmured, a warm smile spreading across his face. "I feel better already."

Her smile widened, the worry fading slightly. "Be mindful of your steps today."

He paused, flattered. "As you command, Your Highness."

Deon felt his heart melt under her gentle care, and it took all his willpower to turn and walk away from her. He moved carefully, determined to hide the pain that still lingered.

Zelana's eyes followed him, her unease growing, as a quiet concern clung to her.

"I can see why you're quite taken with him," came a voice behind her. Natalie stepped forward, her playful smile lighting up her face. "He's got a certain charm… and it helps that he's easy on the eyes."

Zelana blushed, her smile growing timid. "He *is* handsome," she admitted, and the two giggled softly.

"Princess…" Dominic interjected, urging her attention back to the present task.

With a final glance at Deon's retreating figure, Zelana composed herself and turned toward Dominic, moving gracefully in the direction her parents awaited, with Natalie following closely behind. Her mind was undoubtedly swirling with the man who had so effortlessly captured her thoughts.

CHAPTER THIRTY-SIX

New Beginnings

Zelana neared the corner of the garden, feeling an unmistakable aura of unease enveloping the group.

"Allow me to introduce my daughter, Princess Zelana," Lucas announced without any delay.

Zhong rose from his seat and faced her, his posture subtly shifting as his gaze fell upon her, momentarily captivated by her presence.

You're breathtaking, he thought, admiring her allure.

Deon's previous descriptions of her echoed in his mind, but nothing he said had prepared Zhong for the captivating beauty standing before him.

I may have met my match, he mused silently, observing the poise and quiet confidence with which she carried herself. She stood before him, her gaze meeting his without wavering, something he rarely encountered with other princesses.

Zelana observed the distinguished, handsome man before her, noting his Asian descent and royal bearing. *You radiate a blend of strength and charisma, reminding me of Deon,* she observed silently, a spark of curiosity and intrigue growing within her, noting his composure and graceful manners.

"Your presence humbles me, Princess Zelana," Zhong articulated with finesse, taking her hand and placing a delicate kiss upon it. "I am Crown Prince Zhong Yang of Sanshe."

"It is an honor to meet you, Crown Prince Zhong," Zelana replied elegantly, matching his formality.

Zhong stood upright to engage her eyes with unwavering attention.

Before the exchange could deepen, Sophia interjected smoothly. "Your father and I have some matters to attend to. Why don't you take this time to show the Crown Prince around?"

"It would be my pleasure," Zelana affirmed as she smiled subtly, concealing her reservations.

"Thank you kindly for your understanding, Your Majesties," Zhong acknowledged the royal couple's efforts with courtly grace, working to solidify their diplomatic ties.

"We shall reconvene later tonight," the King stated, signaling a continuation of their discussions.

My parents are up to something, Zelana observed them quietly, sensing the carefully orchestrated undertones of the encounter.

With a respectful nod, Zhong shifted his attention to Zelana, ready to explore the grandeur of the Zelonian castle under her guidance. As they stepped into the moment, both royals carried themselves with quiet dignity while silently scrutinizing each other—each aware that this moment held more significance than a simple tour, as they charmed each other without hesitation.

CHAPTER THIRTY-SEVEN

Royals

NATALIE TRAILED DISCREETLY behind Zelana and Zhong, allowing them some privacy as they meandered along the garden path, maintaining an air of formality, yet an undercurrent of mutual curiosity subtly infused their interaction.

"Zelonia's gardens are quite a marvel," the Crown Prince commented, his steps synchronizing with the Princess's, as his gaze lingered appreciatively on her radiant complexion and captivating blue eyes.

"Thank you. It's a haven I find myself running to when I want time alone," Zelana responded, aware of his admiring stare. "How was your journey here?"

"It was quite scenic. We traveled for two days, resting in Eastern Village for a night," he replied, still observing her closely. "The landscapes were breathtaking, yet they pale to the beauty before me."

Zelana offered a small smile, feeling a blush tint her cheeks at his words, but maintained her composure. "I've never ventured beyond these borders," she shared, glancing casually up at him.

Zhong caught her subtle longing and responded with a promise, "That will change soon." His delicate dance of words and glances deepened her curiosity.

"Is my father planning a visit to Sanshe?" inquired the Princess, seeking clarity.

"The King has made several assurances," he revealed, towering over her small frame, as she stared up at him with a curious gaze. He couldn't help resist teasing her in that moment. "If I divulge them, I'd have to take you away from Zelonia."

"Would that be so terrible?" she teased with a smile, following along with his playful banter.

"Quite the opposite, actually," he confessed, laying his emotions bare. "I find myself increasingly captivated by your presence."

His words caught Zelana by surprise as she lowered her eyes, her usual poise and grace momentarily faltering. "I've never met a man who expresses himself so freely."

The Crown Prince smiled, his gaze intensifying. "You live up to your reputation, Princess of Zelonia."

"Crown Prince of Sanshe, what is this reputation you speak of?" she teasingly challenged him with a playful spark in her eyes as she tilted her head up to meet his gaze.

"Ambassador Deon spoke admirably of your intelligence, charm, and wit," he shared, feeling his initial nervousness melting away.

"Did he now?" she inquired, a subtle smile forming on her lips at the mention of Deon's name, intrigued by what else he might have said about her.

"Very much so," he admitted, leaning closer as he softly whispered, "What he neglected to mention was that you're the most beautiful Princess in all the realms."

Zelana's smile deepened as her eyes twinkled, feeling touched. "It seems you both have mastered the art of flattery."

"It's no mere flattery, I assure you." He returned her smile with sincerity and a playful charm.

"Why is it you keep reminding me of him?" she pondered aloud, her voice soft, as if lost in thought.

"Ambassador Deon?" asked Zhong, seeking clarification.

"Yes, you're both hard to read," she murmured with a scrutinizing gaze. "Earlier I asked him why he was limping and he easily escaped my question. Maybe you can indulge me."

"Ah… that," he chuckled lightly. "If I tell you, you must return the favor."

"What is it that you have in mind?" she asked, strangely feeling a bit nervous.

"Keep my company again tomorrow," Zhong responded without hesitation.

"If it pleases you," Zelana agreed, flattered.

Zhong felt overjoyed at that moment. "It pleases me more than you know."

The Princess gazed up at him with a subtle allure, her eyes shimmering. "So, tell me…" she said softly, her voice filled with intrigue, "how *did* he get hurt?"

Zhong hesitated, his eyes flickering with uncertainty whether he should be honest, but he couldn't resist the temptation to please her. "He was on his knees for hours asking my father a favor."

"A favor?" she inquired, concerned. *No wonder you were limping…*

"That favor, I cannot disclose," he said before she could ask, his expression turning serious.

"You and Ambassador Deon are quite mysterious," murmured the Princess, her curiosity unsatisfied.

"It's natural we share certain... talents. We were raised as brothers," he admitted, his tone carrying a blend of fondness and pride. "My father has a soft spot for him... and I do too... on certain days."

Zelana giggled softly, covering her lips with her hand as she nodded thoughtfully. "Sibling rivalry at its finest," she mused, her eyes twinkling. "I had a feeling you two were close the moment we met."

"You will find that I'm the romantic one," quipped the Crown Prince, drawing a sweet laugh from her.

In the tranquility of the garden, a delicate connection started to form, one conversation at a time, between the Princess of Zelonia and the Crown Prince of Sanshe.

CHAPTER THIRTY-EIGHT

Confusion

THE AFTERNOON SUN filtered through the leaves, casting dappled shadows on the ground, creating a serene and almost mystical atmosphere. Kalina strolled down the garden pathways with Miranda following her, but her thoughts were far from the present, pondering back to the mysterious man she had encountered the previous night at Swan Lake.

"What are you thinking about?" asked Miranda, noticing a smile on her Princess's face.

"I can still remember the look in his eyes as he pressed his lips to mine..." murmured Kalina, her eyes dreamy, "It left a lingering sweetness I cannot forget."

"It must have been magical..." she replied, her eyes glossed over with envy.

"It truly was," Kalina admitted, engulfed in the memories of him. She remained oblivious to her surroundings as Zelana's gentle voice called out to her.

"Princess Kalina..."

Kalina was pulled from her thoughts, coming face-to-face with her friend. Her eyes suddenly widened in disbelief upon seeing Zelana accompanied by the very man who had been occupying her thoughts.

As their eyes met, Zhong's composure momentarily faltered, revealing a hint of astonishment beneath his façade. The air around them thickened with unspoken words and concealed feelings.

"Have you both met before?" Zelana asked, noticing the tension in the air.

"Yes, briefly..." Kalina admitted, her voice a whisper.

"I believe you're mistaken," Zhong countered adamantly. "I've never met you before."

Their contradictory responses intensified the tension that hovered awkwardly over them, leaving Zelana perplexed.

"We met at The Lagoon yesterday afternoon," Kalina clarified, feeling slighted by his refusal to acknowledge their encounter.

"I must insist, you're confusing me for someone else," Zhong retorted with a calculated calm, attempting to diffuse the situation.

Kalina stared at him, hurt and in disbelief. He was the man who stole her first kiss, who made her heart sing. Yet, here he was, dismissing their previous encounters without blinking an eye.

"Excuse me," Kalina spoke with a pained expression as she hastened away.

"Princess Kalina..." Zelana called after her, but she continued walking without turning back.

"It's an unfortunate misunderstanding," Zhong remarked, his expression giving away none of the emotions that were swirling beneath the surface.

"I have to check on her," Zelana murmured, not knowing what to think.

"I'll come with you," offered the Crown Prince.

Suddenly, Deon approached with a teasing smile. "Where are we going?"

"Ambassador..." Zelana greeted, surprised to see him so soon. Yet, his presence calmed her heart.

"Am I interrupting?" Deon asked slowly, sensing a strange vibe in the air.

"We were just about to check on Princess Zelana's friend," Zhong responded casually as the men walked on each side of the Princess.

"How's everything coming along?" inquired the Princess, gazing up at Deon.

"Quite well actually. We were able to get everything unloaded and set up. The training sessions will commence tomorrow," Deon explained with pride.

"I'm impressed at how quickly you were able to organize everything," Zelana praised him generously.

"I came with intentions to deliver. This time, I've come to please," Deon replied with a wink.

Every time you wink, my heart flutters, she wanted to say, her eyes lingering admirably on him.

Deon grinned, lost in his own thoughts. *How do I stop my heart from wanting to be yours when you look at me like that?*

The Crown Prince was visibly uncomfortable with the attention his friend was giving Zelana as he felt a pang of jealousy. "I hear it wouldn't have been possible without your influence," Zhong interjected, his voice tense.

Zelana turned her gaze to the Crown Prince, her expression softening. "Ambassador Deon was quite convincing," she responded warmly.

The sparkle of excitement in her eyes tugged at something within Zhong, his intrigue and admiration for her deepening despite the subtle discomfort of witnessing the bond between her and Deon slowly unravel before him.

CHAPTER THIRTY-NINE

COMPLICATED

STEPPING INTO THE royal courtyard, the men were immediately struck by the stunning vista that unfolded before them. The centerpiece was a grand fountain, sending gentle sprays of water cascading into the air, creating a soothing melody that complemented the serene beauty of the surroundings. Benches were arranged with precision around it, offering perfect vantage points to enjoy the view, while the pathways were lined with neatly trimmed bushes, adding to the ordered elegance of the courtyard.

Deon stepped closer to the railing. "This view could soothe any troubled soul," he expressed, as the scene before him evoked a sense of tranquility and longing within him.

The Princess and Crown Prince walked over to Deon, joining in the admiration.

"It's even more breathtaking at sunrise," Zelana remarked, her voice soft and reflective.

"The view is, indeed, incredible," agreed Zhong, his words affirming the shared sentiment.

Their serene moment was interrupted by the sudden creak of a door. Kalina appeared, taken aback at the sight of Zelana in between two distinguished, handsome men, as a wave of envy washed over her, her eyes darting between the three.

Deon was caught off guard as he stared at Kalina, remembering the previous night's clandestine meeting at the lake and recognizing her as the mysterious woman who had captured the Crown Prince's interest at the restaurant. Tension knotted in his stomach as he exchanged a worried glance with Zhong, whose composed exterior betrayed none of the previous night's passion.

Zelana sensed the undercurrents of confusion. "Please give us a moment..." she said as her hand reached out, lightly grasping Kalina's arm, guiding her back into the sanctuary of her room.

As the door closed with a soft click, leaving the men alone outside, Deon quickly approached his friend with concern etched on his face.

"That's the woman from the restaurant—the one you were with last night at Swan Lake," he murmured.

"How was I to know she was a princess?" Zhong muttered in frustration, keeping his voice low while running his hand through his hair. "I encountered her with Princess Zelana earlier and she recognized me immediately. I panicked and denied everything."

"You... what?!" Deon blurted out in disbelief.

"I didn't want Princess Zelana to think less of me," Zhong confessed, his eyes darting nervously.

"Why would she care?" he pressed, struggling to wrap his head around Zhong's behavior.

Zhong took a deep breath, his voice dropping to a whisper. "When I'm in Princess Zelana's presence, I get really nervous... it's quite unsettling," he admitted, betraying a vulnerability he rarely showed.

Deon's heart clenched painfully, a part of him wanting to deny what he had just heard. *Do you have feelings for Princess Zelana?* The thought reverberated through him as he forced himself to remain composed, but each word struck him like a forceful punch to the heart, leaving him momentarily breathless and disoriented.

Zhong's gaze shifted uneasily to the ground as if he couldn't bear to meet Deon's eyes. "She's different. I feel different around her," he mumbled. "No one else has ever made me feel this way."

"You're always like this when you first meet a woman," Deon refuted, unconvinced. Yet, he couldn't help worrying; something about Zhong's reaction unsettled him more than usual.

"Deny it all you want. I know what I feel." Zhong finally looked up, meeting Deon's gaze. "She is everything you described and more. I've never met a woman that makes me feel weak in her presence—yet inspires me to be stronger for her."

Deon's jaw tightened as he fell into a heavy silence, battling to mask the turmoil brewing beneath his calm exterior. The effort to stay unfazed was almost unbearable as the air between them felt thick and suffocating. Every word that left Zhong's mouth felt like a sharp blade stabbing at his heart as he listened to him speak fondly of the very Princess who had also captured his own admiration.

"What about Princess Sierra?" he asked, after a long, tense pause.

Zhong's irritation flared. "Do you have to bring her up right now?" he snapped, frustrated.

"Princess Zelana isn't just some girl to be pursued lightly, Zhong," Deon stated, his voice softening, a hint of pleading underlying his words. "Don't treat her like the others."

"What's gotten into you?" he asked, narrowing his eyes at Deon, confused. "You've been on my case for days now."

"You told me to always be brutally honest with you," Deon

replied, his voice thick with emotion. "But the truth is, you've never been able to handle it."

Zhong's demeanor shifted. "I like her, Deon," he admitted, his voice softening. "I could love her."

The ache in Deon's heart deepened as he tried to process the profound implications of his friend's heartfelt confession. *I have to bury my feelings again,* he thought, knowing he couldn't betray his friend. Yet, thinking about Zhong and Zelana together gnawed at him, sending sharp waves of heartache and pain through his chest.

"Just... make sure she's the one this time before enacting on your urges," Deon said, his voice strained, trying to steady the storm brewing inside. "The alliance between our kingdoms hang by a thread."

Along with our friendship, Zhong, he wanted to say, but the words hovered on the tip of his tongue, too heavy to voice—too dangerous to utter.

Zhong stared at his friend. *Do you have feelings for Princess Zelana?* He searched Deon's face for emotions he may not be expressing as the air between them felt charged, like the calm before a storm.

"Princess Kalina has never met you, so distract her. I need her off my back so I can handle things on my end," Zhong suggested, testing Deon's loyalty.

"It was just a drink at the bar, what's the fuss?" Deon tried to minimize the gravity of the encounter, not wanting to be put in a difficult position.

"We kissed last night, and it was probably her first," the Crown Prince admitted. "You know how significant first experiences can be, especially when they don't end according to one's fantasies."

Deon sighed, upset. "That's why I tried to stop you last night," he lashed out in anguish, staring at his friend in desperation. "You need to stop seeing so many women."

"I got it. You were right, okay? But I'm already in this mess," he murmured, raising his voice. "I'll request to see her tonight and approach the situation with care. Hopefully, we can come to a resolution that allows us both to move on gracefully. I only ask that you please do me a favor and distract her. Better yet, pretend like you're interested until I get a chance to talk to her in private."

"You're kidding, right?!" Deon exclaimed in disbelief, their conversation abruptly cut off as the door swung open, revealing Zelana and Kalina, accompanied by their ladies-in-waiting.

Their attentive eyes swept over the visibly strained faces of the two friends, completely unaware of the internal storm that raged within both men.

Zhong quickly masked his discomfort with a practiced smile while Deon inhaled deeply, trying to regain his composure before facing the Princesses.

Zelana sensed something wrong but wanted to maintain an inviting atmosphere. "I haven't yet had the opportunity to introduce you to my friend, Princess Kalina Ashbourne of Snowy Meadows. This is Crown Prince Zhong Yang of Sanshe and his esteemed Ambassador, Deon Vang."

Deon noticed Zhong's eyes and stepped forward, following through with the Crown Prince's request.

"It's a pleasure to meet you, Princess Kalina. I look forward to getting to know you," he said, taking her hand gently in his and pressing his lips to it, gaining a curious glance from Zelana.

Kalina was momentarily taken aback by the gesture, noting the man's handsome, exotic features. "I'm deeply honored," she replied, as Deon released her hand.

Zhong offered a polite bow. "It's my pleasure to be acquainted." His words were meticulously chosen to match his distant gesture.

"Likewise…" she responded politely.

I will not let you have the honor of indulging in my pain, Kalina thought as she glared at him, noticing the Crown Prince's cold greeting.

As the soft hues of the sunset began to paint the sky, a subtle smile graced Zelana's lips, seeking to ease the awkward tension. "Sunsets are breathtaking here. Would you both like to join us for a stroll?" she inquired, her tone light and inviting.

"I was just about to ask you, Princess Zelana. It seems we share the same thoughts," Zhong replied with a hint of enthusiasm, seizing the opportunity to shift the atmosphere to his favor.

Deon was still caught in the remnants of the earlier awkwardness and merely nodded in agreement.

Together, the group embarked on a leisurely walk with Zelana and Kalina leading and their ladies-in-waiting in tow, while the men trailed behind, following with synchronized steps. The serene beauty of the setting sun cast a warm glow over their faces, softening the earlier sharpness of their interactions.

CHAPTER FORTY

SUNSET

ZHONG GLANCED AT Deon and urged him to approach Kalina. Deon squinted his eyes and shook his head slightly to express his reluctance. With a subtle nudge from Zhong, Deon took a step forward toward Kalina, noticing Zelana turn around with a curious stare.

"Princess Kalina," Deon began with a cautious yet courteous demeanor, walking beside her. "How long have you graced Zelonia with your presence?"

"It's been almost a week," Kalina replied softly, a trace of shyness in her tone.

"What's your impression so far?" Deon inquired, smoothly engaging her in light conversation while Zhong stepped over to Zelana's side.

"The Zelonian court has been exceedingly welcoming," she answered, her eyes briefly meeting his, revealing a spark of intrigue.

"Have you had the chance to see the famed Zelonian farming machines? They're quite the behemoths," ventured Deon, getting a feel for what interested her.

Her laughter was light and genuine. "No, I haven't had that pleasure yet," Kalina admitted, her eyes twinkling with amusement, impressed by Deon's lively and charismatic presence.

"Well, they are rather impressive. How about I show you tomorrow? We could even take one for a spin if you're up for it," Deon offered playfully, seeking to establish a rapport.

"That sounds wonderful," she responded enthusiastically.

Zelana felt a strange knot form in her chest as she stayed silent, listening in on their conversation.

"Don't make any plans for the early afternoon. I'll be doing my final rounds and will come by your place since I know where you live now," Deon teased, noting Zelana's surprised expression.

"I'll be waiting, Ambassador Deon," Kalina replied with enthusiasm, touched by his attention.

Zhong nodded to Deon with contentment as he turned to Zelana and teased, "It seems we need to step up our game, Princess Zelana."

"I'm not sure what you mean," Zelana murmured politely with a strained smile.

"Will I have the honor of knowing where your quarters are?" Zhong asked with a twinkle in his eyes.

Zelana glanced at Deon as he watched her helplessly. "You will be surprised to know that Princess Kalina and I are actually neighbors," she disclosed, her voice carrying a note of casual openness.

"That's quite convenient," Zhong commented with a surprised nod, his gaze sweeping the area.

"And where might the men's quarters be?" Deon interjected, as his eyes lingered on Zelana with an unmistakable glint of interest.

"Across the courtyard," she answered, catching the playful mischief in his eyes. "Why do you ask?"

"Just curious," Deon replied with a wink.

His wink sent an unexpected warmth rushing back to her

cheeks, while the corners of his mouth turned up in a flirtatious smile, the smile that had enveloped her mind for days.

Zhong and Kalina observed their sudden, playful interaction, as a stir of envy bloomed at the apparent closeness between Deon and Zelana.

"I know you, Ambassador Deon. It's not mere curiosity," Zelana playfully accused, her tone exuding suspicion as he smiled and began to step away, heightening the mysterious aura around him. "You're not getting away this time," she assured him, slowly following.

"Whatever are you talking about, Princess Zelana?" Deon turned to face her flirtatiously while retreating backwards, reminding her of their moments in the city.

"I know you're keeping something from me," Zelana pressed, a playful smile dancing on her lips as she narrowed the distance between them, enchanted by his charming evasiveness.

With a sly smirk, Deon reveled in the moment, continuing to walk backwards, leading her to pursue him. "I can't..." he began, his voice trailing off in a tease.

"...wait to tell me?" she presumed, playfully finishing his sentence.

Deon's smirk deepened as he gently added, "Tomorrow..."

"Tomorrow?" she echoed with suspicion and anticipation. "What's so special about tomorrow?"

"Patience, Princess..." Deon murmured with a knowing smile, recognizing her attempt to coax the secret out of him a little earlier than planned.

"Always so mysterious..." Zelana smiled as she stared at him, her eyes teasingly curious.

Their gazes remained locked, prompting Zhong and Kalina to start suspecting the nature of their relationship while they continued to observe and trail them. Zhong noted that his friend was more carefree than his normal self in Zelana's presence.

Deon paused by the lake's edge, resting his arms on the railing as his playful demeanor faded into a more contemplative state, allowing himself to get lost in the tranquil waters. He felt his emotions deepening for Zelana, yet his thoughts drifted to Zhong's earlier confession, feeling a twinge of guilt.

"Is he always like this?" asked Zelana, as she gazed at Zhong with a twinkle in her eyes.

"Ambassador Deon is full of secrets," he jested with a chuckle.

Deon turned around, leaning with his back to the railing. "Claims the man who holds more secrets than anyone," he replied with a teasing smirk at his friend.

"I believe Crown Prince Zhong is speaking the truth," Zelana playfully added, her eyes dancing between Deon and the Crown Prince. "Did you know that Ambassador Deon made me think he was a commoner, only to find out he's not only an ambassador but also a Commander?"

"Never would I have thought Ambassador Deon was both charming and a master of disguises," observed Kalina, joining in the playful exchange as Deon's identity added a new layer of intrigue.

"He's also the son of the General of Sanshe, to be exact," continued Zelana, gazing up at Deon with a mischievous smile. "A Lord by birth, Princess Kalina."

"In my defense, you didn't ask," Deon responded with a wink.

Zhong started to notice that every time Deon winked at Zelana, a tint of blush would color her cheeks.

"The Ambassador can be quite sneaky," Zhong remarked, giving his friend his own sarcastic, light-hearted jab.

"Don't start, Zhong..." Deon challenged with a smirk.

Kalina could tell there was a deep-seated friendship between Zhong and Deon, considering how he called out the Crown Prince's name so casually.

Zhong laughed heartily as he faced Zelana, adding a theatrical tone to his voice. "You see how he talks to me?" His mock indignation intensified the already light-hearted atmosphere.

Zelana leaned her arm on the railing and chimed in, "He was just as mischievous the last time around."

"How mischievous?" Zhong inquired in playful interrogation.

"He snatched the last piece of chicken off my stick, and when I did the same to him, he looked at me as if I did something unholy," she recounted, her smile broadening in amusement.

"How dare you, Deon?!" Zhong exclaimed, his tone exaggeratedly shocked, playing along.

"Just you wait, little girl. Next time, I'll grab two pieces," Deon retorted as his infectious laughter spread to Zelana and Zhong, continuing the playful banter.

A jealousy began to simmer within Kalina as she watched the playful exchange between Zelana and the two men, wishing it was her that was getting their attention.

"It's beautiful, isn't it..." Zelana remarked, turning around to admire the sun disappearing over the lake while both men stood on each side, stealing glances of her.

You're beautiful...

They both thought to themselves, their feelings deepening helplessly.

The lakeside, once a quiet haven, had become a lively stage where friendships intensified, rivalries emerged, and complex emotions subtly unveiled themselves.

CHAPTER FORTY-ONE

Provocation

THE ROYAL HALL was a setting of refined elegance, with wine and desserts enticingly served. The ambience was that of a bustling social venue, alive with the gathering of princesses and princes from the realms that had sought refuge in Zelonia. The warm glow of chandeliers and the soft melodies of a string quartet added a refined elegance to the gathering as Zelana and her friends returned from the lake, drawing admiring glances from around the room.

Chue's face lit up on spotting his friends approaching, their steps light and playful. "Where have you guys been hiding?" he called out with genuine curiosity.

Zhong flashed a teasing smirk, "It seems someone has missed us."

"And how has the evening treated you?" asked Deon with a chuckle.

"It has been quite the social affair," Chue responded, his grin widening. "I've had the pleasure of making the acquaintance of several princesses from diverse realms."

"Men…" Kalina sighed, her voice dripping with mock exasperation and amusement, sparking a round of laughter among them.

Chue turned to Kalina, a flicker of recognition in his eyes. "Have we met before?" he asked curiously.

"Perhaps at The Lagoon?" Kalina suggested slyly, eyes glinting with mischief to entrap him.

Chue paused, momentarily caught off guard as he recognized her from the restaurant. "I would certainly remember if I had met someone as unforgettable as you," he remarked thoughtfully, his gaze sweeping over to his friends to gauge their expressions.

"Princess Kalina Ashbourne of Snowy Meadows," she introduced herself as he nodded in greeting.

"Chue Lor, I'm..."

"Not a Prince but an esteemed Advisor-in-Chief of Sanshe," repeated Jenessa and Anika, walking over.

The princesses' playful statement elicited more laughter as they joined the group with Crown Prince Andreas accompanying them.

"It seems Chue hardly needs an introduction," Deon teased, poking fun at his friend.

"I can't help being the center of attention," remarked Chue proudly, his chest puffing slightly.

Zelana let out a soft giggle as her hand delicately covered her lips, trying to stifle her amusement. Deon couldn't help glancing at her with admiration.

Hearing their jolly voices resonate through the hall, Nikolai turned his attention away from the King and Queen, catching a glimpse of Zelana amidst the lively crowd. Approaching with a drink in hand, he cast a cautious glance at her companions.

"No wonder you weren't in class today, Princess Zelana," the Crown Prince remarked with insinuation.

"I've been occupied with new initiatives we're planning to undertake here in Zelonia with Sanshe," she responded, addressing his implicit question with a poised smile.

"I see," he acknowledged, his gaze scrutinizing the distinguished gentlemen by her side.

"You all look ravishing," Kalina piped in, her eyes sweeping over her friends.

"I know," Andreas responded with a flirtatious raise of his eyebrow.

Jenessa rolled her eyes playfully. "She was referring to me, obviously."

"She meant me," Anika teased, striking a playful pose, trying to catch the men's eyes.

The royal hall buzzed with energy as they introduced themselves and continued to engage in conversation. The vibrant atmosphere was filled with light-hearted teasing, sparking bursts of laughter through the grand hall, forging new friendships.

"If not for their dark schemes, Princess Zelana would be in Frostwald and already engaged to me," Nikolai declared possessively, glancing at her with a smile.

"Interesting," Zhong mused as his voice carried a touch of dark amusement, his eyes drifting from the Crown Prince and settling on Zelana. "The Immortals did me a favor then."

"That's a bit morose, don't you think?" Kalina challenged, her brow arched in surprise.

"All I meant was that my path may not have crossed with Princess Zelana's under different circumstances," Zhong clarified, his gaze softening with undisguised admiration.

"It seems someone is quite taken with our dear Princess," Jenessa chimed in teasingly.

Deon's gaze settled on Zelana, whose eyes were fixed on Nikolai. He caught a fleeting nervousness in her demeanor—a subtle vulnerability he had never observed in her before. Turning his attention to Nikolai, Deon noted the tightness in his expression, a mask of barely restrained anger, clearly visible despite his best efforts to conceal it.

"Aren't we all?" Andreas added with a cheeky grin.

"I am standing right here, mind you," Zelana teased with a playful smile, glancing around at her friends, trying to lighten the mood as laughter echoed around them.

Kalina watched her friend, envious of the attention she was getting from the men.

"Where is Crown Prince Samuel?" inquired Anika curiously.

"I saw him this morning," Zelana responded, noticing her friends' worried expression.

"I overheard King Lucas asking him to investigate the Fire Mines," Deon informed casually.

"I hope it's not a dangerous situation," Anika remarked with a concerned expression crossing her face.

"There's no shortage of charming gentlemen here to keep us entertained," Kalina interjected, her hand grasping Zhong's arm.

"I'm not usually the one that does the entertaining," Zhong remarked with a grin, caught off guard by her bold, flirtatious gesture as he gently disengaged her hand.

"He's more accustomed to being entertained," Deon teased with a smirk.

"Dancers, to be precise," Chue stated with amusement, prompting a ripple of laughter through the group.

"I'm a great dancer," revealed Kalina seductively, placing her hands on her hips, wiggling her body.

"Very impressive," Zhong praised, surprisingly enjoying the movements of her curves.

"Kalina! Kalina! Kalina!" everyone cheered and applauded her.

Zhong turned to Zelana and whispered, "I'd love to see you dance."

"I'm also not an entertainer," she replied playfully with a subtle smile.

Zhong burst into a series of eloquent dance moves, captivating the room with his fluid grace.

"Oh my…" Zelana gasped in astonishment at his dance moves.

Kalina felt a surge of energy as she tried to synchronize her movements with Zhong's seemingly effortless motions. She found it impossible to keep pace and paused to watch in admiration.

"I've never seen a man dance like that," Anika observed with a smile.

"Go Zhong!" Jenessa cheered with enthusiasm.

More applause erupted around the room as Zhong's eyes returned to Zelana, watching her every expression as his dancing ceased.

"How was that for your taste?" he asked with a grin, slightly breathless.

Zelana nodded with a flirtatious smile. "You might have made Azalon's top ten with those moves."

Zhong chuckled as he casually draped an arm around her shoulders.

I wouldn't do that if I were you, thought Zelana. His touch was light but unfamiliar, sending a ripple of discomfort through her. She glanced at Nikolai, seeing his sharp, piercing glare of disapproval.

"Perhaps it's best for you to keep your courtesies more formal with Princess Zelana," Nikolai interjected with a low and stern voice, carrying enough to reach the ears that needed to hear.

Zelana felt Zhong's grip tighten, a defiant assertion against his demand. "Actually, I was hoping to drop the formalities altogether," he challenged, locking eyes with Nikolai's in a silent battle of wills.

The unexpected altercation shocked her friends; they gasped and Zelana instinctively looked at Deon, who was already silently assessing the situation with a stoic expression.

"Do I have to ask twice?" Nikolai inquired, taking a step closer.

Zhong grinned. "Someone's apparently the jealous type."

Please stop, Zelana cried silently, a wave of nausea stirring in her stomach, watching the situation escalate helplessly.

"Take your hands off Princess Zelana before I break them," Nikolai threatened, his stance menacing.

Zelana's mind raced as the vibrant chatter of the hall blurred into background noise and tension coiled around her, tightening like a corset, sending a chill down her spine. Her heart pounded in her chest from an encroaching dread of what might unfold next.

"I implore you to try," Zhong responded calmly, his words laced with provocation.

The escalating tension drew the crowd's attention— along with the royal couple's—as all eyes were on the unfolding scene. In a rapid succession of movements, Nikolai's aggressive lunge toward Zhong disrupted the harmony, causing him to reflexively let go of Zelana to block the punch.

Zelana stumbled backward, her poise faltering under the sudden chaos. In a swift, protective gesture, Deon reached out and wrapped his arms around her waist, pulling her close to him to prevent her fall and shield her from the brewing conflict.

"Princess..." Deon murmured, his voice a low rumble against her ear, filled with genuine concern.

Her mind reeled back from the edge of panic, feeling the sudden warmth and firmness of his body pressing against hers in the hushed silence. Staring up at Deon, her pulse quickened, feeling a cascade of relief wash over her, mingled with a confusing swirl of gratitude and perhaps something deeper.

The men instinctively turned to them, feeling pained to see the unexpected intimacy of their embrace.

"Are you alright, Princess Zelana?" Nikolai inquired, his eyes narrowing in shock.

Deon subtly adjusted their positions, strategically placing himself between her and the Crown Princes as his eyes continued to observe them intently.

Zhong took a step toward Zelana, now partially hidden behind Deon. "My apologies," he said, a hint of regret coloring his voice, his pride slightly wounded.

"Let's get out of here," Nikolai suggested as he moved closer, extending his hand to her.

"Not when you're like this..." Zelana replied as her fingers tightened around Deon's hand.

"I just want to talk," Nikolai said, his gaze tender and imploring as he pleaded to her.

"Princess Zelana clearly doesn't want to go with you," Deon interjected gently, his protective stance unwavering as his hand clasped hers a little more firmly.

"I wasn't speaking to you," he retorted in frustration, trying to reach past Deon's protective barrier.

With a swift and forceful push, Deon repelled him with his hand, sending him stumbling. The unexpected show of strength left the crowd stunned in silence.

"I never said you were," he countered, his voice devoid of emotion.

"How dare you touch me?!" Nikolai shot back, infuriated, as he steadied himself.

"Stay back, Crown Prince Nikolai," Deon warned softly.

"I don't take orders from a mere Ambassador of Sanshe's court!" he replied.

"I didn't expect you to, especially when you can't even honor the Princess's wishes," Deon remarked calmly as the crowd murmured among themselves, impressed by his exhibition of control and maturity in the face of Nikolai's outburst.

What would I have done if you weren't here? the Princess thought, looking up at him in awe.

"Let us not forget our manners," Lucas stepped forward, his authoritative tone immediately restoring order. "Ambassador Deon is an esteemed guest in our Kingdom, as are you, Crown Prince Nikolai."

Nikolai clenched his fist and reluctantly withdrew from the room in shame.

"I'm sorry, Princess," Zhong apologized once more, turning to Zelana with a genuine look of remorse.

"I need a moment," Zelana excused herself and slipped her hand from Deon's while stepping away with Natalie accompanying her.

Seeing the King and Queen approach Deon, Kalina seized the opportunity and grabbed Zhong's arm, leading him away. Chue discreetly followed them, sensing potential conflict.

CHAPTER FORTY-TWO

INTERROGATION

"THANK YOU FOR protecting my daughter. You handled the situation with both cordiality and sternness," the Queen complimented, her gaze sharp yet appreciative.

"It was a regrettable incident, but I would not hesitate to act again, if necessary," Deon replied earnestly, taking a step toward the royal couple with a respectful nod. "And I must add, the hall truly comes alive under your gracious hosting, Your Majesties."

"We strive to make these events memorable for all our distinguished guests," Lucas responded with a broad smile, his eyes twinkling with pride.

"Especially one I've been hearing so much about," Sophia added warmly.

Deon was momentarily taken aback by her words. "It is an honor to be in your presence again, Your Majesty. My mother has always spoken highly of your grace and wisdom, sharing how you championed literacy for women, regardless of their status," he responded with a blend of admiration and formality. "I often wondered from where Princess Zelana inherited her stubbornness and charisma, but now I see where she inherited her beauty, elegance, and intelligence."

Deon's light-hearted jest drew laughter from both royals, easing the tension.

"You are quite eloquent with words, Ambassador Deon. I can see how you've managed to rise to such esteemed positions at your age," Sophia complimented, continuing to observe him closely.

"I deeply relish your praise, Your Majesty," Deon responded with deep appreciation.

"From my recollection, you were just a boy when Lady Sonia and General Yengxue joined us for brunch with King MuaYeng and Queen Kashia years ago. You and Samuel were quite the pair," she added with sweet reminiscence.

"Fond memories indeed," Deon agreed, cherishing those times.

"Have you considered my proposal regarding the Princess's mentorship, Ambassador Deon?" Lucas's inquiry cut through the pleasant chatter, shifting the atmosphere to a more serious tone.

Deon paused. "I've given it some thought," he replied, unsure how to approach the topic.

Sensing that he may still be uncertain, Lucas leaned forward. "I can offer you gold, a house with land and servants—equal to the lavish style you had in Sanshe," the King assured him, negotiating his hand.

Deon acknowledged the proposal with a stoic nod. "Your offer is quite generous, Your Majesty," he said, maintaining a calm exterior, although his thoughts raced.

Lucas studied him intently, trying to gauge his decision. "I heard you're inclined to turn down the position. What else must I offer to persuade you to stay in Zelonia?"

There was a moment of silence before Deon finally spoke, his expression softening. "Actually..." he began, hesitating slightly, "I would be deeply honored to accept the position."

The royal couple exchanged surprised glances, clearly taken aback by his unexpected shift.

"Splendid," the King declared, a broad smile overtaking his

features. "When will we have the pleasure of welcoming you to Zelonia?"

Deon chuckled softly. "I've already resigned from my responsibilities prior to coming here."

"You continue to amaze me, Ambassador Deon," Lucas complimented, astonished by his decisiveness.

"I hope to make a meaningful impact in Zelonia, particularly in Princess Zelana's training," he replied with a nod.

"I understand you were not only an ambassador but also a commander in Sanshe, both highly regarded positions," remarked Sophia, trying to delve deeper into Deon's mind. "What drove you to leave those roles and be Zelana's mentor, if I may ask?"

Deon's expression softened as he contemplated his answer. "My roles were significant indeed, and they remain within reach should I ever choose to return to Sanshe. However, time is of the essence when it comes to mentoring Princess Zelana. Since meeting her, I've recognized her immense potential," he replied, pausing to carefully select his next words. "She is at a pivotal age where intensive, focused training is necessary to hone her combat and tactical abilities, particularly to face the threats from the Krimzon Kingdom."

The Queen exchanged a knowing glance with the King, both clearly impressed by Deon's insight.

"Forgive my arrogance," the Queen began, "but an issue constantly weighs on my mind." She paused, ensuring she had his undivided attention. "Princess Zelana's lineage has drawn many admirers from across Azalon, given our descent from a Goddess. While I have full confidence in your abilities, I worry that personal feelings might impede the rigorous training she requires."

Does she suspect I have feelings for Zelana? Deon wondered, caught off guard by her loaded question.

He paused momentarily, formulating a reply that would convey his sincerity. "I assure you, Your Majesty, that no emotions will interfere with the nuanced training essential for the Princess to realize her full potential," he spoke with thoughtfulness and humility. "I intend to push her beyond her limits so she can protect herself and defend Zelonia when necessity demands it."

The Queen studied him for a moment longer, measuring the depth of his words. "I am eager to see the progress you and Zelana will achieve together, Ambassador Deon," she replied with a hesitant nod.

Deon offered a modest smile. "Thank you for your trust, Your Majesty."

"I still can't grasp how the Sanshe King allowed you to leave," Lucas interjected, clearly impressed by Deon's articulation and persuasiveness.

Deon's expression softened, a warmth filling his eyes. "King MuaYeng has always been like a father to me. And like any father, he supports his son's ambitions," he said with a hint of fondness in his voice.

"Take notes, Father," Zelana teased as she returned to their side, catching the end of the conversation.

"I sometimes wonder why she wasn't born a Prince," the King chuckled, his laughter filling the air.

"We've kept you long enough, Ambassador Deon," the Queen added with a gracious smile.

"Not at all, Your Majesties. I truly enjoyed the enriching conversation," Deon replied, bowing respectfully.

"Enjoy the rest of the evening," Lucas encouraged, still grinning.

Deon felt a warmth spread through his chest as the royal couple departed, leaving them alone.

CHAPTER FORTY-THREE

I Want to Know You

DEON TURNED AND faced the Princess, shifting his undivided attention to her.

"So, what did you talk about?" Zelana asked, looking up at him with a playful glint in her eyes.

"You, you and you…" he teased with a smirk.

Zelana laughed softly, tilting her head up to him. "I should have guessed."

"Shall we grab some drinks?" Deon asked, extending the invitation with a grin.

"I might need three after all the excitement," she joked, her steps naturally aligning with his as they made their way to the bar.

Settling down under the soft lighting of the bar area, Deon's gaze deepened as he studied her.

Zelana's eyes gleamed with amusement. "I noticed you're not limping anymore."

Deon eyed her with a wider grin. "Your miracle candies worked like a charm."

"They're hardly candies, but I'm glad they helped eased some of the pain," she replied, still concerned.

"Thank you for your care," he said softly, feeling a warmth fill his heart.

"I can give you more before you return to Sanshe," she offered generously.

Deon hesitated, conflict flickering in his eyes. *Should I tell her now?*

After a moment of contemplation, he decided against it, choosing instead to stick to his original plan.

"What can I get for you?" the server inquired with a warm smile.

"A Summer Scent, please," Zelana chose casually.

"Make that two," Deon ordered with a charming smile.

"You do realize it's a rather sweet drink, right?" she teased, laughing lightly.

"I want to know what you like," Deon murmured, his voice softening, almost intimate, as he leaned closer, speaking words only meant for her. "I want to know everything about you, Princess."

Zelana's breath caught slightly, her pulse quickening at his closeness and the warmth of his words.

"Why the sudden interest in me, Ambassador?" she whispered with a tease, feeling a nervous tinge.

Deon leaned back in his chair. "I want to know you, not just the Princess everyone sees," he murmured gently. "The things you're passionate about, what keeps you up at night… and everything in between."

Zelana's heart raced at his words—and the intensity in his eyes—she knew he was sincere.

"It's time you got to know me better as well," he suggested, his smile turning tender.

"Aren't you only here for a short time?" she pondered, a veil of sadness enveloping her.

Deon paused while the server returned with their drinks. "Thank you, sir."

"My pleasure," the server replied before stepping away.

"We'll have to be more mindful of our time then, won't we?" Deon responded, handing Zelana her drink.

Their fingers brushed lightly—a fleeting touch that sparked a surge of warmth through them. Their eyes met, a sense of wonder shimmering in their gazes—feeling the undeniable pull of a heart wrenching fate—a bittersweet love that would torment them, while leaving them breathless.

"To new beginnings..." Deon raised his glass, toasting excitedly, unaware of his role in her destiny.

"New beginnings..." she echoed, her heart dancing in her chest, clueless to the heartaches awaiting her.

As their glasses clinked softly and they sipped their drinks, Deon's gaze lingered on her. The soft glow of the bar lights accentuated her beauty, casting a warm aura around her, making it impossible for him to focus on anything but her. The questions that had plagued him all evening since Zhong's confession now seemed insignificant, as the ache in his heart began to subside.

"It seems someone is quite captivated by you," he teased, breaking the intimate silence, as his smile softened, watching her closely for a reaction while sipping his drink.

Who are you referring to? Zelana wanted to ask, her eyes sparkling curiously.

Who are you thinking about? Deon pondered silently, watching her eyes light up.

Deon's smile slowly faded. "So, where do you see Crown Prince Nikolai in five years?" he asked, forcing her to think critically.

The glimmer in her eyes dimmed, disappointed that he was speaking of Nikolai. "I suppose he'd still be in Zelonia, married with children," she answered after some thought, taking a sip from her drink.

"And where do you see yourself?" he pressed, making her glance into her future.

Zelana paused thoughtfully. "I'm destined to be a Queen, ruling a nation and conquering Krimzon," she replied with quiet determination. "The reason for my existence as a demi-goddess."

Deon nodded slowly. "I can tell you're passionate about returning Azalon to a place where we could finally live in peace," he said, gazing at her intently.

"I feel it in every beat of my heart," she murmured with fire in her eyes.

"How does Crown Prince Nikolai fit into that future?" he continued to press her. "Can you see him ruling a kingdom? Are you beside him, sharing a life? Are you both fighting Krimzon?"

Her brow furrowed slightly as she silently answered the questions, and a realization washed over her.

Nikolai isn't part of my future. The insight struck her like a divine revelation.

"You have brought me clarity with just a few simple questions," she admitted, astonished by the ease with which he had unraveled her thoughts.

"I had a feeling you've been conflicted for some time," he remarked gently, holding onto her gaze.

"You continue to amaze me," she uttered softly, her admiration for him deepening.

Deon's expression softened. "You should never settle… always aim to rise to the top. When you get there, those with the same drive and ambition will be standing beside you. Only then can you realize your destiny of destroying Krimzon."

Zelana gazed into Deon's eyes, feeling a connection unlike any she had ever known, a closeness that went beyond words.

"I hope you're standing beside me," she whispered, wanting him to know how much he meant to her.

A warmth filled his heart. "If that's truly your wish, Princess, I will be there."

There was a sincerity in his words that wrapped around her heart, soothing the doubts and fears that had kept her guarded. Her lips curled into a soft smile, parting as if to speak, but no words came.

So… you do see me…

A gentle flutter rose in her chest. Despite his feelings for another Princess, she had also become someone he cared about.

I don't know what life is going to throw at us, if it would change everything between us, but for now, I'll be anyone you want me to be, go anywhere you want me to go, Princess. Deon's eyes remained on her, his heart aching. *I'm going to cherish every moment and hold onto you as long as I can.*

Zelana lowered her eyes, her fingers gently tracing the rim of her glass. "What would I have done if you weren't here today?"

Deon sighed, realizing she was referring to the earlier altercation. "Crown Prince Zhong shouldn't have let go of you like that."

"It seems a bit silly now, but when they were fighting and I was unsure of what would happen, I glanced at you, and somehow… I felt comforted," she confessed softly. "I knew you'd protect me."

"I don't find that silly at all," he responded, his chest tightening.

Zelana lifted her gaze, her eyes meeting his with unguarded emotion. "And when I was stumbling backwards, I felt this strange calm… knowing you wouldn't let me fall."

Deon's breath caught, his heart melting in that moment. "How did you come to trust me like this?"

"I just… do…" she whispered, not understanding it herself.

For a few heartbeats, they sat in silence, the world around them fading away—with every shared glance and every quiet breath, they surrendered further to the intensity of their unspoken emotions. The heaviness they felt in their hearts—unacknowledged yet undeniable—pulled them closer with each passing moment, intensifying the feelings they knew they would not be able to hold back much longer.

The air between them seemed to shimmer with unspoken words, only to be pierced by sharp, familiar voices from across the room. Zelana's eyes flickered past Deon, her expression dimming. The delicate, intimate moment they had been immersed in faded, shattered by the tension around them.

"What is it?" he asked softly, watching a shadow of concern briefly cross her otherwise radiant face.

"Princess Kalina and Crown Prince Zhong seem to be having a heated conversation," Zelana murmured, her eyes narrowing slightly in speculation. "I think there's some history there."

He followed her gaze, his mood sobering as he caught sight of them locked in an intense, emotional exchange. Chue was nearby, casually leaning against a column, his sharp eyes monitoring every nuance of their interaction closely.

Deon took a slow sip of his drink. "Sometimes you have to trust your instincts," he replied, his voice calm yet guarded, choosing his words carefully so as to not confirm or deny her suspicions.

He was torn between betraying his friend's trust and concealing the truth from the woman he cared for so deeply, knowing the conflict would now be ongoing as he remained a man of Sanshe and Zelonia.

CHAPTER FORTY-FOUR

Hidden Talents

IN THE DIMLY lit corner of the royal hall, Zhong's expression was of turmoil, the flicker of the flames from the torchlights reflecting in his troubled gaze.

"I find myself at a loss," the Crown Prince admitted in distress.

Kalina looked up at him, her eyes brimming with unshed tears, concern etched into every line of her face. "It feels as though last night meant nothing to you," she murmured, her voice trembling.

"Of course it did, but what do you expect of me?" Zhong sighed heavily, the shadows playing across his features, deepening his furrowed brow.

Her hand reached out, touching his arm lightly. "I hold great affection for you," she whispered.

Her confession weaved a tumult of mixed emotions inside him as Zhong froze.

Those moments were never about affection, he wanted to say but wavered.

"Honor me with a courtship, Crown Prince Zhong," she pressed, gazing up at him in desperation.

Zhong's heart raced as panic set in. "Can we, perhaps, discuss this later?" he pleaded, visibly unsettled as his eyes darted anxiously, fearful of being overheard.

"When?" she implored, seeking a promise.

"Fuck..." he muttered under his breath as he spotted Deon and Zelana making their way toward them. Trapped, he tried to edge away, but Kalina's grip on his arm tightened.

"I'll visit your chambers tonight," he promised hastily.

Zhong's features hardened as he gently, yet firmly, loosened her hand, extricating himself from her hold, and stepped away.

"Is everything alright?" Zelana inquired, her keen senses noticing the suffocating tension.

"Everything's fine," Zhong managed to reply with a forced casualness.

Kalina tried to maintain a veneer of courtly grace, yet her mind remained a whirlwind of emotions.

Deon glanced at Zhong and then turned to Zelana, noticing a calm in her demeanor.

Zelana knows something's amiss, Zhong.

The tension became unbearable as Deon strode confidently to the grand piano and sat down.

"What's a social gathering without some music?" Deon said, his voice booming across the room.

With effortless grace, his fingers glided over the ivory keys. A lively melody sprang forth, vibrant and captivating, echoing through the elegant room, weaving a spell of exhilaration.

As the music swelled, Zelana and the other Royals formed a circle around him, admiring his talent. Shifting into a slower, more romantic tune, Deon's voice blended with the notes with a teasing glint in his eyes, capturing their hearts with his song.

Amidst the magical ambience, Zhong and Kalina joined the assembly with Chue trailing behind. Kalina's mood darkened, noticing Zhong's gaze lingering on Zelana, who was visibly moved by Deon's heartfelt performance.

As the last note danced in the air, the room erupted in applause and cheers. Deon rose gracefully from the piano bench and offered a modest bow. His gaze found Zelana's eyes gracing him with a look of quiet intrigue and admiration.

I wrote this when I was missing you, he confessed silently.

"That was quite the spectacle," Anika purred, drawing closer to capture Deon's attention with her presence. "Your command of the piano is truly captivating."

"And your voice complimented your playing perfectly," Jenessa added with awe.

"Thank you," he responded with a charming grin. "I'm pleased you both enjoyed the performance."

Kalina glanced at Zhong, who still had his eyes on Zelana, and felt vengeful. "Your fingers seemed to flirt with every note, Ambassador Deon. It makes one curious what other things they can do..." she added with a tease, her insinuation sparking a hint of playfulness among her friends.

Deon chuckled lightly, about to answer, but Andreas chimed in with a mischievous grin. "Perhaps a visit to the men's quarters would reveal a few other talents, Princess Kalina."

"Words of the wise," Zhong teased, coaxing more chuckles from the group.

Deon noticed a blush creeping onto Kalina's cheeks as she glanced at him, clearly smitten.

Kalina seems to be interested in both Deon and Zhong, Zelana observed, feeling a twinge of unease amidst their flirtatious exchanges.

Deon turned to Zelana and noticed her silence—a stark contrast to the lively Princess he had grown accustomed to. He leaned close and whispered, "Did my performance leave you speechless?"

"I'm deeply impressed. You really are good at everything you do," Zelana murmured, her eyes meeting his. "For a moment, it felt as if you let me have a glimpse inside your heart."

"And what did you see?" Deon asked, watching her intently.

"A man in love..." Zelana spoke softly, feeling a sudden pang of envy.

"Perhaps..." he affirmed as his eyes softened with an unspoken confession.

"Who has inspired such heartfelt music, Ambassador Deon?" Kalina asked as she leaned in closer, interrupting their private conversation.

"I'm infatuated with the concept of love," Deon clarified, maintaining his façade.

"Didn't you recently compose that piece? Was it for a certain Princess you rescued from Esperia?" Zhong cut in with a mischievous smile.

Deon chuckled lightly. "Don't get me started with Princess Lenora."

"His new favorite person in Sanshe," Zhong teased with a smirk.

Deon shook his head with a small smile, letting out a sigh of frustration.

"I know the feeling," Jenessa joked, eyeing Andreas.

"What did I ever do to you?" Andreas asked as laughter erupted from the friends once more.

Light-hearted banter continued to echo through the room, but a restlessness brewed beneath the surface as uneasy feelings quietly simmered among the friends.

"Would you care to join me for a walk, Princess Zelana?" Zhong asked with a gentle insistence that drew the attention of those around them.

"I would love to," Zelana responded, following the Crown Prince, stepping away from her friends.

"Sharing my first day in Zelonia with you couldn't have been any more perfect," he confessed with a warm smile, gazing intently into her eyes, leaving her lost for words.

From a distance, Kalina observed them as jealousy slowly consumed her, watching Zhong shower Zelana with sweet affection. The memory of their intimate encounter was starting to lose its significance, leaving her feeling abandoned. She was yearning to feel his closeness.

Since Swan Lake, you haven't sought my company, she thought sadly. *I hope you keep your word and come to me tonight.*

Zhong continued to make Zelana giggle softly as Deon observed them from beside the Royals, the scene stirring an unfamiliar anxiety in him. The sight of Zelana lighting up under his friend's attentive gaze sparked a tumult of emotions within him.

When did you two get so close? He murmured to himself, attempting to keep his feelings concealed, yet that familiar tightness in his chest returned.

The atmosphere in the hall subtly shifted with Dominic's approach and request. "Sorry for the interruption, but the King would like a word with you, Crown Prince Zhong."

"A moment, please," Zhong acknowledged Dominic,

then returned his attention to Zelana. "Remember your promise earlier?"

"Tomorrow, I'm yours," Zelana flirted, her lips curving into a gentle smile.

"What about the day after?" Zhong teased as he chuckled lightly at her choice of words.

"One day at a time, Crown Prince Zhong," Zelana replied playfully with a soft giggle.

"I will come to your chambers at noon, Princess Zelana," the Crown Prince affirmed, grinning, his heart feeling lighter with the promise of tomorrow.

"Perfect," the Princess agreed with a subtle anticipation.

"Good night," Zhong said before turning to follow Dominic out of the royal hall.

Zelana watched him leave, a soft sigh escaping her lips. She turned back to her friends as her gaze found Deon's, watching her. Her heart ached helplessly, the unspoken emotions between them stirring restlessly, pulling at her in ways she couldn't fully understand.

Kalina approached Deon, noticing that he was distracted. "Ambassador Deon, we're still on for the tour of the giant machines, I presume?"

"Yes, of course," Deon affirmed, momentarily startled, yet quickly masking his emotions as he faced her. "I'll meet you around three in the afternoon?"

"Noon would work better for me," Kalina replied with a sweet smile. "Besides, it'll give us more time to get to know each other."

"Noon it is then, Princess Kalina," Deon honored her request politely.

"Would you mind walking me to my room? It's late and I'm not quite comfortable going alone," she murmured as Deon glanced at her lady-in-waiting standing next to her.

"Of course, Princess," he hesitantly agreed as they started toward the doors of the royal hall.

Zelana watched their retreating figures, feeling her chest tighten. Her hand instinctively rose to rest against her heart, trying to calm the ache that deepened with every step Deon took further from her.

Stop longing for him, she whispered to herself helplessly. Yet, the silent plea did little to ease the heartache determined to cling to her.

CHAPTER FORTY-FIVE

SISTERS

THE DIMLY LIT corridor felt long as Zelana followed it to her room with Natalie beside her. Her steps halted abruptly at the sight of Kalina and Deon on the balcony, in quiet conversation.

"Come inside, I have some wine," Kalina coaxed, gazing up at Deon with a tender smile.

"Thank you, but I really should retire. I have an early morning and an afternoon I need to plan for us with the behemoths," he replied with a small smile.

Kalina giggled softly, feeling an unexpected warmth exuding from him. "I look forward to spending more time with you tomorrow, Ambassador Deon," she murmured with a sparkle in her eyes.

"The feeling is mutual," he responded politely. "Have a good night, Princess."

As Deon turned to leave, he unexpectedly found himself face-to-face with Zelana. He halted in his steps, his gaze lingering on her as his heart ached.

What is going through your mind right now? He wondered as he tried to discern her thoughts.

Are you interested in Princess Kalina? She asked quietly, unable to utter the words aloud.

"Good night, Princess Zelana," he finally said with a nod.

"Sleep well, Ambassador," Zelana returned, feeling a strange awkwardness between them.

Deon continued walking and Zelana's gaze inadvertently caught Kalina's, watching her with a pensive expression. Kalina then offered a practiced smile as the complex web of emotions deepened, entangling the two of them with unspoken sentiments and brewing tensions.

"Ambassador Deon would be my ideal if he were a Crown Prince," Kalina sighed wistfully.

"Have your feelings for Crown Prince Zhong waned?" Zelana asked, surprised by her words.

"I talked to him as you suggested, but he's changed," she confided, lowering her gaze. "It seems he wishes to deny our encounter at The Lagoon."

"I'm truly sorry, Kalina," she expressed sincerely.

"Thank you for your care," Kalina murmured softly as she opened the door to her room.

"I've adopted Anika and Jenessa as sisters. I hope to be yours too," Zelana offered, hoping to establish a closer rapport with her.

"Sisters... I'd like that," Kalina smiled, leaning on her door.

"Get some rest. You look like you're ready to grab a pillow and forget the world," Zelana said with a small smile.

"The drama with Zhong tires me," she admitted with a sigh. "Good night."

"Sweet dreams," Zelana murmured as she watched Kalina disappear into her room.

CHAPTER FORTY-SIX

CLARITY

JUST AS THE door closed behind Kalina, it revealed an unexpected figure, making Zelana halt in her steps.

"Nikolai..." she murmured, surprised to see him.

His posture was rigid, his expression barely concealing his anger. Frustration could be seen in his eyes as they stared at each other in a silent standoff, his gaze burning with unresolved emotions.

Zelana held her breath, preparing herself for whatever words he had to say.

"Which Sanshe scum has captured your attention?" Nikolai asked darkly, his voice laced with venom.

"They're strictly here for diplomatic talks," Zelana replied calmly.

"I see the way you look at them. It reminds me too much of how you once looked at me," he remarked, his voice breaking slightly as he stepped closer, the distance between them quickly diminishing.

Zelana maintained her composure despite the emotional storm brewing before her. "There was never anything between us, Crown Prince Nikolai," she murmured, noticing his eyes brimming with a desperation that pierced the quiet of the night.

"Can't you see how much I love you, Princess Zelana?" the Crown Prince confessed, overcome with hurt and jealousy, laying his heart bare as he pushed her to the wall, pinning her against the cool stone.

"What are you doing?" the Princess asked, shocked, looking up at him nervously.

Nikolai gazed into Zelana's eyes with an intensity that spoke volumes of his yearning, his heart throbbing with a desire that left little room for hesitation. He leaned in slowly as her eyes widened, staring at his lips, poised to claim hers, his need for her affection overpowering any sense of restraint.

But just as he neared, Zelana swiftly turned her head, his kiss landing softly on her cheek. Nikolai froze; the sting of rejection pierced through his chest like a dagger. For a heartbeat, he stayed like that, his breath hot against her skin.

The air thickened with a suffocating silence, both unsure what to say or do next, as if the moment itself was holding its breath, awaiting their next words. Nikolai pulled back abruptly, his eyes darkening, hurt as he stared at her in disbelief.

"Why?" he whispered hoarsely, his voice trembling with a raw vulnerability he rarely displayed. His hands still pinned her against the cold stone, but the force in his grip weakened.

Zelana's heart pounded nervously as she turned, her eyes meeting his gaze. "I'm sorry..." she said, her voice a whisper against the cool breeze of the moonlit night. "I can't get there..."

His eyes, wild with frustration, bore into hers. "You're mistaken. How can you not get there when every part of me is screaming for you?" His words were laced with confusion and a deep craving that continued to consume him.

Tears gathered in her eyes, shimmering like dewdrops under the moon's glow, as she lowered her gaze, her pulse quickening in response to the overwhelming intensity of the moment.

"Forgive me," she said, the pain in her voice echoing deeply in his heart.

His hand tenderly reached for her chin, guiding her gaze back to his. "Tell me to wait. Tell me you're not ready. Anything... but that you don't want me," he insisted gently, his voice raw with emotion.

Tears escaped her eyes seeing the depth of his longing and the sincerity of his emotions—emotions she couldn't reciprocate. "This past week has clarified many things for me, and one of them is that I could never be with you."

"I don't understand," he uttered, his voice cracking, his tone hovering between anger and despair as his face contorted with pain. "Every part of me aches for you," he confessed, his tone shaky and desperate.

"You deserve to be loved," she murmured as a thick silence followed. "But that person isn't me."

Nikolai's breath hitched at her words, his hands dropping to his sides, a reality he hadn't been prepared to accept. His lips parted as if to speak, but nothing came. He took a step back, his expression a mask of devastation, knowing that when the Princess of Zelonia made up her mind, there was nothing he could say or do to change it.

Zelana's heart ached at the sight of him—this man who had laid his emotions bare countless times, only to be met with rejection over and over again. She wanted to offer comfort, but knew that her words, no matter how kind, would only deepen the wound.

"I don't understand... I don't think I ever will," he muttered, breathing heavily, his chest heaving with emotions he could no longer contain.

Nikolai felt broken as his gaze lingered on Zelana, hurt and confused. He turned abruptly, storming away. The sound of his hurried footsteps gradually faded into the distance.

Zelana stood still, leaning against the cold stone wall, feeling utterly helpless.

CHAPTER FORTY-SEVEN

COMPROMISE

KALINA SAT ALONE at her vanity, her reflection cast back at her in the mirror, waiting for a man who might not come. The room was aglow with the gentle flicker of candlelight, creating shadows that danced across the walls, echoing her growing uncertainty.

She drew a deep breath, trying to quell the storm of emotions churning inside her as she replayed the events of the evening. Zhong had drawn Zelana close, defying Nikolai's warnings, danced for her when Deon clearly stated he doesn't entertain, and his gaze clung to her throughout the night. Each memory was a sharp sting, a bitter realization that he had become evasive because of Zelana.

I must win his heart completely, she vowed silently, staring at herself in the mirror.

A soft knock interrupted Kalina's contemplation, sending a wave of anticipation through her. She rose to her feet, smoothing her nightgown before approaching the door. Upon opening it, she saw Zhong standing in the corridor, his presence as striking and commanding as ever, while his eyes roamed her body with an unmistakable glint of admiration.

"Perhaps you should come inside before someone sees you," urged the Princess, noticing his hesitation.

Zhong glanced briefly down the corridor before stepping inside and closing the door behind him, leaning back against it awkwardly. His eyes lingered on her, taking her in, while his breath slowed.

"I feared you wouldn't come," she confessed, her voice low and alluring as she stepped closer to him, tilting her head back to meet his gaze, her eyes sparkling with seduction and desire.

"I'm a man of my word," he replied as his gaze continued to linger on the gentle curves visible beneath her sheer nightgown as her blonde hair cascaded over her shoulders.

"Do you truly want to forsake me for Princess Zelana?" she challenged, her eyes piercing into his, loaded with emotion and bold intent. She took his hand and gently placed it over her bosom.

Zhong's throat tightened, feeling her soft suppleness under his touch as his body started to betray him.

"You see, I am every bit the woman she is," she whispered seductively, the candlelight playing across her features, enhancing her allure. The air between them thickened with tension and desire.

"I have no idea what you're talking about," he managed to say, pulling his hand back and lowering it in an attempt to maintain a veneer of indifference.

"You're not the first man to be enchanted by Princess Zelana," she murmured, undeterred in continuing her relentless pursuit of him. "Royal carriages have come and gone. Many have tried to win her heart. They've all been rejected by her. You will be no different, Crown Prince Zhong."

"I'm not here to discuss her," he asserted firmly, feeling frustrated, caught between his feelings and her probing. "I came to apologize for my conduct the other night. Had I known that you were a Princess, I would have behaved differently."

His words, while apologetic, were an admission of the undeniable attraction that had sparked between them, an attraction that now lay bare. Kalina's gaze softened slightly; her strategy was clear—to unsettle him, to make him reconsider, to claim a place in his heart that might rival Zelana's.

Kalina stepped closer, her intense gaze slicing through Zhong's composed exterior. "Yet, I can see your desire for me, a fire smoldering within you," she whispered, her voice a seductive caress as her fingers slowly traced the seams of his suit jacket with deliberate tenderness. "If night patrol hadn't interrupted us at Swan Lake, you would have claimed my chastity."

"I would not have taken it that far," he countered in denial, his voice strained with an effort to maintain control, yet his eyes wandered, drawn irresistibly to the allure of her form beneath the sheer fabric of her gown. "Let's maintain discretion about that night for the sake of your honor. If it's compensation you seek, I can arrange for gold, jewels—whatever you desire."

Kalina's expression hardened, her eyes narrowing slightly as she absorbed his words. "I don't want stones dug from the earth, Crown Prince Zhong," she responded, her voice tinged with a concoction of hurt and defiance. "All I desire is you."

She began to unbutton his shirt, seducing him to her will, yet halting as he grabbed her hands.

"I'm engaged to Princess Sierra in Sanshe," he confessed, marking a boundary he couldn't cross.

Kalina's expression shifted, confusion and hurt flashing across her features. "Why did you come to Swan Lake then?" she asked, her voice trembling slightly. "Why are you pursuing Princess Zelana?"

"I'm sorry. I was drawn to the two of you," Zhong admitted, the apology tasting bitter on his tongue.

A knot tightened in her chest as their memories of Swan Lake flooded back—his charming smile, the way he had touched her, the moment he stole her first kiss, taking her breath away.

"Your fiancée must have been arranged since you were willing to risk the relationship to meet me," she implored softly. "Forget Princess Zelana..." she said, pulling his head down to her in a desperate kiss.

"Don't," he urged with a firm resolve as he resisted and pulled away. "I don't want to further disrespect you, Princess Kalina. Can't we just move forward and forget that night ever happened?"

"I will tell Princess Zelana everything," she said, her voice breaking as tears started to form. "She'll never see you in the same light again."

Zhong quickly turned the tables on her. "Revealing those moments will damage your reputation."

"It may indeed tarnish me, but it will destroy you," she replied in desperation and anger. "After I disclose our encounters to the Royal Council, the newly forged negotiations Sanshe established with Zelonia will burn to ashes."

Her threat hung in the air, a sharp reminder of the fragile line Zhong had walked—one that could now unravel the hard-earned trust Deon had established with Zelonia.

"What must I do for you to let this go?" he finally conceded.

Kalina placed her hand on his chest, her fingers returning to unbuttoning his shirt. He stood rigidly, leaning against the door, a statue of resistance. His shirt came undone as she stared at his bare, sculpted body with lust. Her hand traced a slow, tantalizing path up and down his torso, eliciting a soft, involuntary groan from him.

She pressed her lips urgently to his, drawing him into the depth of her longing. Her relentless tenderness slowly melted his resistance, and Zhong found himself succumbing to her, returning her kisses with a growing passion. Overwhelmed by lust, he flipped her onto the door, his body flushed against hers. Their kisses intensified, driven by both desire and desperation.

"Touch me," she whispered, her breath warm against his skin.

His hands immediately glided beneath the sheer fabric of her nightgown, gently caressing her soft suppleness, drawing gasps from her lips. His touch grew more daring, sliding down her body and between her legs. In seconds, he left her trembling.

Kalina pulled her lips away, leaning against the door as he continued to evoke sensations that overwhelmed her breathlessly.

"Oh my gosh!" she exclaimed, lost in the moments of her ecstasy.

Zhong found himself panting, struggling to restrain himself as he gazed into her eyes and gently disentangled himself from her embrace.

"Don't ever speak of this again," he managed to say, his voice strained as he methodically began to button his shirt, each motion a battle to maintain his composure.

Kalina glared at Zhong as he guided her gently away from the door and exited swiftly. The door slammed shut behind him with a resounding finality that reverberated through the room.

"It's not over…" Kalina murmured as she staggered to her bed, collapsing into its softness.

The pleasure she felt in Zhong's arms vanished as quickly as he left. Kalina lay, tangled in bedsheets, realizing for the first time the intense pleasure that existed and the profound depth of pain that followed. The absence of his warmth made her feel lonelier, a dark reminder of the price of her desire.

CHAPTER FORTY-EIGHT

Chat of Men

CHUE AND DEON were deep in conversation about the initiative within the quiet confines of the men's lounge, wine glasses in hand. Zhong walked in, his stride purposeful as his expression was fraught with perplexity. He quickly settled down beside them and wasted no time in pouring himself a drink.

Deon took a sip of his wine. "I assume you ended it."

"I did, but I think I've further complicated things," Zhong admitted, already regretting his actions as he downed his glass in one go before refilling it.

"What happened?" Chue asked, curiously.

"Why is it that every time I'm honest about my feelings, or the lack thereof toward a woman, it ends with her making threats?" pondered Zhong aloud, taking another sip from his drink.

"You're poised to be the next King of Sanshe," Deon replied, his tone exuding irritation. "Aren't threats part of the territory by now?"

Zhong let out a big sigh. "Not the kind where a noose is tightened around my neck, threatening to dangle me as a spectacle for all to scorn."

"You're being overly dramatic, Zhong," Deon remarked with a dismissive smirk.

"Dramatic, really?" Zhong retorted in frustration. "I've tried everything. I asked Princess Kalina to forgive me for my conduct. I even offered her compensation, yet she tells me I'm what she desires. I confessed that I cannot return her affections because I'm already engaged to another, yet she kissed me. I then pleaded with her to keep our encounters a secret, to protect her dignity..."

"She still professes her desire for you," Chue cut in, completing his thought.

"Exactly, and she seduced me further," Zhong shared as he gulped down his drink.

"As long as you resisted, I'm confident this will blow over in a few days," Deon reassured with a nod.

"But something did happen," Zhong confessed, leaning back in his chair in defeat.

"Zhong... she's a princess," Deon chastised him sharply, rubbing his temple in exasperation.

"Who threatened to expose everything, discrediting me to ruin the diplomatic relations between Zelonia and Sanshe in front of Princess Zelana and the Zelonian court," he confided, venting his frustrations.

"So, you bedded her?!" Chue exclaimed in utter disbelief as he stood up, pacing the room.

"I didn't sleep with her," Zhong clarified. "I simply improvised and managed to negotiate her silence."

"I sincerely hope she keeps quiet," Chue halted his pacing and faced his friends. "We cannot afford to have your father hear about this."

"She won't say a word. I will make sure of it," Zhong promised, his voice trailing off unconfidently.

"For now… what about next time?" Deon asked, losing his temper.

"I appeased her so there won't be a next time!" Zhong replied, agitated.

"You might want to start considering the consequences of your actions. They're going to destroy everything I've worked so hard to establish with Zelonia," Deon remarked, no longer holding back.

"Try seeing things from my perspective for once," Zhong uttered, making himself the victim.

Deon stood up with a resolute expression. "I'm not meeting Princess Kalina tomorrow. You handle it."

"But you must, Deon. She might do something crazy," Zhong pleaded, also rising to his feet.

"Clean up your own mess. I'm done," Deon declared as he left the men's lounge.

"I'll meet her," Chue offered. "Hopefully I can distract her and provide you some relief."

"You never know, you might end up being the King of Snowy Meadows," Zhong said sarcastically.

Chue simply nodded, sipping his wine in a contemplative silence.

CHAPTER FORTY-NINE

Switch It Up

THE DAY WAS beautiful with the sun high in the sky as Chue strolled through the royal courtyard, savoring the fresh air. His thoughts focused on his upcoming rendezvous with Kalina, devising a plan to distract her. As he advanced, he spotted Zhong walking toward him from the opposite direction.

"Off to see the machines and maybe something more?" the Crown Prince teased with a knowing smirk.

"That's the plan…" Chue responded grimly as they both arrived at the balcony.

"Don't come by the lake," Zhong suggested, brushing past Chue to knock on Zelana's door.

The door swung open promptly, revealing Zelana in a stunning gown that elegantly highlighted her figure, rendering both men momentarily speechless.

"Princess Zelana, you look absolutely stunning," Zhong managed to utter as he offered her his arm.

"You're always so generous with your compliments," she responded with a smile, her hand gracefully settling on his arm.

"Good afternoon, Princess Zelana," Chue acknowledged her with a respectful nod.

"Good day, Chue," she greeted him with a subtle inquiry, expecting to see Deon, recalling him supposedly meeting Kalina that afternoon.

"Shall we?" Zhong insisted as Zelana nodded, and they departed with her lady-in-waiting in tow.

Chue gathered his thoughts as he approached the door beside Zelana's. With a soft knock, it swung open, revealing Kalina dressed casually in knickers and a camisole.

"Princess Kalina..." he muttered, his heart skipping a beat at her revealing outfit.

"Chue?" she mumbled, a hint of surprise in her voice. "What brings you here?"

"Deon got held up at the armory and didn't want you to wait, so he sent me to accompany you," Chue explained, masking the truth.

Kalina nodded awkwardly. "I appreciate you relaying the message. Tell him I'll wait."

She was about to close her door, but Chue stopped it with a gentle hand.

"He won't be able to make it today; he specifically asked me to take you," he clarified, hoping she would take the hint.

Her expression shifted to one of slight irritation. "So... Deon is at the armory?"

Before he could respond, Kalina brushed past him with her lady-in-waiting quickly following.

"King of Snowy Meadows, my butt..." Chue muttered to himself, left standing alone in frustration.

CHAPTER FIFTY

COLOSSAL MADNESS

ZELANA AND ZHONG strolled past the armory, their steps faltering, catching sight of Kalina rushing inside. Pausing at the armory entrance, they took a second, more discerning, observation.

Inside, amidst the clamor of metal, Kalina navigated among the men who were working fervently on the machines, her eyes scanning for Deon. She quickly found him, shirtless and engrossed in work alongside the Zelonian and Sanshe blacksmiths, fixing the levers to ensure that the massive farming machinery operated flawlessly. She quietly walked over to him and watched, admiring how his muscles flexed rhythmically with the movements required to fine-tune the machine.

Deon turned around to reach for a tool from the table and was taken by surprise as he saw Kalina standing behind him, her gaze lingering appreciatively on his physique.

"Princess Kalina..." His eyes glossed over her casual yet enticing attire, accentuating her figure. "What are you doing here?"

"I heard you were preoccupied with work and couldn't join me, so I decided to come to you," she explained, her eyes briefly flickering toward a smudge of dirt on his cheek.

"I appreciate you coming, but this isn't really a place where you can assist," Deon protested.

Zelana, standing at the entrance, watched as Kalina grabbed a handkerchief from her pocket and moved toward him. She tiptoed and delicately wiped the sweat and grime from Deon's face, her touch lingering a moment too long, sending waves of discomfort rippling through Zelana. She could see his eyes watching Kalina and couldn't help but wonder what he was thinking.

Are you looking at her the way you look at me?

Inside the armory, Kalina tucked the handkerchief back into her pocket. "There... I knew I could be of use," she said, gazing into his eyes.

"You really didn't have to," he murmured with unease.

"Let me take care of you, Ambassador," she replied with a soft smile as she reached for the water jug from Miranda and poured water into the cap.

"Why all this attention?" Deon asked, observing her curiously.

"I want us to be friends," she said, offering him the water. "You work hard. You must be parched."

Her eyes traversed his sweaty, muscular frame in admiration as Deon reluctantly accepted the cap and drank the water in one gulp. He handed it back to her and she casually placed the cap back on the water jug.

"You're going to spoil me at this rate," he teased casually.

"Perhaps that is my intention," Kalina flirted, gazing up at him seductively.

Deon chuckled lightly. "I should get back to work."

"What are you working on?" she asked curiously.

Deon picked up two metallic pieces and pointed to their

connections. "These parts go together to secure these gigantic wheels in place," he explained, fitting them together seamlessly.

"Ah," she murmured, leaning into him and gently placing her hand on his shoulder. "It fits perfectly."

Back at the entrance, Zelana observed them, feeling a piercing sting in her heart watching Deon and Kalina talking and laughing.

I can't watch anymore, she thought in silence. With a heavy heart, she tore her gaze away from them.

"I wouldn't be surprised if they started courting," Zhong teased playfully, unaware of her emotions.

"Shall we head to the lake?" Zelana proposed, not waiting for Zhong to respond as she walked away, her departure marked by slow, contemplative steps while he began to follow her to the lake front.

CHAPTER FIFTY-ONE

DECEPTIONS

THE LAKE LAY serene, its waters reflecting the gentle blue of the sky as Zelana and Zhong strolled along the curving shoreline. Their conversation flowed easily, mingled with the gentle whispers of the afternoon breeze. Despite their light-hearted banter, her thoughts still lingered on Kalina and Deon.

"You won't forget about me, will you?" Zhong asked, oblivious to the turmoil raging within her.

"I believe it's you who will forget me," Zelana responded calmly, masking her roiling emotions.

"Then I'd have to forget every moment that's ever made me smile," he murmured, placing his hands in his pockets as he walked beside her.

Zelana slowed her steps to a halt, gazing up at him with a subtle smile. "I have to be careful not to fall for your charms, Crown Prince of Sanshe," she replied with a playful defiance sparkling in her eyes.

"You should see me when I'm actually trying," he teased, his eyes meeting hers.

"Like when you seduced Princess Kalina at The Lagoon?" she asked, the smile fading from her lips.

Zhong panicked. "I'm sorry. I never meant to deceive you. When I met her at the bar, she was just a girl I had a casual drink with," he clarified, careful with his words.

"At least you're no longer denying it," Zelana murmured, turning away from him to watch the gentle lapping of the lake's waters against the shore. "Yet, I still don't understand—there's quite a mismatch between her words and yours."

"What exactly did she say?" he asked nervously.

"Princess Kalina told me you were both mesmerized with each other. She is confused by your sudden disinterest and your pretending not to know her," she spoke honestly, her eyes still on the lake, allowing it to calm her emotions.

"Our encounter was insignificant to me. I didn't want to escalate any misunderstandings, which is why I denied knowing her," he confessed, coming clean.

"That's quite cruel…" she murmured softly.

"It would be crueler of me to lead her on," countered the Crown Prince in defense.

Zelana faced him, her confusion deepening. "I was once envious of the two of you."

"There's nothing to envy, I assure you," he replied, feeling helpless.

A small smile graced her lips. "You both could have had it all—love and a lavish lifetime of royalty."

"Love?" he echoed the word as he took a step closer, his eyes piercing deeply into hers. "The feeling that wraps my heart in warmth each time I see you? The ache that takes hold when we have to part?"

Zelana's expression softened, perplexed, not expecting those words from him, as Zhong leaned in, closing the distance between them. Her heart fluttered, surprising her, their faces mere breaths apart.

"I've been holding back the temptation to kiss you, Princess Zelana," he whispered, his voice a gentle caress, lingering in the air between them as his gaze fell to her luscious lips.

Zelana could feel the heat of his breath against her skin as his lips drew closer. *What do I do?*

A sudden loud jolt from an engine shattered the fragile moment between them. Zelana and Zhong turned toward the sound, their gazes locked onto the colossal farming machine coming to a halt before them. To their astonishment, Deon was at the helm. He stood abruptly, his knuckles white from gripping the handlebars, his vest billowing in the wind, a telltale sign of the storm raging inside him.

Zelana's breath faltered as she instinctively stepped back from Zhong, a flush of embarrassment warming her cheeks. Regret immediately settled like a dull ache in her chest, torn between the unexpected allure of Zhong's lips and her lingering emotions for Deon. One thing was certain—she wished Deon hadn't seen her in that compromising moment with the Crown Prince.

For a moment, I thought I could reach you. How foolish of me? Deon scoffed at himself, maintaining an expressionless façade even as his heart was breaking.

The excited glint in Zhong's eyes faded as he noticed a shift in Zelana's demeanor. He glanced at his friend, catching sight of Deon's rigid stance and clenched jaw.

Are you... upset, Deon? he wondered silently, confused, not expecting his friend to be so affected.

Meanwhile, Kalina remained seated, her eyes narrowed, barely unable to conceal her fury.

You're such an ass, Zhong! I can't believe you were going to kiss her right in front of me, she thought, grabbing the basket of fruits by her feet, plucking grapes and eating them with exaggerated motions.

Zelana observed Deon helplessly as he averted her gaze, slumping back into his seat.

Are you that worried about Kalina? Zhong's eyes lingered on Zelana, sensing her growing concern.

"Sweets make me feel better," Kalina murmured, picking up another grape and offering it to Deon.

"No thanks," he said curtly.

"Are you worried about what *she* might think?" Kalina asked, bringing the grape up to his lips. "I'm surprised you thought Princess Zelana would ever choose a Lord over a Crown Prince."

Deon felt his chest tighten painfully. *I still chose to return to Zelonia to be near her and I would do it again one hundred times over.*

The grip around his heart became almost unbearable as he reluctantly accepted the grape from Kalina's hand with his lips, hoping its sweetness would overtake the bitterness in his mouth. He chewed it slowly, his mind swirling with thoughts he could not escape.

Kalina's gesture was undeniably intimate, and Zelana felt her heart constrict painfully as she watched Deon give in—it cut deep. His expression softened as he turned to face Kalina, a rare vulnerability flickering in his gaze, contrasting the stoic mask he so often wore. That glimpse into his guarded emotions twisted the knife further in her chest, leaving her feeling even more hurt and helpless.

For the first time, Deon really saw Kalina—and the pain she was enduring because of his friend.

Kalina stopped mid-bite, sensing his gaze, the subtle vulnerability in his eyes unfamiliar and unsettling.

"What are you thinking about?" she asked nervously.

Deon hesitated, then spoke, "I probably shouldn't say this, but... you deserve to know. Crown Prince Zhong was never serious about you."

Suddenly Kalina's eyes brimmed with tears. "You know more about us than you let up."

Deon nodded in silent acknowledgement, his expression shadowed with shared sorrow as tears spilled freely down her cheeks. He reached over, gently pulling her into his embrace, suppressing his own aching heart. Kalina buried her face in his chest, her sobs quiet but heart-wrenching as his arms wrapped around her tenderly.

Zelana stood frozen, her feelings for him real and raw, suffocating her slowly as she watched him hold another woman in his arms.

Stop longing for him, she reminded herself, yet her heart ached. *He can't be yours...*

Even as she repeated the words, they felt hollow, failing to dull her pain.

Deon glanced up, their eyes meeting briefly. The pain both were enduring was too obvious to hide.

Zhong observed their lingering gazes, a flicker of unease crossing his face, his suspicions deepening.

Deon tore his eyes away from her and shifted gears, the machine roaring to life. He maneuvered the farming machine, thundering away with Kalina leaning closer, craving his warmth.

"I can see them together," Zhong remarked, attempting to lighten the mood with a small smile.

Words were lost to Zelana as she lowered her eyes, drowning in her own thoughts.

The quiet was suddenly punctured by the sound of footsteps approaching from the path behind them. Dominic stepped forward, his face serious, though there was a hesitance in his manner, as if he knew his interruption was ill-timed.

"Apologies, but King Lucas requests your presence, Crown Prince Zhong," Dominic said, his tone respectful but urgent, breaking the fragile stillness that had settled over the moment.

The Crown Prince's eyes remained anchored to Zelana. "Where should we meet later, Princess?"

Zelana lifted her gaze to meet his, her eyes soft but conflicted. "I'll walk to the gardens and wait for you," she murmured, her voice barely above a whisper.

Zhong gave a reluctant nod, the weight of unspoken words hanging in the air between them. With a heavy heart, he turned to follow Dominic, his steps slow and unsteady, burdened by lingering doubts and the looming separation from her that he would have to endure as he prepared to return to Sanshe.

CHAPTER FIFTY-TWO

SECRETS OF THE HEART

ZELANA AND HER lady-in-waiting continued their stroll along the tranquil lakeside, the soothing lapping of the water mirroring the pensive mood of the Princess, whose usual vibrant aura now seemed subdued.

"Are you pondering over the kiss you almost shared with Crown Prince Zhong?" Natalie gently probed.

Zelana kept silent, slightly flustered by her question.

"If only Ambassador Deon and Princess Kalina hadn't interrupted..." Natalie teased softly.

"Actually, I've been reflecting on *them*," Zelana confided, her voice filled with emotion.

"You're worried about Ambassador Deon, aren't you?" Natalie asked, concerned.

Zelana sighed. "Initially, I believed Princess Kalina's affections were reserved solely for Crown Prince Zhong, but she was quite affectionate with Ambassador Deon today."

Natalie paused. "And he's responding in kind..."

"I don't know how I feel about them together," Zelana admitted, a hint of melancholy in her voice.

"She is aware that Deon's a Lord, so she knows there is no future," Natalie reasoned, contemplating the boundaries set for

Royals. "Perhaps she is drawn to the thrill of chasing someone she can't have."

"A forbidden romance..." Zelana murmured, her chest tightening again as she let out a deep breath.

The rumble of the farming machine filled the air, drawing their attention to the behemoth. Zelana's heart skipped a beat, her breath catching in her throat as she saw Deon piloting the massive machinery alone. His expression was unreadable, but she could see the tension in his posture as he halted the machine in front of them, the rumbling engine dying down.

Deon dismounted the machine with practiced ease and approached them with steady steps, though his heart was racing, feeling Zelana's eyes watching his every move.

"Where's Crown Prince Zhong?" he asked casually, keeping it light.

"He went to meet with my father," she replied a bit nervously.

"Princess Zelana, would you care for a ride back to the armory?" he proposed with a hopeful heart.

"I'll meet you in the gardens, Princess," Natalie quickly interjected before Zelana could answer.

"Natalie..." Zelana called to her, but she had already turned, walking away briskly.

Deon sighed, noticing the evident discomfort on Zelana's face.

"Ladies-in-waiting certainly have a mind of their own these days," Zelana murmured awkwardly.

Deon offered his hand in a gallant gesture. Zelana looked up at him, her expression shadowed by the memory of the moments she had witnessed between him and Kalina. The sight of them together lingered in her mind, gnawing at her heart.

"I'm uncertain this is wise," she voiced in a cautious tone.

His throat tightened, sensing the tension escalate as he slowly lowered his hand, disappointment flickering in his eyes. "Crown Prince Zhong will understand."

"Will Princess Kalina?" she countered, still hurting.

Deon froze, taken aback by her question, surprised that she had brought Kalina into the conversation so unexpectedly. "Princess…" he began, searching for words.

"You brought Crown Prince Zhong up first," Zelana interrupted, trying to hold back her emotions, but the crack in her voice betrayed her.

"Because you were going to kiss my closest friend in front of me," Deon blurted out, unable to hold back the tidal wave of jealousy and pain that had been swelling inside him.

"He was going to kiss *me*," she corrected, her gaze unwavering as she looked up into his eyes.

"And you were going to let him," he murmured, feeling defeated, the thought unbearably painful.

"You ate the grape she fed you," she countered, her voice soft yet pained.

Deon let out a weary sigh. "That hardly compares to you and Crown Prince Zhong."

"Nothing happened between us," she shot back, her voice quivering as tears threatened to spill. "While you… it perturbs me that you so easily accept any kind of affection from any woman."

He stared at her in disbelief. "Are you… jealous?" he asked, struggling to keep his tone even, despite his unease with the conversation.

Absolutely! What kind of question is that? Zelana's heart clenched painfully.

"Why are we even talking about this?" she asked, feeling flustered, on the verge of tears. "I should go. I'm supposed to meet with Crown Prince Zhong."

As she turned to walk away, Deon reached out, gently yet firmly grasping her arm.

"Ambassador…" Zelana started, but her words faltered when he pulled her back to him. She stumbled onto his chest, her breath catching, feeling the rapid beat of his heart against hers.

"Zhong can wait," Deon said, his voice filled with a raw vulnerability he could no longer suppress.

Zelana tried to pull away, but Deon tightened his hold on her.

"Don't leave me, please," his plea was soft and pained, melting away her resistance.

She felt the tension in her body slowly ebbing away, surrendering to the warmth of his embrace as she leaned into the steady beat of his heart, her own slowly falling into rhythm with his.

Deon's jaw tightened, his gaze on the fading horizon. "The sun is setting, marking another day that slips past us," he murmured sadly. "And it feels like we're growing apart."

"You're leaving for Sanshe anyways," Zelana whispered against his chest, her voice quivering as she forced herself to accept the brutal truth.

And returning to the Princess you've been longing for…

Deon drew back and gazed into her eyes, tempted to tell her that he was staying, but instead he suddenly placed his hands on her hips, lifting her effortlessly onto the massive machine. He climbed into the driver's seat as she settled down beside him.

They sat in silence, staring at the lake and watching the sun begin its descent, casting the sky in a breathtaking palette of orange and pink hues. The serene waters mirrored the fiery spectacle above, creating a tranquil beauty that slowly unfolded before them.

"Wouldn't you rather be with Princess Kalina before you leave?" Zelana broke the quiet as her heart thundered with emotion.

Deon sighed. "She means nothing to me," he responded softly, his eyes meeting hers.

"I saw how you held her," her voice wavered, fighting to keep her composure and failing helplessly.

"I was merely offering her comfort," he said gently, trying to console her. "Princess Kalina has strong feelings for Crown Prince Zhong. I don't believe she holds any *real* affection for me."

"And yet..." her voice grew more pained. "She brought you water while you worked in the armory. She wiped your face like someone who cares deeply... gestures reserved for someone you... love."

"I didn't realize you saw all that," he murmured, feeling guilty.

Zelana's heart ached, her words revealing a truth he had to finally face.

Deon could see it—the jealousy flickering in her gaze, the raw emotion she couldn't hide. It tore at him, breaking the walls he had built around his own heart as he watched her struggle.

"I wish you both much happiness," she said, her voice quivering, tears filling her eyes as she stood.

The vulnerability Deon had fought so fiercely to bury surged to the surface, spilling from his heart and filling the space between them—overwhelming and unguarded as his hands gripped her waist, pulling her onto his lap. His arms immediately drifted around her, holding her close.

"I must confess," he whispered in her ear, his voice trembling. "I'm most happy when I'm with you."

Tears streamed from her eyes that moment, breaking down and sobbing into his embrace. Her fingers clutched his shirt tightly as her body trembled against him.

"I'm so sorry I hurt you..." he murmured tenderly, tightening his hold of her as tears brimmed in his own eyes, his emotions raw with regret. "Please forgive me..."

"I'm sorry I hurt you too," she choked out her response, her tears soaking into his chest as she continued to bury her face in his warmth.

All Deon wanted was to hold her and never let go, ensuring she knew how much she meant to him.

CHAPTER FIFTY-THREE

Elite Humans

KALINA PACED THE gardens, her thoughts a tempest of emotions as the delegation's imminent departure loomed. The fleeting moments she shared with Zhong ignited a deep yearning within her, more profound than she had expected. She needed to speak to Zhong, look into his eyes to see if there was a glimmer of truth to Deon's words.

Miranda observed her Princess's troubled demeanor and approached her with a cautious smile. "Crown Prince Zhong is approaching," she whispered, discreetly retreating to give them privacy.

Kalina looked up as their eyes met and Zhong greeted her. "Good evening, Princess Kalina."

As Zhong passed her, their hands brushed against each other, sparking an electric jolt that coursed through their bodies as memories of their shared night flickered through their thoughts.

"Crown Prince Zhong, I hear you're leaving this evening," she voiced, sadness looming over her.

Zhong halted and turned to face her. "I am," he confirmed.

"Weren't you going to say good-bye?" Kalina asked, her voice trembling slightly.

Zhong's expression softened momentarily before masking it with a stern resolve. "I wasn't sure I would see you," he admitted, pausing. "Take care of yourself, and I wish you much happiness."

With those parting words, Zhong's gaze shifted to Deon and Zelana approaching from the armory. Their sweet banter and shared laughter drifted through the garden like a soft breeze, warming the air between them. Zhong felt a surge of jealousy as he swiftly moved toward them, leaving Kalina standing alone, her heart heavy with the realization that he was still tethered to Zelana.

"How did the meeting go?" Deon inquired curiously.

"It was productive. We've satisfied all the stipulations of both contracts," the Crown Prince replied with a note of satisfaction in his voice.

"Perhaps next time we should include mechanical arms in the negotiations," Zelana suggested playfully, glancing gracefully up at the men.

"You mean these?" Deon asked, activating and flaunting his mechanical arms with a grin.

"Impressive biceps," Zelana complimented, her fingers tracing the contours of his metallic arm.

Deon nodded with a proud smirk as a flicker of discomfort crossed Zhong's features, observing their light-hearted exchange.

"I want to feel them too, Ambassador Deon," Kalina stepped forward, her hand grasping his bicep and gently caressing. "Wow. You are quite muscular indeed," she declared boldly with a gentle squeeze.

Deon glanced at Zelana and noticed a hint of disappointment in her gaze.

Zhong activated his own mechanical arms, eager to highlight his strength. "Check these out. Considerably larger, wouldn't you say, Princess Zelana?"

Maintaining her poise, Zelana turned toward him with a playful smile and indulged in the comparison, her fingers gently feeling his arm.

"Both of you are quite... blessed," she stated timidly, her gaze darting between Deon and the Crown Prince with amusement.

"Don't be intimidated by the Crown Prince, Princess Zelana," Deon teased with a playful grin, "Go on and speak your mind."

His comment elicited a blush from the Princess, lightening the mood as laughter rippled through the group. The men deactivated their mechanical arms, the jovial atmosphere dispelling any lingering tension and awkwardness.

"Princess Zelana, I've been quite curious about the famed strength of elite humans," Zhong remarked, seizing the moment to test her strength.

"Then allow me to demonstrate, Crown Prince Zhong," Zelana replied with a teasing glint in her eye, an invitation he couldn't refuse. "Please, lift your hands."

With a smirk on his face, Zhong complied and raised his hands. Zelana gently grasped them while locking eyes with him, and suddenly pushed him effortlessly across the walkway, despite his attempts to resist her exceptional strength.

"Incredible... is this really happening?" Zhong exclaimed in astonishment as he laughed, experiencing the formidable strength of the Zelonian Princess first-hand while struggling to push back helplessly.

From the sidelines, Deon chuckled lightly, his respect and enchantment for her only deepening, while Kalina observed silently, shocked by Zelana's extraordinary strength.

Zelana released Zhong's hands as the enchanting atmosphere was further intensified by the deep, unspoken emotions that seemed to swirl between them.

"I still can't believe it," Zhong gasped in awe. "This demonstration has given me a profound appreciation for the unique talents of Zelonia's royals."

Zelana felt a wave of warmth as the Crown Prince regarded her with intrigue and admiration, a sensation that illuminated her presence.

CHAPTER FIFTY-FOUR

LAST MOMENTS

"COULD YOU SPARE me a moment, Crown Prince Zhong?" Kalina requested politely, feeling sidelined.

Zhong turned his attention to her, his expression inscrutable. "I apologize, but I'm about to depart for Sanshe and wish to spend my remaining time here with Princess Zelana."

Zelana cast a sympathetic glance toward her friend, sensing her growing despair. "That was a bit harsh, don't you think, Crown Prince Zhong?" she said, her tone a subtle rebuke.

Zhong tenderly grasped Zelana's hand. "Should I feign affection for Princess Kalina, let her nurture a lie, when my every heartbeat whispers your name?" His voice was a silent plea.

Deon was speaking the truth, Kalina realized, feeling more humiliated as she turned and walked away.

"If that is truly your wish, I will oblige, but the last thing I want to do is hurt you, Princess Zelana," he confessed, speaking from the depths of his heart. "And continuing to be with Princess Kalina would indeed pain you if you cared for me at all."

His confession left Zelana speechless, caught in a whirlwind of emotions as she looked up at him with a burgeoning sense of wonder.

Is he serious right now? Deon pondered, unsure his heart could take anymore.

"From the moment we met, my feelings for you have only deepened. I've been seeking your parents' blessing and they've finally consented," Zhong informed her, his voice filled with conviction. "I wish to pursue you honorably and avoid any distractions that might taint my sincerity, Princess Zelana."

Zelana became caught in a maelstrom of emotions, looking up at Zhong, flustered. He leaned to gently kiss her hand, sending waves of warmth surging through her as her eyes awkwardly met Deon's.

"The carriage for Sanshe is ready, Crown Prince Zhong," Chue announced as he approached them, noticing a strange vibe in the air.

Zelana suddenly withdrew her hand from Zhong's grasp. "I'm deeply flattered that you feel the way you do, but courtship is too sudden. I think indulging in the moment would just complicate things. We should take time to nurture our fondness toward each other and see if there's truly a future for us."

Zhong's gaze softened as he took in the uncertainty and fear shadowing her features. "I would never impose my feelings on you, Princess. My respect for you runs deep. I shall wait patiently for the day you are ready for my affections," he said, his voice steady though tinged with disappointment.

"Thank you for understanding," Zelana replied with a subtle smile, clasping her hands together. "It was a pleasure to meet you. I look forward to more moments when we can truly get to know one another."

Zhong offered a faint, bittersweet smile. "Please take care until my return."

Zelana nodded as Zhong lowered his head in a respectful bow, then straightened. He then turned and walked toward the Zelonian gate, each step filled with a quiet echo of their unresolved emotions.

Zelana's eyes then shifted to Deon, seeking perhaps a final word or gesture, but he, too, hastened toward the gates, following Zhong and Chue, leaving her in silent contemplation.

Outside the gates, Chue stood patiently, holding the door to the royal carriage open as Zhong paused, a deep sigh escaping his lips, a brief flicker of vulnerability crossing his otherwise composed face.

"Beautiful women are definitely much harder to conquer," Zhong muttered, attempting to mask the sting of his bruised pride as he turned to Deon with a hint of suspicion gleaming in his eyes. "Tell me honestly. Was it because of Princess Zelana that you asked to come to Zelonia?"

Deon faltered for a moment, caught off guard by the directness of the question. "I had many reasons."

Zhong's brows furrowed, sensing Deon's evasion.

"Are you serious about pursuing her?" Deon asked casually.

"If I am, are you going to protect her for me, Deon?" Zhong replied with a smirk.

"The things I do for you..." Deon remarked with a tease, maintaining a playful front, although his heart was heavy with the depth of his own emotional turmoil.

With a final nod, the Crown Prince ascended into the royal carriage, the door closing behind him.

Meanwhile, Zelana stood on the other side of the carriage, her thoughts lingering painfully on Deon.

How can you leave without speaking to me, Deon? She wondered sadly, her eyes scanning the area as if hoping to catch one last glimpse of him. *When will I ever see you again?*

Zhong watched her through the carriage window, noticing the turmoil playing across her features, her eyes darting around anxiously.

"Don't miss me too much, Princess Zelana," Zhong called out, his voice breaking her thoughts.

Zelana turned toward him, her expression shifting as she smiled brightly. "I know where to find you when I do," she replied with a light tease.

Her words made Zhong's heart skip a beat, captivated by the radiance of her smile. She had the power to disarm him completely, making it harder for him to part.

"I'll visit often so you don't have to miss me," Zhong replied with a playful grin, trying to hide how much her words affected him.

The carriage creaked and lurched forward, slowly beginning its departure.

Zelana maintained a warm smile, waving gracefully as the carriage rolled away, her hand lowering only when the dust from the wheels had settled. Yet, as she stood there, her heart remained conflicted, her mind wandering to thoughts of another.

CHAPTER FIFTY-FIVE

The Pledge

ZELANA'S EYES UNEXPECTEDLY collided with Deon's across the courtyard. She clasped her hand over her lips, tears spilling down her cheeks as she gasped in shock, relieved at his unexpected presence.

"Princess Zelana…" Deon murmured softly, his steps bringing him closer.

"I feared you left without bidding me farewell," she whispered, her voice trembling with emotion.

"I could never leave you without a word," he gently assured her, the depth of her distress startling him.

"Did you ask me where the men's quarters were because you had already given up everything in Sanshe to mentor me?" Zelana inquired, more tears cascading down her cheeks.

A teasing reluctance colored his response. "Something like that."

"And you were limping when you arrived because you were on your knees for hours in front of King MuaYeng… requesting him to release you from your duties," she accused softly. "Admit it."

Deon hesitated, stunned at her perceptiveness. "How is it that you always see through me?" he murmured, stepping closer and reaching out, his fingers tenderly brushing away her tears.

"You have a lot of explaining to do, Mister Ambassador," she teased him through glistening eyes.

Deon hesitated, his expression softening. "You've become someone I want to protect, someone I want to cherish, Princess. I can't do that from Sanshe," he confessed, the warmth in his voice enveloping her, filling every crevice in her heart with his affection.

"I'm afraid that when the time comes for you to leave, I won't know how to let you go… not after knowing what it feels like to have you beside me," she whispered, her tears unshed, held back.

Deon's heart melted at her words as he reached out, gently taking her hand in his. With an unexpected grace, he knelt before her on one knee, his gaze meeting hers. Zelana's hand flew to her lips once more, her heart pounding, overwhelmed by the sincerity of his gesture.

"From this day onward, I, Deon Vang, promise to be by your side until you're a powerful Queen, respected and revered by all nations, loved and cherished by your people. I promise to serve and protect you with my life, offering my unwavering loyalty until the day you deem it unnecessary, Princess of Zelonia," he pledged from the depths of his heart.

Zelana's heart swelled with affection as a soft smile spread across her lips. "And if I always need you?" she asked, her voice barely a whisper.

"You shall always have me," he affirmed with heartfelt conviction, his eyes brimming with love and devotion as he carefully lifted her hand to his lips, planting a gentle kiss that sealed his solemn vow.

The moment became a sacred pledge between them; a quiet promise to endure whatever trials life would bring with unwavering confidence; that together, they could overcome anything.

CHAPTER FIFTY-SIX

STRENGTH

ZELANA APPROACHED THE Zelonian Academy, her steps slowing as she spotted Deon amid his stretches. She caught herself admiring his less formal, more approachable look—his hair no longer neatly combed back but worn down, framing his face and accentuating his handsome features.

He was strikingly different from the Deon she was accustomed to seeing—dressed in a regal suit. He wore a sleeveless shirt, trousers, and battle boots, lending him a rugged appeal.

"Good morning," Deon said, straightening up and turning to face her, surprised by the deliberate care she seemed to have taken with her appearance.

"Morning, Ambassador..." Zelana replied, her voice trailing off slightly.

"Please call me Deon when we're alone," he corrected her as she nodded with a timid smile. "Did you come for combat training?" Deon asked teasingly.

"Yes, I did," she murmured, her gaze lingering on him, finding herself slightly entranced.

Deon observed her closer. "Why is your hair down and styled?"

Zelana felt a sudden flush of self-consciousness. "I always wear it down."

Her tone carried a touch of nervousness, revealing the meticulous care she had taken in her appearance, particularly when she knew she'd be in Deon's presence.

"Make sure to always tie your hair up for training," he gently advised.

"Yes, sir," she replied, her eyes twinkling with amusement as she reached up and gathered her hair, pulling it up and securing it with the band from her arm.

Deon's gaze then fell to her camisole, his eyes lingering on how the top clung to her voluptuous form, outlining her figure more than he deemed appropriate for training.

"Why did you choose this top?" he inquired, his voice carrying a note of concern.

"The fabric is stretchy and very comfortable," she explained innocently with sincerity.

"It's too tight," he commented softly.

"It feels fine on me," she said, glancing down at her camisole, not seeing the issue he perceived.

Deon exhaled a heavy sigh, then reached for an armor breastplate. "Lift your arms," he instructed.

She obediently complied and he carefully positioned the armor over her chest, ensuring her comfort. He then shifted his attention to her knickers.

"Those knickers look like they were made for you when you were ten," he criticized, disapprovingly.

She paused before responding awkwardly, "I wear this for training all the time."

"I guess they'll have to do," he conceded after a brief consideration.

His eyes finally settled on her high-heeled boots. "Take those off, I don't want you getting injured."

With a puzzled expression, Zelana sat down, slipping off her boots before standing back up.

"Alright, it looks like we can finally start today's training," he announced, setting the stage for the day's regimen. "Before we dive into combat training, we need to work on strength training."

Zelana was taken aback. "Didn't you see how naturally strong I am?"

"Your strength is foundational, but there's always room for improvement," Deon explained as he lifted a pail filled with water. "Raise your arms. Hold this pail above your head to strengthen your triceps."

The Princess reluctantly obliged and extended her arms upward, steadying the pail as he carefully placed it in her hands. "This seems manageable," she remarked confidently.

He smiled encouragingly, hoisting another pail above his own head. "The real challenge emerges over time," he assured her as they both maintained their stances.

As the minutes ticked by, the weight of the pail began to assert its presence, challenging Zelana's endurance. She shifted uncomfortably, feeling the strain intensify.

"How much longer do I need to hold this?" she asked, wavering slightly under the growing pressure.

"Keep holding until I tell you to stop," Deon instructed, his own posture unyielding.

The struggle became evident as her arms trembled and her grip faltered. Suddenly, the pail tipped, cascading water down her front.

"You're wet," he stated the obvious with a smirk.

"I don't want to do this anymore," she pouted, soaked and frustrated.

The smirk on his face broadened, and he lowered his pail, amused. "Let's try one more pail," he suggested.

With a resigned sigh, Zelana raised her arms once more. He positioned a fresh pail above her head with meticulous care. After half an hour, her endurance waned, and once again, the pail tipped, dousing her.

"One more..." Deon encouraged, placing yet another pail in her hands.

Despite the ache in her arms, she persevered, her determination unyielding. An hour into the grueling exercise, her muscles finally succumbed, and the pail slipped from her grasp, splashing water all around her, soaking her for the third time.

Unseen by the training pair, Lucas and Sophia were quietly standing by the door to the Training Academy, observing the session in silence as the practice unfolded before them.

"The more I encounter Deon, the more I appreciate his qualities," Sophia observed in admiration.

"Unfortunately, he was born a commoner and she's promised to someone," Lucas retorted casually.

"You never know what the future holds," the Queen countered optimistically with a warm smile, observing Deon approach Zelana with a towel, gently patting the water off her face.

"They remind me too much of us, my love," the King teased, prompting a small giggle from Sophia as they began to walk away, hand in hand.

Back at the training grounds, Deon lowered the towel, his gaze lingering on Zelana.

How are you still beautiful all drenched in water? he wondered silently, maintaining a stoic facade.

"What's next?" Zelana asked, ready to take on the new challenge.

"We are going to focus on strengthening your biceps, holding pails of water in each hand," he instructed, directing her to the next task with a nod toward the refilled pails.

Zelana felt her fatigue dissipating under the warmth of his gaze and stretched out her arms. He lifted a pail and carefully placed them into her hands, her arms tensing to meet the challenge.

CHAPTER FIFTY-SEVEN

Slash

AT THE BREAK of dawn, Zelana strode into the training grounds, her hair neatly braided against the nape of her neck, her breastplate gleaming in the morning light, and her battle boots thudding softly on the earth. She was the picture of preparedness, embodying the warrior spirit she aspired to perfect. Beside her, Deon matched her stride, his eyes approving her determination. Together, they began with rigorous strength exercises, the clanking of their pails of water punctuating the morning's stillness.

"I want you to commit to an hour of strength training every morning. It's crucial for building the endurance you'll need to combat Immortals," Deon advised with a stoic expression.

"Yes, sir," Zelana replied with a nod and set down her burdensome pails.

With a swift movement, Deon secured two wooden swords, tossing one to Zelana, ready to start basic combat techniques. She caught it adeptly, readying herself for the next phase of her training.

"First, grasp your sword with both hands, one atop the other," Deon instructed with demonstration.

Zelana's hands closed around the wooden hilt, her stance solid and her eyes alight with the fierce desire to learn and excel. Deon observed her with a critical eye and gave a satisfied nod.

"Execute a slash upwards, sweep it sideways, and finish with a block," he directed, watching as her movements were fluid with a blend of strength and grace while continuing to perform the actions.

"Now, keep your eyes on my sword and block my attacks," he directed as his wooden sword sliced through the air toward her.

With swift precision, Zelana raised her weapon to intercept his blows.

"You're learning fast," he observed with admiration.

"Because I have the best mentor," she teased as she fluidly returned to her combat stance.

Deon chuckled, his dance of wood continuing, attacking with a series of slashes and sweeps, each met by Zelana's deft blocks. He then delivered an overhead strike as she hesitated, uncertainty flickering in her eyes. With no time to think, she instinctively turned to the side, evading the blow with a grace that spoke of instinct rather than trained skill.

"Nicely done, Princess," he praised, truly impressed. "Seeing you improvise and adapt in the face of an unfamiliar attack is precisely what I want to see. You must always be ready with quick responses and versatile in your movements."

"How should I defend against a downward strike?" Zelana asked, curious about the new move.

"Change the blocking technique we practiced by elevating your arm higher like this," he demonstrated, positioning his sword so it intersected with an imaginary adversary's. "Make sure your sword is always crossed with theirs to effectively block the strike."

Deon then launched a downward attack and Zelana followed his advice, raising her sword to intercept his blow. After he retreated, she resumed her standard defensive posture. He attacked from above once more, and again she lifted her sword, successfully blocking his advance.

"Good, you observed my actions and anticipated the repeated attack," he acknowledged with a nod, recognizing her quick adaptation. "Keep in mind that slashes are designed to disorient and inflict pain," he explained, demonstrating a swift twirl and jab with his sword, the tip of the sword pointed at her stomach. "But thrusts are meant to be lethal."

Deon paused, allowing his words to sink in. "In this position, with your sword already embedded in your adversary's body, a slash to the right can be devastating. It will likely strike the heart or its major vessels, leading to immediate incapacitation or death."

As his wooden sword mimicked a deadly slide across her stomach to her chest, her breath hitched, a wave of fear washing over her. "It's terrifying."

"That's precisely why you must prevent an enemy from getting close enough to execute a stab," Deon advised, his sword lowering to a non-threatening position.

"How can I avoid it?" she asked, her nerves tingling with the urgency to know.

"Attempt to stab me," he suggested, a challenging glint in his eyes.

Gripping her sword with determination, Zelana lunged forward to stab him, but he swiftly knocked her sword out of her hand with a deft slash.

"How did you do that?" she exclaimed in astonishment.

"Years of wielding swords have honed my sense of distance and timing against an approaching thrust," he explained calmly. "As you grow more accustomed to the feel of your sword, you'll be able to deflect and disarm your adversaries effectively. Given your strength, I have no doubt you'll master this easily," he remarked, encouraging her. "Now try to stab me again. Let's see what you've learned."

Zelana quickly retrieved her sword and lunged forward in another attempt to stab Deon.

With graceful agility, Deon spun, evading her thrust, and countered with a gentle tap of his blade against her back. "You can dodge a stab by spinning toward your adversary to counterattack like this."

"You were so quick," she praised in admiration and respect.

"Skill, speed, and strength are your best weapons on the battlefield," Deon stated sternly.

Zelana repeated the words in her mind. *Skill, speed, and strength...*

She made another swift attempt to stab him, taking him by surprise, but he executed a backward flip, evading her strike with impressive acrobatics. Fueled by determination, she charged at him again, her sword slashing through the air. Deon bent backward, narrowly escaping her aggressive assault.

"Wow," she breathed out in amazement.

Deon quickly straightened and countered with a slash, which she dodged by bending backward, mirroring his previous maneuver. "Not bad," he conceded with approval.

Laughing lightly, Zelana aimed another slash at him. This time, Deon dipped low, sweeping at her feet, causing her to tumble to the ground.

"Ouch…" she pouted, lying on her back, looking up at him with a hint of frustration and amusement.

Deon approached her with a warm smile, extending his hand to help her to her feet. Gratefully, she accepted, and he hoisted her up with a firm pull. Without missing a beat, they resumed their dance of combat, swords clashing rhythmically as they tested each other's skills.

Kalina and Miranda arrived, joining Natalie to watch the training session unfold. The sound of wood against wood filled the air as they observed the intense sparring.

"How long has Princess Zelana been combat training?" Kalina asked with intrigue.

"It's her second day," Natalie replied with a hint of pride in her voice.

Kalina's eyes widened in disbelief, astounded by the rapid progress and natural talent Zelana exhibited in her swordplay.

CHAPTER FIFTY-EIGHT

Close Encounters

DEON ARRIVED AT the Zelonian Academy, surprised to find Zelana already there, holding a pail of water over her head. "Someone's quite determined," he remarked proudly, noticing she had put her hair up in a bun that morning, teasing him with a new look each day.

"I have to keep up with you somehow," Zelana replied with a sparkle in her eyes.

His chuckle broke the morning quietness as she set down her pail of water.

"Today, we'll be shifting our focus from swordplay to hand-to-hand combat," he announced, feeling that progression in their training was due.

Anticipating the physicality of what was to come, the Princess playfully scrunched her nose. "This is going to hurt, isn't it?"

Deon smirked, a playful glint in his eyes. "You might earn a scrape or bruise, but you'll manage," he assured her before delving into the lesson. "We'll start with the grab and throw technique. It's crucial for defending against a frontal attack in close combat."

Zelana nodded, watching his arm movements intently. He suddenly approached her.

"You grab your adversary's arm with your left hand and use your right elbow to leverage under that arm, quickly throwing him to the ground," he said, demonstrating his movements precisely.

Zelana found herself lying on her back, the hardness of the ground not easing her fall as her expression was a blend of pain and admiration, experiencing the effectiveness and force of the maneuver.

"I can't get up..." she pouted, half-joking and half-serious.

His laughter filled the air, helping her to her feet. "Now you try."

With a focused determination, she executed the technique, flipping Deon onto the ground with surprising ease as she gazed down at him. "How was that?"

Deon was still on the ground, wincing. "It was... quite painful," he confessed, impressed.

"I didn't think I threw you that hard," she murmured playfully.

"It's reassuring to know you can handle Immortals with your strength," he quipped, smiling despite the discomfort as he slowly stood up, leaving Zelana with a flushed and triumphant smile.

"Now, let's say your adversary grabs you from behind, choking you," Deon said, setting the scene for the next technique. Without warning, he demonstrated by swiftly moving behind Zelana, encircling her neck with his arm to simulate the choke hold.

"All you need to do..." Deon continued, his voice calm despite the intensity of the demonstration, "...is twist your body toward the open side of the choke, and your neck will slip free."

"Like this?" Zelana caught on quickly and mimicked the movement.

"Exactly!" he praised, pleased with her quick grasp of the technique.

"I never knew it could be that simple," she expressed her surprise with wide eyes.

"Immortals are much stronger, but the principle holds," Deon assured her with a hint of playfulness. "I might suggest you stepping on their toes with those heels you love, giving you more advantage over your adversary."

Zelana couldn't help but giggle. "What if I'm choked from the front?"

"You mean like this?" he asked before gently grasping her neck to clarify.

She held onto his arms, attempting to lessen the grip, and nodded.

"You can't just pry their hands off due to their strength. Instead, tighten your throat muscles and duck swiftly; they'll be forced to release you," Deon instructed.

Following his guidance, Zelana freed herself, looking up at Deon with newfound respect. "You've got some impressive techniques."

"I didn't rise to the rank of Commander based on my good looks alone," he teased with a modest chuckle.

She laughed softly, in awe of his quick wit and the charming way he presented his lessons.

"Avoid being choked from the front and lifted up to the air," he added, his expression turning serious, demonstrating with his hand. "It's a death sentence."

Zelana nodded as a shiver ran through her body.

Deon saw the flicker of fear in her eyes. "Another move that would leave you helpless is when your adversary grabs you, either from the front or back, and squeezes you tight. With the immortals' strength, they would either crush you to death or easily capture you."

"It sounds to me that I should always keep my distance from my adversaries, if possible," she concluded.

"Exactly," he confirmed before introducing the next scenario in a serious tone. "One very important move I need you to master is how to free yourself when your adversary pushes you down onto your back and mounts you."

Zelana hesitated, her eyebrows raised in concern. "Do you want me to lie on my back?"

"If you don't mind," Deon confirmed, encouragingly.

She laid down, her back against the soft earth as she gazed up at Deon with nervous anticipation. He straddled her, an awkwardness apparent in his movements.

"This position..." he began, attempting to maintain a professional demeanor, "...is all about power and balance. The person on top naturally has more power, but the secret lies in shifting the balance."

He paused, ensuring she was attentive. "You need to wrap your arms around me tightly, preventing me from using mine. Then, intertwine your legs around my waist, immobilizing my movement. This way, you can use your body to roll me over onto my back and escape."

Zelana followed his instructions, entwining her limbs with his body to dislodge him, yet she struggled to flip him over.

"I can't..." she admitted, giggling in frustration.

"Use your whole body to push," Deon encouraged her.

Zelana heaved with all her might as her body tensed and she managed to roll Deon onto his back, freeing herself and straddling him.

Deon lay beneath her, a smile of defeat on his face as he acknowledged her success.

"I did it!" Zelana exclaimed in triumph, her face alight with the joy of mastering the move.

He seized the moment to teach her another crucial lesson, swiftly pulling Zelana down to him, grabbing her body and rolling her onto her back, pinning her arms to the ground, reversing their positions as she looked up at him with wide eyes.

"Never allow anyone to pin your arms in this position," Deon warned, his voice stern with a serious urgency. "If they do, escaping becomes nearly impossible."

Zelana's heart pounded nervously, acknowledging his advice with a nod.

The lesson took an unexpected turn as Deon gazed down at her, his pulse quickening as he took in the sight of her positioned vulnerably beneath him. His usual composure was slipping as he stared into her blue eyes, slowly mesmerizing him. His eyes moved down to her luscious lips, parting as if tempting him to kiss them, nearly impossible to resist, blurring the professional lines he had tried so hard to maintain between them.

Deon quickly stood up, extending a hand to help her as they exchanged uncomfortable looks, both acutely aware of the sudden, unspoken tension that had arisen between them.

She slipped her hand into Deon's as he helped her to her feet, the momentum causing her to collapse against his sturdy chest, intensifying the awkwardness. He held her close to him, their hearts beating with the same rhythm.

They suddenly heard the sharp sound of approaching footsteps breaking the tension.

"Ambassador Deon, King Lucas requires your presence in the meeting hall right away," Dominic called out, urgency lacing his tone, redirecting Deon's attention from the intimate moment to the demands of duty as he released her.

"Let's pick this up tomorrow," Deon suggested, his eyes shifting from Dominic back to Zelana.

"Yes, of course," she replied softly, supportive of his service to her father.

With a nod, Deon departed with Dominic, their steps quick and purposeful, toward the meeting hall.

CHAPTER FIFTY-NINE

KRIMZON LETTER

IN THE TENSION-FILLED atmosphere of the meeting hall, Lucas paced anxiously, his usual composure shattered with worry. Sophia sat at the luxurious sofa, her customary poise eclipsed by tears.

As Dominic and Deon entered, Lucas immediately approached them. "Deon, it's rude of me to interrupt your training sessions, but your counsel is imperative right now," the King expressed as his confidence seemed dimmed.

"I am at your service, Your Majesty," Deon responded with attentive respect. "How may I assist?"

Lucas gathered his thoughts and quickly delved into the heart of the issue. "Do you recall me sending Crown Prince Samuel to inspect the Fire Mines?"

"Yes, I remember you asking him to go when we were in the armory," he said, his concern deepening.

With a heavy sigh, Lucas revealed the unfolding crisis. "We acquired the Fire Mines from Lashia, exchanging our weapons to aid their fight against the Immortals. Our operations to mine aluminum have recently commenced. However, we've faced significant disruptions due to protests from the people of Northern

Village and that is why I sent Crown Prince Samuel to address the situation and try to maintain peace."

The King paused, his expression somber as he presented a letter to Deon. "This correspondence came from the King of Krimzon this morning," he disclosed with concern.

Deon's hands were steady as he opened the letter and read the stark words inked on the parchment:

King Lucas of Zelonia,

I have taken Crown Prince Samuel as my captive. He is now at the mercy of my Immortals, his lifeblood sustaining them. Present yourself at the Fire Mines tonight if you wish to see him alive again.

King Marcus of Krimzon

"We need to verify the authenticity of this claim…" Deon suggested cautiously.

"We've already dispatched a scout this morning. The Immortals are indeed holding the Crown Prince captive within those mines," Makeo replied, his voice casting a shadow of dread over the room.

"I am desperate to rescue my son, but what puzzles me is why he's kept alive," Lucas stated, flustered.

Zelana, already dressed in a stunning gown that swayed elegantly with her every movement, entered the room with Natalie that moment, catching the somber note in her father's voice.

"They're likely using him as a pawn," Gaius suggested solemnly.

"To extort me?" Lucas questioned aloud. "But what are they truly seeking?"

"The letter implies they desire *you*, my King," Deon voiced as the Councilmen nodded in agreement. "I fear Marcus is using the Crown Prince as bait to lure you into a perilous trap. If he manages to ensnare you both, he will not hesitate to end your lives."

"Leaving Zelonia defenseless against the onslaught of Krimzon, without a King or a Crown Prince to guide the realm," the King finished his thought.

"Precisely," Deon nodded in agreement. "We must carefully consider all the potential reasons for Crown Prince Samuel's abduction."

"We don't have time to decipher their motives," Makeo challenged, losing his composure.

"We could launch a full-scale attack to demonstrate Zelonia's might," Rowan offered.

"I concur with Commander Rowan. If the Zelonian army overpowers Krimzon, it'll force them to return the Crown Prince to save themselves," Makeo added, throwing in his support behind the idea.

"I fear that may be what Krimzon wants," Dominic countered. "If we're defeated, what then?"

"Commander Dominic raises a good point. They will be prepared, and we could be walking into a trap, losing the Crown Prince along with countless other lives," Deon warned with caution.

"What do you suggest then, Ambassador Deon?" Gaius asked, silence enveloping the room as they turned to him.

Deon's eyes briefly met Zelana's, noting her growing concern.

"Your Majesty... you will have to be at two places at once," Deon suggested, his words causing a murmur to ripple through the room, contemplating the dangerous game of power and survival.

"I am but one man," Lucas said, his features tightening, feeling the weight of Zelonia's future heavy on his shoulders and his son's life hanging by a delicate thread.

"You have me, Your Majesty," Deon consoled him assuredly.

"What do you have in mind?" the King questioned, confused.

"Perhaps I can undertake the rescue mission and impersonate you by leading an army to the Fire Mines and outmaneuvering this trap, while you remain behind and defend Zelonia in case we fail," Deon suggested, presenting a bold strategy. "With the right group of armored warriors and the strategic use of explosives that Sanshe has mastered, we may be able to rescue Crown Prince Samuel and entrap the Immortals with our own surprises."

"Your primary role is to mentor Princess Zelana. I am already overstepping by asking you to participate in our discussions. I can't ask you to risk your life for me," Lucas countered, dismissing the idea.

"I appreciate your concern, but I cannot stand idly by, my King," Deon expressed with heartfelt sincerity. "Zelonia's battle against Krimzon is not just a local conflict; it's a matter that concerns us all. The stability of Azalon hinges on the safety of our rulers and the protection of both our realms."

The room fell silent once more as each word from Deon resonated with unity and hope.

"I have faced death's shadow more times than I can count. My experience as a Commander in Sanshe has prepared me for moments like this," he proclaimed, turning toward the Princess with tender regard. "With Princess Zelana's blessing, I would like to take charge of this mission."

Sophia and Lucas shared a glance, silently acknowledging the fierce respect and loyalty Deon openly and boldly professed to their daughter before the entire Royal Council.

A delicate blush tinted Zelana's cheeks. "Ambassador Deon's leadership and bravery have been proven time and again. I strongly urge you to entrust him with this mission, Father. I believe he can secure my brother's rescue," she affirmed with unwavering confidence.

Inspired by Deon's dedication, Dominic stepped forward. "Permit me the honor of joining Ambassador Deon to serve as your surrogate in this quest, Your Majesty," he requested, his commitment mirroring Deon's courage, knowing the duty and sacrifice the mission entailed.

"Please save our son, my love," Sophia implored softly as she turned to Lucas, silently pleading.

A surge of hopeful determination swelled within the King's heart as he unsheathed his sword.

"Kneel, Ambassador Deon," Lucas commanded, his voice resonating with renewed vigor.

Deon knelt, his gaze meeting Zelana's. *I'm one step closer to you,* a silent vow echoed within him.

Zelana watched him with pride, her eyes shining with admiration. *You were born to lead, Deon.*

Lucas placed the cold steel of his sword on his shoulder, imbuing the act with ceremonial significance.

"I, King Lucas Celeste of Zelonia, hereby bestow upon you the prestigious title of Commander of the Zelonian army," he proclaimed with authority. "From this day forth, you are charged with the duty to serve and protect Zelonia with your life. Will you accept this commandment, Ambassador Deon?"

"I accept your decree and will serve and protect Zelonia all of my days, my King," Deon vowed without a trace of hesitation, proud to accept the profound responsibility offered to him, letting it rest comfortably upon his shoulders.

"Royal councilmen of Zelonia, please welcome our newest Commander, Deon Vang," the King announced, prompting a surge of applause from the assembled dignitaries. "You may rise."

Deon stood with pride, bearing the title of a Zelonian Commander, his stature elevated within weeks.

Lucas observed Deon as he sheathed his sword, feeling empowered to have a man of his talent serving under him, and the applause faded into a respectful silence.

"Commander Deon, I entrust the Royal Guards to your command for this mission," Lucas declared with confidence. "They are well-trained and battle-hardened; I am certain they will perform admirably under your leadership."

"Thank you, your Majesty," Deon nodded respectfully and wasted no time. "I wish to convene with the key members of the Royal Guards at once to strategize our approach."

Lucas gestured to Rowan, standing off to the side. "Commander Rowan is my Lead Royal Guard. He will assist you with the transition."

"We are honored and prepared to follow your lead, Commander Deon," Rowan stated, stepping forward. "The Royal Guards are assembled in the interior parts of the castle. Please, follow me."

Deon glanced briefly toward Zelana, his gaze lingering of a silent promise, before turning and following Rowan, stepping into his new role with a determined and purposeful stride.

CHAPTER SIXTY

EXPECTATIONS

AFTER THE COUNCIL members departed, Lucas approached his daughter with an inquisitive eye.

"You've managed to secure Deon's allegiance remarkably quick. Is there something more we should be aware of?" the King asked with a hint of suspicion.

"I'm not sure I follow, Father," Zelana responded, feigning ignorance.

"Why would Deon seek your permission?" Lucas pressed, intrigued by the visible bond between them.

A subtle smile graced her lips. "Deon has pledged to serve and protect me. His loyalty is mine."

"And what might that encompass?" the King continued, delving deeper.

"I'm not quite sure myself, but I assume he is bound to fulfill any request I make of him," she answered with a subtle smile, her eyes gleaming with the countless possibilities.

The King took a step forward, his demeanor growing solemn. "Do you remember the counsel your mother and I gave you about relationships between Royals and commoners?" he asked, hinting at the longstanding societal norms.

Zelana nodded, reciting the age-old wisdom, "Admire the man with my eyes but safeguard my heart."

"You must remember that you are not simply human, but an elite human Princess and a demi-goddess. You are destined to join hands with a King through marriage, strengthening Zelonia and supporting Samuel's future reign. This is the only way you can honor our distinguished lineage," Lucas affirmed with steadfast conviction.

"But Mother wasn't of royal birth before marrying you," Zelana countered, pointing out the inconsistency in her father's stance with his own life choice. "My support for Samuel would be most impactful if I stayed in Zelonia."

"Our marriage was ordained by our shared divinity," the King disclosed, his face etched with his sacrifice of duty over love.

Sophia rose gracefully, joining the conversation. "I was the mortal offspring of Azar, the God of War, born to a mortal woman, and your father was the only son of Goddess Alexi and King Merci. Our pure celestial blood has endowed you and Samuel with godlike strength, swift healing, and immunity to Immortal compel."

"It's unlikely we can find others with our unique lineage beyond our borders," Zelana murmured softly.

"That's precisely why you must marry a Crown Prince or reigning King," Lucas asserted resolutely.

"Is that why you granted Crown Prince Zhong permission to court me without consulting with me first?" she inquired, still hurt and upset.

"Crown Prince Zhong is the future King of Sanshe. He's a fine young man, adept in both leadership and battle," Lucas reasoned. "What more could you seek in a suitor?"

"Love," Zelana whispered, her word a quiet plea for understanding. "You both promised me that we would discuss my future together before deciding. What changed?"

"You have rejected every Crown Prince who has visited and proposed," Lucas noted, his patience wearing thin.

"I refuse to settle for someone who doesn't move my heart," Zelana responded, her resolve unwavering in her views on marriage and courtship.

The King's voice sharpened, "And yet, you entertain the idea of a Lord? A man destined to serve under Crown Prince Zhong for his lifetime?"

"I am fully aware of his social standing and the expectations placed upon me," Zelana asserted, addressing her parents with great passion. "I'm merely asking you not to dismiss Commander Deon so hastily."

Her eyes were alight with the intensity of her feelings as she pressed on. "He is truly an exceptional man—embodying virtues that distinguish him from the Crown Princes I have encountered over the years. Should our feelings deepen, you would be blessed to have someone of his caliber and talent as your son-in-law."

"Commander Deon's merits are indeed commendable. Were he of royal birth, we would not be having this discussion," Sophia interjected softly, echoing the bittersweet reality of royal obligations.

"It's disheartening to know that a man's worth is gauged solely by his birth and not his character or valor, especially one who risks his life for our family," she murmured, her eyes shimmering with tears.

"Do not speak to me with such insolence!" Lucas thundered, his temper flaring. "I was the first to see Commander Deon's potential, which is precisely why I appointed him as your mentor and rapidly promoted him. I assure you, I hold his contributions in high regard."

Zelana absorbed the force of her father's words, yet her heart was unable to deny Deon.

"My love, please calm down," Sophia interjected softly.

"My intention is not to diminish his worth, but to prevent you from entangling yourself in a futile romance that guarantees no future and will end in heartbreak—distracting you both from your destinies," the King continued, giving her no room for dissent.

"I understand," Zelana replied softly as she bowed and withdrew from the confrontation.

As she exited the room, her heart was heavy with the complexity of her emotions and expectations of her royal duty, a path she was unsure Deon could ever tread beside her.

CHAPTER SIXTY-ONE

The Royal Guard

ZELANA SAT CONTEMPLATIVELY by the water fountain in the courtyard as Natalie stood in silence. The Princess's thoughts swirled like the water's gentle flow, trying to understand her parents' concerns, yet she remained at a loss as she gazed into the rippling waters.

Her introspection was interrupted by the clinking of armor approaching. She glanced up, her eyes meeting the polished gleam of the Royal Guard's armor as he stood under the sun's rays, his presence imposing yet familiar. She rose to her feet, ready to step away.

"Where do you think you're going?" the Royal Guard asked playfully.

Zelana halted, recognizing his voice as she slowly turned to face him, her eyes narrowing slightly.

"Wherever you're going," she teased flirtatiously.

"Do you even know who stands before you?" he challenged as he stepped closer, his armor casting an elongated shadow across the cobblestone path.

"Dominic, perhaps..." she said, tilting her head slightly as her gaze pierced through the metallic visage that obscured his features.

"Try again," he responded, enjoying the playful interrogation and the mystery it presented.

Zelana smiled and guessed once more, "You must be Gaius."

"No," the Royal Guard denied with an air of amusement.

"I was going to say Crown Prince Zhong but he's not here," she teased as the guard hesitated, his façade briefly slipping as he cleared his throat.

"Have you been thinking about him?" the guard asked, his composure wavering.

"No. My mentor consumes much of my attention," she confessed, her eyes intense and searching, piercing through the gleam of his armor.

"What's your impression of your… mentor?" he asked as the air thickened with unspoken tension.

"I am touched by his unwavering commitment and passion in fulfilling his duties," she began, then paused in contemplation. "And I deeply value his desire to support my future as Queen… but…"

"Speak your mind, Princess," the guard requested, his gaze sharpening as he noted her hesitation.

"Sometimes I wish he could see me as more than just Zelonia's Princess," she confided softly, a trace of longing in her voice.

"You're beyond his reach, Princess, but he's easily within yours," he whispered back, his words subtly hinting at a power she wielded, one she didn't even realize she had.

Zelana immediately grasped onto his words and took a step forward, diminishing the distance between them as he remained in place. She paused and observed his signature, stoic composure. With a daring move, she reached out and gently touched his gleaming armor.

"You must return," she commanded, overwhelmed with emotions.

The Royal Guard lifted his hand and gently covered hers, caressing softly, making her heart flutter at the intimacy of his touch.

"Return to me," she added, her voice dropping to a sultry whisper.

"Always," the Royal Guard vowed, his voice rough with emotion.

Zelana rested her head on his chest, seeking the warmth she'd longed for since that day they fought.

Gently, he wrapped his arm around her, pulling her closer into his embrace. "Beside you is where I belong," he murmured softly, tightening his hold of her.

Zelana's heart quickened as she listened to the steady rhythm of his heartbeat, a sound that seemed to halt time as they stood wrapped in each other's presence.

From a distance, the somber call of the battle horn pierced the air, signaling the army's march.

"I must go," he whispered as he slowly unwound his arms from around her.

Their hands lingered together for a moment longer, then slowly slipped apart.

The Royal Guard bowed deeply, holding the pose with solemn respect, then turned to leave as Zelana watched his figure recede with a heavy heart.

"Only under disguise was he able to be honest with me," she whispered, a trace of sadness lining her words as Natalie nodded with a soft smile.

The revelation of his feelings—and the clarity of her own—left Zelana's heart as heavy as the armor he wore, feeling a profound helplessness that frightened her.

CHAPTER SIXTY-TWO

THE TRAP

DOMINIC, MASQUERADING AS King Lucas, cautiously ventured deeper into the Fire Mines with Connor in tow. Their path was lit by the flickering light of their torches while Deon and his team slowly followed them in the shadows at a discreet distance. The Fire Mines were engulfed in a haze, with sporadic bursts of flames illuminating the rich veins of aluminum steel embedded in the walls.

Dominic and Connor followed the small path, leading them toward an open area in the middle of the large, circular cave. Deon's unit followed along the edge of the walls, silently killing the Immortals they encountered hiding in the dark crevices.

They reached the open space, eerily deserted, and halted in their steps.

"Crown Prince Samuel was being tortured right here this morning," Connor said, confused, breaking the oppressive silence.

The ominous quiet was soon shattered by the sound of growls as Dominic witnessed the gleaming red eyes of the Immortals in the dim light beginning to materialize from the shadowy recesses of the cave.

"I see them..." Dominic murmured, his voice tense, noticing their menacing presence closing in.

In a sudden surge of aggression, an Immortal sprang forward.

Dominic swiftly fired at the attacker. The effect was instantaneous; the encroaching creatures' advance stalled at the sound of the shots echoing through the cavernous space. The sight of their fallen comrade quickly spread fear among the Immortals.

The sound of gunshots signaled Deon's team to move swiftly through the shadows of the Fire Mines. Their approach was both silent and deadly as they confronted the Immortals with the sharp whisper of daggers slicing through the air with precision, followed by the soft thuds of bodies hitting the ground. The cave soon became a silent tomb, the quiet punctuated only by the faint groans of the dying.

Strangely, a grim silence filled the air and there was no more movement in the cave.

A single gunshot rang out, the signal for retreat.

Dominic and Connor hurried out of the cave, their footsteps echoing in the hollow space as their faces were illuminated by the flickering light of their torches. As they emerged into the cool night air, they saw Deon's and Rowan's teams already assembling.

"Were there any notable threats out here?" Deon scanned the scene, noticing only a handful of Krimzon bodies strewn across the ground.

"Nothing we couldn't handle," Rowan replied with a nonchalant shrug, wiping his sword clean.

"Back to Zelonia!" Deon shouted, leaping onto his horse as it swiftly galloped away.

The urgency in his voice spurred his Royal Guards into action. They mounted their steeds swiftly, their horses' hooves thundering against the ground in a rapid symphony through the dense forest.

Princess Zelana, I'm coming…

Deon's thoughts raced as the fear lurking in the back of his mind began to envelop him. He silently hoped and prayed that they were not too late.

CHAPTER SIXTY-THREE

The Chaos

ZELANA CLASPED HER trembling hands. Her heart pounded in fear as she and the other Princesses stood helpless on the castle balcony. Below them, the King and Queen—an embodiment of royal courage—stood fearlessly on the battlefield in front of General Gaius and the Crown Princes. Behind them, the Zelonian army lined up, prepared to confront the encroaching Immortals.

"May the Heavens shine upon us this night!" Lucas declared, his voice resonating across the battlefield.

"Blessings abound!" the Zelonians chanted the response prayer in unison.

The air was thick with tension as Marcus's voice boomed across the battlefield. "You were supposed to be at the Fire Mines, Lucas," he roared with chilling scorn. "Where's your so-called fatherly love now? I thought only Immortals were heartless. Seems we've rubbed off on you."

"You know nothing of a parent's love. Fortunately, you will never know its joy," Lucas shot back, unfazed, his words slicing through the air with as much force as any sword.

"Now that we know what kind of a father you are..." Marcus mused cruelly, unruffled by the King's insult, "let's see what kind of a King you show yourself to be in front of your men."

A cart rolled forward, revealing Samuel, bound and visibly broken, his once regal bearing reduced to a pitiable state of defeat with his unkempt appearance and downcast head.

"Samuel..." Sophia's voice broke out in a heart-wrenching whisper, her eyes filled with a mother's anguish as she beheld her son's wretched form.

Gasps of horror rippled through the Zelonian ranks.

"Crown Prince Samuel wasn't at the Fire Mines, as I suspected," Lucas said, maintaining his composure, attacking with psychological warfare. "I knew you'd try to deceive me again."

"What did you expect from me? I'm an Immortal, we're not known for our morals," Marcus chuckled darkly, mocking him.

Lucas clenched his fist. His attempt to unnerve the Krimzon King was met with cold indifference, failing to achieve its intended effect, while the safety of his son hung precariously in the balance.

"By the way, I didn't come for bloodshed. I came to trade his life for yours," Marcus declared, his voice dripping with calculated malice.

"I will give you one hundred chests of gold for my son," Lucas offered, visibly struggling.

"What am I going to do with gold?" Marcus taunted, laughing off the proposition with a smirk. "I will take you or the Queen. Both of you are graying and near death anyway. What's a few years when you can save Samuel, who might rule Zelonia for a few more decades."

"How do I know that if I surrender myself, you'll return my son?" the Queen asked in desperation.

"You don't..." Marcus replied with a sardonic smile while dismounting from his horse and ascending the cart where Samuel was bound. "You just have to pray to your gods that I keep my end of the deal."

The Queen's descent from her horse was swift and powerful, causing the earth beneath her to tremble.

"Don't go, Sophia," Lucas commanded, but she continued walking, her gaze fixed on their son's helpless form, ready to sacrifice everything.

With a heavy heart and slow, determined steps, Sophia advanced toward the Krimzon army. Anxiety pulsed through her chest as she halted before the Krimzonites, casting a final, lingering glance at her husband. In that silent exchange, love, regret, and unspoken words bridged the distance between them, filling the air with a bittersweet understanding.

"I'm sorry..." she murmured as Lucas looked upon her helplessly.

Sophia turned back and faced the Krimzon army, crossing the threshold.

"Your mother is coming to save you," Marcus smirked wickedly, lifting the Crown Prince's head so he could see her approaching.

Tears slid down Samuel's face as he mustered the last of his strength and cried out, "Goddess Alexi's bloodline will live forever!"

His defiant scream echoed across the battlefield, inspiring all those who heard it.

Without warning, the sky became ablaze with flaming arrows, casting a hellish glow over the battlefield, raining down upon Krimzonites from behind.

Sophia lunged forward, her movements swift and desperate. With heavenly strength born to elite humans, she tore Samuel free from the ropes that bound him and threw his body toward the Zelonian lines in a desperate bid to save him.

Marcus quickly ensnared Sophia in his grasp, a triumphant smirk on his lips. "I think you may have just killed him," he sneered, tightening his grip on her with a deathly embrace.

As Samuel soared through the air, Lucas sprang up with godlike speed, catching Samuel mid-air and landing on the ground, sending ripples through the earth. The Zelonian army watched in awe at the celestial display of power, emboldening them to fight the encroaching evil with renewed vigor and courage.

"Attack!" Lucas's command thundered, unleashing the Zelonian army's fury upon the Immortals.

The Zelonian forces surged across the battlefield, the earth trembling beneath their powerful advance. The armies clashed and blood was swiftly spilled, staining the ground a deep crimson.

Amidst the chaos, Zelana's heart sank as she witnessed Marcus subdue her mother. His monstrous fangs pierced the Queen's neck, draining the life force from her once-vibrant form.

Jenessa shuddered beside Zelana. "The Immortals… they're ferocious," she whispered, her voice quivering in fear.

Anika clutched onto Jenessa, tears streaming down her face. "The Queen… she sacrificed herself to save Crown Prince Samuel."

"My mother would do anything for us," Zelana whispered, tears blurring her vision as she stood paralyzed by the nightmare unfolding before her.

"How are the Immortals so strong?" Kalina murmured, awestruck at the horror on the battlefield.

Zelana's heart pounded intensely, watching with bated breath. The Krimzon army was being squeezed between the might of the Zelonian main forces and the strategic assault from behind by the Royal Guards. She could see the battle lines shifting and the night sky intermittently lighting up with bursts of light. She squinted and realized it was gunfire sparking in the distance, signaling Deon's presence as he relentlessly pursued Marcus, who had taken her mother on horseback.

"I see Commander Deon!" Zelana exclaimed, her voice trembling, a surge of relief washing over her.

"Where?" Kalina asked, her eyes widening in surprise as she frantically searched the battlefield.

"Do you see the lights sparking over there?" Zelana pointed toward the bursts of gunfire. "That's his pistol! It's him—Commander Deon!"

Jenessa and Anika's gazes followed the path of Zelana's outstretched hand.

"I see it!" Anika whispered, her voice filled with awe. "He's leading the Royal Guards!"

"Do you think he can get to the Queen in time?" Kalina asked, the tension in her voice clear.

"He has to," Zelana replied, her heart swelling with hope. "He's the only one who can."

"Look! The flashes are moving toward the forest," Jenessa gasped, clutching onto Anika's arm.

Zelana's heart pounded wildly in her chest, her fingers tightening on the stone railing. "The Krimzonites are retreating…"

The Princesses' eyes remained fixed on the distant, glowing bursts of Deon's relentless advance.

The Krimzon forces dwindled under the coordinated attack, retreating toward the forest. In a strategic move, they parted to create a pathway to allow Marcus, with Queen Sophia in his grasp, to make his escape. As soon as he passed through, the path immediately sealed shut, forming a defensive wall designed to block the Zelonian Royal Guards' pursuit.

"What a coward! He used his forces to retreat," Zelana whispered angrily, tears welling in her eyes.

Anika placed a comforting hand on her arm, her expression tense yet compassionate. "It's not over yet. The Zelonian forces are still fighting."

"I don't see the bursts of light anymore," Kalina added softly, leaning into Zelana for comfort.

"Don't lose hope," Jenessa murmured, tightening her arm around Zelana's shoulder.

Tears slid silently down Zelana's face as she stood, forlorn and powerless, her gaze lingering on the battlefield that had once held so much hope.

Behind the protection of his army, the King of Krimzon slowed his horse to a halt, turning around, his expression smug with a sly smirk.

"Come if you dare..." Marcus taunted, his voice dripping with cruel amusement, staring straight at the Zelonian Commander, baiting him to follow and lead the Royal Guards into a perilous trap.

Deon reined in his horse, his eyes locked on Marcus through the narrow slits of his helmet.

"Halt!" His authoritative voice sliced through the chaos on the battlefield, his order swift and decisive.

The Royal Guards, trained to obey without hesitation, immediately ceased their advance, their momentum grinding to a reluctant stop.

"But they have the Queen!" Rowan exclaimed, his voice strained, his hands twitching on his reins as he yearned to push forward.

Deon's jaw clenched, his discipline holding firm, though inside he felt the same desperation gnawing at him that Rowan couldn't hide. It clawed at him, urging him to act, to chase after the Krimzonites who retreated methodically into the protective shadows of the forest. His heart screamed to push forward, but his mind fought to stay in control—one reckless command and they would all be lost.

"Death awaits us in that forest," Deon responded, his voice heavy with the weight of the decision. "We must live to fight another day."

"Commander Deon is right, we don't know what's waiting for us in there," Dominic said, supporting Deon's decision, his gaze shifting to Rowan. "It could be a death trap."

Rowan grunted under his breath, clearly upset as the distant sound of a horn pierced the air, its mournful call signaling the retreat of the Zelonian army.

Deon's gaze drifted toward the castle. He could see the silhouettes of the Princesses standing on the balcony, their figures illuminated by the pale moonlight, feeling their eyes on him.

I'm sorry I couldn't get to her, Princess, he whispered silently, failure constricting his every breath.

The horn sounded again. "Back to the castle!" he commanded with a heavy heart.

Sheathing his sword, Deon withdrew from the ravaged battlefield. The Royal Guards mirrored his movements, their armor clinking softly in the night air as they departed, leaving behind the haunting remnants of the night's violent clash—the blood-soaked ground and those lives, forever gone.

On the cold stone balcony, Zelana stood motionless beside her friends, the knot in her chest tightening, her heart gripped with anguish as her thoughts spiraled to her mother, now a prisoner in the hands of the Krimzon King. She feared for her mother's fate in the days ahead, draped in darkness. Each passing moment deepened her dread, wondering how her mother would endure the cruelty of their enemy.

Down below, Deon dismounted his horse, his gaze sweeping across the battlefield. He felt distraught as a sinking realization hit him—Zelonia wasn't as invincible as he had once believed. Watching the somber withdrawal of Zelonia's army was disheartening. The future felt uncertain and fragile as the once thundering battlefield was now a graveyard of fallen bodies and flickering torches. The silence was eerie, broken only by the soft rustle of wind carrying the scent of blood and smoke.

Something gnawed at Zelana's heart as she stood on the balcony and her eyes traced the slow exodus of her kingdom's forces. It felt more than a military defeat—it was a bitter, foreboding loss. The darkness creeped ever closer to Zelonia, threatening to endanger not only her kingdom but the survival of humanity in Azalon.

CHAPTER SIXTY-FOUR

The Holy Ring

THE DOOR TO the meeting hall swung open, revealing Lucas and the members of the Royal Council already deep in conversation about potential strategies to rescue the Queen. The urgency of their dialogue filled the air until they noticed the Princesses present, prompting an abrupt pause. The young women, sensing the gravity of the situation, quickly exited the room.

"See to it that your brother is being cared for," the King urged, frustration clear in the lines etched across his face.

"Don't worry, Father," Zelana assured him, swiftly making her way toward the door.

As she stepped into the corridor, she unexpectedly came face-to-face with Deon. His figure was marred by the battle—blood smeared across his face, armor, and hands.

Deon gazed into her tear-streaked face, his heart heavy with guilt. "I failed you."

"No... you did what you could," she said softly, trying to be strong for him.

"I'm so sorry..." his voice barely escaped his lips, his eyes dark with anguish. "If I had been alone, I would have chased Marcus all the way to Krimzon, but I couldn't lead the Royal Guards into that forest... knowing—" his words faltered, caught in his throat.

"It was a trap," Zelana completed his thought, her heart aching at the torment etched across his face. "You made the right decision. Don't *ever* doubt yourself on the battlefield, Deon."

A long breath left his chest, her words lifting some of the burden he carried. "I will rescue your mother, no matter what it takes," he vowed, his eyes a quiet fury.

"I know you will," she replied, her confidence unwavering.

Deon reached for her hand, gently caressing it, savoring her touch. "I have to go."

Zelana nodded as he reluctantly let go, slipping into the war room. The heavy door shut behind him, leaving her standing in the silence of the corridor. She sighed softly, gathering herself before heading toward the medical hall to tend to her brother.

Inside the chamber, Deon sat down, his eyes scanning the faces of the Royal Council engaged in a grave discussion of strategy.

Lucas turned to Gaius, his expression taut with concern. "How many men did we lose?"

Gaius's face grew somber. "Less than one hundred, Your Majesty," he reported.

Lucas exhaled deeply, his heart heavy, thinking of the costs of war. "It's tragic nonetheless."

"Krimzon attacked us without warning," Gaius replied with a firm tone. "We'll be prepared next time."

Nodding slightly, Lucas shifted his gaze to Deon. "How many casualties to the Royal Guard?"

"A few injuries, but zero casualties, my King," Deon responded with a grim expression.

The King's eyes flickered with surprise. "That's a relief."

"Any life lost is a wound to us all and the Queen is in their clutches," Deon remarked remorsefully.

"Because you ordered us to back down!" Rowan blurted out, his voice tight with resentment. "We were so close to saving her."

Deon turned to him, his expression calm and assured. "If we had entered that forest, none of us would have survived," he replied, his tone leaving no room for doubt.

Rowan's eyes flashed with anger. "You don't know that. Maybe you just don't care enough about the royal family since you're not from Zelonia," he sneered, his emotions spilling over.

Deon's gaze sharpened as he locked eyes with Rowan. "I take my oaths seriously," his voice was controlled, but he responded fiercely. "Do not question my loyalty."

"If you had to choose between King Lucas and King MuaYeng, you'd side with the Sanshe King without a doubt," Rowan pressed, undeterred.

"That's enough!" Lucas's voice cut through the tension, rubbing his forehead in frustration. "We are not enemies here. We cannot afford division."

Dominic spoke up. "I supported Commander Deon's decision. Leading us into that forest would've been reckless. Marcus is cunning, and it's clear he had contingencies in place. He lured us to the Fire Mines and attacked Zelonia simultaneously. It's clear he's an adversary we must approach with extreme caution."

"We can save the Queen if we commence a full, frontal attack on Krimzon as day breaks," Makeo suggested, his face flushed with anger and determination, the rage in his voice igniting the room.

"Being careless would result in mass casualties on our side," Gaius warned. "We cannot underestimate the Immortals. They have the power to compel our men and turn them against us."

"They can compel two—three at most at a time. And, they are powerless during the day," Makeo stated, insisting they had the advantage.

"True, but the Krimzon King will undoubtedly keep the Queen in the darkest dungeon," Gaius remarked, highlighting another concern. "We would have to penetrate their stronghold, enter their feeding dens, and who knows what horror awaits us inside."

"If we do not show strength, they will keep provoking us, gradually weakening our resolve until they can completely annihilate us," Rowan added, his voice rising, supporting Makeo's proposal.

"I have to agree with the General," Dominic stood firm, backing his comrade. "A blind assault is too risky. We need a well-thought-out plan."

"Are you suggesting we let the Queen die?" Makeo challenged, attempting to provoke the King's wrath as he glanced around the room.

"Don't you dare try to twist my words!" Gaius snapped back vehemently, his usual composure shattered in the heat of the escalating argument.

The tension in the room rose, each man standing at the precipice of his patience.

Suddenly, Deon's voice broke through the chaos. "Allow me to go to Krimzon alone and rescue the Queen." His words silenced the room instantly. "It will minimize our casualties. Marcus will be expecting an army, not someone solo."

Deon's proposal was met with silence at first, a pause too long to ignore as the Royal Council exchanged wary glances.

Rowan scoffed. "One man against the heart of Krimzon? You

can't be serious, Commander Deon. This is a suicide mission and you know it."

Deon met Rowan's skepticism with unwavering calm. "I've studied their movements. They won't see it coming and I have an advantage—Marcus has never seen my face although I've fought him countless times. I can blend in with the Krimzon people, gather intelligence on where they're holding the Queen, and during the day—when they're vulnerable—I'll break into the dungeon with my mechanical arms and free her. We'll be back in Zelonia before nightfall."

The room was engulfed in heavy silence as all eyes turned toward Deon, his plan sinking in.

A grin tugged at the corner of Dominic's mouth, finally breaking the tension. "When did you come up with this plan?"

"While you all were having the heated conversation," Deon replied with a small smile.

"Under Commander Deon's leadership today, the Royal Guards suffered zero casualties. His success was due to well-prepared contingency plans, prioritizing human life over reckless sacrifice," Dominic stated, his words subtly reinforcing Deon's proposition. "I believe we should support Commander Deon's mission to Krimzon, and I'll accompany him, of course."

Makeo and Gaius exchanged glances and nodded in agreement, while Rowan sighed deeply, shaking his head in disbelief at the idea.

"So, what's the contingency plan?" Lucas asked, curious about his thoughts.

"If Commander Dominic joins me, he can wait at Northern Village with the horses, ready for a swift retreat once the Queen is rescued," Deon explained. "If I don't return within three days—though I aim to be quicker—he'll inform General Gaius, who will have the Zelonian army on stand-by in the mountains, prepared to launch an attack. How does that sound?"

Lucas paused to contemplate the plan. "You continue to surprise me, Commander Deon."

Rowan, not yet convinced, raised a critical question. "And what happens if they catch you and compel you to reveal everything? We'd be walking into a trap."

Deon paused for a moment, then raised his right hand, revealing a diamond ring that glinted with an otherworldly sheen. "I'm immune to the Immortals' compulsion," he shared.

A collective gasp rippled through the room.

"I remember my mother telling me once," Lucas said, eyeing the ring closely, "that she gifted King VangKong of Sanshe four Holy Rings, forged from her divine blood, to prevent him and his entourage from being compelled during the village wars. I've never seen one until now."

"Without that ring, Krimzon would've turned Commander Deon into their war machine," Dominic teased with a smile.

"You could take me down easily," Deon said with a grin, glancing at Dominic, sensing he had made a new friend as Dominic chuckled at his remark. "I'll go to the armory and prepare some explosives."

"I'll join you," Dominic replied, rising to his feet.

The tension in the room seemed to ease, only to be shattered by a voice calling from the balcony.

"King Lucas of Zelonia!"

The abrupt summoning made the men exchange uneasy glances before moving slowly toward the balcony, a sense of dread creeping into their steps. As they stepped onto the balcony, the grim scene unfurled before their eyes—the Queen's lifeless body was laid out on a cart in the open field below—her once regal presence reduced to a chilling stillness—flanked by two Immortals on horseback. Their silhouettes loomed like dark harbingers of death against the moonlit sky.

Lucas stared down at the woman he loved—his Queen, now nothing more than a motionless shadow of her former self, his mind struggling to accept the horrific image before him.

It couldn't be.

The King's legs weakened, his knees buckling under the weight of his unbearable grief as Dominic and Deon rushed to his side, steadying him firmly with their hands.

"My Sophia..." Lucas's voice trembled, a fragile whisper of disbelief, his heart breaking.

"King Marcus sends his greetings," Julian, an Immortal Guard, intoned with a chilling calm, shattering the thick silence. "Your Queen has served him well. He returns her body to you in gratitude."

The words were a cold mockery, each syllable a cruel jab at Lucas's shattering heart.

"The end of Krimzon is coming!" Lucas's anguished threat reverberated through the air, echoing across the field, a raw expression of pain and fury that resonated with the hearts of all who heard.

The Immortal Guards absorbed King Lucas's ominous declaration of war, exchanging a brief glance, unfazed, as they turned and guided their horses away. They faded into the shadows, their silhouettes gradually blending into the encroaching darkness of the night.

CHAPTER SIXTY-FIVE

Blood Rings

THE KRIMZON PLEASURE Lounge was a realm of sensuous shadows and forbidden luxuries, reserved for the elite and those of royal blood. Sheer curtains, reminiscent of veils of secrecy, cascaded from tall posts, the room exuding a predatory elegance, cloaked in the seductive interplay of red and black.

Luxurious black leather sofas sprawled across the room, scattered with pillows in the same lurid colors, inviting the occupants to surrender to comfort and excess. Along the walls were beds draped with canopies, their secluded allure promising realms of private pleasure and whispered secrets, each a stage for the night's more intimate escapades.

At the heart of this decadent chamber lay a polished marble floor, starkly contrasting with the darker tones that dominated the room. In its center stood a stage, crowned with a solitary pole that gleamed under the muted light, hinting at the nocturnal entertainments that captivated the Krimzon court, catering to their darker desires.

Marcus reveled in the nightly indulgences the lounge offered, surrounded by his fellow princes and his confidant, Lorenzo. Together, they immersed themselves in carnal pleasure and the allure of blood, satisfying their immortal cravings. Yet, this night promised a departure from their routine as the atmosphere was filled with anticipation and an unusual restlessness.

"What is this Blood ring supposed to do for us?" Vijay asked, his brow furrowing in skepticism.

Prince Vijay Kumar was another Ancient One, an Immortal of the esteemed Kumar royal family. He was once a Ferrian Prince, the younger brother of the Ferrian King who negotiated with Maldev, a dark entity spawned from the depths of Hell, for the elusive gift of immortality.

A sly smirk crept onto Marcus's lips. "Maldev assured me that if we possess these rings, the chill of our undead existence will fade, and rich human emotions will be ours once more."

"Can we walk amongst humans under the sun?" Lorenzo asked, his eyes narrowing. The prospect ignited a spark of hope in his ancient eyes.

"He promised protection from the sun's wrath," the King replied with a confident nod. "We could even indulge in the luxury of sleeping on beds once again."

"I'm going crazy waiting like this," Caspian voiced as he began pacing the room, eager for the promised transformation that lingered tantalizingly just out of reach.

"Patience..." Marcus murmured as he settled beside Lorenzo on the expansive sofa, eyeing him.

Crown Prince Caspian Ravenshadow was an Ancient One and a native of the Krimzon Kingdom, descended from a royal lineage rooted in the southern region of the realm. His family was coerced to forge an alliance with the northern territories, uniting under the rule of King Theo Chamberlain.

"What is taking Dimitri so long?" asked Roland, echoing Caspian's urgency. He hailed from Iron Glades, the eldest of three brothers who were transformed a century ago. He was the last of the Silverbane family, his brothers dying in various Krimzon wars.

The atmosphere in the Pleasure Lounge shifted noticeably as the door swung open, revealing Dimitri, a distinguished leader of the Krimzon Knight's Men.

"Here's the man of the hour," Caspian's voice cut through the tense silence excitedly.

Dimitri Dragomir was an Officer in the Frostwald military before being captured and compelled to serve the Krimzon Kingdom. After ten years of service, he was no longer under compulsion but chose to continue serving Krimzon as a Knight's Man, driven by his own volition.

The Knight's Men of Krimzon Kingdom were human warriors, distinguished by their valor and unwavering loyalty. They were entrusted with leading battles, executing critical missions, and safeguarding the kingdom's interests, forming the backbone of the kingdom's human military elite. Selection into their ranks was based on combat prowess—Knight's Men were often the sole survivors of grueling arena tournaments or those who demonstrated exceptional bravery on the battlefield.

Dimitri made his way toward them, addressing Marcus with a deferential bow. "My King, I have your Blood rings," he said, presenting the coveted items to him.

The men observed with envy and curiosity as Marcus took the eight rings, his gaze fixated on their gleaming ruby red surface. With a chuckle of anticipation, he slipped one of the Blood rings onto his finger and a warmth surged up his arm. His expression morphed from excitement to stunned wonder as the metal seemed to meld with his skin, throbbing as though it were alive.

"Yes..." Marcus murmured softly, his eyes wide with awe, feeling the Blood ring's power surge through him, warm and invigorating, tingling across his skin and re-configuring his undead form.

His heart hammered in his chest, every breath deep and sharp. His veins pulsed with new life, each beat awakening urges long buried. Carnal desires flared to life, blood rushing to his groin. The transformation was all-consuming, flooding him with the raw intensity of human sensations and desires he once thought had been lost forever.

"You seem to be in agony," Vijay remarked, observing the King with concern.

"I feel reborn," Marcus corrected him, marveling at the texture of his skin, already smoother.

"And there's a flush to your cheeks now," Lorenzo observed with a wicked smile.

A light chuckle escaped Marcus as he glanced down at the rings in his palm. "Why are there only eight?"

"Queen Sophia's blood only yielded this many," Dimitri replied, conveying the unsettling results. "I witnessed Maldev drain every last drop from the Queen's body myself."

Dimitri's thoughts returned to that frightful moment when he stood in the Blazen Caves in the south, in front of the fiery lake with Sophia unconscious in his arms.

"Almighty Maldev, Krimzon calls," he announced, his voice echoing through the dark, smoky cavern.

Suddenly, a monstrous beast manifested from the flames of the lake, its grotesque form towering above them. "Queen Sophia..." Maldev chuckled wickedly, his delight unmistakable.

He willed her limp body from Dimitri's grasp. Her unconscious form floated above the blazing lake, suspended in a sinister haze. "Wake..." he commanded, his voice deep and malevolent.

Sophia's eyes fluttered open. "Maldev..." she whispered, clearly frightened.

His dark laughter reverberated through the cave. "Azar, your flesh and blood is mine," Maldev declared, slashing her arms with his pointed nails.

Blood spilled from her wounds, falling into the fiery lake below.

"What evil deed are you doing with my blood?" Sophia demanded, glaring into Maldev's red eyes.

"You will aid in angering the gods, destroying everything beautiful in Azalon," Maldev sneered, his tone filled with a dark promise.

Dimitri remembered shuddering at the words, a growing dread gnawing at him.

"Azar will not let that happen," Sophia countered fiercely despite her visibly weakening body.

Maldev chuckled once more, a deep, chilling sound. "Krimzonites will return to their human forms and bring terror to Azalon, day and night. No one will ever know peace again."

"Azar, hear me now! I need you, Father!" she cried out, tears brimming in her eyes, looking desperately toward the Heavens.

"Azar has been punished for bringing you into this world. He's become deaf and blind for years," Maldev sneered, but as his words hung in the air, a faint ray of light pierced through the stone walls, illuminating Sophia in a warm, divine glow.

Dimitri and Julian had slowly backed away, in awe at the scene.

"Gods of the Heavens, shine your light upon Azalon once more. Evil has been unleashed on the land you created with love and light,"

Sophia prayed, her tears falling as the light brightened, enveloping her in a radiant aura.

Maldev's furious roar reverberated through the cave, shaking the very walls as Dimitri witnessed his sharp claws slash across her throat, blood spilling in a vicious arc.

Sophia's head drooped forward. Like the final flicker of a candle flame in the darkness, her breath escaped her lips in a soft, broken whisper…

"Please… don't turn away from us…"

With a dark growl, Maldev hurled her body to the ground beside Dimitri as he saw the divine light around her slowly dim and vanish as her life faded.

"Goshnosh Zathem!" Maldev bellowed.

From the fires, eight ruby rings rose, floating toward Dimitri. His hands trembled as he accepted them.

"Bring these to Marcus and tell him to bring Lucas to me. I will forge eight more rings from him," Maldev commanded, his voice laced with malevolence.

"As you command, Mighty One," Dimitri had replied, his heart racing with fear, head bowed, and the evil before him vanished.

Julian picked up the Queen's lifeless body while Dimitri turned and left in haste.

"Any last words from Maldev, Dimitri?" Marcus asked, staring at him, seemingly distant.

His words broke into Dimitri's thoughts as he returned to the present. "Yes, he wanted me to convey that he will provide eight more rings once you deliver King Lucas to him."

Marcus's expression darkened, disappointment clear in his tone. "It's unfortunate Samuel's blood wasn't pure enough," he grunted, his frustration simmering beneath the surface.

"I want my ring," Caspian demanded, extending his hand eagerly.

Marcus's hand clenched shut as he rose, his imposing figure standing over the gathered princes.

"These are not gifts," Marcus sneered, his tone dripping with disdain, strangely feeling anger course through his veins. "You've all become complacent. Lorenzo and I are tired of providing for Krimzon."

The men were surprised by Marcus's words, clearly influenced by the Blood ring.

Caspian stood up, his eyes alight with a glint of curiosity. "I've stood by you through countless wars, my King," reminding Marcus of their shared battles.

"Not lately," Marcus shot back, cold and sharp.

"I have ensured a steady flow of women for your feedings," Vijay said, hoping to assert his value.

"And I've always executed all your commands, regardless of their nature," Roland chimed in, emphasizing his unyielding fidelity.

Marcus's gaze swept over them, feeling disappointed in the men for the first time in centuries as the princes each hoped to gain his favor.

"Seize a kingdom and you'll earn a Blood ring," Marcus declared, his tone darkening. "But betray me and I'll relinquish it. What follows... will make you beg for death."

The Princes stared at the King, confused, his declaration a stern reminder of the razor-thin line between favor and fall from grace in the Krimzon court.

"The Blood ring has changed you," noted Vijay, noticing his shift in demeanor.

Marcus smirked, feeling the raw power coursing through him. "You have no idea," he muttered, his voice darker, more dangerous. Even he marveled at the change—the rush of power, the fire in his veins. It was intoxicating.

"It has sharpened my senses to what goes on here," Marcus replied with a smirk.

The Princes stared at him with suspicious eyes, surrendering to the King's ultimatum and his demand for absolute loyalty. Slowly rising, they left the Pleasure Lounge in silent contemplation.

As the room emptied, Marcus slipped all the rings onto his fingers, embracing their power.

CHAPTER SIXTY-SIX

LUST

THE POWER OF the Blood ring had promised more than mere protection from the sun, reigniting the fiery depths of carnal pleasures Marcus once thought were forever dimmed by his immortality.

"Bring her in, Striker!" he called out with a mischievous look in his eyes.

The door swung open. A stunning woman with a fair complexion, long red hair, green eyes, and adorned in scant lingerie reluctantly walked in. Her eyes flashed with apprehension as the Immortal Guard ushered her deeper into the Pleasure Lounge. She stared at the Immortal she was brought to serve—he was much bigger in stature, and his eyes roamed over her body, as if he was human. She quickly braced herself for another feeding, something she had grown accustomed to since her arrival in Krimzon.

Marcus chuckled darkly as he approached the woman with evil intent. With a swift motion, he hoisted her over his shoulder as she gasped, surprised. He carried her to a bed, shrouded in sheer red and black curtains, and set her down.

"Please, be gentle," she pleaded, her voice quivering as the Immortal stared at her with a smirk.

"It's not my nature... to be gentle," he said, caressing her face with his fingers. "I am King Marcus."

You're the King?

Her mind raced as she trembled, surprised she had finally met him, after a year of serving so many Immortals.

You seem more human than the ruthless beast I thought you'd be.

"I will compel you and you will obey," his voice lowering to a hypnotic whisper.

As the words left his lips, she struggled to move, only to be restrained by the force of his compulsion.

"Undress for me," the King commanded.

What? Is this even a feeding?

Her heart pounded, scared, a desperate cry for freedom from his compulsion echoing in her mind as her hands moved on their own, removing her lingerie with him watching intently.

Marcus's breath grew heavier with desire as the straps of her bra slowly slipped from her shoulders, exposing her form. He strangely found himself appreciating her feminine body, something he hadn't taken notice of before he wore the Blood ring.

"You have beautiful skin," he marveled as his hands gently traced her curves, subtly squeezing, feeling her soft skin under his fingertips, rediscovering a sensation that had long eluded him for two centuries—unfamiliar cravings tugging at his groin.

His hands aren't cold like other Immortals, she noticed as a gasp escaped her. His touches were tender yet commanding, her body reacting to his every caress. *And he seems to find pleasure in exploring me…*

"Touch me," Marcus ordered, his voice heavy with yearning.

The woman obeyed, carefully unclasping his royal attire. Her fingers danced lightly across his broad chest and traced the contours of his muscular form.

Fully hardened, Marcus felt the full extent of his arousal—a raw and fierce primal craving surging within him—a stirring in his veins he had almost forgotten.

"On your back," Marcus commanded, his voice hoarse. The hunger was as unrestrained as his thirst for blood as his entire being pulsed with a visceral need.

Wait—he's not going to make love to me... is he? It's impossible!

Her mind screamed, yet she could see desire burning in his eyes. She fought hard to resist him, but her body betrayed her, compelled to obey as she laid down.

The King removed his underpants, slipping them off as her eyes widened to see him aroused. Her nervous gaze only emboldened him as he lifted her legs and immediately settled between them, drawing a sharp cry from her lips. With a satisfied smile, he continued a steady rhythmic dance of intimacy, savoring the emotions that were once lost to him returning in that moment.

The woman's initial cries softened into moans, soft praises of the profound sensations he evoked within her. Her body relaxed, giving in to the pleasure until her warmth constricted around him.

A rush of exhilaration ignited within him, emotions he had not felt in ages. "I miss this feeling."

"You're amazing, my King," she uttered breathlessly, the compulsion still gripping her flawlessly.

Marcus gasped for breath as his movements quickened, staring at her flushed face, fully immersing himself with the intense passions of mortal pleasures. His body was slick with sweat as he continued to make her moan with pleasure. A loud groan escaped him and he exhaled with satisfaction as he surrendered himself inside her, a release that felt more incredible than taking the life of a human being.

Marcus collapsed on top of her, breathless, holding her tightly to him as he rolled onto his back and gently pulling her with him, cradling her in his arms.

"What's your name?" he asked, feeling a strong attraction to her.

"Victoria..." she responded softly, her head resting lightly on his chest.

"Victoria..." he repeated, a small smile tugging at his lips.

"I can't get enough of you, my King," she whispered, unexpected words slipping from her lips.

For the first time in years, a flicker of insecurity stirred within him. "Tell me how you really feel," he demanded, his breath heavy with doubt as he gazed into her eyes.

"I wish you'd release me from compulsion," she admitted truthfully as he requested.

Marcus's heart sank at the sudden honesty. "I release you from my compulsion, Victoria," he said softly, sitting up and leaning his back to the wall, watching her closely as his power lifted from her.

"You're as ruthless as they say," she spat and sat up, covering herself as the spark returned to her eyes.

"A moment ago, you were telling me how you can't get enough of me," Marcus said, smirking.

"You compelled me to say words you'd never hear otherwise," Victoria shot back, her eyes briefly flickering over his naked form, a memory of Deon flashing painfully in her mind.

Marcus's expression darkened with intent. "I want you to be mine exclusively, Victoria."

Her brows furrowed, her thoughts racing. "What does that even mean?"

"You are not to feed or bed anyone but me," he explained, leaving no room for negotiation.

He... likes me. The thought was disturbing, but a glimmer of hope sparked in her eyes.

"Will you be exclusive to me?" she asked softly.

His eyes narrowed slightly. "No."

"How is that fair to me?" she blurted, her question lingering awkwardly in the air.

This one isn't very bright, he thought as he stared at her, finding her question absurd.

"I'm the King. You should be honored that I want you at all," he replied as he stood up, feeling annoyed for the first time in years, pulling on his robe. "There are plenty of women who would accept my offer without hesitation. Let's forget we ever had this conversation."

Victoria was surprised that her strategy of playing hard to get didn't work as she watched him walk away without a second glance.

"If you give me immortality, you can have me anytime you want," she called out to him as he halted and faced her, noticing her seductive gaze.

"Is that what you truly desire?" he asked, surprised by her boldness, taking a few steps toward her. "It requires you to live forever in darkness and thirst for blood the rest of your days," he paused, eyes narrowing. "Never feeling the pleasures of the flesh again."

"How did we just..." her voice trailed off, *have sex?*

Marcus showed her his hand, revealing the Blood rings he wore. "I have these. You won't have any."

Victoria stared at all the rings on his fingers. "You can always give me one."

He darkly chuckled. "You have to earn it, like everyone else."

Victoria watched him step away toward the spa, leaving her alone to contemplate his offer.

Reaching the spa, Marcus removed his robe and lowered himself into the warm water that trickled from the rocks above. Leaning back, he rested his head on the soft towel as a slow smile crept across his lips. His mind reveled in the thought of countless nights in the Pleasure Lounge, filled with unrestrained indulgence and extravagant pleasures stretching endlessly before him.

CHAPTER SIXTY-SEVEN

Queen Sophia

THE AFTERNOON SUN'S rays cast a stark contrast to the somber mood that enveloped the gathered crowd. Thousands had come, each bearing their own dark emptiness in their hearts, to honor and pay their final respects to Queen Sophia. Crafted with elegance befitting royalty, her coffin lay solemn and serene before them.

Zelana stood beside her father, her posture rigid with the effort of composed strength. Inside, she was crumbling, her heart yearning to retreat to the solitude of her chambers, to hide beneath the covers and pretend this was all just a terrible dream. Yet, she remained, her presence a pillar of support for her father and her people, even as her own sorrow threatened to overwhelm her.

Lucas's face was a mask of dignified grief as he approached the podium. The gathered crowd fell into a respectful silence, their eyes fixed on him as he prepared to speak. He cleared his throat gently, steadied himself with a deep breath and began to address the mourners, his voice carrying across the sea of bowed heads.

"We gather here under the warmth of the sun, which seems to defy the cold shadow that has fallen over our hearts with the loss of my beloved wife and the kingdom's mother, Queen Sophia, whose light has been prematurely extinguished by the darkness of our times. As your King, I stand before you, cloaked not in the garb of royalty, but in the shroud of mourning, for I have lost not just my Queen, but my love, my life's companion, and the very heart of our family.

"Queen Sophia was the embodiment of grace, compassion, and unwavering strength. Her spirit was as radiant as the dawn, casting a glow of love and warmth that touched the lives of all who had the privilege to know her. Her laughter a melody that resonated within the walls of our castle, a resounding echo in the silent chambers of my heart.

"To the world, she was a Queen whose counsel was sought and revered, whose benevolence knew no bounds. To Zelonia, she was a beacon of hope, a tireless advocate for the less fortunate, a voice for the voiceless, and a mother figure to the orphaned and downtrodden. She fought fiercely until the end as a Zelonian warrior, unyielding in her love for Zelonia and its people.

"As we stand at the crossroads of grief and memory, let us honor Queen Sophia's legacy by standing united with kindness and love intertwined in our lives. Queen Sophia may have departed from this earthly realm, but her spirit will forever dance in the breeze, whisper wisdom in the rustling leaves, and shine in the eternal starlight that watches over Zelonia."

Tears welled in Lucas's eyes as he turned to the Queen, his voice breaking as he said the final tribute.

"My Queen. My love... may your journey beyond be gentle, and may you find rest in the embrace of eternity, knowing you were deeply loved and will be eternally missed," he began, his tone a mix of reverence and profound sorrow. "Your King, your family, and your nation mourn your loss, enriched by the time we were blessed to share with you."

The afternoon light cast long shadows across the mourning crowd as a gentle breeze drifted through the assembly, carrying with it the faint, collective sobs of the people. It was as if the very wind itself mourned, whispering Sophia's name through the leaves of the trees that lined the royal burial ground.

Deon stood stoically on the other side of Lucas, his eyes occasionally darting to Princess Zelana. She was a shell of the confident young woman he had come to know. In the weeks since he had begun training her, she had always carried herself with an unspoken strength, a subtle smile of confidence gracing her features, as though she was untouchable by the world's darker realities. Now, her innocence had shattered, leaving her visibly broken, her tears unrestrained as she sought comfort in Natalie's embrace.

Deon felt a deep, helpless ache as he watched her. He had equipped her with battle tactics to overpower her enemies, combat skills to protect herself, and negotiation techniques to guard her realm. Yet, as he stood there, it became painfully clear that he could not teach her how to shield her heart from the ravages of loss. The sight of her in such despair tore at him and there was nothing he could do to ease the crushing weight of her grief, a gentle reminder of the limits of his guidance.

Kalina stood quietly beside her ailing mother, her eyes sweeping over the mourners. As she watched the procession, a complex blend of relief and grief welled up inside her, emotions she was careful to hide beneath a composed exterior. Though she mourned Queen Sophia's passing, there was another part of her that found satisfaction in the fragility of those who, before today, seemed so untouchable.

When her gaze fell on Zelana, silently observing the Princess in tears, she felt a flicker of something dark, something resentful and bitter stirring within her.

I have known loss longer than you, a quiet thought crept into Kalina's mind. *Finally, you get a taste of what it means to lose someone you thought would always be there.*

CHAPTER SIXTY-EIGHT

Crown Prince Samuel

AFTER THE SOMBER ceremony of Queen Sophia's burial, the King and Zelana, along with the members of the Royal Council, made their way to Samuel's bed chamber. As they entered, a disturbing sight greeted them—the Crown Prince was convulsing.

"My son, wake up," the King said, settling into a chair beside the bed and grasping his son's hand.

Zelana's heart throbbed with worry, sitting on the other side of the bed, placing her hand soothingly on her brother's arm. "Samuel, we're all here," she murmured softly.

At the sound of their familiar voices, Samuel's eyes fluttered open, the immediate panic subsiding as his gaze scanned their faces. A different kind of pain emerged as tears welled in his eyes.

"Where's mother?" he asked, his voice weak and fraught with concern.

"She's not feeling well, so she couldn't come see you," Lucas replied, the words heavy on his tongue, caught in the cruel bind of compassion and deception.

Zelana glanced at her father, her heart clenching, realizing he was shielding Samuel from further pain.

Lucas stared into his son's eyes, masking his emotional turmoil with a veneer of strength. "How are you feeling?" he asked with concern.

Samuel's voice was frail but calm, tears brimming in his eyes seeing their familiar faces. "I've never felt so weak in my life," he admitted, the vulnerability in his eyes contrasting his usual strong demeanor. "You have no idea how relieved I am to see all of you. I thought I was going to die."

His tears spilled over, tracing paths down his pale cheeks as Lucas's heart tightened at his son's distress. He quickly handed him a handkerchief, which the Crown Prince used to dab away the tears.

"You must have experienced something deeply traumatizing. Do you want to talk about it?" the King gently probed, sensing the dark shadows that haunted his son's gaze.

"The Immortals are the spawn of evil," he spoke, the recent horrors pressing against the forefront of his mind. "They trapped me in the Fire Mines and the Krimzon King... he fed off me."

The Royal Council remained silent yet pained as they slowly absorbed his recount.

Samuel paused before continuing. "The Immortals joined him and feasted on me like I was a banquet. They claimed they felt stronger, feeding off my elite blood," he murmured, his voice barely above a whisper as the memory of the events drained him further.

"Revenge will be ours," assured the King, his heart aching for his son's suffering as he turned to the others, his voice firm yet weary. "I think he needs to rest."

"Get well soon, Crown Prince Samuel," Gaius said, his voice steady and firm.

"You're tougher than anyone I know," Deon encouraged, giving him a reassuring pat on the shoulder.

"Thank you for coming," Samuel responded, his voice low but grateful.

The men nodded and exited the room, leaving the royal family alone.

Zelana observed her brother's frail, bedridden body sadly, a shadow of his former vigor. "I'll be back to check on you later. Do you need anything right now?" she asked, offering a subtle smile.

"You've done more than enough, Zelana. Get some rest," Samuel replied appreciatively.

"Good night you two," Zelana said, exhausted, as she rose to her feet and left the room.

Lucas lingered by the bedside. "Rest and regain your strength," he soothed, his words a balm to the lingering fear still haunting the Crown Prince.

"Father," Samuel's voice broke, a tremor of vulnerability betraying the depths of his shame. "There's something I couldn't bear to disclose in front of the others."

"What is it, son?" The King's voice was soft, his concern deepening.

A shudder ran through the Crown Prince's body as he gathered the strength to revisit the torment. "I had fallen unconscious because of my loss of blood. But when I awoke, I found myself on the ground, my limbs chained to the walls of the cave so I couldn't move."

The Crown Prince's breaths became shallow and labored. "Using his power, the Krimzon King compelled women... humans, to seduce me, leading to coerced fornication," he said, each word soaked in the pain of the memory.

"What a monstrous deed!" Lucas exclaimed at the chilling confession. A shadow of sorrow and outrage sparked in the King's eyes as he slowly absorbed the brutal exploitation his son suffered.

The Crown Prince took a deep, shaky breath, as if the very act of recounting the trauma sapped what little strength he had left. "King Marcus would force an herbal drink down my throat. It was tasteless, like water, but it would cause me to become aroused again and another woman would be forced upon me," his voice faltered, reflecting the depth of his violation and helplessness.

Lucas's brow furrowed in deep horror. "He wants to breed elite humans," he remarked grimly.

The evil plan drew a sharp intake of breath from Samuel.

"How many women were there?" the King asked with concern.

"Five... ten... I don't recall exactly," the Crown Prince admitted, his voice low and heavy with remorse, reminded of the abuse orchestrated by the Krimzon King.

"We'll figure out how we want to handle this," the King murmured, his tone conveying his disdain at the cruel logic behind the barbarity.

"I'm confident that you and mother will find a way to resolve this," Samuel said, his eyes dimmed.

"Rest assured, it will be taken care of," the King replied, retaining his composure. "Get some sleep now, my son. I need you back, stronger than before."

With a weak nod, Samuel's eyelids fluttered close, and after a moment, his breath grew heavier, sleep claiming him.

The King leaned back in the chair beside Samuel's bed—his form a silhouette in the dim light—contemplating his family's dilemma and the enormity of his kingdom's plight. He sighed heavily, his hand absently reaching for a book on the bedside table, a feeble attempt to distract his mind, if only for a moment. However, as he flipped through the pages aimlessly, his eyes skimmed the words without truly registering them. His thoughts, stubborn and unyielding, circled relentlessly back to the daunting challenges weighing on his shoulders.

Will I manage to fill the roles of both mother and father, providing the nurture and guidance my children so desperately need?

Can I find the women who could potentially be carrying my son's legacy?

How do I find the strength to lead Zelonia to victory when my heart is shattered?

Lucas pondered silently as tears welled up in his eyes, wrestling with himself as both a parent and a monarch, feeling the profound emptiness left by his wife's absence.

CHAPTER SIXTY-NINE

Lost

UNDER THE SOFT silver glow of the moonlight, Zelana wandered through the courtyard, her delicate footsteps echoing faintly on the ancient cobblestones. The cool night air carried the gentle scent of jasmine, stirring the memories that lay deep within her heart. Beside her, Natalie walked in respectful silence, sensing the melancholy that enveloped her Princess.

Zelana's gaze was distant, her mind adrift in a sea of memories of her mother, Queen Sophia. This courtyard, with its flowering vines and whispering fountains, had been one of their favorite retreats. As she walked, ghostly images of her mother—laughing as she chased a young Zelana through a shower of falling leaves—played before her eyes like scenes from a forgotten dream.

Nikolai followed at a discreet distance, the rustle of leaves under his feet muffled by the shadows of the towering oaks as he watched over the Princess, concerned for her overwhelming grief.

Suddenly, Zelana's pace slowed and she stopped near the bench where she and her mother had often sat, sharing stories and dreams. The air seemed to tremble with the echo of her mother's laughter—so vivid and warm that it wrapped around her like a comforting embrace. Her knees buckled and she collapsed to the ground, overcome by her longing and loss.

Nikolai gasped, rushing to her side, but breaking from the shadows, Deon sprinted across the courtyard reaching her first. He knelt beside her and gently lifted her into his arms.

"Princess Zelana, are you alright?" he asked softly, fearful and concerned for her well-being.

Zelana looked up, her eyes glistening with tears as she met his gaze. "It was so real, Deon," she whispered, her voice breaking. "I could hear my mother laughing just there, by the fountain. I thought… I really thought she was here until I remembered that she was taken from me."

Deon's heart clenched at her words as he held her closer. "Queen Sophia will always be with you, in your heart and in your memories."

Natalie placed a comforting hand on Zelana's shoulder, her presence a silent pillar of support.

Unbeknownst to them, Nikolai watched silently from the shadows, his heart breaking as he watched Deon lift Zelana up effortlessly and carry her across the courtyard.

A hopelessness crept into his thoughts. *I've lost her.*

Zelana leaned into Deon's embrace as she gazed up at him, tears streaming down her face. "How is it you're always here when I need you, Deon?"

"I promised I'd always be by your side," Deon reminded her, gazing into her eyes lovingly. "The path ahead may seem dark and hopeless, but always remember that you're not walking it alone. We will find the way through the darkness together."

His words brought more tears to her eyes as she sobbed into his chest, clinging to him tightly. Deon held her close, fighting to stay composed, determined to be her strength when she was weakened.

CHAPTER SEVENTY

Found

ON REACHING ZELANA'S room, Natalie quickly opened the door and Deon carried her inside, laying her down on her elegant bed. He took in her grand bedroom, a reflection of her regal status and refined taste. The high ceilings and soft, cream-colored walls made the space warm and inviting, while the luxurious red curtains added a vibrant contrast. The white furniture—including an ornate dresser and matching vanity—was intricately crafted and the majestic bed, with its gold sheets and plush pillows, invited relaxation. Bookshelves lined the walls, filled with works spanning ancient history to modern philosophy, accentuated by delicate roses that added a touch of natural beauty and fragrance.

Natalie drew the curtains close, enveloping the room in a warm, soothing dimness. Deon's eyes lingered on Zelana, his gaze filled with deep affection.

"Try to get some sleep. I'll see you in the morning," he whispered, his voice a comforting blanket in the silence of the night.

As he turned to leave, he felt her trembling fingers clasping his arm.

"Could you stay… just until I fall asleep?" she asked, her voice barely above a whisper.

Her vulnerability tugged at his heart. Without hesitation, he returned to her side, gently sitting on the edge of the bed and enclosing her hand in his, caressing it soothingly. "I'll stay as long as you need."

A subtle warmth swelled in her heart. "Are both of your parents still with you?"

Deon hesitated, his gaze dropping as memories surfaced. "My mother passed away when I was ten. She was very ill," he shared, his voice thick with emotion.

"I'm so sorry," Zelana whispered, her own heart heavy with the echo of his pain.

"Being born and dying... the two things that bring much joy and sorrow," Deon replied, his eyes meeting hers, a gentle strength in his gaze. "It took a long time to accept that I'd never see her again."

"It hurts so much," she admitted, the raw ache of her own loss still tearing at her heart.

"I'll be here for you through the grief, and I'll still be here when it begins to ease," he promised.

"What would I have done if I never met you? I can't imagine going through this alone," she said, a faint smile touching her lips amidst the sadness.

"You're stuck with me. You will never be alone again," he teased with a soft smirk.

A small smile graced Zelana's lips as she sat up and nestled herself against him, her head resting on his chest. He encircled his arms around her, holding her close, grateful to see even the slightest lift in her spirits as Natalie quietly withdrew to the adjoining room, leaving them alone. They remained in the warmth of each other's embrace, finding comfort in the silence together.

"Tell me about Sanshe..." she whispered softly.

"Sanshe..." he echoed, his mind drifting to his homeland. "She sits on the ocean, surrounded by lakes and rivers. We would have so much fun discovering the kingdom together."

"You speak as if you're not from there," Zelana teased, her smile widening.

Deon chuckled softly. "Being buried in royal duties most of my life, I've never truly taken the time to explore and appreciate its wonders."

Zelana gazed up at him, her voice wistful. "I'd love to get lost in Sanshe with you."

A sudden idea sparked in his mind. "Come with me, Princess. Picture us standing in front of the royal carriage as I offer you my hand to help you inside," Deon murmured, excitement lighting his eyes.

"Thank you, my Lord," she replied with a small giggle, playing along.

"Always," he smiled, his gaze lingering on her.

"Go on..." the Princess urged with enthusiasm.

"As you step inside, you sit on a luxurious, plush, maroon velvet seat. I join you, sitting..." he paused.

"Next to me," she completed his thought, her mind drifting away with his words.

"I sit beside you and we depart from the Zelonian castle at dusk, our royal carriage descending the hillside, surrounded by the sprawling green pastures that stretch endlessly toward the horizon," his voice weaved a captivating scene for her.

"Zelonia is truly beautiful," she sighed softly, fully immersed in the enchanting journey.

"Breathtaking," he agreed, continuing with a twinkle in his eyes. "As our carriage winds through the expansive flatlands, we find ourselves enveloped by dense forests, ancient guardians lining our path, leading us toward the rugged mountainous terrain ahead."

Her eyes glistened with wonder. "I've never seen mountains before…"

"I will take you there, Princess," he promised, his voice soft yet certain. "We climb the mountain pass and as we reach the top, we find the sun dipping below the peaks, painting the sky in strokes of amber and crimson."

"Such a mesmerizing view," her eyes lit up, enchanted by the vivid picture he painted.

"It truly is," he nodded with a smile. "Standing at the peak, we look down to see Eastern Village nestled in the lush valley, its lanterns flickering like stars come to rest on earth, encircled by the protective arms of the towering mountains. There, under the canopy of night, we rest for a few nights and enjoy the sights."

"Together…" she whispered wistfully, admiring the beauty of the scene he described.

"Always together…" he murmured, feeling a warmth fill his heart. "When dawn breaks the next morning, the air is crisp and invigorating as we continue our journey, crossing the mountain tops. And there, just as the sun crests the horizon, we encounter a majestic waterfall. It plunges with relentless force toward Eastern Village, a stunning display of nature's power—untamed and beautiful."

"I can hear the rush of the water as it flows thunderously down from the mountain," she whispered in awe, creating a vibrant imagery in her mind.

"I would love to swim under a waterfall one day," he said, his eyes lighting up at the thought.

"Count me in," she replied, her own smile mirroring his, captivated by such a peaceful escape.

"We then descend the mountain and come to a bridge that leads to Cherry Blossom, a village with tunnels of cherry trees, their blossoms a delicate canopy stretching above us," he murmured, sighing as the scenery reminded him of his father... of home.

"It's absolutely mesmerizing," she said softly, moved by the passion in his voice.

"Beyond Cherry Blossom, the landscape opens to rivers that flow into expansive lakes, their waters stretching eagerly toward the ocean. There, beside the ocean, lies Sanshe—a fortress of solitude and strength," he described, his voice deepening with emotion as they reached their destination.

"I can almost see the grandeur of Sanshe in all its splendor," she whispered, dreamily, envisioning the landscape he described. "Are there fireflies there?" she asked, painting a picture of twilight magic.

Deon's smile widened, touched by her imagination. "Yes, there are. How did you know?"

"I've read about them," she shared, her smile soft and reflective as her eyes fluttered shut, watching the enchanting scene in her mind. "They dance in the night like tiny stars, bringing light to dark places."

Deon grinned, awestruck by her poetic description. "Books open worlds."

"Mmmm..." she let out a soft murmur, melting into his embrace.

The room fell silent, the only sound being the gentle rhythm of Zelana's breathing as she drifted to sleep. He watched her, observing her peaceful face, a serene smile on his own lips. Carefully, he adjusted her position, making sure she was comfortable, and gently laid her down on the bed.

Deon pressed a tender kiss to her forehead, his lips lingering a moment, savoring her presence.

"Good night, Princess Zelana," he whispered, his voice barely a breath before standing up.

He cast one last look at her sleeping form and quietly slipped out of the room, closing the door softly behind him, leaving the Princess to her dreams under the watchful stars.

CHAPTER SEVENTY-ONE

DISAPPOINTED

AS THE MORNING sun rose over the training grounds, Deon was already deep into his routine, the clink of three water pails in each hand echoing quietly. The usual bustle of training was subdued, however, with Zelana notably absent.

Lucas arrived unexpectedly, with Dominic beside him, his brows furrowed in concern. "Where's the Princess?" he demanded, scanning the area.

"She had a difficult night," Deon replied, pausing his routine. "I believe she's resting."

"No one rests until the threat from the Krimzon Kingdom is neutralized," Lucas declared, his voice firm with resolve.

Deon stood up straight, facing the King with a respectful demeanor. "I understand your pain, my King, but Princess Zelana's health is crucial. She needs this time to heal, both in spirit and body."

Lucas's expression hardened. "It seems your emotions are clouding your judgment, Commander Deon," he said sharply. "When you accepted this role, you promised me and the Queen that your emotions would not interfere with her training. She must be pushed to her limits if she is to defend Zelonia effectively."

Deon fell silent, choosing not to argue.

"Follow me..." Lucas grabbed two wooden swords and walked off toward the royal courtyard, while Deon helplessly obliged.

CHAPTER SEVENTY-TWO

THE DUEL

IN THE QUIETUDE of the early morning within the royal courtyard, Natalie ascended the stairs to Zelana's quarters, her hands clutching a steaming cup of tea as she hurried.

"Natalie, inform the Princess to come out immediately," the King ordered, shattering the serene silence with his commanding voice.

With a silent nod, Natalie's pace quickened and vanished into the room. Moments later, Zelana emerged, her expression clouded with confusion and weariness as Natalie followed. Slowly, she moved toward her father and Deon, each step seeming to drain her.

"Why were you absent from training?" Lucas demanded, distressed and angry.

"I..." Zelana's voice faltered, her face drawn and pale. "I'm not feeling well..." she managed to say, her voice barely above a whisper as her eyes darted uneasily between her father and Deon.

"There is no time for weakness," Lucas snapped.

A surge of frustration and sorrow overwhelmed Zelana. "Mother has just passed away..." she murmured, her voice cracking under the weight of her grief.

"That is why you need to stand strong," the King retorted coldly. "And yet you chose to rest instead?"

"I couldn't leave my bed," the Princess admitted, choked with emotion, tears brimming in her eyes.

"Your brother is barely holding on because he endured endless torture. What is your excuse?" the King's voice escalated, each word a dagger.

She was rendered speechless, stunned by her father's harshness. The unfolding drama caught the attention of the Royals who began emerging from their rooms curiously, witnessing the heated confrontation.

"Your Majesty," Deon struggled to hold his silence. "It's evident that the Princess is unwell. I implore you to allow her a few days to recuperate."

Lucas's expression hardened as he faced Deon. "You are quite determined to protect the Princess. No wonder she's undisciplined," the King accused, his temper flaring out of control as he flung a wooden sword toward Deon, who caught it adeptly. "I'll punish you in her place," he declared grimly.

Before Deon could respond, the King launched a controlled yet forceful assault, his strikes landing heavily on Deon's arms and chest. Deon stood unyielding, grunting with each blow, absorbing each punishing strike with a stoic calm, making no move to defend himself or retaliate.

"Stop! You're going to kill him!" Zelana cried out, her voice trembling in horror as she witnessed Deon's suffering, his silent endurance a demonstration of his loyalty to her.

Lucas halted momentarily, surprised by Deon's ability to withstand his strikes.

"To be a true warrior, you must withstand pain, both in heart and body," he lectured sharply, his eyes piercing, turning the hilt of the wooden sword to Zelana. "Now, go and train like you're supposed to."

Her father's punishment of Deon only hardened her resolve. With a swift motion, she snatched the sword from his grasp and hurled it to the ground.

"I'm not well enough to train today," she declared with conviction.

"Fine." Lucas's tone was harsh and merciless. "I'll continue to punish Deon until you decide you're ready," he declared with cold detachment, bending down to retrieve the sword and resume his vicious assault. With a ruthless slash, he struck Deon across the stomach, and then his chest.

"Fight back, Deon!" Zelana's voice rang out, steeped in disbelief and desperation as she watched Deon continue to endure the punishment without defense.

The King then delivered a powerful blow to his back, the force snapping the sword in two. The impact was devastating, causing Deon to spit out blood, his sword falling from his weakened grasp. Lucas picked up the jagged remnants of the broken sword and raised them, poised to strike again.

In a moment of desperate courage, Zelana dashed forward and scooped up the fallen sword, raising the weapon to block the incoming strike, drawing a look of surprise on the King's face.

Deon grimaced with pain, watching his Princess position herself between him and her father, holding the sword in a combat stance. The sight of her standing protectively before him, ready to challenge the King himself, deepened the swell of emotions tugging at his heart.

Lucas's attacks grew more ruthless, but Zelana was relentless, swiftly blocking both wooden daggers coming at her from differing angles. The courtyard buzzed with murmurs of disbelief and awe as it echoed the clash of wood and sharp breaths. The Princess's resilience was fueled by her fear and protectiveness, defending Deon with her all, against further harm.

Zelana's arms trembled from the exertion of combat, yet her eyes sparkled with newfound confidence. With each block, she countered swiftly, her wooden blade slicing through the air, each movement a combination of the skills Deon had instilled in her.

Lucas was taken aback, initially attacking with fervor, but now found himself blocking and dodging. His expression morphed from anger to surprise, then to a begrudging respect as he witnessed his daughter's capabilities. The duel intensified as the King threw a blade toward her in a desperate bid to end the confrontation.

Zelana performed an elegant forward flip, her body arching through the air with swift agility as she deftly evaded the incoming attack, the wooden dagger embedding itself into a nearby tree. She landed gracefully on her feet behind the King, spinning around swiftly to face him and pressing her sword against the King's back.

"I won, Father," she declared, her voice resonating across the courtyard as the point of her wooden sword was a mere whisper away from her father's heart.

The King paused, surprised, as his stern demeanor softened and a stunned silence enveloped the courtyard, eyes wide with shock at the unexpected outcome of the duel.

"Now stop this madness, Father," she pleaded, shaking and out of breath.

Lucas slowly turned to face his daughter as she lowered the wooden sword. His face broke into a slight grin of approval, yet he remained firm in his stance.

"As your mentor, Deon is responsible for your training. If you ever skip again, next time I won't hold back, and it won't be a training sword," he threatened, his gaze as sharp as the blade he referenced.

"There won't be a next time," Zelana declared, meeting her father's gaze with a fierce one of her own, standing resilient in the face of her father's scrutiny.

Seeing that she had indeed learned her lesson, the King threw the jagged piece of wood to the ground, the fire in his eyes dimming as he faced Deon. "We have a meeting in an hour. Don't be late."

Recovering somewhat, Deon replied with a guarded expression, "I'll be present, Your Majesty."

Lucas turned and walked away, Dominic trailing behind him like a shadow.

Zelana slowly bent down, tenderly gathering a fragment of the broken wooden sword, and pulled out the other piece from the tree.

"Give them to me," Deon said as he reached out to take them.

"I'm keeping them," Zelana murmured, clutching the broken pieces to her chest.

"Why?" he asked, concerned.

"To remind myself of the consequences of my actions," she revealed, gazing up at him sadly.

I still can't believe you took up a sword to defend me against your father, he thought silently as a profound sense of affection coursed through him.

"Please come to my room," she urged softly, turning and walking to her quarters.

CHAPTER SEVENTY-THREE

Loyal Inflictions

NATALIE GENTLY PUSHED the door open to Zelana's room, swiftly stepping aside to let the Princess and Deon pass. Zelana placed the remnants of the broken training sword on her shelf, a stark reminder of the pain caused by her actions, as a sudden wave of guilt enveloped her.

"Don't ever endure punishment meant for me again," she murmured in remorse.

"You can't ask that of me, Princess," Deon declared, his commitment to her firm and unwavering.

"Then defend yourself. Even if it's my father," she commanded, her voice trembling with emotion.

"As you wish," he replied, noticing a fierceness in her gaze that was new and compelling.

"Take your shirt off," she requested, grabbing an ointment from a drawer.

"I need to prepare for the meeting," he started to decline awkwardly.

"It'll only take a minute," assured the Princess, her voice softening.

Deon hesitated at first, then complied, removing his shirt. His muscular frame was marred by reddened welts and fresh bruises as tears glistened in her eyes, her heart breaking on seeing him suffer.

"It doesn't hurt anymore," he attempted to reassure her, catching her pained expression.

Zelana gently dipped her fingers into the ointment and began to apply it to his wounds. Each brush of her fingers was soft, yet he flinched slightly, betraying his earlier claim. Sensing his discomfort, she blew softly on the tender skin.

"You don't need to pretend with me," she whispered as her eyes met his with a depth of care and concern. It stirred something deep within him that words could not fully capture.

With each gentle touch and soft breath against his skin, Deon's affection for her deepened. His heart ached as his gaze lingered on her while she soaked a small towel in the bowl of warm water sitting on the table and carefully dabbed at the dried blood by his eyes, nose, and lips.

You will never hurt because of me again, she told herself, her hands trembling slightly, betraying her emotional turmoil as tears threatened to spill from her eyes.

"Turn around, please," she whispered and he willingly obliged.

The sight of his cracked skin, marred by the brutal force of the training sword, caused her tears to overflow as his back revealed deeper cuts. With gentle motions, she tenderly treated each wound.

Deon clenched his jaw, the sting sharp, yet he remained silent, not wanting to show his discomfort as she gently smeared the ointment on his skin, her touch like a soothing balm relieving the pain.

After she finished applying the ointment, Zelana stepped back, hastily wiping her tears away, not wanting him to see how deeply affected she was by his suffering.

"Thank you for taking care of me, Princess..." Deon said softly as he began to put his shirt back on, covering the marks of loyalty he bore for her.

Her eyes locked with his. "Come back tonight," she implored with a concerned expression.

Deon paused, feeling his heart clench at her words. "As you wish," he murmured with emotion.

Zelana's eyes softened, and a subtle smile graced her lips as she grabbed a pouch from her drawer.

"One every hour," she reminded him, handing him the medicinal herbs.

Deon nodded with a grin and accepted the pouch, taking one pill out and munching on it. "Tastes like candy."

Zelana smiled, feeling a bit relieved. "Let's watch the sunset together."

"I'll be here," he promised, before opening the door and hurrying toward his obligations.

Zelana leaned against the doorframe, quietly watching him leave.

Deon paused, glancing back to find her still watching him. A warmth spread through his chest, and in that fleeting moment, he was certain his heart beat for her. He smiled, letting out a deep breath, before turning and heading to the meeting hall, Zelana's presence still lingering in his thoughts.

CHAPTER SEVENTY-FOUR

Revenge

IN THE MEETING hall of the Zelonian palace, the atmosphere was dense with tension as the Royal Council convened. The King surveyed the gathered nobles and military leaders with grave determination.

"As you all are aware, our conflict with the Krimzon Kingdom has escalated beyond tolerable bounds with the capture of Crown Prince Samuel and the death of Queen Sophia," Lucas began, his authoritative tone echoing through the hall. "We must end the Krimzonites, securing peace for our people and Azalon."

The King paused, allowing the gravity of his words to permeate the room before continuing. "I have devised a plan that leverages our enemy's current movements against them. Officer Shay has reported that Marcus plans to attack Lashia in five days. We will use this opportunity to our advantage."

The Councilmen looked at each other with concerned expressions.

"Commander Dominic and Commander Deon will lead forces to intercept Marcus on the road before he reaches Lashia," Lucas detailed the strategy with precision. "Assassinating the Krimzon King will disrupt their leadership, sowing chaos within their ranks."

Dominic and Deon shared a glance, recognizing the daring nature of the plan.

"Simultaneously, Commander Rowan will launch a full-scale assault on the Kingdom of Krimzon, cutting off any reinforcements. This dual strike will cripple our enemies on both fronts and Krimzon will be left with no one to defend it," Lucas elaborated with vision and foresight.

The Council members nodded in agreement, absorbing the strategy with optimism.

"This operation will demonstrate our strength to allies and foes alike," Lucas stated, his tone imbued with a rare intensity. "The future of our kingdom and the stability of Azalon hangs in the balance."

His gaze then settled on the young warriors tasked with this critical mission. "Commander Dominic, Commander Deon, and Commander Rowan—you've been training for challenges such as these. Your skills, courage, and resolve will be the cornerstone of our success."

The Commanders stood, their expressions one of unwavering resolve.

"I will not fail you, my King," stated Dominic with a bow.

"I will uphold the honor and strength of Zelonia," added Rowan, bowing.

"We will execute this mission flawlessly, Your Majesty," vowed Deon as he also bowed.

Lucas nodded with pride as he looked upon his Commanders—three of the most skilled fighters in the land, carrying the heavy burden of Zelonia's fate and shaping the future of Azalon.

"Two separate, focused discussions will commence here tomorrow afternoon, so prepare your ideas and come ready to share them," he concluded as he stood up and the Royal Council filed out of the room.

Lucas approached Deon with a solemn expression. "This morning's actions were not personal," he began, his eyes searching Deon's for understanding.

"I may not agree with your methods, but I do understand your reasons," Deon admitted, his response measured, careful not to escalate the tension.

"With the ongoing threats, the Princess must be fully prepared," he explained with a deep sigh. "The horrors that befell Crown Prince Samuel—I shudder to think what would happen if the Princess fell into the hands of the Immortals."

Deon paused to consider his words carefully, reflecting on his own experiences. "Hardship taught me resilience, but it was love that shaped me. I urge you, my King, do not let fear sever your relationship with Princess Zelana."

"Your words strike deeper than you know," Lucas murmured as Deon nodded and left the chamber.

CHAPTER SEVENTY-FIVE

THE POOL

THE GENTLE RIPPLE of water echoed through the royal pool as Deon sliced through it, his strokes graceful and powerful. Each lap was a bid to wash away the pain that clung to his body. Beside the pool, voices of Jenessa, Anika, and Kalina drifted to the serene atmosphere, followed by their ladies-in-waiting.

"Who is that?" Anika asked, halting with Jenessa, intrigued by the rhythmic flex of his sculpted arms.

"It appears to be Commander Deon," Kalina noted, pausing beside her friends as she leaned over the railing to catch a better glimpse of the man in the water.

"It is the Commander," Jenessa replied, her eyes tracing the contours of his athletic build. "His movements are so powerful," she murmured, more to herself than to her friends.

A dreamy smile played on Kalina's lips. "I suddenly find little appeal in attending classes today," she declared, her voice carrying a hint of rebellion as she made her way toward the pool area.

"Kalina..." Jenessa's voice trailed off, caught between concern and curiosity.

"Lord Makeo won't be pleased if we're late," Anika cautioned. Yet, her words lacked conviction as she was also drawn toward the pool.

The Princesses reached the poolside just as Deon completed his lap and paused by the pool's edge, slicking back his wet hair. "Aren't you ladies supposed to be in class?" he chided lightly.

"Perhaps we're more interested in a more hands-on type of instruction today," Kalina retorted with a blend of defiance and allure.

Deon emerged from the pool and the Princesses gasped at his well-defined muscles glistening with water droplets under the sun's rays.

"Shall we start with those biceps?" Jenessa suggested with a smile.

"I'm more interested in studying his abdominal muscles," Kalina replied, a playful twinkle in her eyes.

Deon chuckled at their banter. "Hardly the kind of remarks one expects from Princesses," he said, grabbing a towel and drying off.

The Princesses exchanged playful glances, continuing to admire the chiseled perfection before them.

"No words could do justice to what I'm thinking," Kalina quipped, her mischievous gaze lingering.

"We should get to class before the Commander decides we need a lesson in discipline," Anika chimed in nervously. "We saw him with the King—definitely not someone to cross."

"Oh, Commander Deon, please do discipline me," Kalina blurted out impulsively without thinking.

"Kalina!" Anika exclaimed, clearly shocked and embarrassed by her friend's audacity.

Deon's expression was a blend of amusement and a hint of admonishment as he shook his head. "Be careful what you wish for, Princess Kalina."

Kalina grinned, unfazed. "How naughty do I need to be to get punished?"

Deon's eyes narrowed slightly, though the corner of his lips twitched with a hint of mischief. "Trust me, Princess, you don't want to find out," he replied with a playful edge, leaving just enough of a warning to make her wonder.

Suddenly, the gate to the pool opened and Connor stepped in, disrupting their playful banter.

"Sorry for the interruption, Commander Deon, but the King requests your presence in the royal lounge," Connor announced with a serious expression.

Deon nodded, glancing back at the ladies. "Fun's over. Now off to class, Princesses."

The Princesses giggled as they grabbed onto each other's arms and hurried away toward the academy.

CHAPTER SEVENTY-SIX

KING'S GIFTS

DEON STEPPED INTO the royal lounge, his gaze shifting between Dominic, Rowan, and Gaius already there, waiting. The room was thick with unspoken tension as a flicker of suspicion ignited within him, particularly when Gaius rose to his feet with a gentle smirk.

"Gentlemen," Gaius began, the smirk never leaving his face, "the King wishes to express his gratitude for your dedicated service in protecting Zelonia and its people. Before you depart to battle in Lashia, His Majesty has personally arranged a two-night stay for each of you in the Royal Suite—a privilege reserved only for visiting kings and their guests."

The announcement took the Commanders by surprise, each exchanging looks of astonishment and slight discomfort at this unexpected indulgence. Gaius clapped his hands three times and the doors opened. The air filled with a subtle, alluring fragrance as six stunning young women entered, each dressed in a beautiful gown—sheer and seductive. The gowns flowed elegantly as they glided into the lounge, their presence further unsettling the gathered men.

"Thank you for your unwavering loyalty to Zelonia," Gaius continued as he glanced at his men. "Please proceed to the Royal

Suite and experience the Royal Treatment, gentlemen—you've earned it."

With those words, Gaius exited the royal lounge, leaving the Commanders with their unexpected companions as the room shifted subtly from surprise to mild apprehension. The distinguished men pondered the implications of this sudden luxury thrust upon them as the poised and graceful women began to engage the men in flirtatious conversation.

Tracy Fletcher, a blonde woman with a graceful ease, approached Deon curiously. "Commander Deon, I presume?" she said softly, "I'm Tracy. The King insists I take special care of you."

"I'm grateful, Tracy, although the King's generosity is quite… overwhelming," he managed to say.

A brunette with an infectious charm, Adela Walsh, stepped forward, gazing up at him with brown eyes as mysterious as shadows in the night. "I'm Adela, Commander Deon. I hadn't envisioned you to be quite so striking. I can't wait for us to explore each other further."

Her words deepened Deon's unease. *I can't believe King Lucas is attempting to mend our strained relationship with women,* he thought, feeling more apprehensive.

"Your presence is appreciated, but General Gaius has left. Please enjoy the rest of your evening as you wish," he replied with a stoic expression.

Dominic approached and chuckled, clapping Deon on the back. "Relax, Commander Deon. It's the calm before the storm. His Majesty wouldn't arrange this without good reason."

"Embrace it. Not every day are we treated like kings," Rowan grinned broadly.

As his comrades left the chamber with their companions, silence enveloped the room. Deon glanced at the two beautiful women, struggling with the undeniable allure of the situation.

No one would know if I rejected them, he thought to himself, devising a plan.

"Ladies, while I appreciate the King's generosity, please understand that I am preparing for a significant battle and must remain focused on my duties," he said, remaining detached.

"You're carrying a heavy burden, Commander. Let us help ease your mind," Adela replied with a calming voice.

"Thank you, but I must decline," Deon responded as he started toward the door.

"The King would be gravely displeased if you don't at least appear to appreciate his gifts," Tracy shared, trying to use reason to persuade him.

Deon's steps halted as his mind raced. *Could I really fall out of favor with the King?*

Tracy realized her words had made him question his resolve and actions. "The King hears everything," she added, laying on the pressure.

Reluctantly, Deon sat down on the plush, blue velvet sofa, lost in thought. *How do I handle this?*

Unnoticed by anyone, the door to the royal lounge opened slightly as Kalina peeked inside, searching for Deon. Her eyes widened and her heart raced as she spotted him in the company of two beautiful women. She hesitated before silently closing the door, leaving just a narrow sliver through which she could watch, hidden in the shadows, observing the scene in secret.

"You seem to be in deep contemplation," Adela murmured

softly as she sat down beside him, gazing at him seductively. "Allow us to distract you, even if only for a night."

Tracy approached and seated herself on the other side. The women's closeness was overwhelming as the atmosphere in the royal lounge grew more tense.

"Relax and indulge in the moment. Don't fight it," Tracy urged, traversing her hand up and down his leg, gently caressing, feeling the tension coil beneath his skin.

Adela grasped his left arm and ran her fingers down its length. "You're so muscular." She leaned close, her breath warm against his ear. "You're making me drip with desire, imagining you strong in all the right places," she murmured suggestively, her voice lowered to a gentle whisper.

Her words made Deon's body react, his breathing growing heavier as her lips brushed softly against his earlobe, igniting an unexpected spark of desire within him. She continued to trail down his neck, kissing and sucking, ensuring to leave her mark.

Deon's resistance faltered, his gaze drawn to the way her dress clung enticingly to her form as her suppleness bulged from her corset, tempting him to undo the lace holding them back.

"The Royal Suite is calling us," Adela reminded him softly, noticing his eyes on her.

Kalina observed them with growing intrigue, envy enveloping her. She was spellbound by the visible struggle she could see on Deon's face, overcome with conflicted desire.

Tracy cradled his face with her hand and turned his gaze to her, pressing her lips to his.

"Don't," Deon stated firmly, turning away from her.

"Do you not find me pleasing?" she asked, his rejection slightly hurting her pride.

"You are both stunning," he admitted earnestly, "but I'm not a man who compromises his principles for a night of pleasure."

Adela leaned closer, her head softly resting against his lap. "I was asked to seduce you, but it seems you've seduced me," she confessed, gazing up at him with a sparkle in her eyes as her heart raced.

Deon's jaw tightened. *She's got trouble written all over her.*

As he gazed down, he couldn't deny the physical attraction he felt toward her. He gently lifted her head from his lap and stood, his posture rigid as he fought to maintain control.

Adela quickly stood up and grasped his arm. "The Royal Suite can be as innocent or as dirty as you want it to be, Commander. You make the call," she purred, her words a dangerous lure.

Deon hesitated, his gaze lingering on Adela. The temptation was undeniable, but his instincts screamed at him to walk away.

"I promise to behave," Adela assured him with a playful tease.

With a resigned breath, Deon finally relented. "Lead the way."

The royal escorts smiled and glanced at each other with mischief in their eyes as Deon started walking toward the door and they trailed after him.

Kalina quickly pulled Miranda with her as they retreated into the shadows of a nearby corridor before they could be seen.

CHAPTER SEVENTY-SEVEN

FORGIVE ME

AS THE ROYALS navigated through the hushed corridors toward the royal lounge for a much-deserved rest after classes, they inadvertently encountered Deon accompanied by two lovely ladies. They halted in their steps, their gazes following them, taken aback by the exquisite gowns, leaving little to the imagination.

Deon's eyes briefly met Zelana's, and in that fleeting moment, a storm of unspoken words passed between them.

Forgive me, Princess Zelana, he wanted to say, his gaze filled with apology and regret.

What are you doing, Deon? She asked silently, her expression faltering as a surge of emotions threatened to unsettle her.

Deon forcibly returned his attention to the escorts, masking his turmoil with an indifferent expression while maintaining conversation despite his heart racing with silent apprehension.

"Commander Deon has good taste in women," Andreas observed, his awe undisguised.

A soft shadow of disappointment crossed Zelana's features, yet she maintained a composed façade.

"How can anyone be that pretty?" Anika remarked with envy.

"It's just make-up," Zelana murmured, feeling jealous.

"Did you see how they were dressed?" Jenessa commented, slightly irritated.

"Obviously intended to seduce a certain man..." Nikolai murmured, his gaze lingering appreciatively on the retreating figures in the distance before turning to Zelana. "Why do you think he's with them?"

"How am I to know why a man does anything?" Zelana replied carelessly, gazing up at Nikolai with an annoyed expression before walking toward the royal lounge with the Princesses trailing behind.

"What an absurd thing to ask her," Andreas immediately chided him.

"Those women have to be royal escorts," Nikolai said, keeping his voice down. "What happens when you're alone with an escort? Let alone, two?"

"It's not our business," Andreas replied as he rushed after their friends.

CHAPTER SEVENTY-EIGHT

Royal Suite

KALINA AND MIRANDA walked down a less frequented corridor that led to the Royal Suite. They quickly hid behind a statue when they saw Deon checking in at the reception area. He turned around and handed the key to Tracy.

"Enjoy the room, ladies," Deon said, his voice suddenly devoid of its usual warmth.

"Wait," Tracy looked up at him, perplexed. "You're not staying?"

"I have a prior engagement," Deon informed, maintaining a stoic expression.

"We'll be up all night waiting for you," Adela assured him with a hopeful smile.

Deon paused, his expression unreadable. "I'll return tomorrow," he said before turning away.

"Is it because you have a woman?" she pressed, feeling desperate.

Deon smirked, continuing to walk away, his farewell a mere wave over his shoulder.

Tracy exhaled in frustration as she watched him disappear around the corner. "What now?"

"I suspected Commander Deon might prove difficult," Adela admitted, the rejection stinging more than she had expected.

Back in the secluded corridor, Miranda turned to Kalina, her eyes wide with revelation. "Those women are royal escorts appointed by His Majesty to specifically entertain visiting kings in the Royal Suite."

Kalina's features darkened with jealousy. "No wonder they're dressed so provocatively. I can't believe women like that are allowed such easy access to Commander Deon."

"But it appears he is not inclined to accept such… companions, since he's continuing to reject their advances," Miranda murmured with respect. "Such admirable restraint."

"Why would the King arrange such a gift for Deon?" Kalina mused aloud, furrowing her brows, troubled by the implications of the Royal Suite.

"Perhaps it was to smooth things over after the altercation this morning," Miranda speculated.

At that moment, Kalina's eyes caught sight of a familiar face approaching the Royal Suite. "Isn't that man the General of Zelonia's army?"

Near the reception area, the escorts approached Gaius, who was concluding his review of the guest list.

"General, may we have a word?" Tracy asked reluctantly.

"What seems to be the problem?" Gaius inquired, recognizing them to be escorts by their attire.

"It appears our guest has declined our services," Tracy admitted, slightly embarrassed.

Gaius raised an eyebrow. "Who were you accompanying?"

"Commander Deon," Adela revealed. "He told us he had a prior engagement and left."

"Let me see what's going on," Gaius assured them, suspecting where Deon might have gone.

As Gaius departed to investigate, Kalina stepped out from hiding. She approached the escorts, ready to confront them and uncover the truth behind their presence.

CHAPTER SEVENTY-NINE

KEEPING HIS WORD

DEON WANDERED THROUGH the tranquil courtyard, his steps leading him toward Zelana's room. With each stride, his mind raced trying to piece together the right words.

How do I explain why I have to keep these women company without casting blame on her father? A sigh escaped him. *And how do I justify having to see them again tomorrow?*

As Deon approached her balcony, his pace slowed, each moment heavier with hesitation. He ascended the steps, unprepared for the delicate conversation that awaited. He paused in front of her door, his heart heavy with uncertainty, and just as he was about to knock, the door creaked open.

"Commander Deon, Princess Zelana has been waiting for you," Natalie announced softly.

Deon froze, catching sight of Zelana's warm smile through the doorway. His heart clenched with guilt. He had missed the sunset with her and now the burden of having to explain his entanglement with unwanted temptations weighed even more heavily on him.

"How did I know you'd be here?" A familiar voice cut through the cool night air as he emerged from the dark shadows of the courtyard.

Deon was caught off guard as he hesitated, seeing his friend approach. "I was just coming to bid Princess Zelana goodnight," he said, masking the discomfort he felt under Gaius's scrutinizing gaze.

Through the slightly ajar door, Zelana caught sight of Gaius and stepped closer, trying to discern what they were discussing.

"Aren't there other places you're supposed to be tonight?" Gaius hinted darkly, alluding to the Royal Suite. "Rejecting the King's hospitality is the same as rejecting the King himself."

"I would never dishonor the King," Deon responded sincerely, pressured by the subtle threat.

"I didn't expect you would," Gaius replied, his arm resting on Deon's shoulder, a gesture that seemed both brotherly and calculated. "Let me walk with you," he suggested, a subtle insistence in his tone.

As they prepared to leave, the door swung fully open and Zelana stepped into the night, her presence sending a chill through the warm night air.

"Did my father send you to check on Deon?" she demanded, her emotions raw with suspicion.

Gaius's demeanor softened as he withdrew his arm from Deon, turning to address the Princess. "The King is genuinely worried about Commander Deon's injuries, especially with war imminent."

"Commander Deon wouldn't be hurt if not for my father," the Princess reminded him sharply.

Gaius's stance hardened. "Princess, please know that the King's decisions and actions, however harsh, were with good intentions," he insisted gently, hoping to clarify any gap in misunderstanding.

The sorrow in Zelana's eyes intensified on hearing Gaius's voice rise, almost in disrespect.

Deon's heart clenched as he noticed her struggling to maintain composure.

"Perhaps this isn't the best time for these heated discussions. We should all take the night to reflect," Deon suggested as his gaze tenderly rested on the Princess. "Sweet dreams, Princess Zelana."

Zelana nodded, feeling helpless, watching Deon reluctantly turn away, pulling his comrade with him.

A cold realization washed over her. *My father is intent on keeping us apart.*

As Deon's retreating figure blended into the shadows of the night, she quietly withdrew into her chamber, the door whispering shut behind her, sealing her in with her growing frustrations.

CHAPTER EIGHTY

Concession

DEON MADE HIS way back to the Royal Suites with Gaius keeping pace beside him, his mind continually swirling with thoughts of Zelana, worried how she might perceive him after tonight. Spending a night with royal escorts wasn't something he had ever envisioned for himself.

Adela would be there. His mind drifted to her, worried, knowing the chemistry between them was undeniable.

Should I keep this a secret from the Princess? He asked himself as he let out a sigh, his footsteps echoing slightly in the quiet corridor as he neared the suites.

Gaius observed Deon closely. He was unusually quiet, his expression one of concern, while he kept his hands in his suit pocket, seemingly lost in thought.

Gaius paused. "As a fellow King's Guard, let me give you some friendly advice, Commander Deon."

Deon halted his steps, removing his hands from his pockets and facing his comrade, listening intently.

"Keep your distance with Princess Zelana and cease the midnight rendezvous immediately. It doesn't look good on you or the Princess, and if it continues, it may cost your life," Gaius warned, his words harsh and merciless.

"I won't take your advice lightly," Deon replied, maintaining his composure.

"Tonight will reveal where your loyalty lies," Gaius remarked sternly. "Choose carefully."

Deon nodded, reading between the lines, and stepped up to the host's desk. "I seem to have misplaced my room key," he said, feigning casualness.

"Not a problem, Commander Deon," she reassured him, recognizing him instantly. She flipped through her parchment ledger before handing him another key. "Here you go. Enjoy the Royal Treatment."

"Thank you for your assistance," Deon responded as he accepted the key.

Deon glanced at the General before stepping away to walk down the dimly lit hallway. He felt a troubled ache throb in his heart as he steeled himself for whatever confrontation the King had orchestrated behind these closed doors. Each step toward the Royal Suite was weighed down by the realization that he was bound by a royal command that might win him favor with the King but irrevocably damage the delicate bond he had nurtured with Zelana.

As Deon reached the door to his Royal Suite, he paused, his hand hovering over the handle with reluctance. His thoughts raced, desperate for an escape, but he knew none existed. With a heavy heart, he finally turned the key. Hearing the soft click, he let out a resigned exhale and stepped into the unknown, readying himself for the unimaginable things awaiting him in the suite.

CHAPTER EIGHTY-ONE

The Seduction

THE ROYAL SUITE unfolded before Deon in shades of black and gold, its opulence accentuated by the dim glow of candlelight. The room had sheer cascading curtains tied back against the walls, framing the grandeur of the space, exuding stately elegance. At its center, a large bed commanded attention, its linens shimmering gold and maroon under the flickering light, inviting an air of undeniable luxury.

As Deon moved further into the suite, his gaze swept over the meticulously arranged setting, each detail curated to impress and comfort its guests. The air was scented with a subtle rose fragrance, reminding him of Zelana, making the ache in his heart deepen.

In a synchronized motion, the women stood up from the bed and let their gowns slip to the floor, revealing delicate lingerie. Deon let out a gasp, his eyes unintentionally tracing the contours of their figures before he could stop himself.

Self-restraint, he reminded himself, experiencing both desire and guilt.

The women slowly approached, moving their hips with grace as they walked, swaying seductively, adding to the sensual tension.

"Welcome back, Commander Deon," Tracy said softly, grasping his arm while gazing up into his eyes.

"I'm here for the Royal Treatment," Deon spoke hesitantly, fully aware of the control he'd have to maintain moving forward. "I'm not entirely sure what it involves, but I'm willing to explore it."

"It demands a full surrender—emotionally and physically," Adela said softly, staring up at him.

"You assured me that nothing would happen without my consent," he replied with quiet confidence.

"You can decline any unwanted gesture, but you must allow us to ensure you're pleasured—it's our service to the King—do with us as you please," Adela replied with an inviting sparkle in her eyes.

Her words made Deon's throat tighten nervously.

"Many are hesitant at first, but they often find the experience… intoxicating," assured Tracy as she glided toward the in-room bar, filling three glasses with rich, dark wine, and returned, offering one to each of them. "I propose a toast to an evening filled with new experiences…"

"And new memories," Adela added, raising her glass.

Deon already felt regretful as he lifted his glass. "Cheers…" the word barely escaped his lips while he clinked his glass against theirs before downing it in one gulp.

Adela noticed an inconsistency in his stoic composure. *You will surrender to me, Commander,* she vowed to herself as she took the glasses and set them aside.

"The King insists on only the best service for his Commanders," Tracy remarked, her hands moving to his jacket as she slowly unbuttoned it, letting it slide off his shoulders and placing it on the nearby plush chair.

"Let us fulfill your every desire," Adela whispered as she stepped closer, her hand sliding down his torso, her touch already awakening him.

He gasped as she lowered herself, her hands moving to unbuckle his belt while her eyes remained on him. Each movement was slow and enticing.

Deon's nervousness deepened as his trousers slid to the floor, revealing more than just his underpants.

A look of satisfaction spread across Adela's face as she lifted her gaze to his once more and gently rubbed her hands up and down his legs, making his bulge expand. Her lips parted with insinuation, awaiting his permission.

Deon's heart throbbed in his chest, gazing down at Adela, her proximity unsettling him. Just as he felt his resolve weakening, his mind drifted to her... *Zelana*. Her pained expression filled his thoughts, anchoring him back to a reality far beyond the suite's alluring walls.

"Adela..." he whispered, breaking through the sexual tension as he offered his hand to her.

Adela reluctantly placed her hand in his. He pulled her up with a gentle firmness as her body melded into his embrace. The moment was intense as their eyes locked and her fingers wandered across his skin, delicately tracing the sculpted lines of his chest, taking in the full measure of his muscular frame.

"You are like a god," she whispered, exploring his body with an undisguised look of admiration.

"Gods enjoy massages," Tracy teased softly as she turned on a soft fountain, creating sounds of waves crashing gently on a distant shore. "Why don't you lie down on your stomach, Commander Deon?"

Deon stepped away from Adela and positioned himself onto the bed with caution. As soon as he settled, Adela straddled him. His body instinctively tensed up at the unexpected closeness.

"Imagine you're by the ocean, Commander," she leaned forward, her voice a soothing whisper to his ear, while her jasmine scent slowly intoxicated him. "You're lying on the beach, feeling the gentle caress of waves washing over you."

As Adela's voice wove the hypnotic imagery of the ocean around him, he closed his eyes and allowed himself to be carried away by the fantasy. He envisioned the fading sunlight in the sky as he lay on the serene beach with Zelana in his arms, watching the gentle waves lapping soothingly toward the shore.

Adela expertly applied warm, scented oil to her hands and began a fluid, rhythmic massage from his lower back up to his tense shoulders as Deon's breath grew deeper, more relaxed.

"You're holding in a lot of tension," she observed softly, her skilled touches drawing deeper breaths from him with each pass of her hands.

"Your touch feels... incredible," Deon murmured appreciatively.

Adela smiled, her fingers working deeper into the muscles of his shoulders.

She leaned down to his ear. "If you find this enjoyable, you will be enraptured with what's coming," she promised in a whisper, her lips brushing his earlobe lightly, sending a shiver down his spine.

His eyes fluttered open, breathing heavily while staring at the flickering candlelight casting soft shadows that danced across the walls.

Tracy joined them, her touch light yet firm, expressing a quiet admiration for his biceps, gently massaging each muscle while appreciating his form.

As they continued to tease the tension from his body, his breath deepened and his eyelids shut once more, succumbing to the relaxation and getting carried away by the enchanting sensations washing over him.

CHAPTER EIGHTY-TWO

CHAT OVER WINE

A SOFT KNOCK DISTURBED the silence around Kalina's chambers. Miranda cautiously opened the door only to see her friend, Natalie, her face brightening with a subdued smile.

"I brought some leftover wine from dinner," Natalie whispered, her voice carrying a hint of excitement.

"Shhh... Princess Kalina is asleep," Miranda responded in a hushed tone, motioning for Natalie to back up onto the balcony for a bit of privacy.

Natalie quickly filled two glasses, raising hers in a silent toast. "Isn't it just divine?" she murmured after taking a sip.

Miranda tasted hers, the rich flavors enveloping her senses. "It's like being swept off my feet and floating among the stars," she said, her voice filled with a wistful longing.

Natalie giggled softly. "Why is it always me bringing the treats?" She took another sip.

"Princess Kalina usually drinks hers too quickly," Miranda said, her tone turning somber. "She's been under so much stress with her mother's illness and all the drama tonight."

Natalie's curiosity piqued, her smile fading into a concerned frown. "What drama?" she asked.

"The drama with Deon, you haven't heard?" she replied, her voice low, filled with surprise.

"This morning's confrontation with the King?" Natalie guessed, her face scrunching in thought.

"That was just the beginning," she added, draining her glass in one long sip. "It led to everything that unfolded tonight."

"What happened?" Natalie asked, hurriedly pouring her another glass. "You can't leave me hanging."

Miranda leaned in closer, her voice barely above a whisper. "The King gifted royal escorts to Commander Deon," she revealed, taking a cautious sip of her wine.

"What?" Natalie's eyes widened, nearly spilling her wine. "To appease him?" she muttered, shocked.

"Apparently," she responded with a tease. "You should have seen them. They were beautiful."

"We should go inside before the guards start their rounds," Natalie suggested, wanting to tell Zelana.

Miranda nodded as the ladies-in-waiting's movements were swift and silent, slipping back inside their rooms, leaving the balcony and its whispered secrets.

CHAPTER EIGHTY-THREE

Mystery Woman

DEON COULD FEEL the stress melting away under the skilled ministrations of their hands, tracing paths of relaxation up his torso, spreading across his shoulders and to his arms, like the warmth of the sun on that secluded beach he had imagined. The Royal Suite, his worries, and the impending war seemed to dissolve into the ambient sounds and scents, leaving him adrift in a sea of tranquility. Unbeknownst to him, another woman had entered the suite.

"I'll take over, Adela," Tracy offered softly as they exchanged mischievous glances.

Adela gently stood up, allowing the mystery woman to straddle Deon's back.

Unseen by him, the woman discreetly shed her top, smoothing warm oil over her body before resuming the massage, gliding her hands up his back. Adela moved down to attend to his legs with tender, firm strokes, meticulously traversing the length of his muscles, easing their tension.

A low groan escaped Deon's lips as the combined efforts of Adela and the mystery woman began to melt away the stiffness and strain that had accumulated over weeks of stress. The woman lowered herself onto him, allowing the soft, oiled curves of her body to slide over his back.

Startled by the unexpected intimacy, his eyelids fluttered open. "What are you doing, Tracy?" he asked with caution, sexual tension escalating with the enhanced sensations of her bare skin caressing his.

"Relax, it's a special technique," Tracy whispered into his ears, easing his mind.

The woman exhaled gently, her movements growing increasingly intimate, enveloping Deon in a wave of desire. She continued to press her body against his, massaging with a sensual tease as his resistance slowly faded into a haze of relaxation.

The line between a massage and sexual indulgence blurred as Deon felt her hand slip down to his crotch. His eyes snapped open and in a swift motion, he turned, causing her to tumble onto the bed. She quickly snatched a robe and covered herself, her eyes registering a shock that matched his own.

"Have I displeased you?" the woman asked, her voice soft and apologetic.

"Who are you?" he demanded, sitting up abruptly, taking in the unexpected sight of a third woman, her face hidden behind a mask adding to the mystery and discomfort.

"Lace is new. She joined us midway," Tracy quickly interjected, trying to assure him and smooth the unexpected disruption. "You seemed so at peace. We didn't want to interrupt your relaxation."

Deon's surprise morphed into suspicion as he eyed her cautiously. "Why the mask, Lace?"

"It's standard for new escorts, allowing us privacy until we're more settled," Lace responded softly as she slipped on her robe, pulling it to cover her bosom.

"Thank you for the evening, ladies," Deon stated firmly, shifting to the edge of the bed to get dressed.

"Please, don't leave," Adela implored, grasping his arm to halt him, a hint of desperation in her voice.

Lace straddled him with her robe slightly open as he inhaled sharply, surprised at her boldness.

"Forgive me," came a soft, sultry apology from Lace.

Her hand found the back of his neck as her hips started to move rhythmically against him, each movement deliberately provocative to rekindle his arousal.

Adela and Tracy sat on the bed, one on each side of him. They leaned in, kissing his shoulders and tracing a path to his neck, their actions heightening the already intense atmosphere, calming him.

"I didn't consent to an additional escort," Deon managed to say, despite their seductive gestures.

Lace leaned into him, her face brushing lightly against his skin. "Take me, Commander Deon," she whispered softly to his ear, continuing to move her body tantalizing against his.

"Mask off…" he commanded, facing her, his breath warm against her lips.

Lace ignored his request as she pressed her lips to his, but he evaded her, his patience snapping.

Deon took hold of her thighs and swiftly lifted her from him, standing up as her body slid down his.

Her feet found the floor with a soft thud as Lace immediately grasped his arm. "Commander…"

With decisive movements, he pulled on his trousers. "I must retire," he declared, his tone devoid of the warmth it had held earlier.

He swiftly put on his jacket and adjusted it with brisk, precise movements before striding toward the door, pulling it open and exiting, letting the door slam shut behind him with a resounding echo.

Tracy turned to Lace sharply. "Why didn't you just take off your mask?" she hissed, irritated.

"He should respect my preference," Lace responded in a subdued voice.

"And you touched him!" Adela exclaimed, visibly frustrated. "I was clear about the rules—no intimate contact unless the guest initiates."

"He seemed so at ease with you; I thought he wouldn't mind," Lace responded, trying to justify her actions as the others began to gather their robes.

"You're not participating tomorrow, Lace," Tracy directed, slipping on her robe.

"You can't stop me," Lace retorted defiantly.

"I will not allow you to ruin things for us again," Adela stated, one hand resting on her hip.

Lace's eyes narrowed with determination. "I will ensure the Commander stays the night tomorrow," she asserted confidently. "He won't be able to resist me."

Adela and Tracy exchanged a look of disbelief, sensing a new rival in their midst.

CHAPTER EIGHTY-FOUR

JEALOUSY

ZELANA HURRIED THROUGH the lavish corridors of the palace, her heart pounding with every step. Natalie's words echoed relentlessly in her mind.

"Miranda told me that Commander Deon was gifted royal escorts."

The thought gnawed at her and she felt betrayed—not just by Deon but by her own father, for orchestrating such a situation for him, especially knowing the depth of her feelings for the Commander. She finally reached the host, slightly out of breath, barely managing to keep her composure.

"Which room is Commander Deon in?" Zelana asked, her voice strained from the turmoil inside her.

"I'm sorry, Princess, but I'm not at liberty to divulge that information," she replied, her smile faltering.

"Then I shall have to search each one," the Princess declared, leaving no room for negotiation.

The host's eyes widened in panic. "Please, Princess Zelana," she pleaded softly, visibly flustered by the potential consequences of her actions. "Don't make it difficult for me. I could lose my position."

"I will handle any fallout," Zelana assured her with an intense gaze.

The host hesitated, her fingers trembling as she paged through the ledger. With a glance around the corridor, she leaned closer, lowering her voice. "He's in 7. But please… be discreet, Your Highness."

"Thank you," Zelana murmured, turning to leave, navigating down the luxurious hallway.

Reaching the room, Zelana's hand trembled slightly as she knocked, her heart heavy with dread, afraid of what she might find behind the door.

The door swung open, revealing a striking brunette whose expression shifted from curiosity to mild surprise upon seeing her.

A wave of insecurity crashed over Zelana and her breath caught in her throat as doubt flickered in her chest, glossing over the brunette's flawless beauty, her eyes involuntarily taking in her alluring figure.

"Princess… Zelana," Adela greeted her with a polished smile and cautious tone. "What brings you to the Royal Suites?"

Jealousy gnawed at Zelana as she fought to maintain her composure. "Is Commander Deon here?" she asked, trying to keep her voice steady despite her emotions.

Adela's polite smile wavered. "I'm sorry, but we can't reveal the information of our guests, even to a princess," she responded with a hint of intrigue and subtle defensiveness.

Zelana's gaze quickly darted past Adela, sweeping over the room, catching sight of the disheveled bed which spiked her anxiety. Just then, a blonde woman emerged from the shadows of the room, further intensifying the tension.

"Commander Deon certainly knows how to give and enjoy the Royal Treatment," Tracy purred, her tone dripping with insinuation, wanting to add fuel to the already raging fire in the Princess.

The casual cruelty of the remark drained color from Zelana's face. Her heart sank at the thought of the unspoken implications. Steadying her heart, she gathered her poise, pushing her way into the chamber.

"Perhaps you're both not fully grasping the situation, so let me enlighten you," Zelana began, her voice calm and commanding, her gaze cold as it settled on Tracy.

"You may find it easy to speak disrespectfully to me now, but remember this—there will come a day when I am Queen. And on that day, you will regret your words and actions, *begging* for forgiveness as you bow before me," she declared, her voice like ice, her eyes flashing with a promise of vengeance.

Adela's confidence faltered, her composure visibly cracking under the intensity of Zelana's words.

"Commander Deon left half an hour ago, Princess Zelana," she conceded quickly, softening her tone.

The confirmation of Deon's presence felt like a blade to her heart. Feeling more lost than ever, she spun on her heels, making her way to Deon's personal quarters, seeking answers only he could provide.

CHAPTER EIGHTY-FIVE

Avoidance

ZELANA WALKED THE endless halls toward Deon's room, her mind a tumult of unsettling scenarios, amplifying her fears with each echoing step. Her heart pounded against her chest as she finally reached his door, her hand pausing before the soft knock.

Silence greeted her, tightening the knot of anxiety in her chest.

She knocked again, more urgently. "It's me, Princess Zelana," she whispered through the door, her voice quivering with emotion. "Please, if you're there, open the door, Commander Deon."

Still, only silence answered her plea, deepening her sense of isolation.

Confusion and creeping dread gripped her as she considered the possibilities of his whereabouts this late at night. After a few tense moments spent pacing in front of his room, hopelessness washed over her. With a heavy heart, she turned and made her way back across the Zelonian courtyard to her own chambers, each step heavier than the last.

As she reached her balcony, she cast a desperate glance back toward the men's quarters, her eyes catching a dim light flickering in Deon's window. A cold realization washed over her that moment.

He was home… he purposely avoided me.

Stepping into her room, the tormenting images intensified, unsettling her, as tears blurred her vision.

The escorts were beautiful, Zelana thought silently. *And you're still a man.*

The pain of such thoughts was excruciating as she slid down against the door slowly into a crumpled heap, sobbing uncontrollably. The gnawing fear that Deon might have been swayed by their allure, that he might prefer their company over hers, was too much to bear. Her heart felt as if it were shattering within her, leaving her to face the engulfing darkness of her insecurities.

CHAPTER EIGHTY-SIX

GUILT

DEON SAT IN the dark, the only light in his room, a sole candle, keeping him company. He perched on the edge of the sofa, motionless. His hands clasped tightly together, each finger entwined as if holding together the fractured pieces of his resolve as his mind wandered back to moments ago, the soft, hesitant knock at his door, leading to the faint sound repeated, more urgently, and then her voice, delicate and fraught with worry.

"It's me, Princess Zelana..."

"Please, if you're there, please open the door, Commander Deon..."

Deon wanted nothing more than to rush to the door, to see her face, to reassure her, and to feel her close. But another part of him, the part shadowed by the remorse of the evening's indulgences, held him back. He was a man accustomed to control and command, yet he was helpless in the Royal Suite and had been ensnared in unwanted pleasure, challenging his morals.

How can I face you, Princess Zelana? I gave in to seduction, all to appease the king.

Seeking a small solace, Deon reached into the drawer of his bedside table and retrieved a small red velvet box. Inside lay a beautiful diamond bracelet, exquisitely crafted and glinting softly in the candlelight—a token of affection he had the Royal Jeweler custom-made in Sanshe. Holding it, he allowed himself a moment of vulnerability as his mind drifted to Zelana.

"I miss you... I miss us," he whispered into the night as the warmth of their memories pierced through his defenses, igniting a pang of longing to see her, even if briefly.

Deon carefully closed the box, setting it down on the table, before rising and placing his hand on the window frame, his gaze drifting outside with the faint hope of catching a glimpse of her. Her chamber was dark—an empty shadow of the cold isolation he had left her with.

His gaze lingered, the stillness of the night heavy around him, as shame tightened its grip, a relentless reminder of another night of temptation awaiting him, the guilt tormentingly unsettling, inescapable.

CHAPTER EIGHTY-SEVEN

Speed

As THE FIRST rays of morning light bathed the training academy in a soft glow, Zelana was already immersed in her rigorous weight training routine. The echo of water pails clinking resonated through the quiet space as she set them down, a bead of sweat tracing her brow.

The Princess glanced up, her posture stiffening to find Deon approaching. She quickly masked her emotions with a composed façade.

"You're up early today, Princess Zelana," Deon greeted casually, his eyes avoiding hers slightly, realizing the night had been as restless for her as it had been for him.

"I needed to do something to distract my mind," Zelana admitted, trying to draw him to tell her about the night in the Royal Suite.

"I'm happy to see your dedication to your weight training," he noted, keeping the conversation focused and professional. "I think it's time we introduce a new element to your regimen, speed training. It's designed to sharpen your reflexes and improve your agility."

"What does it involve?" she inquired, pausing to dab the sweat from her forehead with a towel.

"Let's move to a more open space," he suggested, leading the way as the Princess followed. "I'll toss balls from different directions and at various speeds, and you try to catch them," he confirmed, setting the tone for the session. "This will not only test your agility but also your ability to stay focused under pressure, mirroring real combat situations where threats can come from anywhere at any time."

Zelana nodded. "I'm ready," she stated, embracing the challenge as she positioned herself in the center of the designated area, her eyes alert and following his movements closely.

Deon went easy the first few throws, each at a moderate pace, to let the Princess get a feel for the movement. As she caught each ball, he gradually increased the speed and varied the angles, making each catch more challenging, forcing her to react swiftly.

As the session progressed, her response times improved, but the intensity of the exercise took its toll. Despite her best efforts, she stumbled a few times, the surprise of a particularly fast throw knocking her off balance. Each time she hit the ground, he instinctively stepped forward, extending his hand to help her up. However, she'd wave him off, pushing herself up without accepting his assistance.

Deon couldn't hide the flash of pain that crossed his expression, recognizing she'd taken a step back from the closeness they once shared. Each catch, each fall, and each recovery mirrored their personal struggles, their mutual pain, and the unspoken truth they both struggled to face alone.

They resumed the training, both throwing themselves into the exercise, unsure how to mend the emotional distance growing between them. As they wrapped up their rigorous training session, they both were visibly worn out, their bodies weary and their spirits heavy with unarticulated feelings.

"Apparently, I don't have much stamina," the Princess remarked, her tone subdued with frustration.

"You did exceptionally well today," he assured her with admiration. "Stamina builds with time and consistent effort."

She offered an appreciative nod as she gazed up at him, noticing bruises on his neck. "Does that hurt?"

"What hurt?" Deon's voice held a note of hesitation, sensing her suspicions.

"You have red marks all over the left side of your neck," the Princess observed, dumbfounded.

Deon instinctively covered his neck with his hand, realizing the faint bruises left behind were from Adela's lingering kisses and gentle bites.

Zelana's heart sank as the silence that followed was heavy with unspoken words. The once charismatic Deon she had come to know—always articulate and certain—was now silenced.

"You've changed," the Princess accused as she gathered her things and turned to leave.

"Princess Zelana…" Deon called out, his voice weighed down by reluctance.

Zelana halted, her heart breaking, feeling suffocated, as though the air had been stolen from her lungs.

"I have a meeting with the Royal Council and you have class," he murmured, sensing her unspoken suspicions. "Perhaps we could discuss this tomorrow?"

Tears welled in Zelana's eyes. *Because you're returning to the Royal Suite, aren't you, Deon?*

She needed to look him in the eye as she faced him. "Are you seeing someone?" she asked, her voice trembling with emotions.

Deon's heart sank, a sense of helplessness washing over him as he held her gaze. "Something like that," he admitted, burdened by the secret he kept.

Her heart screamed, aching to say the words that lingered painfully on her lips.

Do I mean that little to you? You spend a few hours with them and now they matter more than me?

The silence between them grew unbearable; the warmth that once bound them now cold, as though frozen overnight.

I will never care for you the same again, Zelana wanted to say, tears finally spilling from her eyes.

But even as the words formed in her mind, her heart ached, torn by the truth that she wasn't ready to let him go, no matter how much it hurt. She forced herself to walk away, each step pulling her further from him as she clutched her heart.

Stop longing for him, she told herself. Yet, her heart resisted, as if trying to hold onto him even when she felt he was already slipping away.

Deon immediately regretted letting her go but he stilled himself, fighting back the guilt that was ripping him apart inside.

Keep walking, he told her silently. *Just like that. Don't look back, Don't let me hurt you anymore.*

But as the distance between them grew, the quiet longing in Deon's heart whispered of what they could have been, a future slipping away before his eyes.

CHAPTER EIGHTY-EIGHT

BATTLE PLANS

IN THE GRAND Zelonian meeting hall, Lucas listened with rapt attention as Deon and the defense team meticulously outlined the strategic plan for the upcoming battle.

"We plan to leave tomorrow. Given the unpredictable nature of the Krimzonite forces, we have opted to split our defense group," Deon began, using pens to demonstrate his vision on the grand map table.

"Force One, under the command of Dominic, will fortify the gates of the Lashia Kingdom. Concurrently, Force Two, which I will command, will clandestinely position itself within the forest, approximately half a mile from the anticipated route of the Krimzon army," he continued, detailing the tactical deployment. "We intend to lay traps along their path to incapacitate as many Krimzonites as possible before launching a direct assault. At the optimal moment, Force Two will strike, aiming to eliminate Marcus before he can reach the gates of Lashia."

Deon further elaborated, "Should our initial assault falter, I will fire a single, piercing shot from my pistol as a signal to Force One of the imminent threats. The remnants of Force Two will then retreat deeper into the forest, feigning defeat. This maneuver is designed to provoke the Krimzon army into a hasty charge toward the gates of Lashia, where they will meet a united front as Forces One and Two converge to vanquish the enemy."

"Well thought out. Execute the plan," the King declared, nodding with approval as he observed the shared determination between Deon and Dominic. "Should the circumstances become dire..."

"We will withdraw, my King. Rest assured," Dominic responded confidently with a resolute stance.

Lucas's expression softened. "I want both of you to return unscathed," he implored. "Commander Rowan is riding to Krimzon to block their reinforcements as we speak."

The Commanders nodded, their expressions showing relief as they realized that everything was progressing as planned.

Lucas turned his attention to Deon with furrowed brows, approaching. "How are your wounds faring?"

"They're much better, thank you for your concern, Your Majesty," Deon replied, expressionless.

"I noticed that you seem more relaxed. Did the Royal Treatment meet your expectations?" the king inquired with a hint of curiosity.

"It was quite the experience," Deon affirmed, nodding appreciatively. "The women are beautiful."

"I personally chose them based on exceptional recommendations from former guests," the king mentioned with pride and a touch of regret. "Unfortunately, you didn't stay the night."

Deon was surprised how swiftly the news had reached him. He paused, choosing his words with care.

"I was simply too fatigued last night, Your Majesty, and didn't wish to overextend their graciousness," he explained casually.

"Tonight, I intend to stay up late and fully immerse myself in every aspect of the Royal Suite experience."

The King's laughter resonated warmly through the hall. "I'm pleased to hear that. As a Commander, you must find time to indulge in pleasures to ensure you're at your peak performance when confronting our adversaries. Don't let my gifts go to waste," he said, his eyes twinkling with mischief and wisdom.

Deon bowed slightly. "Thank you for your thoughtful generosity, my King," he replied, shifting the conversation toward more personal concerns. "How fares the Crown Prince?"

A weighty sigh escaped Lucas. "He remains frail, suffering from a persistent cough that the royal medic fears may be pneumonia. It's unlikely he'll be fit for battle anytime soon."

"That's concerning indeed," Deon nodded in agreement. "But it is vital he recovers fully before engaging in wars."

The King's tone softened, touched by an unusual slur that hinted at an unspoken weariness. "Deon, I must commend you," he began, his eyes reflecting a deep admiration. "Since you began mentoring the Princess, her prowess in combat has notably improved. It's impressive to witness such progress in the short time you've been here."

Deon's gaze momentarily dropped at the mention of her, his posture shifting as he gathered his thoughts.

"The Princess is remarkably quick to absorb new skills and she's incredibly diligent, both in her training and studies," Deon praised, his voice carrying deep respect and admiration as his eyes met the King's once more. "I have no doubt that Princess Zelana will stand as one of your most formidable allies on the battlefield, my King," he added with conviction.

Lucas observed Deon's respectful and composed manner, nodding in approval.

Despite the recent additional responsibilities I've imposed upon you, and the challenges in the Royal Suite to test your loyalties, you continue to express gratitude and willingly participate without question. I can't feign ignorance to your demonstration of strength and resilience, including the lack of bitterness in you, Deon. You possess qualities that I value highly as an authoritative figure in my court.

CHAPTER EIGHTY-NINE

SECRETS

STOP CARING...

Zelana kept telling herself, yet her heart betrayed her with every thudding beat as she moved through the palace corridors. She halted, glaring down the hall, her eyes resting on the letters on the wall.

The Royal Suites.

After her intense training session with Deon that morning, her curiosity had only grown stronger. Despite her attempts to fight it, the thoughts gnawed at her relentlessly, wondering about his encounters with the royal escorts behind those closed doors.

You gave up everything to mentor me. How could one night in the Royal Suite change you?

Her thoughts darkened, slowly consuming her, making it impossible to ignore the women who had so easily captured his attention... and perhaps, even his heart.

"Leave me, Natalie," Zelana whispered as her eyes remained fixed on the hallway.

Natalie slowly glanced down the hall, realizing the Princess had private matters to take care of. She nodded silently and left the Princess, her steps echoing softly as she stepped away.

Zelana's curiosity was filled with dread, jealousy, and fear, afraid of what the truth might reveal. She also burned with a desperation for clarity, drawing her inexorably toward the Royal Suite.

"Princess Zelana…" the host greeted her with a nod, observing the Princess turn with quiet determination, making her way down the corridor to room 7.

Reaching the door, Zelana hesitated in front of the woodwork's intricate carvings. With a deep breath that did little to calm her racing heart, she raised her hand and knocked firmly on the ornately carved door, the sound sharp in the quiet hallway.

It swung open, revealing the beautiful brunette once more, whose initial surprise quickly morphed into a sly grin, her eyes dancing with a mischief that seemed to mock Zelana's turmoil. Leaning casually against the mahogany frame, she held the polished door slightly closed, obscuring the suite from the Princess's curious eyes.

"Another visit? To what do we owe the honor?" Adela teased, eyeing the Princess with a provocative arch of her eyebrow.

The Princess's expression remained unreadable. "You're expecting Commander Deon this evening, I presume?" she inquired, each word a dagger cloaked in velvet.

"I am," Adela confided without hesitation, her smile faltering into a cautious expression as she gauged the fire burning in Zelana's eyes.

Not waiting for an invite, the Princess pushed past her, stepping into the suite, venturing into the heart of uncertainty, ready to confront whatever awaited her inside.

"You can't just barge in, Princess Zelana," Adela exclaimed, a flicker of concern crossing her features as she hastily let the door swing shut and hurried after the Princess into the depths of the suite.

Zelana moved with silent grace, her regal poise undiminished as she stepped further into the opulent chamber. Her gaze swept across the room—soft candles flickering, rich, dark drapes framing the bed, and lavish furnishings whispering of indulgence and secrecy. She crossed to the bed and sat down, her fingers trailing over the silk sheets, feeling their softness teasing her skin, whispering of luxury and comfort—designed to seduce and lure Deon into succumbing to his desires. Her gaze returned to the escort, who stood uncertain.

Adela was momentarily caught off guard by the Princess's deep scrutiny, her confidence faltering slightly. "Is there something I can assist you with?"

Zelana's expression remained a mask of royal composure, though a storm of emotions swirled within. Her gaze absorbed every detail of the escort—striking green eyes framed by her long brunette hair cascading over her shoulders. Her slender figure was accentuated by her voluptuous curves, draped in black, sexy lingerie beneath a loosely tied robe, radiating a dangerous allure that could easily captivate any man, including Deon.

"What's your name?" Zelana questioned, her voice icy and sharp.

"Adela," she murmured, offering a faint smile.

"How many of you are serving the Commander?" Zelana pressed, her tone demanding yet composed.

"There's three of us," came a voice from behind Adela.

The blonde escort stepped forward, her confident stride unwavering as her eyes met the Princess's without hesitation.

"I'm Tracy," she introduced herself smoothly, then gestured toward another blonde emerging from the shadows. "And this is Lace."

Zelana rose from the bed, her gaze sweeping over the women, as if assessing their merit on a scale only she could measure. She noted their contrasting beauty with blonde hair and the vivid green of their eyes to their modest, yet undeniably seductive figures when dressed provocatively in black, sheer lingerie.

"It seems you take quite an interest in Commander Deon," Tracy observed, closing the distance between herself and the Princess, her movements graceful and unhurried. "He must mean a great deal to you since you've come to visit us twice."

"He's my mentor," Zelana confessed without pause, a flicker of vulnerability in her eyes. "I needed to see for myself if the escorts handpicked by the King are truly worthy of his time and attention."

The women exchanged curious glances, wondering if there would be consequences if they overstepped with the Commander.

"He's definitely found the Royal Treatment tantalizing. Why else would he keep coming back for the experience?" Tracy murmured, more cautiously.

"What is this... experience?" Zelana asked, trying to maintain an expression of indifference.

"Anything and everything a man wants and desires," Adela replied with an alluring smile. "The promise of seductive dances, lingering kisses, and pleasures of the flesh."

Adela could see her words tearing at Zelana's heart, confirming her suspicions.

So you're the reason the Commander has been hesitant.

Zelana fought to stay composed, embodying the dignity of her royal lineage, continuing to face potential rivals for Deon's affections.

"Why are you wearing a mask, Lace?" Zelana asked, her voice poised with grace.

"I'm new," Lace responded with a small, hesitant smile.

The familiarity in Lace's voice tugged at the Princess's senses, igniting a spark of suspicion.

"Still learning the ways to a man's heart," Zelana remarked, a subtle smile playing on her lips.

Without hesitation, Zelana reached out and swiftly removed the mask. As it fell away, the face beneath was one she had never expected to see.

"Princess Kalina?" Zelana gasped, her disbelief echoing in the tense silence that immediately followed.

The escorts, caught off guard, circled around, their expressions shifting between confusion and curiosity, each trying to make sense of the sudden revelation before them.

"You're a princess?" Adela asked, her brows furrowing in bewilderment.

"You lied to us..." Tracy added, her voice sharp with disappointment.

The consequences of the deception began to settle in as the escorts glanced at each other, knowing the situation could damage their standing with both the King and the Princess.

"I was curious about the Royal Suite," Kalina began, trying to justify her actions. "I had no idea that Commander Deon would be the guest."

Adela's eyes narrowed, disbelief hardening her features. "You knew it was him, that's why you insisted on joining us. Don't try to insult Princess Zelana with more lies."

"It's the honest truth," Kalina protested adamantly.

"And you blatantly disregarded our code of honor with the Commander yesterday," Adela added, defending herself and Tracy. "Your intentions were clear—you wanted to bed Commander Deon."

"That's absurd," Kalina snapped back, her voice tight with desperation as the accusations piled up.

"No wonder you hid behind a mask, using a fake name to disguise yourself," Tracy accused mercilessly. "You were afraid the Commander would recognize you."

Kalina's eyes darted to Zelana, seeking an ally in her gaze. "You know I have feelings for Crown Prince Zhong. Why would I do what they're accusing me of with Commander Deon?"

Zelana's gaze flickered uneasily between them, each statement a stone in the growing wall of mistrust.

"They're merely escorts, trying to save their own skin," Kalina continued, her voice pleading. "I trust you'll see through their deceit, Princess Zelana."

"That's bullshit," Tracy muttered, clearly frustrated.

Words became lost to Zelana that moment as she watched Kalina quickly retreat to the dressing room.

"Princess Kalina wouldn't have gone through all this trouble, pretending to be an escort, for a man she didn't desire," Adela murmured softly with intent.

Zelana's gaze settled on her. "I can see it in your eyes. You desire him too," she whispered, suspicion lacing her words.

"I will be completely honest with you, Princess Zelana. If Commander Deon gave me a reason to leave this life, I would do it in a heartbeat," Adela confessed without hesitation, a subtle smile gracing her lips, her eyes glinting with a quiet determination.

So you're the reason Deon's changed... Zelana thought as the realization stung, igniting a flame of jealousy that burned deep in her chest. It was hard to accept the bitter truth—he may have fallen for Adela's seductive allure.

The Princess he yearned for in Sanshe may have been beyond his reach, but Adela certainly wasn't.

CHAPTER NINETY

YOUR SONG

ZELANA WALKED BACK from the Royal Suite, her emotions still raw and unsteady. Each step felt heavy, weighed down by the thoughts swirling within her. As she neared the royal lounge, her steps faltered, hearing the familiar melody drifting from the partially open door—a song Deon had played the other day. The haunting notes seemed to pull her in, compelling her to approach. She leaned against the wall, her breath shallow, listening quietly from the shadows.

Inside, Deon's voice melded with the soft, flowing music, his fingers moving effortlessly across the piano keys. There was a sadness woven into the romantic melody, and as he sang, Zelana could hear the depth of emotion in his voice, the unspoken longing in every word. The song touched her deeply, more than she expected, and tears began to well in her eyes.

I didn't realize you could feel so deeply for a woman you just met, Zelana thought silently, her heart aching unbearably as tears flowed from her eyes. Each note, each word that left his lips intensified her affection for him, her heart swelling with emotions she could no longer suppress, pulling her deeper into the feelings she had tried so hard to bury.

As the last notes echoed through the now silent lounge, Deon couldn't stop thinking of the woman his heart continued to crave.

Princess Zelana...

She continued to linger in Deon's thoughts, though his lips dared not to speak it aloud. He sat at the piano, trying to calm the emotions raging inside him as his fingers still rested on the ivory keys.

Back in the corridor, Zelana wiped away her tears, taking a deep breath to regain her composure. Straightening herself, she prepared to leave, when suddenly, the door to the royal hall opened. Deon stepped out, and they nearly collided.

Zelana's breath hitched in her throat, her heart pounding as their gazes met. In that brief moment, no words were needed. His eyes—guarded that morning—now brimmed with emotion, mirroring the pain she felt inside. It reminded her of their first fight at the lake as she saw a vulnerability in his expression, tearing at her heart.

"It was beautiful," she murmured softly, her voice thick with emotion, breaking the quiet. "I hope... the woman in your heart... appreciates it."

Her words struck Deon harder than he expected, leaving a bitter taste in his mouth.

Zelana lowered her gaze and walked away, her figure retreating slowly into the dimly lit corridor.

Deon's heart raced as he turned around, wanting to call out, to stop her, to explain.

Every note I played was for you...

He wanted to say, yet his jaw clenched, fear gripping him—the fear of exposing his heart kept him frozen, letting her go once again.

CHAPTER NINETY-ONE

THE REPORT

THE SOMBER THRONE room of Krimzon, dark and foreboding, was illuminated only by flickering candles, casting long shadows across the cold stone. At its center, a warming pool, bordered by lush greenery and benches, served as a stark contrast to the room's chilling atmosphere.

Marcus was sitting on his throne, in deep conversation with his officers.

Julian's voice echoed slightly in the vast hall as he relayed the recent events. "After we returned the Queen's body, King Lucas declared, 'The end of Krimzon is coming'," he reported solemnly.

Marcus stood abruptly, his movement swift and sharp. "What did Lucas say?" he demanded, his tone laced with disbelief and rising fury.

"The end of Krimzon is coming..." Julian repeated firmly.

A cruel laughter burst from the King, his voice echoing menacingly off the stone walls. "That's not a way to show appreciation. I bring him his wife and he dares to threaten me? That man has no idea what I'm capable of now."

The room tensed as Julian continued, albeit hesitantly. "Moreover, Cedric, who recently escaped the Fire Mines, reported that the Zelonian soldier masquerading as King Lucas was armed with a pistol," he disclosed, the weight of his words palpable in the air.

Marcus stroked his chin thoughtfully, his gaze distant yet calculating. "Interesting," he mused quietly. "I fought a Zelonian Commander with a pistol as well."

"It seems Sanshe and Zelonia are forging an alliance," Silas observed, the Lead of the Royal Council.

"We must stop them. Keep your eye on both kingdoms. We need to know their every movement," the King's voice, though soft, carried an ominous undertone, hinting at the storm that was brewing beneath his calm exterior. "We'll leave for Lashia one day early. We need our sustenance, and we cannot afford any mishaps."

CHAPTER NINETY-TWO

ALL IN

THERE WERE THREE knocks on the throne room door.

"Come in," Marcus called out, his voice commanding.

Striker entered with Victoria at his side. She knelt gracefully in front of the King, her gaze lifting to meet his with a seductive gleam.

"Victoria claims you're expecting her," Striker announced with a neutral tone.

Marcus scoffed, knowing all too well that he hadn't summoned her.

You found your own way to me, he mused, irritated by her boldness.

"Everyone, out!" Marcus commanded, his voice cold and final.

The guards and Striker filed out, the heavy throne doors closing behind them as Marcus rose from his seat, his gaze locked on Victoria.

"How dare you lie your way to me?" he growled, eyes darkening to crimson as rage stirred within him.

Victoria stood slowly in desperation. "You haven't requested me since that night. I didn't know any other way to see you," she whispered, a tremor in her voice.

"I know you were with Crown Prince Caspian last night," he hissed, his anger intensifying. His fangs elongated as he stepped toward her, closing the distance, his predatory nature awakening.

"I couldn't bear to let him feed off me. I couldn't stand him touching me after being with you," she confessed, gazing up into his eyes, hoping to crack his cold heart. "I accept your offer."

"It's too late, Victoria," he snarled mockingly, circling her like a predator toying with its prey.

"Let me be yours and yours alone, my King," she pleaded softly, fear beginning to tighten in her chest.

Hesitation flickered in Marcus's eyes. *Is it me you want or is it something only I can give you?*

She swallowed nervously as he halted in his steps. Her heart pounded with him towering over her, feeling his gaze burning into her. She knew what was coming but was powerless to stop it.

With one swift motion, he pulled her to him, his fangs sinking into her neck with brutal force. The taste of her blood ignited something primal within him as he drank deeply, draining her life with every pull.

Victoria's eyes fluttered shut, her breath shallow, clinging to the last remnants of life as her body weakened, slipping into a limp state in his arms.

"Save me..." she begged, her voice a whisper, staring up at him through blurry eyes.

Darkness closed in, swallowing her whole as she succumbed to Marcus, her vision fading, his face the last she saw as the world slipped away.

CHAPTER NINETY-THREE

SURRENDER

DEON HALTED HIS footsteps outside the door of the Royal Suite, his hand resting on the handle for a moment longer than necessary. *I have to stay the night,* the troubling thought weighed heavily on his mind. With a deep breath, he hesitantly unlocked the door and pushed it open, stepping inside.

The suite was dimly lit, bathed in the soft glow of candlelight, with a slow alluring melody playing in the background by three men––one with a flute, another using a violin, and the last on a timpani, setting an intoxicating ambience. The three beautiful escorts awaited him, each dressed in flowing, silky garments that whispered against their bodies with each subtle movement.

Adela and Tracy posed themselves against the ornately carved posts of the grand bed, their movements graceful and alluring, their gestures a visual enchantment to tempt and entice him.

In the center, Lace used the bed as her stage. Her blonde hair cascaded beautifully down her shoulders, brushing against the soft bedding, as her eyes met Deon's—her gaze a silent invitation as her arms swept above her head, gracefully gliding down her sides while she swayed to the music, her hands caressing over her own curves seductively, tracing lines that beckoned his gaze to follow.

Deon's heart pounded fiercely against his chest as he absorbed her graceful movements.

Tracy and Adela elegantly broke away from the bed and stepped toward him, their hips swaying rhythmically to the music while they began to dance around him, slowly undressing. One by one, their robes fell away, revealing provocative lingerie that clung to their curves.

"Surrender yourself to the Royal Treatment, Commander," Tracy whispered, her voice soft and tantalizing as her fingers traced a daring path along his arm, delicately slipping his jacket off his shoulders while Adela eased his trousers down.

Deon was exposed and vulnerable, left with only underpants on, lingering under the dim light. His heart pounded as Adela stood before him, her eyes burning with desire. She rested her hand on his bare, muscular chest, her fingers trailing delicately along the defined lines of his body, savoring every curve with lingering appreciation.

Her touch sent shivers through Deon, stirring emotions he struggled to restrain, whispers of temptation both thrilling and unnerving him. He feared he couldn't resist the undeniable chemistry between them as her hand wandered down his torso, her boldness making his heart pound harder. Before he could stop her, she reached his groin, her grasp sending a surge of conflicted desire through him. His body betrayed him, immediately responding to her touch.

"Stop..." Deon whispered breathlessly. His hand instinctively grabbed hers, trying to halt her from arousing him further.

From the bed, Lace watched with rising jealousy, turbulent emotions swirling within her as she observed Adela's brazen actions. Deon's resistance was clear, but Adela was relentless.

"Give in to your desires. I know you want me," Adela urged softly, gazing deeply into his eyes. "I've been waiting all night for you… craving you so desperately."

Her words slipped past Deon's weakening defenses, his resolve slowly crumbling as he stared into her eyes, seeing them ablaze with lust, drawing him closer to the edge of surrender.

"Don't let this night waste away, Commander," Adela whispered, her lips parting slightly in anticipation as she grabbed his neck and pulled his lips to hers.

"Commander!" Lace called from the bed, her eyes filled with possessiveness, unable to stand idly by.

Lace's voice disrupted the seductive spell Adela had casted on Deon. Rising from the silken sheets of the grand bed, her slender, voluptuous figure commanded Deon's attention as she descended toward him.

Adela followed Deon's lingering gaze, realizing as her heart sank that his attention was no longer on her. Annoyance flashed in her eyes as she turned to Lace, her gaze sharp with accusation.

You promised you would only observe, her eyes seemed to say, filled with unspoken frustration, yet without a word she stepped aside, conceding the moment to Lace.

The sheer fabric of Lace's attire clung to her curves, outlining her enticing figure. Her voluptuous suppleness bounced provocatively with every step and movement, a mesmerizing vision even his disciplined mind struggled to ignore.

You're more enchanting than I remember, Deon thought in that moment, captivated by the seductive power she wielded so effortlessly.

Reaching him, Lace stared into his eyes, her expression unreadable under the mask. She began swaying her body to the soft music, unbuttoning her garment, her movements slow and intentional, ensuring Deon's eyes followed every contour of her body as she dropped her robe to the ground. He gasped at the sight of her voluptuous curves.

Forgive me, Princess Zelana, he murmured silently, unable to tear his eyes from her suppleness, barely concealed, dancing before him. With each twirl and dip, she challenged his last shreds of restraint, igniting a slow-burning desire within him of unspoken pleasures.

"I want to see your face," he whispered softly, his fingers reaching for her mask.

Adela and Tracy gently, but firmly, pulled him down onto the plush chair. The suddenness of the motion jolted him, but the soft touch of the chair's velvet embraced him like a seductive promise.

"Behave, Commander Deon," murmured Tracy with a purr.

"Or we might have to bind you," Adela added with a tease.

Deon chuckled lightly, amused by how the escorts transformed into protectors of Lace's secrecy, guarding the enigma that stirred his desires. But his curiosity wouldn't be silenced so easily.

"I dare you to remove your mask," he challenged her once again, needing to unveil the woman that stirred desires within him he could no longer suppress.

A mischievous smile danced on Lace's lips as she paused in front of him. "Since my mask seems to trouble you, perhaps Tracy should continue?"

Before she could move away, Deon swiftly pulled her to his lap, guiding her to straddle him.

Lace gasped, startled by the boldness of his gesture. Her pulse quickened, feeling his undeniable desire throbbing beneath her, stirring unfamiliar emotions. She attempted to rise, but he gently tugged her back down to sit, his grip tightening possessively on her hips, grounding her against him.

"You're here for the experience, aren't you?" he murmured, his voice low and intimate.

Lace's heart raced nervously, unsure what to expect as the air between them thickened with unspoken desire, her breath quickening as she felt his gaze penetrate her mask.

"I swear your eyes were green," he breathed out, resistance and indulgence blurring.

"They've always been blue," she whispered softly, her voice sultry and inviting, her eyes filled with a sensual allure that drew him in.

Deon slowly leaned into her, the faint scent of roses suddenly enveloping him, stirring his heart in a way that made his breath catch—a fragrance he knew all too well.

Myztica...

Deon's heart pounded harder as he slowly drew back, his gaze tracing her features with growing certainty. His fingers reached up, brushing delicately against her cheek, lingering as he absorbed her presence. His eyes fell on her lips—soft and luscious—and in that moment, the mask she wore vanished in his mind. He no longer saw Lace, only the woman who filled his every thought.

How did you find out? Why are you even here?

The thoughts made his heart ache with longing as she stared at him with innocent eyes.

I don't care about the reasons. I'm not going to let myself regret this moment again.

He leaned in slowly, the space between them diminishing, his eyes never leaving hers until their lips met, kissing her softly. He paused, pulling back slightly, sensing her hesitation and inexperience.

"Leave us," Deon ordered, his command echoing through the chamber with no room for dissent.

Tracy and Adela exchanged a glance of resignation before quietly exiting the chamber with the musicians, leaving the two alone in the candlelit intimacy.

As the door clicked shut, sealing away the world outside, time seemed to slow—their lips were breaths apart, making her more nervous with each passing moment, seeing an uncontrollable desire burn in his eyes.

"Forgive me…" he whispered softly as he let go of all restraint.

Deon reached out, his fingers slipping to the nape of her neck, pulling her into him with need. As their lips brushed, his tongue teased them, parting her lips, claiming her sweetness with a hunger that was raw and undeniably intimate. The spark between them ignited into a fire that burned with passion. Their kiss deepened and grew more urgent, fueled by the closeness they had both been denied as she gripped his shoulders, expressing emotions she had never dared to before.

Deon's hands slid to her waist, pulling her flush against him, their bodies melding together, a dance of tongues and lips filled with craving and unspoken emotions they had been holding back. He gripped her hips, gently moving against her, conveying the growing hunger he could no longer contain.

Overcome with desire, he swiftly lifted her, her legs wrapped around his waist, as he carried her toward the opulent bed. He lay her down on the silken sheets, hovering over her small frame, their bodies almost touching, his gaze never leaving hers.

"You're so beautiful," he whispered, his eyes darkening with desire.

His fingers gently caressed her face and grazed her neck, trailing down and sliding over her voluptuous softness as she flinched slightly at his touch. He paused, gazing tenderly into her eyes.

"Are you sure you're an escort... Lace?" he teased softly.

"I... haven't been this close with anyone before," she said hesitantly, vulnerability clear in her eyes.

Her words only intensified his arousal, stirring something primal in him as his lips claimed hers once more, his kiss deep and consuming. She melted into him, her hands instinctively finding their way to his chest, feeling the racing of his heart beneath her fingertips.

The room was drenched with sexual tension—the scent of roses, the flicker of candlelight, the way their bodies moved against each other, and the intimate caresses tempting them to surrender to the night's promise of forbidden pleasures.

Deon stared into her yearning eyes, his desire for her unbearable. Yet, a small part of him hesitated.

You're destined to be a Queen, he thought to himself silently. *I could never take that from you.*

He captured her lips once more, kissing her breathlessly and with a passion that conveyed both his love and restraint, brimming with unspoken devotion, choosing to protect her chastity.

As the night deepened, they both understood the consequences that dawn would bring, but let the world beyond fade away, finding comfort in the warmth of each other's embrace.

Lace found herself surrendering to his lips again and again, drawn to his tenderness. Gradually, the intensity of their passion softened, giving way to the gentle rhythm of shared breaths. Wrapped in each other's arms, they drifted to sleep, lost together in the shadows of the night.

CHAPTER NINETY-FOUR

Sweet Secrets

As THE SUN shifted outside, promising the start of a new day, Deon's eyes slowly opened, a gentle smile spreading across his face at the sight of her beside him. His heart swelled with a rush of affection as he gently fixed the mask that now covered only a part of her face, ensuring her comfort.

Your secret is safe with me.

He smiled warmly, wrapping his arms around her, snuggling closer, savoring the warmth of her presence in his embrace for a moment longer.

Lace stirred slightly, her eyes fluttering open as she felt his arms tighten around her. Memories of the night before came flooding back to her.

"I will never tire of being in your arms..." she whispered, a subtle smile gracing her lips.

"Lace..." he said her name softly as she turned her head to him, only to be met with a gentle kiss.

He pulled away slightly, his gaze filled with admiration. "I wish I could stay all day in bed with you," he whispered silent confessions, tugging at her heart.

"Your wish is granted," she teased as he shifted to hover over her.

Deon leaned down and kissed her passionately, their shared breaths filling the room along with the soft rustle of fabric, as his lips made her breathless while he slowly shifted in between her legs.

"I've never desired anyone as I desire you," he breathed, his voice breathless with restraint.

Words were lost to her, her heart thundering in her chest as she felt his strength, his need, sliding insistently against her, his suggestive movements becoming a wordless declaration of his craving for her as she melted under him, wrapped in his embrace.

Deon hesitated, his gaze lingering on her. "Leaving is harder than I thought," he murmured, reluctant to return to the world—to his duties, yet he forced himself to stand, each movement paining him.

"I wish the night didn't have to end," she whispered sadly, feeling his warmth leave the bed as she watched him resume dressing, each movement pulling him further from the intimacy of the night.

Deon paused, feeling a tug at his heart as his eyes met hers once more, reminded of the very words he had once whispered to her in the city.

"It doesn't have to end," he replied as a fire of determination flickered in his eyes. "I will earn my way to you," he declared with visible longing.

"What if you forget me?" she inquired softly, capturing his heart with her words as he quickly returned to her side, gently pressing his forehead to hers in a tender gesture.

"With each sunrise, you will be my first thought," he confessed, "and my last under the moonlight."

She pressed her lips to his, a silent confession that she felt the same. Deon returned her kiss with a promise—of something more beyond the momentary escape of the Royal Suite.

Reluctantly, he pulled away and stood, adjusting his jacket with slow movements, as if arming himself against the world. His footsteps echoed through the quiet room as he moved toward the door. Before leaving, he paused, his eyes lingering on the beautiful woman sitting on the bed, his heart swelling with an unspoken love.

"Next time, that mask is coming off," Deon said with a playful wink, his words hinting at the sweet secrets they were both keeping from each other.

A soft smile touched her lips, mirroring the gentle smirk that broke across his face, softening his features. With a heavy heart, he finally stepped out of the room, carrying her memory with him.

The soft sound of the door closing behind him marked the end of their stolen night—one that Lace wasn't ready to let go. She slowly removed her mask, her fingertips brushing over her lips, as she let out a breath she didn't realize she'd been holding.

A tender smile spread across her face as she lowered her hand to her chest, feeling her heart beating rapidly beneath it, each beat full of aching clarity.

"I love you…" she whispered with emotion as the truth in her heart became undeniable.

CHAPTER NINETY-FIVE

AIM HIGH

DEON WAS MIDWAY through his second set of weights when Zelana entered the training academy, her hair pulled back in a tight bun, her expression morphing into a timid smile. He placed the weights down with a deliberate clank, staring at her with a knowing gaze.

"You're late," he noted, the edge in his voice softened by a hint of amusement.

"Sorry, I overslept," she fibbed, her voice faltering slightly as a blush tinted her cheeks.

Deon grinned as he shed his shirt, revealing his muscular chest glistening with sweat.

She couldn't help but admire him, her mind returning to the memory of her fingers caressing his chest.

"You shouldn't look at a man like that," Deon chided, catching the intensity of her gaze.

"Like what?" she replied innocently, quickly turning away to hide her embarrassment.

He chuckled softly as he motioned toward the shooting range. "Follow me. Let's get started."

He walked to the makeshift shooting range as she trailed him, admiring his broad shoulders and his muscular arms, the arms that held her closely in an intimate embrace all night.

"Before I depart for Lashia, I want to be certain you can handle a pistol," he stated in a casual tone.

Zelana watched as he smoothly withdrew his pistol, the metal gleaming under the sunlight. With precise gestures, he began explaining the mechanisms and safety features with a calm authority as she attempted to focus on his words but found herself captivated by the movements of his lips. Her mind drifted to the tender kisses those lips lay on her body and the way his closeness had left her breathless.

Noticing her prolonged stare, Deon experienced a surge of mutual longing as his expression softened while handing her the pistol. "Let's work on your stance and grip," he suggested, stepping closer.

Accepting the pistol, their hands touched briefly and the rapid beating of her heart intensified.

Deon positioned himself closely behind her, closing his eyes and taking in her rose scent, pressing his chest lightly against her back, feeling comforted with her warmth against him, calming his heart.

"Hold it steady like this..." he instructed as his hand covered hers, guiding her grip with careful precision as he aligned the pistol at the target. "Aim, and when you're ready, gently pull the trigger."

His voice was firm yet tender as she felt his breath warm against her ear, sending a shiver through her, stirring memories of his affectionate whispers.

BANG!

The deafening sound of the gunshot resonated through the academy, momentarily overshadowing the quiet intensity between them, her eyes wide with the raw force she had just unleashed.

"It's so powerful," she marveled in awe, her hands trembling slightly from the recoil.

She turned to him and found his lips inches away from hers, feeling his presence engulf her.

"It was designed to be lethal," Deon spoke, his expression stoic. "But its true power lies in protecting lives—defending those we love."

Zelana gazed into his eyes, her expression deep and thoughtful, clearly moved by his words. "Then I must master the pistol," she replied, his emotions resonating with her.

Deon's eyes softened, a gentle warmth flickering across his features, refocusing their attention. "Let's try that again. Hit the mark, not just the board," he directed firmly.

He adjusted her stance and guided her arm, raising the pistol and aiming together. With a deep breath, she pulled the trigger once more.

BANG!

The shot rang out, hitting just outside the intended mark.

"Getting there," he encouraged warmly as he drew another pistol.

BANG!

Deon demonstrated with flawless precision, puncturing the very center of the target.

"Impressive," she gasped, amazed by his skill, her admiration for him deepening helplessly.

"Try to keep steady when you pull the trigger. The less you move, the more accurate you'll be," he advised, motivating her with his demonstration.

Zelana steadied herself, aiming and pulling the trigger.

BANG!

"How's that?" she asked, seeing the bullet hit the edge of the target.

Deon's expression was unreadable for a moment. "You can't kill Immortals with that aim." He took her hand and directed the pistol to his heart. "It needs to be here." His voice was soft but serious.

Zelana quickly lowered the pistol, her hands trembling slightly.

"You must perfect it in time," he demanded, yet his gaze was gentle. "I don't want to have to worry."

"I won't disappoint you," Zelana assured him with a small, seductive smile.

The look she gave him tugged at his heart, tempting him to pull her to him and kiss her senseless.

Deon shifted his eyes away from her. "Let's add some complexity to the moves," he remarked, picking up a shield and tossing it to her. "Hold the shield at an angle so I can demonstrate."

Zelana gripped the shield, her eyes following Deon's every move.

"You'll need to run and use the shield to propel yourself into the air and fire behind enemy lines," he instructed as he backed away and dashed toward her.

Her eyes widened in awe as she watched him effortlessly perform the maneuver.

He landed on the ground with perfect posture and turned to face her. "This technique is crucial when you're confronting enemies entrenched behind cover," he added in a serious tone. "It requires you to maintain shooting precision under physical duress. Now, you try."

Zelana hurled the shield toward him; he caught it and positioned it as she ran at full speed, propelling herself using the shield as a ramp, but landed too swiftly to take a shot. She repeated the sequence, each time struggling with the same issue.

"Try to propel yourself higher. That'll give you the time you need to aim and shoot," Deon coached, adjusting her approach and posture.

With each attempt, Zelana's confidence surged. Her jumps were higher and her shots sharpened, each bullet inching closer to its target under Deon's watchful guidance.

She tumbled to the ground once more, her hair slipping loose from her bun, a sight of graceful defeat as she lay fatigued in the soft dirt with heavy breaths.

It's so hard not to want you, he sighed, trying to calm the ache in his body that longed for her.

"I worry I may never master this move," she murmured, feeling disheartened as she slowly sat up. Her hair cascaded freely around her shoulders, framing her face in a disarray that accentuated her beauty.

"You can," he said softly, his eyes never leaving her as his pulse quickened. "You will."

The simplicity of his words drew Zelana's gaze and she caught the intense look of desire simmering in his eyes—the very same look he had the night he kissed her.

Why is he looking at me like that? She wondered as her heart quickened, her breath slowing.

Deon's chest tightened as he took in her disheveled appearance, finding it impossibly alluring. Every part of him wanted her, but he fought back his emotions.

"Let's go again," he urged, offering his hand.

Zelana reached for it, and as Deon pulled her to her feet, they found themselves standing inches apart, the tension between them thickening, electric. Neither moved, neither spoke, but the unspoken pull between them felt undeniable, their thoughts wandering back to that unforgettable night of passion.

Connor suddenly burst into the training grounds, his arrival abrupt, his breath ragged from haste.

"Is something amiss, Officer Connor?" Deon asked casually, trying to compose himself.

"The forces en route to Krimzon were ambushed and Commander Rowan's fallen," Connor reported urgently, his voice tight with panic. "Some soldiers were captured and taken to Krimzon, but the majority have retreated to Zelonia. We need you back at the meeting hall immediately; the King demands an urgent council."

Deon retrieved his pistol from the ground and sighed, casting a worried glance at Zelana, who watched him with a growing sense of unease.

"Let's go," he said, leading the way to the meeting hall with Connor trailing behind.

CHAPTER NINETY-SIX

AMBUSHED

THE MEETING HALL was tense as Lucas stood by the grand map table, his gaze fixed on the marked paths leading to Krimzon, each route a potential thread to the fabric of his kingdom's fate.

Deon stepped into the hall hearing the low murmur of the Royal Council as they spoke in hushed tones, while the King's attention was elsewhere, directed toward the heavy doors at the end of the chamber.

The doors burst open with Makeo and Gaius entering, their expressions somber, as their usual poise was replaced by concern.

"Your Majesty," Gaius began, his voice steady despite the weight of his words. "The Krimzon Army left one day sooner than planned and ambushed our army. We are retrieving Commander Rowan's body as we speak."

A heavy silence enveloped the room as the gravity of the news settled among the assembled council. Lucas clenched his fists, his knuckles whitening, and he hit the table with rage.

"March to Lashia immediately," Lucas commanded, his voice carrying a sharp edge of urgency.

Makeo stepped forward and quickly advised, "We must reconsider. Without the support of Commander Rowan's troops to block Krimzon's reinforcements, advancing to Lashia and executing the plan to assassinate Marcus is no longer viable. We risk too much with too little support."

Lucas paced briefly, his steps echoing in the stillness of the room. He stopped, facing the large window overlooking the palace gardens, his back to his men. "We cannot afford to lose Lashia," he said, more to himself than to anyone else. "General Gaius, please accompany Commander Dominic and Commander Deon to Lashia. The success of this mission rests in your hands now."

"As you command, Your Majesty," Gaius nodded, the resolve in his eyes matching that of his king.

Deon felt an urgent need to share his insight. "We need to bolster our intelligence. If Krimzon can catch us off guard like this, we must be ready to anticipate their next moves more accurately."

"I will send additional spies to Krimzon," Lucas agreed as he returned to the map table.

"They should be capable of reaching Marcus, even in his sleep," Deon added as the men nodded in agreement, the room filling once more with murmurs.

"Women," Lucas mused, catching on to Deon's suggestion. "Officer Connor, recruit some attractive, capable women."

"I will see to it, Your Majesty," Connor stated with a bow, quickly exiting the chamber.

"We will prepare for immediate departure," Deon declared with a heavy heart, as he, Gaius, and Dominic bowed, before swiftly leaving to rally the troops.

CHAPTER NINETY-SEVEN

The March

THE ZELONIAN ENCAMPMENT stretched across the valley, banners fluttering in the cool breeze. Tents were lined up in perfect rows, the smell of smoke from morning fires still lingering in the air. Beyond the camp, the towering kingdom gates loomed like silent sentinels, standing guard over the valley. The sun cast long shadows across the terrain, reflecting off the soldiers' armor as the low murmur of their conversations filled the air, preparing for battle. Every clink of metal, every thud of a boot on the dirt was tense with the urgency of their mission to defend Lashia.

The Commanders convened at the heart of the Zelonian encampment, near the towering gates of the majestic kingdom. Deon adjusted the strap on his armor, his expression unreadable, as Gaius and Dominic approached.

"Commander Deon," Gaius began, his voice steady but grave. "It's not like you to be this silent before battle."

"Just thinking of the road ahead," Deon replied hesitantly. "We're walking into a battlefield, outnumbered, without a clear plan except to charge forward. It doesn't sit well with me."

Dominic nodded thoughtfully, watching Deon secure his sword to his belt. "This won't be the first time we've fought outnumbered."

"Not having a proper strategy troubles me more than the numbers," Deon replied in a low tone, not wanting to cause panic among the soldiers. "When we reach Lashia, we need to meet with their King and military leaders immediately to assess their defenses."

"They no longer have a monarch. I think Princess Lulu is ruling the kingdom now," Dominic replied.

"I remember King Lucas saying as much," Gaius confirmed. "Both the King and Crown Prince fell in the last defense. Tragic."

Deon shook his head in disbelief, his resolve hardening. "We must hurry, then."

One by one, the Commanders mounted their steeds, their formidable presence commanding respect and bolstering the morale of their men. The metallic clank of armor reverberated through the encampment, a powerful display of strength and readiness. The Commanders were positioned at the forefront, prepared to guide their forces through the dangerous journey ahead as the low, steady blast from a horn called the army to formation.

The Zelonian army spread out flawlessly, a disciplined and courageous sea of warriors ready to face the peril that awaited them beyond the kingdom's gates. Thousands of soldiers formed an unbroken line that stretched beyond the horizon.

"Move out!" Gaius commanded, his voice cutting through the afternoon air as the horn sounded again.

The ground trembled beneath the thunderous beat of hooves, sending clouds of dust swirling up into the sky. Deon's horse trotted along with the formation, his body moving forward, but his heart remained behind as his thoughts drifted to Zelana… his chest immediately tightening.

"We need to arrive before dusk. I assume Krimzon will launch a full attack at night," Gaius said, trying to brainstorm a strategy on the whim.

"Ideally, we'll be defending from behind Lashia's walls," Dominic replied calmly. "Field battles rarely go in our favor."

Deon tried to focus on the battle discussion, but the pull of his emotions was relentless, a tide he could no longer resist. The battlefield was calling, but so was she, as an unshakable feeling kept gnawing at him, making his heart clench in his chest with a sudden, overwhelming need.

I must see her before I leave…

"Go on without me. I'll catch up," Deon said with a quiet resolve as Dominic and Gaius exchanged puzzled glances, observing him with furrowed brows.

"What is it?" Dominic asked, frowning.

Without responding, Deon's grip tightened around the reins, and with a sharp tug, he urged his horse to turn abruptly, spurring it into a swift gallop. He raced back to Zelonia with renewed urgency, leaving his comrades watching in silence, bewildered, as the dust from his horse's hooves hung in the air.

CHAPTER NINETY-EIGHT

CHERISHED

KALINA SAT DOWN next to Zelana, her movements tense as they both awaited the start of their class. Yet, her thoughts were far from the lesson ahead.

"Curiosity led me to the Royal Suite, but I never anticipated to find Commander Deon there," Kalina said softly, her eyes searching Zelana's for a glimpse of forgiveness.

Zelana turned to meet her gaze, the hurt in her eyes unmistakable. "It troubles me that I don't know how honest you've been with me, Princess Kalina."

"Can you handle the truth?" Kalina challenged her, her expression serious and unwavering.

Zelana paused, about to respond, as she suddenly heard the clatter of horse's hooves approaching.

A Commander's sudden presence drew the eyes of the Royals to the entrance of the courtyard, their expressions shifting from casual interest to profound curiosity as he slowly removed his helmet with graceful composure.

Deon's gaze was as commanding as it was tender and intense, sweeping over the gathered nobility and settling on Zelana, whose eyes met his with unspoken longing.

"Princess Zelana..." he called to her, his voice deep and resonant, echoing across the courtyard as the cluster of Royals rose to approach the railing of the balcony.

Zelana moved toward him, the sunlight catching the delicate features of her face, highlighting her ethereal grace. They parted, forming an elegant pathway as Zelana reached the balcony, her poise as majestic as it was vulnerable under his intense gaze.

"May I have a word?" he asked with a gentle urgency that belied his calm exterior as murmurs resounded around them.

"Yes, of course," Zelana replied, flushed with emotion as she gathered her composure.

Kalina glanced at Zelana, feeling a tinge of jealousy.

"Can't you see she's in class right now?" Nikolai burst out with annoyance.

"Hush," Jenessa countered, curious and intrigued by Deon's presence.

With a hint of hesitation, Deon guided his horse closer to the expansive balcony. "The Zelonian army is marching to Lashia as we speak."

"So, war is imminent." Zelana's voice was barely a whisper as her heart started to ache.

"You must remain strong during these trying times," Deon murmured softly, sensing her anxiety.

"Are you saying you're going, Commander Deon?" the Princess asked in desperation.

He paused before speaking. "We cannot escape tomorrow because we avoid responsibility today."

More murmurs encompassed the balcony as Zelana gazed at him helplessly.

Deon reached into his pocket and grabbed a red velvet box, presenting it to her. "I've been wanting to give you this," he revealed with a warmth that drew the gaze and admiration of those around.

Zelana reluctantly accepted it, and as she opened the box, she found a beautiful, luxurious bracelet, rich with sophistication—a masterpiece of delicate craftsmanship, elegantly wrought with fine gold. It featured small diamonds adorned with larger diamonds exuding flawless clarity spread along the bracelet. The gems sparkled, catching and reflecting even the faintest light with dazzling clarity.

Deon's gesture caused a ripple of surprised gasps among the Royals.

"I had it customized in Sanshe," he revealed, his voice subtly softening.

You thought of me while you were in Sanshe. Her heart overflowed with warmth as the blush of delicate pink on Zelana's cheeks deepened.

"It's beautiful. I've never seen anything like it..." she murmured as she gently placed it on her wrist. "I will cherish it deeply, Commander Deon."

"Don't forget me," Deon teased her with a light-hearted grin.

"Never... even for a brief moment," Zelana replied with a gentle smile, her eyes never leaving his.

Soft giggles filled the air as he was slightly embarrassed by the attention he had garnered.

Deon offered a bashful grin, gazing at Zelana timidly. "I should go."

"Please tilt your sword," she implored tenderly as he obeyed. She grabbed her handkerchief, tying it to the hilt of the sword. "Carry me with you... keep me close always..."

"I will take you with me wherever I go... Princess Zelana," he vowed softly, touched at her gesture.

Zelana became overwhelmed with emotions as she tried to remain strong, blinking back tears.

Deon's gaze was unwavering, etching every detail of her face to his mind—the sparkle in her blue eyes, the curve of her alluring lips, and the way the sunlight danced through her lustrous blonde hair.

Your lingering gaze, your reluctance to leave, and your unexpected tenderness leaves my heart aching with worry... unsettling me, she thought in silence. *What's behind those expressive eyes, Deon?*

I've never wavered in battle before, but somehow, leaving you this time fills me with a strange unease, he murmured to her silently.

"You must return," she whispered, her eyes simmering with deepening emotions.

"Beside you is where I belong, Princess," he said softly with a subtle smile, slipping his helmet back on to hide the insecurities that haunted him as his eyes lingered on her for a moment longer.

Zelana brought her hand to her heart, feeling a surge of longing envelop her as tears welled in her eyes.

Deon offered her one final bow, pausing in deep reverence. Slowly, he raised his head, allowing his gaze to meet hers one last time before guiding his horse to leave. With a swift kick, his steed galloped back to join the ranks of the Zelonian army, leaving more than just the dust in his wake.

"I never suspected that beneath that stoic expression, the Commander would possess such a romantic soul," Anika whispered as she watched his figure vanish in the distance.

"There's something about him in armor..." Jenessa murmured with admiration.

"It's rare to meet men like Commander Deon," Zelana confessed with affection, her voice quivering as her eyes glistened with unshed tears, already finding his absence unbearable.

Zelana's words sucked the air from Nikolai's lungs as he walked back to his seat with Andreas awkwardly accompanying him.

"If only he was royal..." Kalina sighed, her voice trailing off with longing.

The Princesses turned to Kalina, startled by her words.

"I would ask him to be King of Snowy Meadows," Kalina murmured, confessing to the wind.

Zelana struggled to hide the sharp sting Kalina's words ignited within her. Her gaze returned to the gate from where Deon had departed as her fingers gently traced the intricate contours of the bracelet, finding comfort in his last words.

"Beside you is where I belong, Princess."

CHAPTER NINETY-NINE

Lashia

THE COMMANDERS OF Zelonia arrived with their legion to find the sky over Lashia dark, thick with the stench of smoke and the clamor of battle, chaos reigning supreme. Fires roared at the kingdom's gate as they were greeted not by the Lashians, but by the brutal ongoing assault of the Krimzonites.

"May the Heavens shine upon us this day," Dominic prayed under his breath.

"Blessings abound," Deon and Gaius concluded the prayer as they observed the ferocious onslaught.

With their meticulously devised plans already rendered obsolete amidst the unfolding devastation and Lashia's defenses faltering, the Zelonian Commanders were left with no other recourse but to launch a covert offensive from the enemy lines in a desperate bid to reclaim the besieged kingdom.

"Surround them!" Gaius commanded, his voice slicing through the clamor.

Dominic wielded his sword and stood shoulder to shoulder with his troops, fighting fearlessly alongside them. He sliced through their enemies mercilessly, driving the Zelonian forces forward to close in and surround the Krimzon army as the ground turned a grim red with spilled blood.

Deon cleaved through the ranks of the Krimzonites with precision, each swing cutting down enemies that stood in his path, demonstrating his formidable skill. His sword dripped with the blood of the fallen as he solidified his role as a Zelonian leader—a relentless beacon of strength and courage in the heat of battle.

Arrows suddenly whistled through the air, their sharp tips finding their mark in the Krimzonites who pursued him relentlessly from behind. Deon noticed a figure moving with lethal grace, darting toward him. With an acrobatic flip, the young woman landed effortlessly by his side.

"Thank you for coming, Zelonia," she murmured, her voice steady despite the frenetic scene around them as she addressed the armored man beside her.

Deon paused, momentarily taken aback by her beauty, even as he continued to engage the encroaching enemies. "Commander Deon Vang, at your service."

"Crown Princess Lulu Lee," she revealed, surprising him as she fought bravely at his side. Her sword sliced through the air, cleanly severing the head of a Krimzonite targeting them.

Deon's gaze lingered on her delicate features, her long black hair falling gracefully around her slender face. Her light brown eyes held a quiet depth, betraying the weight of the burdens she carried. He couldn't help but notice her agility, her petite, slender frame moving with an effortless grace that only heightened her allure.

"Forgive the delay," he said, his blade continuing to plunge into their enemies with merciless, deadly thrusts. "The news of Krimzon's shift in tactics reached us far too late."

"The fact that you still came means everything to us," Lulu expressed, her voice carrying a note of relief and intrigue for his skill and composed demeanor. "We've been battling them all night."

"Your perseverance is truly admirable, Princess Lulu," Deon commended, as they stood side by side, repelling wave after wave of Krimzonites. "Hold the line with me just a while longer."

Caught off guard by his unexpected praise, Lulu turned to glance at him, a momentary distraction that almost cost her life as a Krimzonite charged at her.

Deon swiftly stepped in, deflecting the blow as he thrust his blade into the assailant's chest. He extracted his sword from the soldier as the body collapsed on the bloodied earth.

Lulu suddenly felt empowered with him beside her, determined to protect what remained of her kingdom as they continued to stand together, forming an indomitable front against their foes with the clash of metal on metal. Her blade sliced through their adversaries while Deon's rapid succession of slashes and jabs cleaved Krimzonites with ease.

The battle grew fiercer, the clashing of steel and the cries of the wounded filling the air, creating a tense and suffocating atmosphere. Lashian and Zelonian soldiers fell around them; the ground soaked in blood. Amidst the chaos, Deon's eyes widened in disbelief as he caught sight of a figure he never expected to see under the sun. The King of Krimzon was aggressively pursuing Gaius with his overwhelming skill and strength across the battlefield.

"How can Marcus be day-walking?" Deon muttered aloud, astonishment coloring his voice as he tried to make sense of the impossible. His grip tightened on his sword, his mind racing as the realization of the danger they faced intensified.

Before Lulu could respond, Deon activated his mechanical arms, a fierce determination flashing in his eyes as he charged toward the intense confrontation where Marcus was dominating Gaius mercilessly. The battlefield blurred around him, the sounds of battle fading into the background as his focus zeroed in on the brutal scene unfolding ahead.

Blood streaked across Gaius's face, his body battered and bruised, each strike from Marcus landing with devastating precision. Gaius's strength waned under the weight of each crushing blow and kick, leaving him staggering and ultimately collapsing as another punch landed on his jaw with unrelenting ferocity.

"Once Lashia falls, Zelonia will be next..." Marcus declared as he stood menacingly over Gaius, a dark chuckle escaping his lips, sending chills through the air.

Mechanical arms suddenly clamped around Marcus from behind, their powerful grip catching him off guard, locking him in place.

"Sanshe?" Marcus spat, bewildered, struggling and thrashing against the unexpected restraint.

"Back to the Lashian walls!" Deon shouted across the chaos, keeping his grip firm around Marcus.

Gaius grimaced in pain, trying to rise from the ground, but collapsed again as he clutched his ankle, which appeared to be sprained. His face twisted in frustration and agony.

"Lorenzo!" Marcus's strained voice echoed across the battlefield as Deon's mechanical arms constricted further.

At that moment, another ancient Immortal emerged—whose presence was unexpected during the day, defying everything Deon knew about their kind and deepening his confusion.

Lorenzo rushed to the Krimzon King's side, his movements swift and determined. With a powerful yank, he peeled Marcus free from Deon's mechanical grasp. The sudden force threw Deon off balance for a heartbeat, but his instincts kicked in as both Immortals attacked without pause.

Deon dodged their blades in a dizzying series of twists and turns, narrowly avoiding the fatal strikes aimed at his vital points from their coordinated attacks. Each blade came perilously close, slicing at him with lethal intent. He retaliated with a swift double kick that struck both Immortals squarely in the chest, forcing them to stagger back, giving him a moment's respite to catch his breath.

Dominic charged toward Marcus with his sword drawn, ready to aid Deon. But before the blow could land, Marcus grabbed the blade mid-strike with his bare hands, snapping it effortlessly into two, stabbing one end into Dominic's stomach as blood seeped from the wound.

"Fuck..." Dominic cursed under his breath, shocked at the raw strength of his adversary.

Deon quickly drew his pistols, firing rounds and forcing the Immortals to hastily seek protection behind their shields. The Krimzon Army swiftly moved in, surrounding them on all sides.

"Retreat, Princess Lulu!" Deon shouted, sensing a critical shift in the enemy's tactical formation.

Without hesitation, Lulu reached for the horn strapped to her belt and blew into it—the sharp sound resonated through the battlefield, ordering a strategic retreat. The allied forces dashed toward the safety of the gate, with the Krimzonites in close pursuit.

Once at the wall, Lulu's voice rang out, "Archers, release!"

A relentless storm of arrows rained onto the advancing enemy, providing cover for the retreating soldiers just as the gates sealed shut behind the retreating forces.

Dominic watched in awe as Deon audaciously charged toward the front lines, skillfully using the Krimzonite shields to catapult himself into the air. He unleashed a flurry of bullets upon the disoriented soldiers mercilessly, their bodies littering the ground, disrupting their formation.

Dominic seized the moment, helping Gaius to stand as they limped together toward the gate, the sounds of battle roaring all around them.

Deon landed gracefully among the Krimzonite ranks, but the moment of victory was short-lived as the enemy soldiers immediately regrouped, forming a tight circle around him and his fellow Commanders.

Marcus lowered his shield and charged forward, his blade slicing through the air in a lethal arc aimed at Dominic and Gaius. Gaius managed to raise his sword in defense, shooting a stern look at his comrade.

"Leave me!" Gaius commanded, his voice ragged with exhaustion, his strength waning.

Before Dominic could protest, Marcus's blade severed Gaius's head in a swift, clean stroke. His lifeless body fell to the ground, marking the tragic end of a fierce warrior.

"Gaius!" Dominic screamed. In a desperate move, he swept Marcus's legs out from under him, sending the Krimzon King crashing to the earth.

Marcus rose to his feet as Deon sprinted toward them, pistols blazing. Bullets tore into Marcus's chest, each impact causing him to stumble and groan in pain. But before Deon could finish him,

Krimzonite shields rushed in, forming a protective barrier around their fallen King.

"Who the fuck are you?!" Lorenzo shouted, his face twisted with rage as he emerged from behind cover.

"Commander Deon of the Zelonian and Sanshe army, Lorenzo!" Deon responded fearlessly, standing tall despite the chaos that swirled around him.

Lorenzo let out a primal scream as he charged, his shield raised to block the incoming bullets Deon fired with precision. As he neared, he quickly engaged with slices and slashes.

Deon swiftly sidestepped and spun around, delivering a powerful kick to Lorenzo's backside, sending him reeling forward to the ground in disarray, losing his shield.

Without wasting a moment, Deon opened fire again, the rapid shots tearing through the air toward Lorenzo, who rolled and scrambled for cover, dodging the deadly bullets. He dove behind the shield wall once more to deflect the oncoming fire.

The wall of shields tightened mercilessly around the Zelonian Commanders, locking together to form an impenetrable wall as they moved in, effectively entrapping them inside. Time was not on their side.

"You must warn the King of the day-walkers," Deon murmured, his breath ragged with urgency, recognizing the severity of their situation.

Without waiting for a response, Deon grabbed Dominic and, with a swift and desperate motion, hurled him out of the tightening circle of shields.

The force of the throw sent Dominic soaring through the air, his body tumbling over the Krimzonite soldiers before landing with a thud on sacks of sand strategically placed to fortify the castle's defenses. The Zelonian soldiers quickly rushed to his side, helping him toward the protective embrace of the castle walls.

High atop the wall, Lulu watched anxiously as Deon maneuvered toward an escape, rushing to the shields. Her heart pounded in her chest as she saw him make a daring leap for freedom, but in a heart-stopping moment, the Krimzonite King reached out and clutched Deon's leg, yanking him back into the deadly circle.

"Commander Deon!" Lulu's scream pierced the air as the allied soldiers turned their heads in alarm.

Dominic quickly scrambled to the top of the wall in a frenzied rush, his heart in his throat as he watched the struggle unfold below. Deon wrestled free from Marcus's grasp and tumbled to his feet, immediately retaliating with another barrage of bullets aimed directly at the Krimzonite King.

The fury in his eyes remained undimmed as Marcus snatched a shield from a Krimzonite soldier. With deft twists and twirls, he skillfully deflected the onslaught of bullets from Deon. He stalked his prey, pacing methodically within the shrinking circle of shields, each step drawing him closer to Deon as the deadly enclosure tightened.

"You're mine!" Marcus hissed through clenched teeth as blood dripped steadily from his wounds. His eyes were blurry from the loss of blood, but he was determined not to show weakness.

A hush fell over the battlefield and Deon could feel all eyes upon him as the soldiers held their breaths. They awaited his next move as the oppressive weight of impending doom settled on his shoulders, but his expression remained calm. With deliberate slowness, Deon reached up and removed his helmet, letting it clatter to the ground with a dull, metallic thud. His gaze lifted to the walls of Lashia, where Dominic and Lulu stood motionless, appearing stunned and helpless.

Deon's heart raced as the walls closed in, but his spirit remained unbroken and his resolve hardened. This was a battle of wills as much as strength, and he would not go down easily. With a sudden burst of raw strength, he launched himself at the barrier with ferocious intensity, pushing his way toward the castle wall. The allied forces observed in astonishment, watching as Deon's strength forced the Krimzonites to falter, their soldiers sliding and tumbling to the ground under his relentless attack.

The wall of shields slowly collapsed, buckling under the sheer force of Deon's determination. But no sooner had the line broken when another wave of Krimzonites rushed forward, hastily filling the breach. Shield upon shield, soldier pushing against soldier, they layered their defense, pressing inward with an unrelenting force—a living wall, designed to overwhelm and crush him.

Lulu's heart pounded as she witnessed Deon being suffocated and entrapped. "We must do something," she said urgently, turning to Dominic, but her words faltered when she saw him clutching to his bleeding wound, barely able to stand.

Determined, Lulu grabbed a rope from her belt and tied one end of it to a column on the castle wall and attached the other end to an arrow. She shot it into a sturdy tree at the battlefield's edge. Slinging her bow onto the rope, she pushed off, sliding swiftly toward the ground.

"Princess Lulu!" Dominic's voice cracked in alarm and admiration, watching her daring descent, while his face contorted, struggling with his own wounds.

Deon turned at the sudden movement, his eyes widening, as he saw the Lashian Princess gliding down onto the battlefield with effortless grace. Her landing was a blur of motion as she immediately drew her bow and unleashed a flurry of arrows at the Krimzonites who were maintaining the outer circle of the shield wall. Her rapid, precise attacks thinned their ranks, causing gaps to form, and their once-impenetrable formation faltered.

"Get the Princess!" Marcus roared, redirecting his troops toward Lulu.

The Krimzonites surged forward, their shields raised in a tight formation to block her continued assault.

Deon's heart clenched as he witnessed her becoming the target of the enemy's fury. His eyes darted rapidly, seeking any sign of vulnerability in the wall of shields. With a surge of adrenaline, he unleashed a series of punches and kicks against the metal barriers. Each strike left dents in the metal, forceful enough to momentarily unbalance the soldiers and briefly disrupt their formation. Yet, they quickly moved in to enforce the wall.

Lorenzo unshielded and darted toward Deon. Their swords clashed, metal meeting metal with a sharp, jarring ring. Deon blocked the incoming jab with his sword, swiftly countering and stabbing Lorenzo, slicing his blade across his stomach. Blood gushed out from Lorenzo's wound as he collapsed, his blood pooling beneath him as the Krimzonites rushed in to enclose him behind their protective shields.

Meanwhile, outside the circle, the Krimzonites reached Lulu and she drew her sword, wielding it with deadly precision. She dodged stabs and countered with her blade swinging through the air, slicing her adversaries with lethal efficiency. With each swing of her blade, another enemy fell, but their numbers were growing, the sheer mass of them threatening to overwhelm her.

The Lashian Commanders saw her valiant efforts and quickly rushed out of the gates, rallying to her side. The sound of clashing steel and battle cries filled the air as they joined the fray, bolstering her defense.

Amidst the chaos, Lulu reached for another arrow, quickly securing a rope to it, her eyes unwavering with determination as she dashed toward higher elevation.

"Commander Deon!" her voice cut through the clamor as his head snapped toward her, spotting her on top of a huge rock in the field.

With a swift motion, she sent the arrow soaring into the air, over his head, embedding itself into a distant tree. She quickly tied the end of the rope to a nearby tree, pulling it taut.

Deon's instincts kicked in, realizing what she was doing as he quickly stepped on shields, propelling himself into the air, grasping the rope in a desperate bid to swing out of the encroaching circle.

Marcus imitated his movements and with a quick strike of his blade, severed the rope. Lulu's heart sank as she witnessed them plummet back into the circle of death.

Deon quickly regained his footing as the hope he held onto started to slip away. "Save Lashia!" his command rippled across the battlefield, his voice thunderous, igniting a spark of urgency among the Lashian forces.

Deon caught sight of the Lashian Commanders pulling Lulu back toward the safety of their walls, ushering her through the gates which slammed shut behind her, cutting off the possibility of further danger—and assistance—from Lashia.

Marcus lunged forward and the two formidable warriors clashed fiercely, their blades meeting with an explosive force, sparks flying as metal met metal.

Deon channeled all his strength into each blow, swiftly attacking with a combination of punches and kicks along with slashes and jabs, driving Marcus to be on constant defense.

Marcus thrust his sword, narrowly missing Deon's chest, before he shifted and stabbed Marcus in the side with devastating accuracy. Pain shot through Marcus's body as Deon unleashed a barrage of bullets at him, forcing him to cower behind shields once again.

Deon's grip tightened around the hilt of his sword, his fingers brushing against the soft fabric of the handkerchief tied around it—gently reminding him of Zelana. Her familiar scent seemed to linger in the air, filling his lungs and pulling at his heart. His gaze flickered downward as his chest tightened, an ache forming deep within him as his thoughts drifted to her.

Princess Zelana... this might be the end of me.

As the words echoed in his mind, the chaos of the battlefield blurred and faded, leaving only her presence—the warmth of her smile, the softness of her touch, the depth of her love... the love he couldn't protect. Each heartbeat felt heavier, more painful, realizing all that he was about to lose, breaking him from within, threatening to tear him apart.

"Zelana!!!" Deon cried out to her in a raw anguish, his voice tearing through the battlefield with desperation, reverberating with the unbearable, excruciating pain of his heartbreak.

Tears welled up in Dominic's eyes as he watched helplessly from the walls. Hearing the emotional torment in Deon's voice made Dominic realize the depth of Deon's love for Zelana.

Lulu rushed up the stairs, her heart pounding as she reached the top of the wall, witnessing Deon hurl his pistols toward Lashia.

They arched through the air and landed with a dull thud just inside its protective barrier of the kingdom's walls.

Every Zelonian and Lashian scattered along the wall stood immobilized, their faces etched with horror and sorrow. The sight of the fearless Commander being overwhelmed by the relentless might of the Krimzonites intensified their fear.

Blood continued to seep from Marcus's stab wound, but he showed no sign of pain. With a swift, brutal motion, he grabbed one of his soldiers and sank his fangs deep into the man's neck, feeding ravenously. The soldier's scream was brief, his life drained in seconds as Marcus tossed his limp body aside, his own wound healing rapidly.

"This monster is who you choose to serve?" Deon shouted, his voice cutting through the horror on the battlefield, turning to the Krimzonite soldiers, his words exuding defiance and disgust, challenging their allegiance to the bloodthirsty King. His piercing gaze swept over them and for a brief moment, a disturbing stillness crept onto the battlefield.

The Krimzonite soldiers, who moments ago had fought with relentless loyalty, exchanged uneasy glances, doubt creeping into their eyes. Yet, fear also flickered in their expressions.

Marcus wiped the blood from his mouth, his eyes gleaming with renewed strength as he stood tall, his confidence unshaken. "They know the odds," he sneered, his voice dripping with malice. "Human lives are too fragile to be fighting on the wrong side." His gaze swept over his soldiers, daring any of them to defy him, while his cruelty pressed heavily upon their conscience.

Deon's jaw clenched as his eyes narrowed with cold fury. "Our lives may be delicate, but your immortality doesn't make you more powerful—only hollower," he began, his voice unwavering, carrying the strength of his convictions. "You rule by instilling fear in your people, inflict cruelty to control them, and use them to fight your wars, but you will never earn their love or loyalty."

The truth struck a nerve as Marcus's face contorted with rage. He lunged forward once more, his blade flashing through the air. "I will find Zelana and feed off her while you watch from hell!" he taunted, his voice dripping with venom as his sword thrust forward with deadly intent.

With unwavering determination, Deon blocked his strike with his mechanical arm, the resounding clash of metal piercing the air. He countered swiftly, delivering a fierce kick, sending Marcus stumbling.

"Move in!" Marcus barked, frustrated, as the shields closed in even tighter around Deon.

Only a few steps from each other, their swords clashed once again, each movement sharp and deliberate. Deon was undeterred by the overwhelming odds against him. His strikes were unrelenting, each slash and thrust aimed with precision, forcing Marcus to be on defense again.

With a fierce cry, Deon rammed his sword into Marcus's chest, but as Marcus growled in pain, he seized Deon by the throat with an iron grip, lifting him off the ground with terrifying ease.

"Commander Deon!" Dominic called to him from the top of the Lashian wall as tears streamed down his face. He collapsed to his knees, overwhelmed by the pain of watching the man who had become a brother now hanging between life and death on the battlefield.

The Zelonian and Lashian soldiers' morale plummeted in that moment, seeing a warrior—an unshakable, inspiring vision, standing strong against overwhelming adversity—now vulnerable, helpless, suspended in the air with his feet dangling above the blood-stained earth. It shattered their hopes of ever overcoming the Krimzonites.

Marcus's grip tightened around Deon's neck, crushing the breath from his lungs. "Now, where is this… Zelana?" His taunt was a weapon in itself as he glared up at Deon, searching for any sign of weakness.

He doesn't know who she is. The thought provided Deon a small, bitter comfort amidst the torment.

Defiance burned in Deon's eyes as he struggled, desperately clawing at Marcus's hands, attempting to loosen the hold around his throat. His thoughts were heavy with the unspoken regret of all that was and could have been. His vision began to blur into darkness.

Never did I imagine I'd be taken from you so soon.

A tear slid down his cheek as his mind drifted to the night they shared in the Royal Suite, a night of unfulfilled desires. Her lingering kisses had overwhelmed him, filling him with a promise of a passionate love… ending before it could even begin. Suddenly, he heard her voice—soft and soothing, whispering to him, melding with the wind's own sighs across the battlefield, amid his dying breath.

I love you… Princess Zelana…

Deon finally confessed, feeling her warmth slowly fade as his life began to slip away. His eyelids grew heavy, each breath more labored than the last. As his consciousness flickered in and out, Zelana's image lingered in his mind—he clung desperately to her love as the darkness consumed him, and with a final, trembling breath, he faded into silence.

In the hushed stillness that enveloped the battlefield, the horrifying image of Deon's limp body brought tears to the eyes of all those who bore witness—a memory that would haunt them for years to come.

Although we only met briefly, it was enough to know that you were a legend, Lulu thought silently as tears flowed down her face, watching Deon's head finally fall forward in a heart-wrenching defeat.

With fury burning in her chest, Lulu notched three arrows onto her bowstring and drew back with fierce determination. She released them in rapid succession, the arrows cutting through the air and plunging deep into the Krimzon King's back, piercing his tough skin.

Marcus roared in agony as he slammed Deon's lifeless body to the ground with a shattering force, the impact jolting Deon's heart, a faint flicker of life sparking deep within him. Marcus released the body, turning to face Lulu, his face twisted in rage while blood dripped from his gaping wounds.

"I'm not done with you, Princess Lulu," he growled, seething with malevolent intent. "Those walls won't keep me out much longer. I give you three moons," he sneered. "By that time, you will be mine."

CHAPTER ONE HUNDRED

Krimzon

In THE VAST expanse of the grand plaza, the Krimzonites—both Immortals and humans—gathered as the air vibrated with their cheers, the sound thunderous and exhilarating. Marcus exuded a regal and imposing aura as he sat upon his throne, basking in the glory of victory. The excitement surged to a crescendo as the assembled crowd chanted his name.

"Marcus! Marcus! Marcus!"

Marcus rose to his feet, his presence charismatic and commanding as he raised his right hand, a gesture that brought an instant hush over the masses.

"Yesterday, I stopped Zelonia's army!" His voice echoed across the throng, resonant with triumph, sparking a wild eruption of cheers from the crowd. "Today, I defeated Azalon's greatest hero!"

Amidst the cheers, Julian maneuvered a cart, bearing a lifeless figure tied to a column onto the stage. The atmosphere was charged with intrigue as the noise slowly faded back into a breathless silence, eyes fixed on the unexpected stranger beside their King, prompting soft murmurs of astonishment and curiosity among the crowd.

"I bring you a trophy!" Marcus announced, his gaze sweeping over his people, each word gripping their attention as he gestured toward the figure beside him. "This is a man, once revered in Zelonia and Sanshe—a god-like warrior who stood in our way for years… but no more!"

Once again, Marcus's words ignited an enthusiastic response from his people. The crowd's cheers of victory grew louder and louder, celebrating a new era of terror in Azalon, shaking the very foundation of the grand plaza.

"Behold the legendary Commander Deon!" Marcus thundered, his proclamation resonating with power and conviction as the cheers morphed into a harmonious chant.

"Deon! Deon! Deon!"

In the castle, a figure emerged from the shadows. The incessant chanting and cheering had finally drawn her out from the quiet solitude of her chambers after years of seclusion.

Stepping onto the balcony overlooking the grand plaza, she gracefully rested her hand on the ornate railing, her piercing hazel eyes sparkling like stars against the night sky. Her long and wavy light brown hair cascaded down her shoulders, framing her delicate face with effortless grace. Her fair skin seemed to glow, almost luminescent under the soft caress of the moonlight, while her lips, as red as freshly spilled blood, were gently pursed, exuding a quiet yet captivating allure.

"Who is this… mortal?" she murmured to herself, her voice barely a whisper against the cacophony of chants swelling from below.

She gazed down at the gathered masses with a composed sigh, her expression cool and unfeeling, with a blend of interest and slight irritation. The name, unfamiliar yet spoken with such passion by her people, sparked a flicker of intrigue in the depths of the enchanting Princess Faleia Chamberlain's eyes.

Below, the crowd continued chanting Deon's name in mockery, celebrating his defeat. He hung limp against the column, battered, bruised, and broken—but no one noticed the subtle movement of his bloodied hand, tied above his head, slowly clenching into a fist.

Not defeated…yet.

List of Characters

ZELONIA

King Lucas Celeste (55 years old) – King of Zelonia

Queen Sophia Visconti (50 years old) – Queen of Zelonia

Crown Prince Samuel Celeste (23 years old) – Crown Prince of Zelonia

Princess Zelana Celeste (18 years old) – Princess of Zelonia

General Gaius Cornelius (55 years old) – General of Zelonia's army

Commander Dominic Dupont (35 years old) – Commander of Zelonia's army/King's bodyguard

Commander Rowan Campbell (45 years old) – Commander in Zelonia's army/Lead Royal Guard

Lord Makeo Kamaka (60 years old) – Advisor of Zelonia's Royal Council

Officer Connor Williams (25 years old) – Officer in Zelonia's army

Adela Walsh (20 years old) – Royal Escort

Tracy Fletcher (21 years old) – Royal Escort

Natalie Martin (20 years old) – Princess Zelana's lady-in-waiting

ROYALS TAKING REFUGE IN ZELONIA

Princess Kalina Ashbourne (19 years old) – Princess of Snowy Meadows

Miranda Contini (22 years old) – Princess Kalina's lady-in-waiting

Princess Anika Sharma (20 years old) – Princess of Star Haven

Hema Verma (23 years old) – Princess Anika's lady-in-waiting

Princess Jenessa Guardcrest (19 years old) – Princess of Ember Falls

Letisha Jones (24 years old) – Princess Jenessa's lady-in-waiting

Crown Prince Nikolai Kuzmin (22 years old) – Crown Prince of Frostwald

Crown Prince Andreas Fadel (24 years old) – Crown Prince of Glimmerock

King Leigh Ashbourne (60 years old) – King of Snowy Meadows

Queen Isabel Wallace (55 years old) – Queen of Snowy Meadows

LASHIA

Crown Princess Lulu Lee (20 years old) – Crown Princess of Lashia

FERRIA

Crown Prince Emeric Vitus (28 years old) – Crown Prince of Ferria

SANSHE

King MuaYeng Yang (65 years old) – King of Sanshe

Crown Prince Zhong Yang (25 years old) – Crown Prince of Sanshe

Princess Huashi Yang (18 years old) – Princess of Sanshe

Kalia Xiong (20 years old) – Princess Huashi's lady-in-waiting

Commander Deon Vang (25 years old) – Commander/Ambassador of Sanshe

Chue Lor (28 years old) – Advisor-in-Chief of Sanshe

General Yengxue Vang (65 years old) – General of Sanshe's army

Victoria Schulz (21 years old) – Deon's ex-girlfriend

Herald (55 years old) – King's assistant

ROYALS TAKING REFUGE IN SANSHE

Crown Prince Winston Thornblade (25 years old) – Crown Prince of Esperia

Princess Lenora Thornblade (21 years old) – Princess of Esperia

Gwen Evans (22 years old) – Princess Lenora's lady-in-waiting

Crown Prince Esteban (26 years old) – Crown Prince of Mesa Valley

Princess Sierra Alanis (20 years old) – Princess of Mesa Valley

Elena Lopez (21 years old) – Princess Sierra's lady-in-waiting

KRIMZON

Maldev – also known as the Evil One, a spawn from Hell

King Marcus Chamberlain (30 years old) – King of Krimzon

Princess Faleia Chamberlain (21 years old) – Princess of Krimzon

Prince Caspian Ravenshadow (30 years old) – Prince of Krimzon

Prince Vijay Kumar (28 years old) – Prince of Ferria

Prince Roland Silverbane (32 years old) – Prince of Iron Glades

Commander Lorenzo Vargas (30 years old) – Marcus's right hand man

Knight's Man Dimitri Dragomir (28 years old) – Lead Knight's Man

Julian – Immortal Guard

Striker – Immortal Guard

Cederick – Immortal Guard

MENTIONED CHARACTERS

King Merci Celeste (70 years old) – King and Founder of Zelonia

Goddess Alexi (70 years old) – Queen and Founder of Zelonia

God Azar (21 years old) – Queen Sophia Visconti's father

Bellarose Visconti (40 years old) – Queen Sophia Visconti's mother

King VangKong Yang (80 years old) – Late King of Sanshe

Queen Kashia Hur (55 years old) – King MuaYeng Yang's late wife

Lady Sonia Alderidge (50 years old) – General Yengxue Vang's late wife

King Theo Chamberlain (55 years old) – Late King of Krimzon

Queen Katherina Hawthorne (50 years old) – Late Queen of Krimzon

Lady Maychee Cha (45 years old) – Princesses of Sanshe's Mentor

ACKNOWLEDGEMENT

I WOULD LIKE TO thank God for blessing me with a passion for writing and giving me the strength to persevere, finally completing my first book in the Azalon series, bringing it to life.

To the amazing people in my life who stood by me through every late night and early morning, thank you from the bottom of my heart. Your unwavering belief in me kept my fire burning.

To my incredible editors—your honest feedback, sharp insights, and tireless efforts polished the novel into something I could be truly proud of. And to my publisher, Nu Voice Press—a special thank you for not just championing my vision but believing in the heart of this story and helping me share it with the world.

Finally, to you, my readers—thank you for stepping into Azalon with me. Your imagination is what breathes life into this story, giving my characters a world beyond the pages. Your continued support means more than words can express, inspiring me to keep creating and exploring new worlds together.

Thank you all... for being part of my journey.

Love always,

K. Vang

Author Biography

K. Vang is an American entrepreneur, author, and filmmaker. With over two decades of experience, she has crafted novels and movie scripts in diverse genres including romance, drama, horror, and fantasy. She holds a Master of Science in Information Technology, specializing in Web Design and Development, from the University of Denver. Her creative and technical skills resonate domestically and internationally, reflecting her multifaceted talent and love of storytelling.